EARTH
REBOOT

T. SCHARRER

Earth Reboot

This is a work of fiction. Although some actual towns, cities, and locations may be mentioned, they are used in a fictitious manner and the events and occurrences were invented in the mind and imagination of the author. Any similarities of characters or names used within to any person past, present or future is coincidental.

Published by:
T. Scharrer

FIRST EDITION

Email Address: earthreboot2@gmail.com

ISBN-13: 978-0-578-19075-4

Library of Congress Cataloging-in-Publication Data

Category: Science Fiction, Psychological Religious Intrigue

Edited by: T. Scharrer

Cover Design & Book Formatted by: Eli Blyden | www.EliTheBookGuy.com

Published & Printed in the USA

*This book is dedicated
to
The SCHARRER family.*

~

*I am eternally grateful
for
my cousin Sue Scharrer
who proofread my final draft.*

Chapter 1

Maggie Wheeler could have spent the rest of her life in bed. She cuddled against her husband Clay's six-foot frame as she had done almost every night since they were married. She loved his warmth and snuggled closer knowing it was almost time to get out of bed. Maggie would soon have to give up her warm embrace, prepare the family's breakfast, and get their sons off to school.

She carefully slid away from her husband. Not wanting to awaken him, she scooted to the edge of the bed to stretch out her legs. She reached the corner of a comforter on the foot of the bed and pulled it over Clay, so if he chooses, he could sleep another half hour. Besides, she felt it was her responsibility to fix breakfast and start each day off for her family. Clay's responsibility was to provide a living and take the lead as a husband, breadwinner and father. He needed more sleep.

Maggie, an old-fashioned stay-at-home mom liked being the family caretaker. Although she had turned down the furnace thermostat a few degrees before they retired for the night, the house felt like a walk-in freezer. God, she thought, it might be warmer outdoors than it is in here.

Maggie hugged a thick robe around her body and shuffled barefoot into the hallway bathroom alongside their main bedroom. Enough sunbeams shone through the window canceling the need to turn on a light. All the bedrooms were on the second floor leaving the first floor as the main living area. The extra frigid toilet seat sent chills up her spine. She hurried about her business, flushed, and then washed her hands in low-pressure water that never got hot. The water continued slowly flowing out of the faucet. This was not surprising. They had a 255-foot deep well instead of city water. Maggie assumed the pressure gage on the twenty-gallon holding tank had not dropped enough to start the well pump.

Gazing into her never flattering medicine cabinet mirror, Maggie's eyes made a quick once over of her long brown tousled hair. Cripes, she hated how she looked after getting out of bed. She added a few drops of water to her still wet hands, splashed some on her face and rubbed her fingers through her hair. Some of the spikes disappeared. She decided to wait until later to brush it, and besides, the water was still too cold.

Maggie appeared several years younger than her thirty-five years. Isolated country living and good eating habits, combined with daily exercise kept her body lean and strong. She inspected a secret spot of gray hair hiding at her left temple. Other than a few minor wrinkles forming around her eyes, her complexion was light and clear. Maggie still could pass for a woman in her twenties and was carded as a minor in many stores when buying alcoholic drinks.

"God, I look ragged...today is going to be a real crapper." She said aloud while flicking a few more drops of the icy water on her face and wiping it off in an attempt to come alive for her challenges of the day. After drying her hands on the blue thread-worn towel, Maggie returned it to the brass rack just above the toilet. The time for indulging herself was over. She would wake up the children and get their hungry mouths fed.

While walking back into the hallway, the coldness reminded her of a house-haunting documentary, she had watched on PBS last Sunday. PBS and Animal Planet were the primary networks that managed to get her attention when Maggie watched television. The television usually remained off during the school week so the children would concentrate on their studies. She stepped into hallway, and looked at the thermometer on the thermostat. Although it would normally be 68 degrees, it read a mere 54. It was not cold enough to be concerned with freezing water pipes, but there was something wrong. The kids would be cranky.

Maggie tried to turn up the heat on the thermostat, pushing it as high as the indicator would go with no results. She flicked the switch from "automatic" to "manual/on" position. Nothing happened. The familiar snap of the ignition coil igniting the propane gas did not sound nor did the blower motor start. The furnace was not working.

Maggie left the hallway, rewrapping her robe, drew it tighter, and entered the twin's room on the other side of the bathroom. Detroit Red Wings hockey team posters covered the back wall. Detroit Tiger baseball pictures, posters, and a few autographed baseball cards adorned the wall opposite of the clothes closet. Their dad was a lifetime Detroit Tiger fan and shared the love of baseball with his children. A collection of autographed baseballs sat on the oak shelf below the cards. The pride of Clay's collection was one signed by Al Kaline. He also had an Alan Trammel, a Cecil Fielder and Charlie Maxwell autographed baseballs. Clay's twin boys loved Michigan sports almost as much as their dad did. Maggie respected the masculinity of the boys' bedroom and its sports décor.

Eric and Joey were sound asleep. Eric was taller and heavier than his fraternal twelve-year-old twin. His days revolved around being meticulous, detailed, and scrupulous, reading many books. Joey, like his brother had his mother's hair and light skin tone and features. Joey's tendency was to be impulsive and hyperactive. Eric was more serene. Neither of the boys resembled Clay, but since he had been Maggie's only lover, and she had had no immaculate conception, they had to be his sons.

Joey's bare foot hung out from underneath his quilts and dangled over his shoes where he had set them beside his bed before going to sleep. His dirty socks remained draped over both sneakers. Maggie instinctively picked them up and dropped them in the dirty clothes hamper sitting in the corner of the boys' bedroom. She knew if she had not picked them up, her son would have worn the socks yet another day. She hated to contemplate how many days Joey could wear a pair if she did not follow this routine every morning. She also made sure both boys had deposited their underwear in the dirty clothes hamper. Clay had jokingly told the boys they could wear their under shorts more than one day, by just turning them inside out and wearing them again. Although the boys did not take him seriously, Maggie was not about to take chances.

Maggie lifted Joey's exposed foot, feeling its coldness in her hand and tucked it under the sheet. She covered him back up with his blanket. His skin had felt ice-cold. She did not want to awaken Joey or his brother just yet. She left the room, ambled quietly across the beige nylon carpet back into the hallway, and tiptoed into their daughter's room.

Kaya was a robust three year-old girl who was fast discovering the world around her. She sported her dad's almost black hair and dark brown eyes, olive complexion and round face. Someday, thought Maggie, she will be a real heartbreaker.

Kaya was awake and restless. Rubbing her eyes at her mom as she entered the doorway she smiled and said, "I'm hungry, Mommy."

"Come here Sweetie. Let mommy hold you for a minute. Are you cold Kaya? You need to get out of your pull-ups and put on your big girl panties. Mommy will take care of you. Did you sleep well? Mommy loves you, yes I do!"

Maggie reached down and picked up her daughter, who gave her a big hug around the neck. Kaya's body felt warm to her touch. After giving her little girl a kiss on the cheek, Maggie put Kaya back into bed and opened the chest of drawers, bringing back a flannel jumpsuit from her drawer. Maggie slipped Kaya into it. This would give her some added warmth on this cold morning. Maggie picked up Kaya and marched downstairs into the kitchen. Kaya gave her mom another big hug and kiss on her cheek.

"Love you Mommy," she said.

"I love you too, Sweetie."

The carpeting felt unusually cold under Maggie's feet, but everything changed when she stepped onto the tiled kitchen floor. The iciness was so cold it reminded Maggie of her childhood, when during a hot summer day, she had licked a Popsicle bought from an ice-cream boy vender who had it stored in dry ice. With the first lick, her tongue stuck to the Popsicle. Her feet felt the same this morning. Maggie wished she had worn her slippers or a pair of Clay's socks before venturing out of their bedroom. Most days she enjoyed the freedom of walking barefoot, but not this morning.

The playpen sat next to the kitchen table where Maggie safely put Kaya when she cooked meals. Although Kaya was big enough not to need confinement, Maggie felt safer with her in the playpen. Kaya's vocabulary exceeded most or her peers and she was mentally mature far beyond an average three-year-old child. After dragging some toys away, Maggie sat Kaya on a blanket and handed her a favorite Minnie Mouse stuffed toy. Kaya clutched the doll and gave Minnie a hug.

"I will be back in a minute Kaya. If you need mommy, just holler real loud... okay?"

Kaya nodded, "Yes, mommy, please hurry back." She turned her attention to Minnie Mouse.

Clay and Maggie had decided Kaya would be their last child. The surprise of expecting another child after giving birth to the twins had thrilled Maggie. Knowing it would be her last child, she had expected to have another son. During her seventh month of pregnancy, Maggie had an ultrasound examination. The doctor found no problems, nor did she find a scrotum. Maggie and Clay were ecstatic. The birth of a daughter was fulfilling their childbearing goals. Kaya became precious to the entire family. It was good for the boys to have a sister. Maggie knew it would be safe to leave Kaya in the playpen, so she went back to her bedroom to wake up Clay.

"Clay, please get up. There's no heat in the house and it's too cold for the kids. Kaya's in her playpen so I have to get back to the kitchen. I didn't wake the boys yet."

Clay rolled over, pulled his blanket higher around his neck, and spoke without opening his eyes. "Maggie, come on, you know I worked late yesterday. Can't you take care of it? Give me a few more minutes, babe." He rolled back on his side, away from her, pretending to go back to sleep.

"Clay, please get up. It's freezing in here. The electricity is off. I don't know if a circuit breaker has kicked off or what happened. Won't you at least get up and light the gas fireplace for me? That'll take the chill out of the house and keep us comfortable until you get the power back on."

She waited for a response, but did not get one. "Come on, Honey, please! You know I don't usually ask you to help me get the boys off to school in the morning, but today I just cannot do everything by myself. I have to get Joey and Eric out of bed and ready for school. The school bus will be here in an hour. With the house as cold as it is, I know the boys won't cooperate with me."

Chapter 2

Clay opened his eyes. "Ah, all right. Donald, my construction supervisor was a real asshole yesterday. He made me work through my lunch break to finish the sink installation in the half-million dollar estate in Gaylord that he's building. He said we were close to his deadline for completing the house and didn't want to lose his bonus for not finishing on time. Donald was supposed to leave my apprentice to help me. Instead, he took my apprentice with the rest of the crew for a couple of beers and a greasy burger for lunch. If he doesn't pay me for working through my lunch hour I'll call my union steward and write a grievance tomorrow. I'm sick of it. I've carried his sorry ass long enough at work. The only reason he wanted to finish the job early was so he and a couple of the carpenters could go to the titty bar after quitting time. As a journeyman plumber, I won't put up with his shit much longer."

"Clay, please don't talk about the strip bar to me. I think it is disgusting and silly for men to shove their hard-earned money into the thong of a nearly naked woman. On the other hand, maybe Donald doesn't have a good wife like you do." Maggie leaned over Clay and gave him a quick kiss on the cheek. "Please don't bring your work home with you. You know it just makes you angry and upset. Okay honey? I need your help this morning."

"I know. I know it isn't your fault. Donald is the worst crook I ever worked for. Someday, I will start my own plumbing business and he can go to Hell." Clay sighed, rolled over and supported himself on his elbows, kissed her and continued; "What did you say about the furnace Babe?"

"It doesn't work, Clay. I believe the electricity is off. Would you mind getting up, going downstairs, and lighting the fireplace? I have to get back to the kitchen. Kaya is by herself in her playpen. I don't like leaving her alone for long -- I've already been gone longer than I should have."

"Just give me a second to get up."

"Thanks. I'm going to wake up the boys and go back downstairs." Maggie lovingly rubbed her hands though his hair, continuing down to his face. She gave him another quick kiss and left the room.

Clay sat up; rolled to the right side of the bed, throwing back the covers. He dangled his feet over the edge of the bed, shifted his weight and stood up. His pajama bottoms started to fall down. The elastic around the top had stretched and worn out after too many machine washings. Clay grabbed them with his left hand and held them up. He didn't care what shape they were in, he only wore them to sleep in. If it were up to him, he would sleep naked like his ancestors before him. However, Maggie bought his pajamas, so he would wear them to please her.

The bathroom was his first target. Then he'd dress and see what was going on with the furnace. *Burr ... Maggie was right.* It had gotten cold in here. Damn cold. Clay decided it was too cold to be naked and too cold for just his worn out pajamas. He picked up his bathrobe from the chair at the end of his bed and wrapped it around his body tying it tightly to keep his pajamas up. Hopping on one foot, Clay put on his soft-soled moccasins. Something caught his eye. His Dream Catcher sat on the carpeting just below their bedroom window.

His Dream Catcher was old, almost timeless. It was passed down from Shaman to Shamans of his Huichol Indian ancestors until it reached Thunder Eagle, a tribal Shaman in Mexico, of whom Clay was a descendent. Before Thunder Eagle died, he gave the Dream Catcher to his granddaughter Clay Bird Spirit, who married a white man, Steve Mellon. Steve took Clay Bird Spirit to Michigan where she gave birth to Lisa. Lisa married Henry Wheeler when she was fifteen years old. Henry and Lisa had one son named Rob. They may have had more children had Henry not been killed while fighting in the Korean War. Rob Wheeler married Sandra Johnson and honored his grandmother by naming his only son after her, and her grandfather, Thunder Eagle. Clay Eagle Wheeler was born. No pictures of Thunder Eagle existed. If they did, the pictures would show an uncanny likeness to Clay. Clay married Maggie and fathered three children.

Clay Bird Spirit bypassed her children and grandchildren, giving 10 year-old Clay Eagle Wheeler the Dream Catcher. She died one year later after celebrating her one hundred second birthday. From that day forward, Clay always kept the Dream Catcher in his bedroom, bringing it with him after he married Maggie. After building their family home in the Michigan woodlands, Clay hung the Dream Catcher on their bedroom window.

"Clay Eagle Wheeler, my grandson," he remembered Great Grandma Wheeler's voice as if it were yesterday, "Take care of this woven circle. Hang it on bedroom window. When you sleep, it guards you from evil dreams. When sun arises in morning, it destroys the evil dreams. In addition, my grandson, it serves to catch good spirit dreams." In his mind, Clay could still see the wrinkled smile from her full lips as she spoke to him. "Good dreams seep through the center hole. Evil dreams caught in web around center. Good dreams float down the feather and bless you with peace at night. You bring great honor to your ancestor, Thunder Eagle, who was the greatest of all Shamans. He sent me a sign saying, Give Dream Catcher to Clay Eagle. Through him, it must pass."

Clay Wheeler did not believe the legends, but he honored Great Grandma Wheeler's memory by displaying his Dream Catcher as she requested. After Great Grandma Wheeler died, he missed her wisdom and listening to the stories of his ancestors. It disturbed Clay to know he did not write down any of the tales after she shared them with him. To Clay, the Dream Catcher had great sentimental value and beauty, nothing beyond that. Someday, he would pass it down to one of his own children. Clay hung the Dream Catcher on his easterly facing bedroom window. It presented its glory every morning when the sunshine blasted through the windowpane and magnified the image of the Dream Catcher as a shadow on the opposite wall of the bedroom. The shadow danced as a shimmering image from the top of the wall and slowly moved downward toward the floor as the sun rose. However, this morning it was different. The Dream Catcher was on the floor. A place to the best of his knowledge it had never been before.

Although not a believer in traditional Indian folklore and religion, finding his Dream Catcher on the floor bewildered Clay. He remembered securely attaching it to the glass. He recovered the Dream Catcher from the carpet and reattached it to the window. Without further thought, Clay left the bedroom and hurried down the stairway, not stopping at the first floor, but continuing into the basement to check the furnace. A few moments later Clay strolled back upstairs into the kitchen where Maggie was preparing breakfast. Their children were dressed and sat at the table.

"Maggie, Honey, I checked the electrical panel and found all the circuit breakers on. The power must be off somewhere outside our home. That's the reason the furnace isn't working, so I'll light the fireplace. Where are the damn matches? I'll get the fireplace going if you help me find them."

"Just a second and I'll get them for you," replied Maggie.

"It's getting goddamn cold in here, Maggie. Sometimes I wonder why we didn't move to Arizona or Florida after getting married. Michigan sucks during the fall and wintertime. Did you find the matches, Honey?"

"Here they are. I took them from the mantle over the fireplace and lit the burners on the cooking stove. I'm glad we opted for the propane gas cooking stove rather than the electric range." Maggie pulled a couple of the matches out of the box, putting them on a shelf above the sink in case she needed them while cooking. She handed the rest of the matches to Clay.

"Please watch your language in front of the kids. They are starting to mimic the construction slang you use."

Clay gave his wife a quick unhappy glance and snatched the matchbox from her hand. He strolled over to the playpen, reached down and gave little Kaya a hug and quick kiss, "How's daddy's baby girl today, huh? I love you, Kaya Bird."

Clay stood up, gawking at Kaya as she smiled back at him. Kaya scrunched up her nose and whispered, "I love you too, Daddy." His daughter was the pride of his existence. Besides, she resembled him and he was proud to show her off to his friends. Clay Eagle Wheeler sported an olive complexion with a large crop of straight black hair on his head. His hair was cut just below the top of his ears, reaching his shirt collar at the back of his neck. His high cheekbones betrayed his ancestral ties to Indian heritage. He appreciated his complexion every summer when he saw his work partners sporting sunburns. He never burned, his skin gradually darkened to brown. Kaya also had black hair, long and straight, without a hint of curl. Her completion was an olive hue like Clay and darkened to a bronze color during the summer. There was no refuting that the Indian DNA was dominant in her genetic heritage. Clay's family was perfect, with two sons to carry his name and a beautiful daughter. Maggie and the children shared his happiness and continued to teach him the meaning of love.

Clay went into the living room and started lighting the fireplace. If the electricity were on, he would just turn on the gas, push the ignition switch and "poof" it would light. Clay turned on the gas, opened the screen and threw a match under the fake logs. The gas ignited with a popping sound, scattering some of the dust from the bottom of the fireplace. The imitation logs began to glow a dull orange color, casting small flickers of light throughout the room. Heat permeated the living room and seeped into the combined dining and kitchen areas. He returned to the kitchen and handed the extra matches to his wife.

"It will be warming up in a bit, Babe."

Joey and Eric sat at the dining table. They giggled and punched each other on the shoulder, impatiently waiting for their mom to fix their breakfasts.

"Dad, Eric just hit me, can I hit him back? Hey dad, this is cool! Do we have to go to school today? Huh? Huh? Can we stay home?"

"Dad," interrupted Eric, "Joey hit me first. He always does it to get me in trouble. Can I punch him back?"

Clay couldn't ignore their punching and teasing this morning. Under different circumstances, he would have ignored their bantering and drink a cup of coffee. Today was different. Yesterday was a bad day at work and today there was no electricity. The cold house shortened his temper.

"You boys shut-up and quit your bickering. Your mom and I don't wish to hear your complaints all the time." Clay's loud voice betrayed his impatience. "Joey. You just asked me three questions and I will ignore them all. So please go and get your Walkman radio. Tune it to WKEO, and see if the school buses are running. The power might be off all over the county."

"What could be better than a day off school?" replied Joey as he jumped out of his chair intending to run and get his Walkman. Before he left, he lightly punched Eric on the arm with his fist, being careful to make sure his dad was no longer watching him. It seemed only seconds before he was back in his chair.

"I can't hear anything dad, my batteries must be dead." Joey turned the switch on and off several times, but not a sound came from the radio speaker.

Clay thought for a moment. "Go look in the top drawer of my desk, Joey. There's a four-pack of Walgreen alkaline double "A's" there. You will find them under my checkbook. Don't touch anything else. Bring the batteries here and put them in your radio."

Clay kept an unloaded handgun in the second drawer, which he kept locked. He had trained the boys how to handle firearms. Clay loved his children and Maggie. He was trying to be a good father. He would protect his family from all crime and the degenerates who meandered throughout modern society. Clay owned 2 Mossberg shotguns and a 30-06 Remington hunting rifle with a 4X Weaver scope. He also had a couple of Remington twenty-two rifles, which he used to teach the boys gun handling and how to hunt small game. Clay never kept a loaded gun in his house, and the bullets and shotgun shells were locked in a separate cabinet for safety.

Before Joey had a chance to get the batteries, Eric blurted out. "I told you not to listen to music in your Walkman last night after we were in bed. I told you, didn't I, Joey. I knew the batteries were almost dead. I told you, but you didn't listen. Huh, didn't I tell you, huh, didn't I?" Not stopping there, he turned his smiling face towards his dad.

"Dad, he was listening to his Walkman last night after you told him not to." Still smiling, he glanced at Joey, sticking out his tongue and making a face at him.

Joey countered back. "No, I didn't, Dad. I was going to but I didn't turn it on. I just shoved it under my pillow and went to sleep. Really, Dad, I didn't listen to my Walkman last night. Don't believe Eric. He always wants to get me into trouble."

Eric countered by kicking Joey's left knee.

"OUCH!" yelled Joey. "He kicked me, dad. Real hard, too!"

Clay faced his boys. He crossed his arms and gave them a stare of total exasperation. Perhaps there was something to finding his Dream Catcher on the floor of his bedroom after all. It was time to stop this power struggle. "Shut up, Eric. Quit tattling on your brother. You know better. Brothers should be sticking up for and protecting each other, not opponents."

His eyes shot at Joey. "Put down the damn Walkman and quit screwing around. Go and get those batteries as I told you to. You're wasting time. I've had enough of your petty arguments, boys."

Joey put the Walkman on the table, pushed back his chair and left the dining room, this time, ignoring his brother. Maggie reached into a cabinet below the silverware drawer, bringing back a small saucepan. She filled it half-full with milk from the refrigerator and sat the pan on the burner. After the milk began to steam, she picked up the pan and poured part of it over a bowl of instant oatmeal, topping it off with a sprinkling of brown sugar.

Maggie got Kaya from her playpen and put her into her booster chair. Kaya loved oatmeal and toast, especially if the toast had butter and grape jelly piled on it. Today, there would be no toast. A slice of bread topped with jelly would have to do. Maggie filled Kaya's plastic glass half-full with the remaining warm milk and presented it to her little angel. "Here baby doll."

Kaya smiled as she started eating breakfast. It wasn't the first time she heard the bickering of her brothers. Her smile was one of confidence, passive intelligence, and patience.

The twins and Clay preferred waffles, but without the toaster, she could not fix them. Maggie bought prepared frozen waffles rather than making them from scratch to save time preparing breakfast on school days. Today she would serve something else. She cracked some eggs into a fry pan, placed it on the still flaming burner and cooked them solid. Once done, she slid them on plates for her men. More bread, more butter, jelly and some napkins.

Maggie started to fix coffee. However, after realizing the electric coffeemaker would not work she retrieved the half-used jar of instant Maxwell House coffee and heated some water on the stove. She came to the table bringing with two steaming cups of coffee, handing one to Clay.

Clay sat at the head of the table with his family. They bowed their heads to say a brief prayer. "Joey, would you say the blessing for us this morning, son?

"Sure dad!"

Joey bowed his head. The room got quiet. With a loud voice, Joey said, "BLESSING! AMEN. Let's eat."

Clay glanced quickly at Maggie and chuckled. Maggie interjected, "Let me continue for my ungrateful son, Lord. We thank you for this food, and thank you for providing nourishment for us. Amen."

Joey fought back a snicker. The rest of the family except Clay followed with another "AMEN."

"Clay, I wish you never taught him that "blessings" joke. You know how I hate to make fun of religion. I know you're not a believer but please have respect for the rest of us."

"Ah babe, you know the boys don't take it seriously. Besides, whoever or whatever the Lord is, if he exists must have a sense of humor; maybe he doesn't approve of electricity either. He didn't give us any today."

Maggie gave him a "don't say that in front of the kids" look. Her disapproval of his lack of religious beliefs mattered not to him. It was time for Clay to change the subject.

"Joey, Clay asked, "did you get your Walkman working?"

"Something must be wrong with your batteries too, Dad. My radio is as dead as the owl that slammed against our windshield last week when we were going to the grocery store."

Clay stopped eating. "There is nothing wrong with those batteries, Joey. Moreover, there is nothing funny about the owl we killed with our car. When I was a child, my great-grandmother, Clay Bird Spirit told me an owl is the symbol of death. Killing an owl with my car was not a good omen. You cannot kill death, my son. Let's get back to the subject of your Walkman, Joey. You probably dropped and broke it."

Clay forced a disgusted glance toward his son. It was important for him to teach his children the value of taking care of any equipment they owned.

"Dad, I know it ain't broken. I didn't drop it either." Joey's shoulders dropped and his eyes began examining the eggs on his plate, picking at them, not eating. He began pushing them around in his plate with his bread, knowing his dad was not happy with him.

After reading the faces of the boys, Maggie said, "Joey, the word is; ISN'T not AIN'T. Now please, eat your breakfast."

"Listen to your mom, son. She knows proper English. She corrects me all the time," interjected Clay. "I know those batteries in my drawer are good, Maggie. I get so tired of the lack of respect for items I buy this family."

"Clay, please don't get angry today. You know this is hard on all of us. Besides, perhaps Joey is telling the truth about his Walkman. Did you consider that?"

"Don't push me, MAGGIE. You don't need to get me going today." He gave his wife a disgusted stare but quickly realized he was wrong. It was time to smooth over the bumps in the plumbing connections, as he would say in the plumbing business. He paused for a moment of silence and composed his emotions.

"I'm sorry Maggie; nothing is going right for me. Please forgive me Babe; you know I love you and the kids. It just seems problems are building on me quicker than I can dump them off. Sometimes I feel that I'm standing in a bucket of shit up to the top of my head, and I can only see with a periscope."

Maggie gave Clay a disbelieving stare for what he just said at the breakfast table. Yet, Clay could see the forgiveness in her eyes. Joey and Eric were laughing at their dad's reply, almost to the point of rolling off their chairs.

"Boys, just ignore what I said and hurry up and finish eating. I don't want you to be late for school. Babe, I'm going outside to see if the power line is down somewhere on our property. Keep the kids inside until I get back. I want to make sure there is no danger of electrocution."

Clay quickly drank the rest of his coffee, wiped his hands with a napkin and stood away from the table. Maggie stood up long enough to take a step over to him, giving him a quick hug.

"Okay, Clay. Please be careful. I love you."

"I love you too, Babe. If you have the boys ready for school when I get back, I'll walk with them to the highway this morning."

He returned her hug with a kiss, staring yearningly into her loving eyes. I'll be back soon, Babe. I'm going to get my coat and leave in a second."

Maggie removed the dirty dishes from the table and put them in the sink. "Joey and Eric, do what your father said. We're already late. I'll clean up the kitchen while Kaya is finishing her breakfast. At least we have a gas fired hot water heater and I can wash the dishes."

Clay, who was just exiting the house, overheard what Maggie said. He could not resist one last dig before leaving. He turned grinning at Maggie from the living room. "You haven't noticed that our water pressure is getting lower have you, babe? Picture what you just said. If we have no electricity, we have no electric well pump; there will be no water, hot or cold in a few minutes. I swear, you may have brown hair but your roots are blond." His smile projected his love to her.

"Clay, I have enough work to do without your words of wisdom. Yes, there was water when I washed my hands and when the kids washed up; the water flowed slowly. There was enough water to make coffee. I suspect it will quit flowing as soon as the tank pressure drops because no more is being pumped out of the well. Nevertheless, there still is some pressure in our pressure tank. So there, I have brown hair after all."

She turned her back with a teasing and playful mannerism, ignoring Clay and giving her attention to the twins, who were not in any hurry to get ready for the school bus. "Boys! Please don't make me tell you again. Get moving, now!"

Chapter 3

Clay and Maggie had inherited the 160-acre parcel of land from her grandfather when he passed away from a massive stroke at the age of 84. Grandpa Harrington felt pressure and pain in his neck. Ralph Black, his next-door neighbor took him to St. Mary's hospital. Grandpa Harrington sat in the waiting room while Ralph was showing Grandpa's insurance card at the admitting desk. Suddenly Grandpa Harrington grabbed the left side of his neck and said; "It's starting to hurt again."

It was the last sentence he spoke. A massive blood clot rushed into his carotid artery blocking the passageway into his brain. Death was almost instantaneous. He slipped off the imitation leather chair and slid to the floor as his last breath exhaled from his mouth. Six months after probating Grandpa's estate, Clay and Margie applied for a loan from the First Solidarity Bank to finance their home construction. It took Clay two-years to build their two-story three-bedroom frame home. A few of his construction friends helped him, exchanging their expertise for plumbing jobs Clay promised to do for them.

Their house stood in a small opening in the woods. Several jack pines, a few white pines, and birch trees with their beautiful peeling white bark surrounded the home. Several huge oak trees provided food for squirrels and chipmunks. In the fall, acorns rained from the oak trees, pattering the house's roof with a sound like birdshot. They rolled into the rain gutter and journeyed though the downspouts to gather in piles at the corners of the house. Clay's favorite trees were the fifty-year-old sugar maples that he tapped every spring and boiled the sap into maple syrup and candy. The children loved it.

Their house nestled a half-mile from the highway and gave them total privacy. It was expensive to put the driveway through the trees and out to the main road, and a challenge to keep the driveway clear of snow during winter months. The advantage of living in the rural country setting is the seclusion from highway noise, neighbors, and the rest of the world. They were at peace with the land and the wild animals.

Their home site was beautiful during the summer, but when the fall season arrived, the driveway filled with leaves. A few weeks later Mother Nature blanketed it with snow.

Clay bought a snowplow for his four-wheel drive Chevy truck. Without it, they were snowbound after a snowstorm. The massive amounts of leaves that fell from the trees in the fall were less of a concern. Clay often jested if Maggie's God planted the trees; it was his job to move the leaves from his driveway with a good wind when they fell to the ground. By summer, much of the leaves had rotted into fertilizer for the wild plants and foliage.

Michigan winter month often resulted in large blizzards and lake effect snow. Sometimes the storms leave up to three feet or more of snow on the ground. This year would be no different. Clay and Maggie were prepared with extra food and other supplies. An extra set of warm clothes, a blanket, and a shovel were stored in the truck in case they were stranded on the highway.

Their house sat about thirty miles east of Lake Michigan. The closer one lived to the lake, the more snow he had to plow.

Clay opened the front door and walked outside to his pick-up truck. He could examine the power line better by walking the driveway rather than driving, so he gave his truck a passing glimpse. Everything was quiet . . . unusually quiet. He searched where the power line is connected to a short insulated rod at the peek of the roof. He saw no problem. Clay breathed deeply through his stuffy nose and smelled the slight pine scent of the woodlands as it floated through the morning air. There was no pungent smell of burned varnish in the air, which would indicate a burned-out electrical transformer.

Clay saw his exhaled breath as a heavy fog. His Uncle Joe used to say; "When you go outside and see your breath, you will know that your Aunt Linda and I are heading to Arizona for the winter." He often thought about them on cold days. One year when Uncle Bob and Aunt Susan went to Arizona, they never returned to Michigan.

The cold damp air caused his nose to drip. Clay pulled out a red hunting handkerchief and wiped his nose before stuffing it back in his pocket.

Hell, that's all I need is a damn cold, he thought. Clay dismissed the thought, preferring to believe it was just the cold morning air kicking butt with his sinuses.

God, he loved this place. He loved nature, the out-of-doors, and studying the trees and his garden as they grew. He often took strolls around his property, exploring the wildlife, thinking about existence and life itself. He could see the beauty in a blade of grass. He studied the annual growth of trees and watched the squirrels and birds feasting at his bird feeder just outside the dining room window. This was Clay's small part of paradise. However, it was not the time for daydreaming or meditating. His thoughts left the metaphysical world and came back to the reality of "now" and his search continued to seek what caused the electrical power outage.

Clay tightened his belt and started walking down the two-track gravel driveway to check the power line running from the house to the highway. His trousers always had a tendency to slip down as he walked. Maggie told him he didn't have an ass. She also said his small ass was much better than having a big one. He remembered how she laughed every time he cinched up another notch in his belt to keep his trousers from falling down.

His final destination was the power pole at the highway's edge. Perhaps a motorist knocked it down overnight. Perhaps a tree limb fell on the wire between the highway and his home breaking the wire. Clay watched where he was walking so he would not be electrocuted.

The sun shone brightly in the eastern sky but the temperature was deceptively cold. A light frost had thrown a white blanket over his vegetable garden during the night. Clay saw his beefsteak tomato and green bell pepper plants had died and the plant stems were drying up. He had stored plenty of vegetables his family had picked from the garden for the long winter. They would keep for several months in the root cellar behind the house. The warm weather had lasted two weeks longer than normal for northern Michigan. The "Farmer's Almanac" was correct again.

The large pumpkins that Joey and Eric grew as part of a 4H Club program sparkled with wet dew. The boys planned to enter a couple of the pumpkins in the County Fair in August, but their pumpkins developed too late for a successful entry. Next year the twins would start seedlings early in the season, growing them in the house before transplanting them to the vegetable garden. Maggie would make a pumpkin pie or two with this year's crop if the deer didn't eat them first.

South of the house, a wild turkey grazed. Where there was one turkey there would be others. Several smaller turkeys appeared out of the wild ryegrass and started to graze and glean the field with their mother. Clay's movement spooked the turkeys sending them running into the tall wild grass where they disappeared.

Clay stopped as he came to the shoulder of Highway 2. The morning air had a slight smell of ozone, as if a lightning storm had recently passed. Everything else seemed to be the way it always had been. On the other hand, was it?

All the wires and the transformer on the power pole at the end of the driveway were intact. However, the normal hum and buzz of the alternating current from the power transformer was absent. Whatever caused the electricity to fail in his home was not something close. It was somewhere between here and Edison's power generating plant, or perhaps beyond. Clay stood for ten minutes at the shoulder of the roadway expecting at least one car or transport truck to pass down the highway. The road was empty.

No traffic came from either direction on the highway. This was never the case. He looked to the north and then to the south and saw nothing. He listened but heard no sounds of traffic coming or going. There was an unnatural stillness surrounding him as if Clay was caught somewhere between two different realities. Clay envisioned quietness when building their home in the wilderness. Now it was too quiet. This was eerily different. It was as if he were on a movie production set of the old X-Files television series.

"Hey, Fox Mulder, are you messing around with Scully behind one of my trees? Get out here and tell me what is going on." It was too bad that Maggie was not here to eavesdrop. If Maggie were here, she would laugh at his silliness.

A brief smile crossed his lips. Clay was glad no one was listening. Once more, he peered up and down the highway. There was nothing to see. He put his hands in his pockets, sneezed again, removed his red handkerchief and wiped his nose. Clay turned back to his driveway and started walking home. Damn allergies, he thought.

Walking back to the house, Clay's thoughts wandered to the normal preparations he and his family made for the cold weather. The driveway would require several more loads of gravel. If not, next spring it would become a bog pit. He learned the hard way during their first spring when Maggie had driven into the driveway after a warm spring thaw and buried the truck up to its axels in mud. It took over an hour using a winch tied to an ancient oak tree to free the Chevy truck.

He looked for the turkeys but they had not returned. They remained hidden in the tall golden ryegrass or among the hard maples. Clay's favorite summertime hobby was hiding and taking pictures of turkeys and deer. He was proud of his photo of a turkey grazing the cornfield with the morning sun just above its head. The photograph hung on the left side of his bedroom wall next to his Dream Catcher. The right side of the wall had a picture of a doe with two fawns standing in his small cornfield.

Clay took one more glance at the power line connected to his house before going back inside. He left the driveway and returned to the porch. He opened the front door and entered the living room.

Chapter 4

Maggie finished cleaning the kitchen and gathered the schoolbooks into a pile for the boys to grab as they ran through the front doorway. She stood up as Clay entered the living room.

"Maggie, something uncanny is going on here. The power lines are intact but it's as if we're living on Robinson Crusoe's deserted island. I was out on the highway for ten minutes and nothing was moving."

"Didn't you see any traffic?"

"There wasn't a car or truck in sight. I saw no airplanes or helicopters either. The only sounds I heard were birds. It was as quiet as the day I was taking nature pictures in Fox Valley animal reserve last summer. Babe, it gave me chills up and down my spine."

"You're kidding, right?" Maggie frowned.

"Nah, the highway looks stranger than shit on a church hymnal. I have no idea what happened but something did. I bet more people than just us are without electricity. Whatever happened appears serious. Maybe there was a terrorist attack somewhere in Michigan last night. I could speculate forever, but you know me I have to know the truth about everything, not conjecture."

Maggie cocked her head sideways and tightened her lips in displeasure at his crude church hymnal humor but said nothing. Clay's defense mechanisms of humor and sarcasm during times of stress helped him cope with the unknown. Maggie recognized Clay's apprehensiveness when he had no answers. This was one of those times.

"Should I send Joey and Eric out to wait for the bus? They usually announce school closings if there is a problem. Without a working radio, we have no way of knowing whether school is in session. I wish we had more than one battery powered unit. The telephone isn't working either."

"I'll buy a spare radio the next time we go to Mackinaw City," replied Clay. "You're right Babe; we should have more than one radio."

Clay had no plans to send his sons to the highway to wait for the school bus alone. "Tell me when the boys are ready to go and I'll walk them to the highway. If the bus doesn't arrive we'll be back here in a short while. I want you to stay in the house and lock the doors until I get back. Something is not right. Until I find out what's going on, I'm not going to go to work and leave you and the kids home alone today."

She put her arms around him and squeezed. Clay hugged her back. He peeked into her reassuring brown eyes. He told her they reminded him of the eyes of a deer fawn, bright, shiny and full of love.

"I'll check on Kaya and see if the boys are ready to go, that is if you will let go of me, Clay!"

Clay released her. "Just send them outside when they are ready, Babe. I'll wait on the front porch."

Clay opened the front door and went outside. He examined his surroundings, inhaling the fresh air through his partly closed sinus cavities. He strolled over to the wooden rocker in the corner of the porch and sat down. Clay and Maggie often sat together on the rocker during summer evenings, watching the sun go down until mosquitoes forced them to go inside for protective cover.

His eyes scanned the desolate horizon. Clay reached into his shirt pocket for a cigarette. Although he quit smoking five years ago, the old habit of reaching for a smoke when tension arose still held him. His last cigarette was after the funeral services for his former employer, Frank Justice.

Frank had started Clay on cigarettes, too. It was common for many professional builders and plumbers to smoke. The hard labor often caused them to seek stress relief with a tension reducing nicotine fix. Frank got Clay off the cigarette habit just before the grim reaper took Frank away with lung cancer. He missed his old friend and longed for those extended discussions with Frank during work hours about nothing and everything. Frank had an answer and solution for every problem, whether it was job related, religious, political or social. The solution was a verbal bashing of conservatism, blaming the religious right and the Republicans for all the woes of the world. As a union man, Frank was a lifetime Democrat who was quick to bash anything that was not liberal. The discussions were always fun and rarely serious. Frank had no solution for the lung cancer that took his life within a year of its discovery. Just before he died, Frank said his final achievement in life was convincing several of his friends and co-workers to learn from his pain and quit smoking. Frank would live many years in Clay's memory.

Joey and Eric exited the house with their schoolbooks, closing the door behind them. They found their dad sitting on the rocker staring off into space as if he were entranced. Eric's voice startled Clay back into the present.

"Dad, let's go. The bus will be here in fifteen minutes. Hey, do yah wanna race us to the highway? Huh? Let's run!"

"Not today boys," said Clay, as he stood up. "Let's walk together this time. Don't run out of my sight. Hey guys, do you think it's summertime? Button up those jackets; it's cold out here. We don't need any sick kids."

Both of the boys stopped, put down their books, zipped up their jackets, and began to lag behind their dad. Clay looked back at his sons. "A little faster guys. Move it. Just because you can't run doesn't mean you can't walk fast. The buss might not be running on schedule today. It could arrive early."

A quick burst of speed and they were again with Clay. The walk to the highway was uneventful; almost a mirror reflection of the one Clay had taken by himself a half hour earlier. Nothing had changed since his first trip except the sky was brighter and the turkeys were "LONG GONE," as the Detroit Tiger baseball announcer, Ernie Harwell would have said.

One of Clay's favorite pastimes was listening to the Detroit Tiger baseball games. Sure, they had a lousy team, but they were the Michigan home team. Baseball has everything, statistics, patriotism, and enough strategy to excite fans to second-guess both the managers and the umpires. Clay thought about the hundreds of hours he spent listening to Ernie Harwell, the voice of Tiger radio broadcasts before he retired after the 2002 baseball season. Ernie never failed to raise the adrenalin in Clay's body when a Detroit Tiger player hit a home run ball. He could still hear Ernie's voice in his memories shouting from his broadcast booth, "IT'S LONG GONE!" Ernie's expression had become part of Clay's vocabulary. Today it seemed civilization was also "LONG GONE!"

Joey and Eric played tag as they ignored Clay's instructions and began racing down the driveway. The twins became aware of the stillness around them and they joined their dad once more. The boys felt tension because of the lack of highway noise that under normal conditions filtered through the trees toward their home. The trio reached Michigan Highway 2 and saw neither cars nor trucks traveling down the road. Clay waited, watching the expressions of the boys' faces as they tried to ponder this unusual happening.

Joey broke the silence, "Dad, it is weird out here. Can't you feel something is wrong? It's like being in a scary movie."

"I know son, but there is nothing to be afraid of. When we three men are together nothing can bother us. Right, Eric?"

"Yeah, right dad. You know, if Joey says this is weird, it's weird. Are we going to stay here long?"

"Nah, not long at all," said Clay, as he resumed looking in both directions down the highway, seeing nothing. A few moments later, he put a hand on each of his sons' shoulders. "No school today, boys. Let's go home."

"Yeah, DAD! Thanks! Cool!" Joey shouted.

"You're it," said Eric as he tagged Joey on the shoulder. He broke into a dash back toward the house. Joey ran after him, his books flopping in his arms. The boys' apprehension vanished. They were far ahead of their dad. Clay jogged behind them. Keeping up was not a problem for him if he had wanted to run. He began coughing and once more, he blew his nose. He looked in his handkerchief. The mixture had a little blood in it.

Chapter 5

The more Maggie tried to do her household tasks the more frustrated she became. The vacuum cleaner could not run. It was dark and cold in the upstairs bedrooms. The fireplace only heated the first floor and was the least efficient means of staying warm.

The air was warmer on the main floor and it no longer felt damp. Maggie turned off the propane gas to the fireplace. At $3.20 a gallon there was no sense in wasting the precious fuel. She gathered the kid's dirty clothes, walked down the stairway into the basement, and dropped the dirty clothes on the floor. She grabbed a kerosene lantern from a storage shelf next to the washing machine, lit the wick and hung it on a hook screwed into the floor joist near the laundry area. Maggie gathered and stuffed the soiled clothing into the washing machine, poured in a cup of liquid Tide and turned it on. Nothing happened. She pulled the clothing back out of the machine and stuffed them into a laundry basket.

"Goddamnit . . . Nothing works in this house." Maggie said aloud. She was glad Clay walked the kids to the highway and didn't see what she had done. She shut her eyes and shook her head, took a deep breath, and composed herself enough to reach down and turn off the gas to the hot water heater.

The tank still had about 50 gallons of water left in it. Nevertheless, they'd need to drain it out of the valve at the bottom of the tank to gather hot water.

The boys and Clay opened the door and walked in the house. That meant there would be no school today and Clay would not go to work either.

"Clay, there's no more water." Maggie shouted from the basement.

"What a surprise, huh?" He said sharply.

"Clay, for once in your life quit the smart ass comments and let's work together. I meant to say the pressure tank is empty you jug head. I was afraid the hot water heater could catch on fire so I turned the gas valve off. Would you mind coming down here for a minute?"

Clay took the last step down into the basement. "I'm glad you thought about the hot water heater. It was a good idea to turn off the gas until we get the power back on." He smiled yearningly at his wife.

She gave him a quick kiss on the cheek. "If you're not going to go to work would you mind keeping an eye on Kaya while I clean the basement?"

"No problem, take your time, Babe." He loved little Kaya. Her sweet high-pitched voice reminded him of birds singing. If Kaya had been born two hundred years earlier, her totem would be the dove, symbol of peace. Clay called her "Kaya Bird." The name would have brought great honor to his ancestors, especially Thunder Eagle, and the Huichol Nation.

They hustled through their chores for a few hours and Maggie fixed a quick lunch. She made bologna sandwiches covered with mustard for Clay and peanut butter sandwiches for the boys. Unlike most little kids, Kaya hated peanut butter. She joined her dad eating some bologna, but she preferred saltine crackers with slices of thin cut processed cheese instead of bread. During the remaining daylight hours they prepared for a possible extended power outage and watched for any human who might be stirring outside the house.

Suppertime came and the kids complained to their father that they were hungry again. Clay waved them off as he held the phone to his ear. Several times throughout the day, Clay had tried to call his boss to tell him he would not be coming to work. The line was dead. The failure of all electrical works in his home reminded Clay of the famous "blue screen of death" his computer presented to him when the program committed an unrecoverable error. He hated

Microsoft. That damn blue screen that occurred when his computer system crashed was his nemesis. The computer had to be powered down, powered up; rebooted, run scandisk to clean up the errors on the hard drive and then it would start to work correctly. Perhaps the life cycle of Planet Earth functioned similarly. Maybe a blue screen of death hit the Earth and the ecology system is rebooting itself. Maybe the world needed a social and physical scandisk of the entire planet. Then, just possibly, it would start running in good order again.

Chapter 6

After supper, Maggie joined Clay and the twins as they walked to the highway together. She bundled up Kaya and let the twins put on their heavy coats and knit caps. Maggie loved the out-of-doors. She loved walking, exercising, and stayed physically fit.

Kaya's young mind grasped all the new and unique ideas, sights, and sounds of the world around her like iron to a magnet. Life was exciting, adventurous, and a total learning experience. She spoke little. She visualized sights and sounds she did not understand as if they were memories rather than experiences. She daydreamed of an endless sandbox, strange huge green plants with few branches resembling the fingers of a hand spread endlessly before her across the horizon. Holes dug out of the larger branches of the strange plants made by colorful birds making building their homes. The driveway and the trees lining it replaced her imagination. Kaya was back with her family walking to the highway.

Kaya threw her head back and gawked at her mom and dad, marveling at their gigantic size. Her brothers seemed so big and old. She loved everyone. Hate did not exist within her.

The smells of the woodlands were breathtaking. So many things of Kaya's world is new experiences. The bird's tweets sounded like bells tinkling on her toys. Listening to a bird as it sang was awe-inspiring to her. Kaya marveled at the colored leaves lying on the ground and the sounds of broken twigs snapping under her feet. She watched a field mouse running past her and quickly disappearing into a small mound of fallen leaves.

Something caught Kaya's attention on the driveway. She bent down and picked up a three-inch round stone not more than a quarter inch thick. She stared at the symmetrical round markings imbedded in the ancient coral petoskey stone. Kaya wiped the dirt from the stone on her jacket, spit on it, and wiped it again. The colors jumped out at her. She started to throw the stone but thought better of it. Looking closer, she saw a small hole at its edge large enough for a string. She squeezed the stone tightly in her hands, kissed it, and hid it away in her pocket. She would keep it for the rest of her life and someday wear it around her neck with other treasures. Kaya resumed walking and hurried to catch up to her Mom and Dad. Suddenly she stopped, knelt down, put her knees on the ground, and began staring straight ahead down the driveway.

Maggie turned to see Kaya several feet behind them. "Clay, wait a minute. Something must have gotten Kaya's attention. She just stopped."

Maggie and Clay went back to where Kaya was kneeling. Kaya raised her right hand and slowly pointed towards the end of the driveway where it exited at the highway.

In a low subdued voice she whispered, "Look Daddy."

"What is it Kaya Bird?" Clay whispered as he knelt down beside her.

"Deer, Daddy. Deer, Daddy." Kaya replied. She continued to point - not moving a muscle.

Clay searched the area with his eyes where Kaya was pointing but saw nothing. There was no movement. He saw no deer. He looked down both sides of the driveway expecting to see a spooked deer fleeing from their approach. Still there was nothing.

Clay watched as Kaya, smiled and shook her head in an up and down motion as if she were saying, "Yes." She ignored her parents and her brothers. Kaya gazed as if she was seeing far beyond the range of normal vision. Finally, she said; "Okay, good-bye." She waved her hand, stood up, and continued walking down the driveway not saying anything.

"What was that all about?" Maggie asked. "It has to be something from your side of the family," she said to Clay and laughed.

"Yup. You're right, Babe. I'll take full credit for all of my kids." He said with a subtle smile.

Kaya continued to explore nature as she moseyed ahead of her parents and behind her brothers. She stopped twice to turn around, exploring with her eyes and smelling the air, mimicking what the deer did while communicating with her. To Kaya, the message had been clear and understood. She would be the one who would lead the way.

Chapter 7

Clay's thoughts went back to his Dream Catcher. Kaya had the blood of Thunder Eagle in her veins maybe more so than her brothers did. Perhaps she did see a deer that only showed itself to her. Clay knew Kaya had an open and pure mind, receptive to ideas that would appear beyond reason and logic to adults. He remembered having similar reasoning when chatting with Great Grandma Clay Bird Spirit as a child. Perhaps it was wrong for him to dismiss the old traditions once he reached adulthood. It would serve no purpose for Clay to discuss this possibility with Maggie. Yes, it was probably from his side of the family.

Clay could not see his nearest neighbor's house which was about two miles north of him. He had never seen the house at all. There was an old two-track driveway coming out to the road and he assumed a home was at the end of the path. He did not socialize with his neighbors, preferring isolationism and enjoying being autonomous. Perhaps it was because of the Huichol Indian DNA. Without the ability to be self-reliant and self-sufficient, Clay felt his family had no business living isolated in the Michigan woodlands. His family and self-reliance took precedent over acquaintances.

Maggie reached the end of the driveway first. The highway seemed more desolate than Clay and the twins described during their first visit. She gently touched Clay's arm. Maggie slid her hand down and interlocked her fingers with his hand. Clay turned and faced her. He put his other arm around her and gave her a hug.

"Everything is going to be all right, Babe. I'll take care of you and the kids. Don't worry."

It was easy advice for Clay to give. Nevertheless, he realized that Maggie needed answers. He knew she was more apprehensive than afraid.

The twins played as if nothing had changed except for the unplanned day off from school. This was unusual during the late fall season but often happened throughout the winter months because of snow and icy road conditions. Clay and Maggie were fortunate to live on a highway that was plowed first during snowstorms. It had yet to snow this year, but Maggie knew it would happen any day.

The sparse leaves still gripping the giant oak tree branches vibrated gently in the breeze. A few continued to fall and land like colorful butterflies on the ground below. Most of the acorns had already fallen. The chipmunks, squirrels and other ground animals were gathering and storing the nuts in secret places for the long winter months ahead. Michigan white tail deer liked to chew on the acorns, but it was not their meal of choice. Clay knew a human could die of eating acorns, whereas many animals thrived on the nuts for their nourishment until springtime arrived, when Nature would again begin restocking their food supply.

The wind moved through the trees and swirled around the stumps and broken branches that had fallen during summer storms. The breezy air created a ghostly whisper, as if the Wind Goddess herself were trying to tell the family what caused the electrical power loss.

Maggie squinted and stared across the highway toward the western horizon as the sun continued to drop below the tree line causing a dark shadow to work its way across the highway toward the five humans. Old Sol resembled an orange balloon as evaporated light crystals from Lake Michigan magnified its form. Clouds briskly moved across the sky. It soon would be dark. Maggie shivered. She bent down, picked up Kaya, and held her tightly.

Clay grasped his wife's hand. Maggie put Kaya back on the ground and they turned back toward the house. When they reached the house, Clay climbed into his truck, put the key into the ignition, and tried to start it. His truck would not run. The horn and lights worked. The engine was dead. Something was wrong with the world.

Chapter 8

The next morning Maggie pulled her perishables from the refrigerator and cooked them before they could spoil. They kept a meat filled chest freezer down in the basement for an emergency. Its contents would stay frozen without electricity for several days. Maggie hoped this status was not an emergency but she would begin her planned crisis procedures as if it were. She decided if the power did not return by Thursday night, she would dry the meat into jerky to preserve it. If the power stayed off for an extended period, there would be enough dried meat sticks to help feed her family during the coming winter.

Clay had built a large pantry to store a quantity of sundry goods and food while confined inside the house during the occasional Michigan blizzards. He added enough storage space for the canned fruits and vegetables they prepared from their one-acre garden. This was a good harvest season and Maggie canned quantities of tomatoes, beans, dill pickles, beets, and sweet corn.

She also made raspberry and other wild berry preserves. Maggie made candles with the paraffin sealer. She wasted nothing. She had an eerie feeling her frugal homemaking was about to pay off in a vital way, perhaps as crucial as saving their very lives.

Chapter 9

Maggie and Clay had gone to bed early on the second day of the power failure. They threw extra covers on the twin's beds and moved little Kaya into their room. Clay lay in their king-sized bed, staring at the ceiling unable to sleep for more than a few minutes at a time. During those precious few moments of sleep, he dreamed.

A recurring dream had Clay jumping backward and forward from the days of Thunder Eagle to the present time. Sometimes he sat beside Thunder Eagle hearing the wise man preach his many prophecies. At other times he was his great-grandfather himself when Indians lived off the land and man was part of nature. It was a time when men took what they needed for the day and left the rest for tomorrow. It was comforting to live with nature for necessities. Clay believed his dreams were influenced by the stories told to him by Great Grandmother Clay Bird Spirit when he was a boy.

Sometimes Clay dreamed in full color where the multicolored blankets made by the village squaws reflected an orange hue as he sat around the tribal campfire. Occasionally he would dream about the beautiful olive complexion of the Huichol squaws who danced all-night circling the fire. He could see their almost naked bodies glistening with oil to fend off mosquitoes. Clay listened to the mesmerizing sounds of bare feet pounding Mother Earth as the drummers pounded out repetitive beats from their deerskin drums, giving honor to nature and the essence of life. Sometimes his dreams included Maggie who joined the dancers. Occasionally Maggie would be there, but with dark complexion as if transforming from a

Caucasian into a Indian squaw. Her beauty stood above all others in the tribal dance.

Clay shot back into modern times and was seated with Maggie in front of their living room fireplace. In an instant, he was pulled back in time where he was trapped in a strange hut behind Thunder Eagle's village. The hut looked out of place . . . out of time. It had no fire pit. Instead, a small heating stove with a metal chimney extending through the ceiling sat close to the wall. A bed stood on the opposite side of the room. Its mattress and mats were made of cotton instead of straw. He tried to open the door and leave the hut. The door was locked. He had no key and Clay could not leave.

He entered a small bathroom with a toilet and a little imitation ceramic washbasin. There was no shower. Clay saw an opening about a foot in diameter in the wall. Peeking out of the hole, he could see the Huichol Nation's village in the distance. Around the boundary of the hut, many oak and maple trees stood in an unnatural setting. At the edge of the village, the familiar cacti foliage with sand and rocks spread out to the horizon, as it did where his great-grandfather's nation had lived in Mexico.

The hut should have been hot but it was cold. He shivered. Yet, through the hole-in-the-wall, he saw swirling waves of heat radiation, distorting the view of the Huichol Village and its people.

Clay raised his foot and kicked around the hole to break away the wood. In the distance, Clay saw Thunder Eagle's eyes on him, bowing his head in despair. The hole was now big enough for Clay to exit. He plunged out of the opening and landed on a mound of rocky sand. As he stood up a diamondback rattlesnake slithered from beneath his feet toward a small opening underneath the hut. The building now resembled a sweat lodge. Out of fear of the snake, Clay shut his eyes and did not move. The snake disappeared. He opened his eyes and the hut was gone. The image of Thunder Eagle sprang into Clay's consciousness and spoke; "The hut is a refuge, nothing more. The rattlesnake is a danger that may or may not pass. You will know the way you need to go."

Clay woke up and found himself in bed with Maggie. He got out of bed and walked in the darkness on the cold carpet to the bathroom. The strange dream had him shaking his head. He splashed cold water on his face and started to walk back to bed. His toe swept against something on the floor. He cringed in pain. He looked down and once more saw his Dream Catcher on the floor. How could it fall again?

Clay picked up the Dream Catcher, turned, and left the bedroom. He tiptoed downstairs to his living room and sat on the couch. Clutching his Dream Catcher and gently stroking the feathers brought back memories of his Great Grandmother Clay Bird Spirit. Her words entered his thoughts, almost as if she were sitting in front of him again. Long ago, after Clay Bird Spirit became physically blind, which was five years before her death, she said, "One sees with more than eyes. There is an inner-world, my grandson, which is one of truth, knowledge and destiny. Seek it with mind, not eyes." She stared at him with her sightless eyes. Clay thought about the difficulties faced by Clay Bird Spirit's blindness. However, sometimes without the distractions of visual sense, he believed she perceived the world with greater intuitiveness. This was the lesson Clay Bird Spirit was teaching her grandson.

Clay continued to be annoyed that his dream vision had faded into obscurity. Whether it had been a warning from the mystic world, or just his mind's way of coping with stress and his personal biological demands he did not know.

Clay's thoughts returned to the pressing events threatening his family. He decided to go back to bed and wait for morning. If he could not sleep, at least he could stay warm. It was too cold to sit here on the couch.

Clay reentered their bedroom and reattached his Dream Catcher on the window again. He climbed back into bed and crawled under the covers.

He spent the remaining hours before daylight tossing back and forth under the blankets. He curled up next to Maggie's back and put his arm around her laying his right hand on her left breast. When he fell asleep, he slept the sleep of the dead.

The sun arose the next morning and shined through the trees into the bedroom casting the shadow of the Dream Catcher on the opposite wall. Maggie was the first to get out of bed. She awakened Clay and asked him to light the gas fireplace.

Clay got up without complaining and lit the fire. He shared a quick breakfast with the family and helped get the twins ready for school. Once more he hiked with his sons down the long driveway to Highway 2 while Maggie stayed home attending to Kaya Bird's needs.

The trio got to the highway and everything was the same as yesterday. No cars, trucks or school buses were visible. To Clay it seemed as if his family was the only remaining humans living on the planet. He and the boys jogged back to the house. Nothing had changed.

He walked the kids back to their house and told everyone he was calling a family meeting in a few minutes. Little Kaya Bird was agitated and restless. She pulled Joey's hair and kicked him in the chins. Joey just laughed but he did not enjoy the kick. Kaya laughed back at him before going over to tickle Eric. Afterwards, she ran to her dad for refuge from the boys and gave him a big hug. Clay picked her up, returning her hug. "I love you Kaya Bird, very, very, very much!" She smiled.

"Love you CLAY," she said. "Love mommy too!" She gave her dad a wet slobbery kiss on his left cheek.

"Hey, I'm DADDY to you kid," he replied knowing she loved to tease him by calling him by his given name. It always worked for her when she needed his full attention. After considering the slobbery kiss Clay countered by making a funny face at her, and an exaggerated "Yuuuuuuky." Clay kissed Kaya on her forehead and put her back down on the floor.

Chapter 10

Maggie watched Clay's interaction with Kaya with emotional acceptance. After the birth of the twins, she knew Clay had also wanted a daughter. Several years later, Kaya was born. Maggie was pleased to see the love Clay shared with his children. A strong bond existed between Clay and their daughter, Kaya. She had named the twins, so Clay named their daughter. The Kaya part she liked, but Maggie wasn't overly pleased when Clay gave her the middle name of "Bird." Clay told her the middle name was taken from Clay's Great Grandmother Clay Bird Spirit. After considering it, Maggie decided it was a great honor for Kaya to share the name.

It was time for Maggie to get back to her housework. This moment of observing Kaya and her daddy bonding together etched into her memories and was recalled many times in later years. Love always leaves the best memories.

Once again, Joey and Eric began their playful teasing of each other. "Joey and Eric, please sit down and behave. This is a serious moment and your dad has something to say. Kaya, would you please come here and sit with me? This is important."

The boys did as their mother asked. Kaya jumped off her dad's lap. She went running across the carpet, grabbing Maggie's leg, gave it a hug. Kaya quickly retreated from her mom and leaped onto the recliner, and looked in earnest at her dad, for an important moment in her life.

Chapter 11

Clay sat down on the loveseat and Maggie sat beside him. He sat for a moment, allowing his family to settle down before addressing his concerns to them. He started to speak, and then stopped, trying to gather his worries into sentences. There would have to be a plan of action, but he had not made a decision. Sometimes ideas would develop as he spoke. He had hopes it would happen now.

"Maggie, Joey, Eric, and of course, KAYA, this is important so please pay attention." He had stressed Kaya's name, while returning her smile. "We are in a situation that has no parallel in my memories. First, we must assume, because there are no vehicles on the highway, there is a massive power outage throughout Michigan and perhaps a large part of the country. We have no idea how long it will last. Since all of our electronic equipment no longer works, even on batteries; and I apologize to you Joey because I now know you didn't break your Walkman. I must find out what happened and when the power will be restored."

Joey smiled, and kicked his brother Eric's knee.

Eric just ignored him.

"I assume," continued Clay, "this power outage is more serious than I can imagine. First, we must consider our family's safety with the weather getting colder and storms coming any day now."

Maggie reached over and grasped Clay's left hand with hers. Their wedding rings touched and made a slight noise, showing togetherness and unity. "Clay, I could stay with the kids while you visit some of our neighbors and see if they know what's happening. Just tell me what to do, and I will do it."

Clay hesitated, letting the idea take root before responding. "Babe, that was also my thought," although he knew it was she who just suggested it. Nevertheless, it sounded logical and reasonable.

"I'm considering walking down the highway to the two-track path that is a couple of miles north of us. I don't know if it is a two-track firebreak in the woods or if there is a house there. If somebody is living there, maybe they will know what happened." He hesitated, making plans as he spoke.

"Maggie, honey, if you have a better idea just let me know. If not, this is what I propose: Eric and Joey, I need you boys to stay inside the house while I'm gone. Do NOT leave for any reason and do NOT open the door for anyone. You boys can play some of the board games we bought for you last Christmas, you know, the ones in the top of your closet that you still haven't played with. Also, please help your mom keep an eye on Kaya Bird. This is important, so don't fail me. I'm counting on both of you to be the men of the house while I'm gone."

"Clay, is this necessary? Why can't we just go with you? I know Kaya is small, but if she gets tired, you and I could take turns carrying her."

"Not this time, Babe. There are too many unexplained events occurring. I would feel better knowing you and the kids are safe here with the doors locked. Don't open the door unless it's someone you know and trust. You have the key to the shotgun cabinet. There are shells on the shelf above the guns. If anyone is too persistent in trying to get inside our home, get the shotgun, not one of the rifles. Load it with buckshot and don't worry about aiming it. One of the most feared sounds to an intruder is hearing the racking of shells into a shotgun breach. They will crap their boxer shorts at that sound. Besides, you cannot miss when you shoot a shotgun."

Joey and Eric burst out laughing at what their dad said. "Hey cool dad," both boys jumped over to where their dad stood and offered him 'high fives.' Eric continued, "Never heard that one before, dad!"

"Okay, boys, calm down, this is a crisis. I thought I'd throw an off-color statement in to relax everyone a bit. Please don't repeat what I said. Sorry, Maggie but the slang I used wasn't intentional, although it did seem to relax everyone." Clay smiled sheepishly and continued; "Getting back to the subject: Boys, return to your seats. Remember, you must cooperate with your mom. This is important and when I get back home, I don't want to find out you didn't follow her directions. You must remember that as a family everyone has to do what must be done to protect each other."

Maggie lowered her eyes to the floor, and spoke to him as her hands were slightly trembling. "Clay, I don't know if I could shoot anyone."

Clay slid closer to Maggie, their hand and wedding rings still touching. He searched her eyes and found the familiar qualities of compassion and empathy first noted during their high school dating ritual. Those qualities found his heart. It was those attributes he was asking her to put aside, until the world again became normal. He wondered if she could protect the family by killing someone who would hurt them.

Clay's eyes gazed over at Joey and Eric, before focusing on little Kaya. Looking back at Maggie, he said. "Don't consider yourself Babe; just protect our kids. I know the love you have for everyone, but sometimes love is not returned by strangers."

Clay leaned closer and gently kissed Maggie on the cheek. "Don't worry Babe; there is nothing which would keep me from coming back to you guys. Without you, I have no existence. I know you're strong, otherwise I would never leave. Our love gives us hidden strengths to carry us through any crisis."

They shared a kiss, an eternal bond between them. Clay stood up from the couch, and faced his children. He leaned down and gave the boys a hug followed by a hearty handshake.

"Boys, after I go, take good care of your mom. You know I'm counting on you. I'm not leaving just yet. I have to prepare to leave which shouldn't take too long. Love both you guys." There was sadness and concern in his face.

"Ah, Dad, don't worry about it. We men can handle everything," replied Eric. Joey sat back down and said nothing.

Clay picked up Kaya, giving her a squeeze and gentle kiss on her cheek. He whispered to her; "Take care of your brothers, Kaya Bird."

Kaya grinned, and said; "I will Daddy," and kissed Clay on his chin. "Yuk, whiskers!"

Two hours later, Clay was ready to leave. He put on a pair of cotton socks, covered them with a wool pair and struggled into his insulated boots. He retrieved an eight-inch hunting knife with a razor sharp blade from his gun cabinet. Clay had used the knife to dress out several deer. He put the leather sheath on his belt and fastened it around his waist. Clay could legally carry the knife as long as he didn't hide it under his clothing. The knife raised his self-assurance enough to start his journey. He put on his wool jacket and warm deer hunting gloves. Clay's preparations were completed. He hesitated before walking toward the front door. If he remained inside the house with all the warm clothes on, his body would soon start to perspire and the dampness would make him colder once he went out-of-doors.

Maggie grabbed his arm; "Clay, here is some food I packed for you. It's not much, but it will keep you from getting hungry on the road. I put in two tubes of saltine crackers, four cans of Vienna sausages with pop tops, and three sealed bottles of drinking water. Those were left over from the case we bought at Wal-Mart last summer." She handed him the small sack with the items. He placed the sack into his backpack.

"Thanks, Babe. I hope that I won't need it, but it sure wouldn't hurt to be prepared if something happened. Hmmm. Four cans of baby dicks, huh. Little artery cloggers, but they taste good."

"Okay, talk dirty, but you know they'll taste great when you get hungry, Clay. You always asked me to buy those sausages for your lunch at work. They remind me of you during our SPECIAL moments." Her voice contained levity, which helped break the seriousness of the occasion.

"Personally, I thought that I was much bigger than a Vienna sausage, but then, if you . . . ah, never mind. I guess it would be best not to continue this conversation when I'm already so far behind schedule." He smiled, knowing she had scored more points than he had on the invisible joke meter.

Again, he hugged her for a longtime, but did not kiss. Clay released Maggie and stood at the front door. He opened it and started to leave. For one moment, he hesitated. "Be sure to lock the door after I leave. I love you."

Chapter 12

Clay abruptly turned his head away from Maggie and sneezed onetime into the cold air before leaving the house. Maggie thought she saw small tears in his eyes. She watched him meander down the driveway. Maggie felt stranded and isolated in the wilderness. Loneliness was gripping and expanding her inner fears.

It was difficult for Maggie to hide her emotions and insecurity from the kids, but she knew it was necessary to pretend nothing was amiss. Clay had been gone about fifteen minutes when she decided to get busy doing something, anything.

"Joey, you and Eric help me clean up the house. Stay indoors as your father instructed and don't open the door to anyone. I'll tend to Kaya's needs and we can finish the housework together. Perhaps we'll play some Monopoly when the work is done."

"Mom, look at Kaya!" Eric shouted. Kaya was trembling and was staring into the fireplace. Her back turned towards her mom and brothers.

Maggie hastened to her daughter, picked her up and holding her in her arms. "Kaya, honey, are you all right? What is wrong? My God! You're as cold as ice. What is it baby?"

"Mommy, Daddy sick. Daddy sick. Daddy sick. Daddy sick. Daddy sick. Daddy cold. Daddy cold."

"No baby, Daddy is all right, I know he is - Eric, go upstairs and fetch a blanket for Kaya. I'm going to sit on the couch and hold her for a while in front of the fireplace. Daddy is okay baby, trust mommy." Clay was okay, wasn't he? Why was Kaya so cold?

Kaya searched her mom's eyes, saying no more. Maggie felt confused. A moment of nausea, and mental disorientation caused her body to shudder as if Kaya was transmitting a telepathic message to her. The message was enigmatic. Only little Kaya Bird could know its real meaning.

Kaya's spell was broken when Eric returned with a pink cotton blanket. Maggie wrapped her into it, cuddling her. Kaya could feel the coldness of her Daddy in her own body because of her strong empathy and awareness of the macrocosm of all existence. Those inner perceptions remained hidden from Maggie.

Kaya Bird was special; Maggie recognized unique qualities within her daughter. It was as if nature was guiding her with strange powers of perception, which had long since vanished from modern society. Perhaps the natural earthly elements, which are part of every person's physical body, were in harmony to the frequency of Kaya's senses. Maggie believed that Kaya unknowingly sensed and received some of the basic hidden messages and truths of the cosmos into her psyche although she had no proof.

Maggie sat on the living room couch, continuing to hold Kaya and staring into the fireplace. She watched the flickering orange tipped flame dancing a colorful ballet on the fake wood. It reminded her of the many times she sat beside Clay, watching the fire with the lights off and sharing intimate touches and conversation with him. She thought about the love she had for her mysterious Kaya. What if there was something wrong with Clay? Was Kaya Bird correct? What would she do if Clay never returned? What could she do? She loved him so much. Sometimes Clay reminded her of a little boy, yet he made her feel complete. Without him, she would be empty, void of wholeness.

Kaya was back to her good-natured self. Maggie picked Kaya up and put her into the playpen. She turned off the control valve to the fireplace to save the propane gas. Maggie would keep busy and the house would stay warm from the oven, while she made the beef jerky. She lit the gas oven and set the temperature at 130 degrees, then slid in a tray full of marinated beef to dry. Eric was the target of Maggie's next plan.

"Eric, would you go upstairs and close all the doors up there? Let's try to keep it as warm as we can here on the first floor. Joey, your turn bud, would you make sure all the closet doors are closed and the basement door is also shut?"

"Sure, Mom;" Eric said as he started running at full gallop up the stairs.

"Walk, don't run, boys."

Before leaving to do his chores, Joey blurted out; "Do you think Dad will be home tonight, Mom?"

"I don't know, Joey. I assume he will be home, but even if he isn't, your dad doesn't want you to worry about him. You know he can take care of himself. Now, remind your brother when he comes downstairs not to run in the house. We don't need anyone getting hurt."

The first day after Clay left, Maggie felt she was living in a slow motion world. Time seemed to move slowly; unlike it does during normal everyday living. A high school philosophy teacher once told her the reason time move slower during some events rather than others was because during those times, there are new unique experiences occurring. These current events befalling the Wheeler family were both new and unique.

Maggie cherished the security of living a set routine. She tried not to think about Clay. Those thoughts depressed her and made her sad. She had to appear strong for the sake of her children, even if she felt weak inside.

Every small sound put Margie's nerves on edge. The rustling of the wind and rubbing of the branches of a hundred-year oak tree against their storm gutters filled her with apprehensiveness. Her neck and spine felt as if a poltergeist was using its slightest touch to rub cold, dead fingers up and down her back. She felt the hairs rise on the back of her head when a squirrel ran across the metal fascia above the porch. She could not let her anxiety take control. Clay had said she had strength; Maggie would not let him down. Maggie found herself doing repetitious tasks around the house. She would check the outside doors repeatedly to make sure they were locked. It was a compulsive behavior action of which she was not aware.

Joey and Eric completed their tasks for the day, but they didn't cooperate with mom. She watched as the boys practiced professional wrestling moves on each other in the living room. After Eric picked up Joey and slammed his body on the sofa, Maggie threatened to drop kick their butts with her size seven shoes if they did not quit the madness.

Maggie decided, contrary to the advice that Clay had given her, it would not be good to keep the boys inside the house too long without being able to go outdoors and play. They needed to roam the woods and give her a break from the confusion. She would change the rules if Clay did not return tomorrow.

"Joey and Eric, please come here."

"What is it mom," said Joey as Eric echoed the same question.

"We are going to live on the first floor to conserve propane. I need you boys to drag your mattresses downstairs, but leave your box springs in your bedroom. Bring your mattresses into the living room and put them on the floor. Also, leave the sheets on your mattresses and bring your bedding down here. Don't rush, make a couple of trips upstairs. If you boys help each other, you can make the job easier. I'll bring Kaya's mattress down here myself. I'm glad your dad convinced me to buy a couch that makes into a bed. I plan to sleep on it until your dad returns."

"Right now, Mom?" Joey asked.

"Yup, get moving boys. When we're done, I'll help you block off the second floor, this time there will be no air leaks. We must save all the heat we can down here. Please do it, guys."

The boys were eager to follow their mom's instructions. It would be like camping out in the living room with everyone together. It wasn't long before the living room resembled a motel room. Having everyone sleeping in one room together was more practical and gave Maggie comfort, knowing she would be within easy reach of her children if an emergency developed. With Clay gone, it was safer for them to be together on the ground floor. They had a battery powered smoke alarm located on the ceilings of each floor of the house. Maggie pushed the button on each to test the units, but discovered they did not work. She lit a match and held it in front of the smoke detector in the living room ceiling. The results were the same. Nothing. What was going on? New batteries were installed on September first, so like the Walkman, the smoke detectors were useless. Safety concerns were another reason it was best to keep the family on the first floor of the house.

Suppertime came. The milk stored in the refrigerator was spoiled. Maggie removed the remaining gallon and disposed of it. After turning on the faucet to rinse the milk stain from the stainless steel sink, reality struck her. How long would it take her to break the habit of trying to get water out of the tap? There was no water.

She would have to depend on the shallow well that Clay had driven about two hundred feet from the house, near the barn. For the last couple of days before he left, both he and the boys had been bringing in several buckets of water a day, which they drew from the well. Clay had agreed with her suggestion about leaving the hot water tank full, to be used in an emergency or to prime the well pump if needed.

When he first built the house, Clay considered raising a couple of hogs for the family's supply of meat. He drove a shallow well to a depth of twenty-five feet behind the house. He intended using it to water the garden and the animals. He never did buy any livestock. However, having a well and hand pump in the backyard gave their home the appearance of an old-time farmhouse. Not all was lost. It also proved to be a second source of water if the main well or pump failed to work.

Maggie changed Clay's plans about raising animals by telling Clay the story of her Uncle Dick. Maggie's Uncle Dick had raised hogs; it was easy to find his house, because one could smell the pig shit for a mile down the road. She remembered how her Uncle Dick had little regard for his home, waking in on the carpet with pig shit stuck on the soles of his shoes. As long as she could buy bacon at a store, that would not happen in her house. One of her worst memories of childhood was viewing her Uncle Dick castrate the hogs. Even now, she ate little pork.

Clay then considered raising a couple of steers. Raising cattle was expensive. The idea of raising livestock became just a pipe dream. A "well pipe dream" as Clay would refer to it later because only the "well" became a reality. Clay put a hand pump on the wellhead and let the boys play with it. He did pump some water into pails and used it for the tomato and pepper plants when they first started growing in the garden each spring. During summer dry spells, it was much easier to hook a hose to the house and used the deep well when all the crops needed watering.

Having a hand pumped well brought back hidden memories engrained in Clay's DNA from the days of Thunder Eagle. "This is like the old ways," he often told his family when pumping a pail of water.

The shallow well was useful. The twins enjoyed playing with the hand pump. The leather seals were pliable and Clay had a couple of spares stored in the barn among his plumbing supplies. When the well was completed, he sent a water sample to Lansing, where it was tested. Although it contained excessive minerals, including high concentrations of lime, it was safe to drink. The hand pump was an inconvenience but at least they had an unlimited backup supply of freshwater.

Clay had shown Maggie and the boys how to prime the pump, being careful not to leave the handle in a down position so it would lose its prime during warm weather. With the cold weather coming, they would let the prime out of the pump every time they used it, so it would not freeze and break. She was sure the boys would get tired of the pumping chore if they had to do it all winter, but she didn't expect it to happen. Little did she know the well would continue to be their only source of freshwater for many years.

*****

Kaya Bird missed her Daddy. She would wander around the house searching for Dad. Sometimes she would stare out of the living room window. In her mind's eye, she saw him. Daddy was sick. Daddy was cold. Last night, her daddy's image disappeared from her perception, as if he had vanished from the surface of the Earth. Daddy was missing, as if he was there, yet not there. Her mind searched for him, but he was gone. Nevertheless, Kaya knew Daddy was alive and this is what mattered to her.

Chapter 13

Eric and Joey took greater interest in playing with Kaya. Television, radios, and computer games no longer occupied their leisure time. Fear was bonding the family, creating an unbreakable unit. This was essential for survival and protection. Maggie, who was observing, saw a difference in the boys' conduct towards their little sister. They were more protective, watchful, and responsible towards Kaya Bird. The boys were learning to become imaginative, playing "pretend" games and relying on one another for amusement. If it were not for their reluctance to obey mom, it would have been a welcome change in their personalities.

Kaya watched the boys entertain each other from her playpen. She also had her own means of amusement. She spent hours playing with the educational toys her dad insisted on buying her. Tension was disappearing because of the quietness of the home. Love bonding, rather than peripheral objects unified the family.

Maggie thought of the days when her grandparents didn't have all the noisy distractions that nowadays occupied much of humanity's waking hours. Her Grandma, who died four years ago at age 87, told Maggie stories about everyday living during her childhood. During the long summer days, Grandma would play outside until darkness would force her into the house. Sometimes she would play hide-and-seek with her friends in the vacant lots in her neighborhood. At other times, she would walk through the fields, picking wild flowers and catching butterflies. During the late evenings, she and her best friend Maria would take an empty pint jar and capture fireflies. Maggie also tried to capture fireflies when she was a young girl, but they were much harder to trap than described by Grandma.

Grandma's only toy was a cloth doll with a plastic face, hands, and toes. Some of the fingers were missing on her doll's left hand but she didn't care. Grandma would sit with her doll, who she named Brooke, playing house on a small mound of sand in her backyard. As the weather turned colder, her outdoor activities moved inside the house. During the winter months, Grandma and her family would sit around a small wood heater in their home, listening to the "Lone Ranger" and "Sergeant Preston" on their old RCA tombstone shaped radio. A good time was a glass of water, bowls of popcorn, and using one low wattage light bulb to light up the room. It was a time when everyone used their imaginations, creating visual images in their minds from the words described in the radio programs. In many ways, Maggie believed radio was a better entertainment medium than television. Television did not stimulate one's imaginativeness as radio did. Television lulled one into a mindless trance, as time flittered away into a visual wasteland of advertisements, flashing images of death, immorality, and suggestive sexual activity. When it became bedtime, Grandma would take Brooke to bed and cuddle her tightly. Sleep came quickly and without nightmares.

Grandma said popcorn was the snack of choice during the old radio days because of its low cost. If the family wanted potato chips, she said her mom made them by slicing fresh potatoes into thin strips and then dropping them into boiling lard for a few minutes. Sprinkle on some salt, and "the taste far surpassed store-bought potato chips," Maggie remembered her saying.

About once a year, Grandma said her mom and dad would buy each of the kids a bottle of soda pop, which was a special treat. The kids would go to the General Market and each of the children could choose their favorite flavors. In those days, black cherry, grape, and strawberry exceeded Coke and Pepsi as the best-sellers. Grandma said she would spend much time pulling several bottles of pop out of the icy water storage unit, where they were stored in the market, before choosing her favorite flavor, black cherry. She would examine several of the glass bottles before finding one that was new, unscratched, and without blemish. This was an important family ritual, so it behooved her to take her time. As time passes, living patterns change. A simple exercise such as choosing a favorite bottle of soda no longer had importance to it.

Maggie realized today's society drank too much soda, which was no longer a special treat; ate too many processed potato chips, and did not use their creative imaginations while watching too much television. Perhaps this is why Americans are overweight and not physically fit. Maggie was determined never to become part of modern society. She was raising her children to have better eating habits and training them not to waste their time with frivolous entertainment.

With the fresh milk gone, Maggie was pleased about having purchased a case of powdered milk, which she originally intended to use for baking bread and other pastries. She also had two cases of condensed milk she bought on sale when Crabtree's Grocery Store had gone out of business three months ago. She opened a can of condensed milk, diluted it with 40 percent water, and poured its contents over some cornflakes, giving it to Kaya. After sprinkling a teaspoon of sugar over the cereal, Kaya seemed not to notice the difference as she ate it.

Kaya Bird Wheeler would be Maggie's last child. After experiencing a pregnancy filled with physical problems, she and Clay had decided to have her fallopian tubes tied after the baby was born. Motherhood would be limited to three children, which Maggie intended to live long enough to enjoy.

The rest of the day was uneventful. Maggie used the fireplace sparingly to conserve the gas stored outback in their 1000-gallon propane tank. She lit the fire in the morning, using it long enough to get the chill out of the house. The constant drying of Jerky in the oven also helped keep them warm.

The boys wore sweaters and sweatshirts. Maggie put two shirts and a couple pairs of pants on little Kaya to keep her warm. The family was amassing a large supply of beef Jerky. The oven was running at a constant 130 degrees, drying a new batch about every eight hours. If she had not started making jerky the thawing meat in the freezer would have spoiled. She would store the jerky for a longtime in sealed containers, to keep it from getting moldy.

The loneliness was worse after the sun went down. Maggie missed the companionship of Clay and the quiet whispered conversations they shared in bed when the kids were asleep. With Clay gone, Maggie laid her head on her pillow and grasping Clay's empty pillow, she would go to sleep clutching it to her breast. She could smell the scent of his hair on the pillowcase. She refused to wash it until he returned.

Three days later, Clay still had not returned. The three days turned into two weeks. The electricity was still off, and Maggie had doubts it would be back on. Something terrible must have happened to Clay. Frost was on the ground almost every morning. The weather had turned nasty after Clay disappeared. Maggie remembered that freezing rain and some snow sporadically fell for a couple of days after he left. She could not recall if he prepared for the rain event. She knew better than to go searching for him. Maggie's three children were her priority and it wouldn't be fair to put them in jeopardy by searching for their father. If Clay could have returned, he would have. It would not be long until the Michigan weather would get colder and snow would be collecting to great depths on the ground.

Sometimes they would get a major snowfall in late November and it would cover and insulate the ground until early April when the spring thaws began. The snow would thaw and create mud. Maggie preferred the snow. It was much easier to shovel and clean up than the endless mud, which was everywhere when the spring rains arrived.

Maggie was worried about Clay. Perhaps he had gotten hurt, killed, or something terrible happened. At times, she would cry, but she was careful not to let the children see her anxiousness. Panic was contagious, and she didn't want to scare the children. Clay was right, Maggie was strong, and for the sake of her children, she would get stronger.

Four days after Clay left, Maggie knew it was the correct decision to relax the rules for Eric and Joey, allowing them to play outside the house for a couple of hours each day. It gave her time for other necessary chores.

When Maggie was a child, her mom didn't have a clothes drier. She remembered helping Momma hang clothes during the winter months on clotheslines strung from one side of the basement to the other. During the warm summers, Maggie helped her mom hang the laundry on the clotheslines behind the house. Even now, she could remember the pleasant aroma of sun dried sheets. Rather than the normal one-hour drying time, Maggie could count on with her gas dryer; she knew it would take a couple of days for her laundry to dry. In the manner of what her mother had done during the winter months, Maggie strung a rope across the basement. If her momma could dry her clothes in this manner for a lifetime, Maggie could do it until the electricity was restored.

Maggie washed the family laundry in a tub, using an old broken broom handle as a makeshift agitator. She wished for a scrub board similar to what her momma had, it would make the chore much easier. When the boys were finished playing outside, they helped with the laundry, eager to use the stick.

Eric and Joey took turns bringing water from the well, carrying it into the basement. Maggie had an abundance of washing soap, buying large volumes of it when it was on sale. She had amassed an untold amount of paper towels and toilet paper stored in the basement. It made her family's life much easier by never running out of important sundry products.

Her fears mounted as she realized Clay might never return. In addition, although the propane tank was almost full, getting more propane gas might be delayed due the power failure. Unknowing to her, the tank would never be refilled. If there was anything good to say about the conditions Maggie faced, it was her unpaid bill for the last propane gas delivery. Without postal service, the invoice would never arrive.

During the second week of Clay's absence, a couple of teenage boys wearing hunting clothes stopped by her house. They were the Wheeler family's first visitors. Maggie didn't know them, but they told her they lived about four miles south, just off the Cedar Swamp Trail, which was a familiar snowmobile route running southwest towards the town of Broken Rocks. The boys were hunting squirrels and requested permission to hunt the back section. They confirmed what she and Clay had already discovered. No automobiles were able to run anymore. All electrical power was still gone. Much to the dismay of Maggie, they could not tell her anything about her beloved Clay nor what caused the power failure.

They shot two gray and three fox squirrels in a large grove of oak trees about a half of a mile behind Maggie's house. They gave Maggie one fox and one gray, which she accepted. Eric, Joey and Kaya would have fresh meat tonight. The two young men left and did not return. Maggie would not see them again for several months.

After gutting and skinning the animals and soaking them for several hours in saltwater to remove the blood, she parboiled them in a kettle of water. Maggie rolled the meat in flour, sprinkled on some black pepper and fried them in a skillet. Maggie fetched a couple of potatoes and onions from the root cellar, adding them to the skillet. Eric and Joey were used to eating wild game and eagerly consumed the good meal. Kaya, although not much of a meat eater, chewed on a small tender piece and didn't complain.

The longer Clay was away, the more Maggie began to accept the leadership role of the family. Her children were her primary responsibility. She valued her children's welfare above the lives of her husband and herself.

"Eric and Joey, yes, you too Kaya, it's time for another family meeting. Please sit down."

The boys sat in the same position they had during the last meeting with their dad.

"As we know, your dad hasn't returned and I don't know what happened." Maggie glanced at Kaya, who nodded her head up and down as if confirming what her mom said. "Before you ask me, I know he is all right, so don't worry. We will survive this." She hoped her children believed what she was saying about their dad.

"Eric and Joey, we have to make a few more family rules. Kaya is included, but mostly these will apply to you boys. "

Joey lowered his eyes toward the ground and spoke. "Mom, do you think Dad got killed? Do you believe Dad is dead?" Tears were coming to his eyes, but his face did not show that he was crying. Joey had courage, which he used to mask his fear. He didn't want his mom see his emotions, but this time his tears betrayed him.

"No Joey, I don't believe he got killed. I can feel your dad in my heart all the time. I know if he could do so, he would contact us."

"Mom," Eric interjected, "Are you sure, are you sure? Is dad all right?"

She nodded. "Boys, I also know your dad wants me to take care of you guys, no matter what has happened. For the last time, I know your dad is alive."

Kaya pulled at her Mom's leg. "Daddy alive. Daddy sick. Mommy, Daddy sick."

Maggie was surprised to hear Kaya. She remembered Kaya saying something similar the day Clay had left. She touched Kaya's face with her fingertips, prompting her to say more. "Can you see your Daddy, Kaya?"

"Daddy sick. I see Daddy, but I don't see him. He is, but he is not here," was all she said.

Maggie gave Kaya a reassuring hug before turning her attention back to the twins. "Joey and Eric, from now on, you must always obey what I tell you and not argue. I know your dad taught you how to use guns. We'll need a regular diet of fresh meat. We have many pounds of beef jerky, but I'm sure you kids won't like eating just dried beef."

"Eric, you will take your dad's Remington 22 rifle and go with your brother to hunt squirrels. You boys must take five bullets with you and ONLY use them to shoot game. Do not target practice with the bullets or waste them shooting trees or cans. Make your shots count. When you shoot two squirrels, save the rest of the bullets and bring them home. If you see a stranger on our property, avoid him or her if possible. Never argue if they approach you. Remember, your lives are worth more than a couple of dead squirrels. If anyone starts to chase you, throw down your game and run as fast as you can. He or she will probably just pick up the squirrels and leave you alone. It should distract them long enough for you to get away."

She hesitated, thinking about what to say next. They learned hunting skills from Clay, which both boys were eager to put to use. Given the responsibility to hunt game took their minds off worrying about their dad. As Clay had told them, they would be the men of the house until he returned.

"Okay, mom. You don't have to worry about us. Can we start tomorrow?" Eric was eager to begin.

"Just a second, boys, I've got more to say. Starting tomorrow, we will have classes here at home. I'll teach you history, writing, and other subjects. We'll use some of my old college textbooks. I knew keeping them would eventually be to my advantage. I'll sort out the information you'll need to learn and you'll be able to understand it when I'm prepared to teach."

Joey shrugged and dropped his shoulders, letting out a disgruntled sigh. "Ah, Mom. I thought we didn't have to go to school. Can't we just wait until classes start sometime again? Huh? Can't we? Huh?"

"No. You don't have a choice. I don't plan to raise children who will be stupid. You kids are going to be smart when I get done."

Maggie intended to control her household as a dictatorship, not a democracy when it came to educating her children. "You will be home schooled until I find out what is happening with our civilization. Boys, get ready for bed, it'll be dark soon."

Tomorrow would bring its own challenges. Maggie's mouth was dry and her throat constricted as she thought about Clay. She bit her lip but said nothing. If Clay never returned, she knew it wasn't because Clay did not love his family. Something must have happened to keep him away from her and the children.

Chapter 14

JIDON, BRESHAWN, AND IKE

Jidon Gibbons was hanging out with his cousin Breshawn and their friend Abe in a second story apartment in Orlando, Florida. Jidon's mother would not be home for three more hours. Two hours from now the electrical power would fail at sunset. For the trio, the lights had gone out several hours earlier after puffing up four hundred dollars' worth of crack cocaine.

Jidon sat on the pink flowered, nylon living room carpeting with his back propped against the wall. A large drop of spittle was dripping down his chin and into his closely cropped goatee. Boogers were dripping out of his nose and a long, partially dried stringy one was hanging down below his lower lip.

Jidon's eyes began to lose their dilatation as he was coming down from his crack induced high. His large black, muscular body was dripping with sweat. He knew his heartbeat could still exceed a hundred-forty beats a minute. If he continued this lifestyle, Jidon's heart could eventually rupture like an overfilled water balloon. It did not matter. God, the rush is damn well worth it! He thought. All his insecurity disappeared in one suck on the crack pipe; with two, he forgot about being an oppressed young black man. Life is good.

Jidon tried to raise his drooping head from his chest. He forced his eyes open into small horizontal slits. His dilated pupils caused him to squint at the evening sunlight filtering through the window curtains. As the room came into focus, Jidon saw his cousin Breshawn

Racheed lying near him on the living room floor. Jidon stretched open the neck of his sweaty tee shirt, brought it up to his nose, and deposited the snot on the inside it. He wiped his face with a clean area of the shirt before putting it back. He gradually left his drug induced world of exquisite sensual euphoria.

Chapter 15

Breshawn, his blood cousin, was lying next to the wall on the living room carpet. Breshawn quit high school during his senior year. He stayed in school to play football and other sports, not to become scholastically wise. If it were not for Mr. Watson's African-American history class, Breshawn in all likelihood would have graduated. He hated the confinement of sitting at his desk. He also hated his social studies teacher, Mr. Watson. Every Thursday morning, during first hour class, Breshawn would carry an eligibility form to take to each of his schoolteachers to sign, so he could play in the football game Friday night. Over a year ago, just before the third game in September, Mr. Watson refused to sign the form. Breshawn became ineligible to play.

It wasn't Breshawn's fault; it was the screwed up system. Breshawn believed only black teachers should teach black history. Only they could convey the inner feelings of the black man's oppression and explain it with compassion and empathy. A black teacher could feel the anguish, know the oppressiveness that Breshawn felt in his own life, and sympathize with those feelings. Mr. Watson had no such sympathy. Mr. Watson was white.

Breshawn expressed his feelings to other students and the school newspaper. His mantra became, "Black Students Need Black Teachers." It didn't make any difference. Nobody cared. Breshawn was banned from writing further newspaper articles when the school's Principle told him his words could cause racial tension in the school. Racial tension my ass; it was always there and would always be there as long as white teachers taught black history.

Thursday arrived. Breshawn would not play football Friday night. Today would be the end of Breshawn's high school education when he would spit in Mr. Watson's face. The old, fat honky man had gotten too close to him, invaded his personal space, and yelled too many times at him for not finishing his homework assignments.

It started during his 9:00 A.M. class when Mr. Watson asked for the students book reports for last week's reading assignment. The class homework was to read the book, "To Kill a Mockingbird" by Harper Lee and write a report. Breshawn became angry while reading the book. The story told of an oppressed black man accused of raping a white woman during the 1920's. He wasn't going to write a goddamn report about what he reasoned to be racial inequality. A white woman wrote the book, which was enough reason for Breshawn not to read it.

Mr. Watson confiscated Breshawn's eligibility form and sent him to the school counselor's office. Mr. Jeffery, the boys' counselor was also a honky. He told Breshawn to sit down until Mr. Watson arrived for the disciplinary hearing.

Mr. Watson arrived. The two men sat down in front of Breshawn as if he was a defendant on trial. Mr. Watson and Mr. Jeffery stared at him without saying anything. Breshawn knew it was an intimidation technique often used against black students. Instead of making him cower down in humble fear, the bullying made him angry. They were playing him. It would not work this time, fuck no.

Mr. Watson, being the closer of the two, leaned toward Breshawn and smiled. "Breshawn, what can we do to help you with your studies? It's time to take control of your life and evaluate your priorities, young man. High school is more than just playing football, you know."

Mr. Watson leaned closer, staring into Breshawn's eyes. His denture breath seeping into the young man's nostrils with each word he spoke. Breshawn could see Rolaids stains on the man's lips, with white chunks sticking between his ceramic teeth. Mr. Watson constantly chewed Rolaids because of a chronic acid reflux problem. It was disgusting. He could at least wipe his mouth.

Breshawn stared back. The man was in his space, in his face, and needed to be put in his place. Without answering, he cleared his throat and greeted Mr. Watson with a big gob of spit that landed on the man's large pockmarked nose, where it stayed.

As Mr. Watson jumped backward, Breshawn stood up, causing his chair to fall. One of the oak spindles broke, as the chair landed with a loud sound on the hardwood floor. Breshawn backed up towards the office door, keeping his eyes on both teachers. I have to protect myself if they attack me, he thought. With one hand on the doorknob, he raised the other one, closed his fist and extended his middle finger, presenting it to both teachers with the All-American resounding yell of "FUCK YOU, MOTHERFUCKERS!"

Breshawn turned his back to the shocked teachers and strutted out of the office and onto the streets. This is where his home would be. Breshawn would never finish his senior year. Breshawn could find a better life on the streets with his friends. Here his friends were all black. On the street, he had choices. They were his choices, not specified by a honky schoolteacher who was trying to manipulate his life. Life would be better because he commanded his own world.

As he sat on the floor of the apartment, Breshawn was roaming in a drug-induced fantasy, subsisting in a mystical world of young beautiful black women, with his dick ready for action. His fantasy dream world included plenty of booze and dope for everyone. All the women loved him. They loved his shaved head, his muscular body, and his masculinity. The colors in his drug-induced dream world are intense; blues are extra blue, and greens - very green. The scantily dressed black women's bodies glistened with oil and perspiration as they danced in the rainbow colored lights, pulsating to the rhythm of the music blasting in the room. He left the world of solids and his body became transparent. Breshawn was floating, viewing the scene from the lights in the ceiling, and then from the floor. He felt himself in the middle of the caldron, embraced by all the nubile women dancers who saw and desired him. The rap music playing in his mind caused extreme sensuous pleasure mimicking reality. He was more than a part of the dream hologram projected within his mind, it was his world, and he was dominating everything. A limitless expanse of imaginary sensuality, only found within the deepest parts of drug-induced pleasure. A world sought by many among the carnal reality, but only found in fantasy. Breshawn was on his way down from his drug-induced pleasure.

*****

Jidon forced his eyes open and turning his head, saw the silly grin on Breshawn's, face. He's fantasizing about money, pussy and parties again, Jidon thought. Jidon opened his mouth, drew in a deep breath, speaking with great difficulty. "Breeeshhhaan" expelled out of his lips in a high-pitched squeal. Jidon didn't recognize his own voice, hearing the unnatural pitch because of the crack cocaine he smoked. His intent was to awaken Breshawn from his catatonic fantasy. Breshawn did not respond. Jidon decided to clear the confusion from his own mind for a few seconds before trying to arouse his cousin again. He didn't need to be sounding like no woman. No sir! His second try was an improvement.

"BRESHAWN, gets up man, you done pissed all over yourself! Do get up, bro. If my momma comes home and finds that you done pissed on the flo, we will all be in deep shit, man. Common bro, get up man."

Breshawn remained unconscious, enjoying his fantasy domain. The ebony babes were hugging and kissing him. They removed their bras standing topless before him. Hot damn! One babe, resembling a girl who once sat behind him in Black History class, began a lap dance. He grinned with excitement as her perky breasts rotated, slapping him across his face. Breshawn listened as a distant voice called his name. Why should he listen to the sound coming from the other side of a dark veil? Was it cousin Jidon? It's party time, to be sure! Although he could not see him, Breshawn invited Jidon to enter his adventure, speaking to him with a slow slurred voice while keeping his eyes closed:

"Join me bro, nuff pussy for both of us." Jidon vanished from Breshawn's virtual world. The babes remained, needing his full attention. Oh, well, don't need him anyways, thought Breshawn as he drifted back, reintegrating into his fantasy. The black princess giving him the lap dance was only wearing a pair of thong underwear after removing her long silk stockings. Both of her hands massaged his head and neck.

Chapter 16

Jidon began to understand what was going on in his friend's mind. He would love to join Breshawn in his fantasy world, but one's dreams and delusions are their own. They are shared by talking about them after they happen, but they could never experience the dream world together. Jidon would have to bring Breshawn back to reality. He was afraid his cousin might have taken too many hits on the crack pipe. He couldn't afford to get caught in his mom's apartment with Cousin Breshawn's brain fried. He knew Breshawn could travel so far into his illusionary macrocosm that he could not make the trip back to cognitive consciousness. Jidon would have to take action to see it didn't happen.

Breshawn's urine soaked trousers stank. He tried to raise his head from his chest, where it was resting. His eyes were fluttering, causing his closed eyelids to resemble a manicured lawn with a mole running under the soft grass. His body shuttered and jerked a couple of times. He drifted deeper into his unrestricted world of pleasure and did not awaken.

Jidon leaned forward trying to stand up, but fell back against the wall. The second try was a success. He was wobbly, his body rocking back and forth. It reminded him of the time he got seasick when fishing in the Gulf of Mexico out of St. Petersburg, Florida a few years back. A black youth counselor had sponsored the trip. It was free and some babes were on the boat. He never did fish. On the other hand, seasickness prevented him from having fun with the babes.

Jidon grasped Breshawn's shoulder with a firm grip of his hand and pleaded. "Goddamn man, c'mon get with the program dude. We got to get outahere, Bro." A sudden noise distracted Jidon. A third companion entered, coming from the small kitchen, into the living room.

"Hey Abe, what's be happening, bro?" Jidon smiled and forgot about Breshawn, gazing at his other friend.

Abraham Washington Jefferson walked towards both men, with Jidon leaning against the wall and Breshawn with his back propped against the wall. Abe was more sober than Jidon and Breshawn but far from being normal. "Hey Jidon, it looks to me that Breshawn is having a bad trip. You know what I mean, brother. Glad to see you coming down, Bro. We have to get Breshawn up on his feet and moving around. I told him he was smoking too much shit, man. Help me get him on his feet, Jidon. Jidon, bend down here and get Breshawn's right arm and I'll get his left. Let's like, pick him up and like, make him walk around. You know what I mean? Ah hell, the motherfucker, he has done pissed his pants. Did you know that? You must have, Bro. You be sitting right next to him. Goddamn, he stinks. Shit. . . Grab his fuckin arm and help me." He said disgustedly. "Get your shit together, Jidon. We don't have long before your momma be here. You know what I mean?"

Jidon did know what he meant. If his mamma came home and found them all doped up, there would be trouble. Although he was of age and could live on his own, Jidon still felt responsible to help care for Momma as she did for him when he was growing up. This time he had broken the rules with his friends in her home. He did not want to dishonor Momma with their doings. He would have to hurry. She would be home in a couple of hours.

Helping Abe, Jidon pulled Breshawn to his feet. Breshawn's head snapped from side to side like a bobble-head doll. With part of his weight on his legs, he opened his bloodshot eyes, looking at his surroundings.

"That be some good shit we had, Bros. Goddamn, goddamn, GODDAMN, I feel good. Opps, I gunna puke."

Abe grabbed the kitchen wastebasket and held it in front of Breshawn who hacked up the contents of his stomach, which included a partially digested pizza. He held Breshawn's head over the pail and watched him vomit into the plastic liner.

"I told you guys not to eat before we smoked our shit. You know what I mean? Damn, neither of you listens to me. Take a breath Breshawn - take a breath, Bro. You will feel better after getting rid of that stuff. Goddamn it stinks in here. I might even puke myself. Your puke stinks like a motherfucker to be sure, you know what I mean?"

Breshawn coughed once more, spitting chunks of cheese and pepperoni out of his mouth. His fantasy faded from his inner mind. Looking at both of his companions, he said; "I loves you, Bros."

"You better mean we're just best of friends, otherwise there be some serious ass kicking here for saying that shit;" said Abe jokingly.

"Let's get him out of those stinking clothes Jidon, before I start puking myself. Hurry before your mama gets here. Move your black ass, Brother. Then get rid of that basket of puke. Don't forget to put another plastic bag in there. I knew those Wal-Mart bags were good for something."

Jidon and Abe dragged Breshawn into the bathroom, where he collapsed with his rear end on the checkered linoleum floor. With Jidon's help, Abe stripped Breshawn naked, throwing his soiled clothing into a pile.

Both men, with their forearms under Breshawn's armpits, helped him into the shower stall. They sat his bare ass just above the drain, his back resting against the back of the stall. Abe reached up and turned on the water full blast. The shower began spraying cold water on their friend's face and body, splashing some droplets onto the floor.

Breshawn's fog congested mind took note. His body tensed and jerked alive. The shock of the cold water caused him to jerk his head back so violently it cracked one of the plastic tiles in the stall.

"Holy shit, Bros, you trying to drown me or something? Goddamn, I'm freezing to death."

He was slowly gyrating, twisting in the stall, not trying to stand up. The cold water soon turned to warm. As it did, he relaxed and opened his eyes wider. Breshawn allowed the spray to awaken his senses. He opened his mouth and filled it with the water. He swished it around and spat it near the shower drain, trying to remove the taste of vomit. His friends succeeded in conjuring him back to the real world. Breshawn was alive.

"Turn off the water Jidon, and help me get Breshawn out of the shower. Let's sit him on this here toilet lid. He's rinsed off, that's good as far as I'm concerned, unless you fancy washing him up, that is."

Jidon glared at him. "Hell no. Don't be a joking around like that, Abe."

Jidon grasped Breshawn's wet arms and with a little coaxing, was able to help him out of the shower stall. It did not take much convincing to get him to sit on the lid of the toilet stool.

Breshawn sat with water dripping onto the floor. He grasped his face with both hands and rubbed his palms against his temples. "My head hurts," was all he could say.

"Jidon, go get a pair of your khakis out your dresser and brings them here, don't be a wasting time. We got to hurry, remember your mama's coming home," said Abe.

Jidon hurried into his bedroom. He opened his chest of drawers and carried back an old thread worn pair of blue jeans. He was not going to give his best stuff to a man who might just piss in them again, even if he was his first cousin. When Jidon returned to the bathroom, Abe had Breshawn dried off with a towel.

Abe gathered Breshawn's soiled trousers and underwear from the bathroom floor and inserted the clothing into another plastic Wal-Mart sack. Jidon threw the haggard blue jeans into the bathroom where Breshawn slipped them on. This time he did so without putting on underwear, which his cousin had not offered to provide anyways.

An hour later, it was starting to get dark. The three young men were sitting in the dining room drinking coffee. For some reason, the coffeepot did not work, so they heated some water on the gas stove. It took longer to boil than it normally did but the trio didn't take notice. The flame was only about half its normal intensity.

Abe found a jar of instant coffee and scooped a huge teaspoonful, adding sweetener and dry creamer in each cup. The sugar would help the trio raise their blood sugar levels after their drug binge. Abe poured steaming hot water into the cups and served them to his companions, saving one for himself.

Jidon's momma still had not come home. He was worried. She was always home just before dark. Two of his mamma's many qualities were punctuality and honesty. Where is she? It would have broken Mamma's heart if she had walked in and saw her son drugged up. Where is she?

Jidon shoved his chair back, stood up, carrying his coffee with him. He walked to the doorway, extended his arm to the light switch on the wall, flicking it on. Nothing happened. He flicked it upward again nothing happened. "Shit, something's wrong with this damn thing and I ain't no electrician."

Jidon flicked the light switch up and down several times, as if the added clicking would send power to the bulb. He gave up, slapped the wall with his open hand returned to the dining area. Jidon sat down with his friends. To hell with it, he just as soon sit in the dark anyways. He would listen to his two friends' bullshit stories until Mama came home. Today, he would just listen, adding little to the conversation.

Abe took another sip of coffee and started talking. It may have been him talking, or the drugs talking, it didn't matter. Friends shared intimate moments after drinking, taking drugs, or playing cards. Abe, Breshawn and Jidon were often talkative after a session of drugs and booze. Today was no exception. It mattered not what is said, but talking was important. "Breshawn, are you sorry you done quit school, Bro?"

"Abe, what make you think about that right now? I ain't never been better in my life. I learned all I know from the streets, that's enough. You sure be weird, brother." He laughed. "I never think about school. Shit man, never. Sometimes you ask some of the strangest questions. To hell with school, if I had it to do again, I wouldn't have stayed there as long as I did."

Abe frowned. "I just asked . . . you know, I graduated and wish that I had gone to college and my life would be different. You know my daddy is still in jail. I expect to be there with him someday. He told me to go to college and thinking back, it was the only good advice he gave me. Hell, the old man never did anything with his life, except end up stamping out license plates in prison. He doesn't do that anymore since the State started putting the damn plastic stickers on vehicle license plates. Someday, maybe us three can go and visit the old man. He's over in Tampa State Prison, you know. Maybe daddy will save three rooms for us! Hey, wouldn't that be a funky time, Bro!"

Breshawn had listened to Abe's story about his daddy many times. "Abe", replied Breshawn, "forget about college and your daddy, man, it just gunna drive you crazy, Bro. College is for white folks, not us. The white man has a better playbook for life. His rules are less rigid, the playing field for whites is bigger, and favors him to win. If I had black teachers, maybe it would have been different for me. That was then, and this is now. Next you'll be considering getting married, having a house full of carpet crawling brats and all that family shit."

"That not all bad, you know, Breshawn. That is, if I can find the right woman for me."

"Oh, I found her, I did," replied Breshawn with a grin. "She was doing a lap dance on me when you and Jidon almost drown me in the damn shower a little while ago."

Abe laughed, slapped a high 'five' on Breshawn's raised hand and both men continued to enjoy the moment.

"Bet she was something, bet she was Breshawn. I know she would have preferred me instead of you, if I'd been there, Bro."

Jidon continued listening to his friends banter, staying out of the conversation. He did not want to get married, nor was he willing to muse about his daddy who used to beat the hell out of him before he disappeared. The only duty Jidon had was to help his mamma. Where was she? Beulah Gibbons still was not home. Jidon knew in a pinch, Mamma could take care of herself. He wanted to be similar to his mamma, a stand-alone person, one who can make it in life without the help of others. Friends were good, but she had the self-confidence to exist in this world even though life sucked. Who could ask for more? Yes, he needed to be like his mamma, but Jidon wouldn't be poor like her.

Jidon sipped his coffee as Abe and Breshawn continued to talk bullshit. His thoughts drifted back and forth from his momma to his friends. The bullshit stories was often repeated while the trio sat around, planning their next drug venture. With little meaning in their conversations, Jidon enjoyed listening to his friends.

Abe finished his coffee and his conversation with Breshawn. He stood up to go back into the kitchen and get more coffee. The air-conditioner was not working. The apartment was getting oppressively hot. Abe decided to open a window overlooking the parking lot behind the apartment complex.

"Jidon, get over here and look out the window. Everything outside is dark, no streetlights, and I don't see any cars running either. What I mean is, there ain't no electricity to be had in the whole hood. This is our opportunity to be sure. You know what I mean? Why are we staying here in this damn hot room, when we can go "SHOPPING! Now, I know you know what I mean, Bro!"

Jidon grinned. He could get some money to buy more crack, both to deal and use. Besides, his momma's rent was due next week. If he got enough cash, he could entertain one of the bitches who danced at Andy's Strip Club. In the back of his mind, Jidon knew the bitches would do anything for him if he provided weed and some spending money. A good lay was worth the good pay. If they put out, it was worth it. Jidon never brought the bitches back to his mom's apartment. Momma would never approve of him banging women here. He and his friends had broken the rules today. He would never let his friends do drugs in her apartment again. He loved his mamma.

"Breshawn," said Abe. "Are you are up to this? You must have your head on straight by now so let's go, brothers. Without power, the security systems in Orlando will not be active."

Without further consideration, Abe and Jidon headed towards the door. Before leaving, Jidon retrieved a flashlight from the cabinet, just above the old Westinghouse stove. He flicked the switch on and off a couple of times to see if it worked. He watched with fascination as the 2-cell alkaline powered beam flashed in his eyes. It seemed much brighter because drug dilated eyes. Jidon left a couple of candles and another flashlight on the countertop for his momma to easily find when she came home from work. With personal business to take care of, he no longer worried about her. Beulah Gibbons had excellent fortitude and could take care of herself.

The trio left the apartment, locked the door and quietly walked down the back stairway past the mailboxes. Breshawn carried the Wal-Mart bag with his soiled clothes in it, and threw it in the hallway trashcan. They exited the building, being careful not to draw the attention of anyone. It would not be good to be seen leaving if they intended to go "shopping."

Chapter 17

Abraham Washington Jefferson had finished high school with high academic marks to his credit. His mom named him after two of America's greatest and most loved Presidents. He was born with the last name of a president anyway. On the other hand, all three of the Presidents were white. Although he knew Abraham Lincoln freed the slaves, he also learned that George Washington was once a slave owner. Therefore, Abraham Washington's name was a paradox. Abraham is a Jewish name and he wasn't Jewish. However, President Jefferson was a slave owner who occasionally dipped his wick in some of his black women. Still, to Abe, it didn't make Thomas Jefferson an honorable white man. Quite the contrary, Abe hated him for what he did. Some of Abe's Black Muslem friends avoided him because of his name. What the hell, you cannot choose your name. His name made him tough. As a youngster, he was teased. Abe learned to fight and kick ass. No one teased Abe anymore. He kicked many asses.

After he graduated from high school, Abe had intended going to junior college. Like many goals, the dream faded with time. One year turned into three years. He would never go to college. The craving for immediate financial wealth resulted in Abe dealing drugs.

Abe spent what money he made from selling drugs on booze and babes. After some months, he started using some of the crack he was selling. It did not take long before Abe realized a drug dealer could not safely work alone. He became acquainted with Jidon Gibbons. They became partners.

A few weeks later, Breshawn Racheed joined them. Breshawn was the son of Elizabeth Racheed, Jidon's aunt. Breshawn became part of the team because he was a first cousin to Jidon. There was nothing stronger than blood. It was stronger than sex, marriage, and friendship. Blood gave Breshawn creditability and trustfulness to become part of their growing drug cartel. Breshawn provided several prospective customers. The trio would soon be driving flashy automobiles, fondling the beautiful babes and most of all, respected in their community.

Abe had watched the "Godfather" movies and marveled at how the "Don's" financial wealth earned him the respect of his peers. Why wouldn't it work in the black community? Someday all his friends and neighbors would be calling him "Don Jefferson." He would be the black Godfather. Money brought great power and respect in the inner-city ghettos. So far, he had accumulated little wealth, but was building a drug habit that could destroy his credibility.

In the near darkness, the parking lot had appeared empty from Jidon's second floor apartment. Once they were on the street, the lot was far from empty. Several people were trying to get their vehicles started. Abe and his companions could see opened car hoods with human heads stuck underneath them. A fat man, wearing blue workpants, was bending over, wiggling the spark plug wires on his engine. When it did not help, he decided to remove the air cleaner cover. Abe snickered, getting a three-inch view of the man's ass crack. Too bad, it wasn't a sister showing her booty, he thought.

Some of the worried drivers shined flashlights on the engines, tinkering with this and that. Doing something was better than doing nothing. Abe saw an old man sitting in a six-year-old blue Buick with the windows open. "Hey old daddy, what be happening here?"

The old man turned, saw Abe and then turned away, most likely figuring him to be a gang member. An old woman with silver corn rolled hair was sitting next to the old man. Although she appeared to be scared, the old woman opened the car door and responded to Abe.

"Please don't bother us, sir. If you young men know anything about cars, would you help us get ours running? I have to take my husband Elijah to the doctor because his pacemaker is acting up. The pain started just about the time the electricity went off in our apartment. He is sweating and in pain. We have been married 55 years and he is all I have left. We need help. Can you young men help us, please?"

Abe started walking toward the car but Jidon grabbed him by the shirt. "Common Bro, we got to take advantage of the situation while we can. You can't be messing around with them old people. Time be a wasted, brother. The old dude is going to croak anyways, if not tonight, then in a day or two. Don't be talking to anyone else. Here we are, trying not to be noticed and you open your big mouth to the first people you see. Shit man."

As they left, Abe glanced back at the old woman and shouted, "Hey momma, I will call a wrecker for you from a filling station."

Jidon frowned, grabbing Abe's arm, tugging on it to hurrying him along.

The old woman may or may not have heard Abe, who knows? Abe could see her holding the wrinkled hand of her husband Elijah. She closed the car door to wait and hope for a miracle. Abe saw on the old couple the faces of his granddad and grandmamma. These were the faces of all older black people who had ran out of time in this life, waiting for the next one where life might be better. Hoping for an afterlife world where those oppressed might somehow find equality and justice.

Abe doubted he would get old. The drugs and booze had made him feel eminent today, and he was feeling good now. This is all that mattered to him, not what he might be doing forty years from now.

"Let's go brothers," said Breshawn.

Abe walked out of the parking lot and on the street with his companions. He intended to call an auto service wrecker. As the old people slipped outta sight, they vanished from his consciousness as quickly as they had entered it. He would make no phone call.

The view of Franklin Street was sobering to the three young men. Cars, trucks and a couple of motorcycles were sitting abandoned.

Many of the owners had decided to walk to their destinations. There were no streetlights functioning. It was past evening and getting darker. Jidon kept the flashlight turned off. There was no reason to advertise their presence.

No stores were lit up. Darkened traffic lights were swaying back and forth in the breeze, like pendulums in ancient clocks. The silence almost drove them insane. Not a horn was honking, or a ghetto blaster sounding. The background noise of the city, which everyone takes for granted, did not exist. There was only silence and more silence broken by the gentle footsteps of Jidon, Breshawn, and Abe.

Like the din of an orchestra getting ready for a concert, the banter of a few voices gradually began sounding. The voices sounded like confused whispers. Although unintelligible, the whispers intensified in the serenity. The sounds were strange, as if a new muffled language was born. This would change.

Abe strolled up to an abandoned Dodge truck, opened the driver side door and tried to turn on the headlights. A slight glow illuminated in front of the truck, fading to blackness within seconds. He tried a Ford sedan and a Honda minivan with the same result. Seemingly, the electronics must have all failed at the same time on these cars. He noticed all the vehicles he tried had their ignitions switches turned in the "ON" position, which would drain the energy from a battery.

"Hey cousin," said Jidon while looking up into the sky. "Looks at those flashing colors up there, bro. They be the aurora borealis. Maybes they be from a U.F.O. I read a book one time that said cars and trucks don't run when there be a U.F.O. flying above. What do you think?"

"I think, you've been reading too many of them goofy books, Jidon. There ain't no flying saucers. Do you see a flying saucer, Jidon? Next, you will be saying you see Ronald McDonald and his flying fucking hamburger out here. Your imagination is screwing with your head for sure. You know what I mean? Maybe your brain is stuck in the *Twilight Zone*." Although Breshawn lectured his cousin about UFO's, he was surprised to see the weird lights flickering in the Florida sky. This was not normal. Florida never had a display like this. Any showing of the aurora borealis was an oddity at this latitude.

Chapter 18

Jidon ignored Breshawn's comments and kept walking. He glanced back up at the sky, but his priority was still ripping off some goods to sell. Fear gripped his stomach and wrenched his guts. Again, he thought about his mamma, hoping she was either somewhere safe or on her way home. If he saw her as they traveled downtown, he would escort her home, allowing his companions to go ahead and complete their business.

An extensive flash of orange and red light burst through the upper atmosphere above the city. This time it caught the attention of Abe, the leader of the group. "This has to be some serious shit happening here, brothers. Forget about the aurora borealis, Ronald McDonald, and all that U.F.O. crap. We don't have time to waste. Let's go and take down Fat Roland's Pizza shop. We can get some cash and cigarettes there. Those damn Pizza owners are rich anyways; some of them own baseball and hockey teams. How do they make so much money selling those goddamn pizzas? Must be the snot they use for cheese and bleached newspaper they squash into crust. Forget about the goddamn sky, brothers, we don't have time to waste."

"I know you're right, Abe" replied Jidon. "I've got a better idea. Forget the pizza shop. We could rip off a couple of drug dealers and get enough shit to last for weeks, maybe get enough cash to leave Orlando. I yearn to go to New York City, or Miami or Washington D.C. Do you know in Washington D.C., the blacks outnumber the whites? I hear it's beautiful in the springtime, with the cherry blossoms. In the winter, it gets cold and everything is covered with snow. You know, I ain't never seen a snowstorm in my life. It doesn't snow here in Orlando, Florida, but I sure would like to throw a snowball someday. Besides, it's about time I left my momma and went out on my own. I would still send her money, you know."

"I agree with you, Jidon," said Abe. "I hear the sisters in D.C. are hot for studs like us. This is our chance to get cash for the trip. If we get enough money tonight, we could start our own drug business. Hell, D.C. is already corrupt with those damn politicians. Are you brothers with me? It's imperative that we do this while it's still dark. Do you know what I mean?"

Breshawn laughed and repeated one of Abe's words. "Imperative? Imperative you say. You mean it's time to get the shit done, brother! What is with this "imperative" bullshit? Don't be a talking like a honky." He rolled his body as he laughed and grabbed Abe's shoulder, giving it a squeeze with his hand.

Nothing would be the same. Abe planned to obtain great riches tonight in Orlando, but he also knew the city could also give birth to massive rioting. Jidon remembered reading about the killings and lootings occurring after the Rodney King trial and a couple decades later in Ferguson, Missouri after a brother got shot by a cop. Conditions were favorable for unrest. Matters could get out of hand in the culturally mixed city of Orlando. The trio would have to be careful.

Chapter 19

Abe, Breshawn and Jidon continued walking down Franklin Street. They lowered their voices, trying their best to be inconspicuous. It is strange how so many streets in project areas and inner cities are named after dead presidents, money, and civil rights leaders. The story was always the same, rename the street and you will change the social structure of the neighborhood. However, it rarely happened. It was common to honor the dead but forget the needs of the living.

Franklin Street was choked with dead automobiles, pick-up trucks, eighteen-wheelers, and taxicabs. A city bus stood at a darkened traffic light with its doors open. The public transit was built to pacify the financially poor people of the city. It was the white man's answer to poverty. "Provide public transportation, it will bring stability to our inner-city neighborhoods" had been the slogan of the city commissioners. The brainchild solution to inner-city instability never worked to improve social conditions. Except for the homeless, few residents used public transportation. The homeless did so to stay warm during the few cold, sometimes freezing nights during Florida's winter months. You could always ride the bus for a buck. That was not a bad price for a warm place to sleep all-night.

The closer the trio went to the inner city, the more people were visible. Teenage kids were consorting in the streets. The whispering din transformed into shouting, with an occasional gunshot echoing among the buildings. Groups of young adults and old people are meandering down the sidewalk looking at the sky and peeking into store windows. Older people walked away as

Earth Reboot

gangs walked unafraid down the streets. At any moment, all hell will transcend upon Orlando.

The rioting started at once, as if someone fired a starting pistol at a track meet. Some of the large transport trucks stranded in the middle of the street were being broken into and robbed of their cargo. It did not matter what was inside, furniture, food, or electronics. People were stealing everything.

For the first time in years, here was racial equality. Whites, Blacks, Chinese, Japanese, and members of all ethnic groups were taking advantage of the blackout.

An Italian furniture storekeeper stood in front his store, with a shotgun across his arms, looking scared but daring anyone to enter his property. Most of the businesses were without guards. The employees and managers locked their doors and left after the electricity failed, presuming it would be off the rest of the night. If the Italian storekeeper had any sense, he would also leave.

As the trio approached Wealthy Street, they watched a couple of kids scramble out of Willie's Pawnshop. Like several businesses down the block, the plate glass window is broken and looters were coming out of the shadows to loot the buildings. They exited with their arms full of merchandise. Some looters pushed shopping carts filled with good to take home.

One pudgy fourteen year-old black teenager, wearing cargo pants, exited the building in front of Breshawn. He was wearing a panty hose mask over his face, carrying an Apple Tablet. Abe and his companions stopped walking and watched with interest as the young man carried the unit behind a dumpster. The young thief crouched down and tried to turn it on. Nothing happened. Again, he pushed to button to turn on the unit. Once more, nothing happened. With heightened anger, the boy stood up, picking up the unit, smashing it on the ground behind him. If that were not enough, he repeated the act, scattering components and plastic pieces on the cement sidewalk. The screen shattered.

"You goddamn piece of junk. Don't work then, fuck you. You'll never work now!" When the kid's rage subsided, he quickly glanced at the trio, who saw visions of themselves when they were the boy's age and roaming the streets looking for action. Seeing the three men, the kid panicked. He shouted back at them. "What's you be looking at? Don't be a worrying about what I'm doing."

Breshawn shouted back, "Hey brother, be cool. We won't be a messing with you. We got our own gig."

With fear emanating in his voice, the kid replied. "No use getting stuff out of there. Nothing in this place works." He turned his back to the trio and began running down the street.

Abe watched the kid leave but said nothing. Did a simple power outage cause the chaos or was it something else? Abe remembered studying the stories of the race riots in Detroit and other cities during the 60's. At least back then, the automobiles ran and radios and televisions worked. Yet, this wasn't a race riot, it was anarchy. The crack cocaine he smoked did not affect Abe's thoughts, his head was clear. He would focus, not on the present, but on the future. Anarchy or not, they must grasp opportunity when it behooved them to do so. Abe looked to Breshawn, only to find his friends were missing. While Abe's mind had been wandering, so were his two comrades. Where in hell did Breshawn and Jidon go? It would not be long before he would find out.

"Hey, Abe . . . over here," shouted Breshawn. Breshawn, with his muscular strength, had a 55-gallon metal trashcan in his arms. He was hurling it towards the display window of Stein's Jewelry Store. With a resounding snap, the plate glass cracked vertically from the sill to the top of the window frame. Breshawn retrieved the trash can, thrust it against the cracked glass, opening a hole large enough for the trio to enter the building. He threw the trashcan into the opening, and watching it bounce several times before rolling to a stop against a display case. Breshawn kicked the remaining edges of the glass window with his boot, so as not to be cut when he entered the building. "Hurry up before someone sees us," he said to his comrades.

Breshawn entered through the opening with Jidon and Abe following him. No alarms sounded. A ghostly light is shining from an emergency lantern hanging above the back door of the jewelry store. The battery was old and the light would soon go out. They were the first ones to enter the building since the power failure.

Jidon grabbed a plastic bag from behind the counter, reached under the display glass, and began filling the bag with watches and rings. He could not hold back his excitement, "goddamn! We be rich brothers"

Breshawn and Jidon are fanatically grabbing everything colored silver or gold in sight. Wedding, engagement and platinum rings were their first target. They gather neck pendants, diamond earrings, bracelets and several Rolex watches, stuffing them into the bag. They would sell or trade this jewelry on the street.

"Grab the jewelry as fast as you can," shouted Abe. "There is enough for each of us. You know what I mean? We can divide it after we get out of here. Brothers, you know this place will be fair game for others too, with that broken window out there for God and everyone else to see. I hope that damn kid doesn't come in here, I don't want to kick his ass. This is our take, no one else's."

Abe knew insanity was gripping the city. The trio was taking risks never considered a few hours ago. He remembered an old axiom, "cover and protect your own ass." They were exposing their asses by their lack of planning in this robbery. Abe knew that robberies, looting, and killings were in all likelihood happening throughout Orlando. His heart raced, almost as quickly as it did when he was smoking crack.

Jidon carried the bag containing the loot. It was time to leave the building. He froze. He raised his head, sniffing the air, trying to recognize the odor. "Do you smell something, Breshawn?"

"Just your stinking bad breath, cousin," taunted Breshawn.

"Quit screwing around, you two, I smell smoke. There's a fire somewhere," replied Abe. He watched an orange flickering glow reflecting from the glass countertops to the ceiling of the room. The air is beginning to fill with wisps of smoke in the fading light of the emergency lantern. "Let's get the hell out of here." Abe led his friends out of the store. Looters are everywhere. Within the last few minutes, circumstances changed. Most of the city's inhabitants felt the same courage and confidence as Abe's group.

A few people began throwing gasoline filled pop bottles stuffed with burning rags at buildings, automobiles, and each another. In the middle of Wealthy Street an abandoned police car is on fire. J&R's hardware store is blazing and paint cans on shelves are igniting, strengthening the flames.

Small propane canisters caught fire. The canisters resembled miniature cruise missiles as they propelled out of the hardware store into the walls of adjacent businesses, exploding on impact. The destruction is escalating, with more fires compounding the carnage. A propane canister shot into the unbroken area of the plate glass window of Stein's Jewelry store where Breshawn, Abe, and Jidon just exited. The building caught fire.

Two young looters sporting afro-haircuts came running out of J&R's hardware store. The intense heat caused their hair to ignite and their clothing to blaze. The two human torches continued running until each fell and lost consciousness. No one tried to help them. No one could help them. Their bodies smoldered, giving forth a stench similar to burned pork.

"Follow me." Abe shouted to his friends. They would go back to Jidon's apartment house. More fires were springing up around them. One automobile would explode, igniting one or two more. One building would ignite, causing others to catch fire. Gunshots permeated the air; looters were brandishing knives and clubs. The quietness, which overwhelmed the trio when they started their quest, was replaced by screaming and shouting, as people became desperate. Sporadic gunshots continued echoing between the buildings. Humanity lost all sense of reason.

Two older white women are fighting over a box of expensive silverware. Tall woman kicked short woman in the groin, knocking her to the street next to the maple silverware case. Short woman opened the lid, grabbed a long fork from the assorted silverware and brought it upward from her crouching position, shoving it into tall woman's ribs. Blood flowed from the wound, cascading into the silverware case. Tall woman instinctively raised her foot and kicked, removing most of the shorter woman's teeth and shattering her nose. There was no winner.

A middle-aged white man wearing a camouflage shirt ran past Jidon. Without breaking stride, the man grabbed the bag containing the stolen jewelry from Jidon's grasp. Camouflage shirt tucked the sack under his left armpit and broke away from them, not looking back.

Jidon screamed, "What the hell. Hey, that motherfucker stole our stuff! I will kill you, honky!" He took off running down the smoke-filled, darkened street after the thief. Breshawn and Abe following, but Jidon was the fastest of the trio, leaving them far behind. Jidon continued screaming at the man, but because of the long-distance running, he was winded. His breathing intensified. His anger caused him to ignore caution. Camouflage shirt slowed down, Jidon would get him. Once more, he screamed, "If you want to live, better stop, right now, man!"

Jidon was pissed. He was so angry he did not see camouflage shirt turn, pull out a Smith and Wesson, stop as requested, aiming the gun at Jidon.

He pulled the trigger. His aim was true. Jidon's face squinted in surprise as a third eye opened right above the bridge of his nose. A much larger hole appeared in the back of his head, projecting brain tissue and broken parts of his skull on the back of his collar and spraying the air with blood.

Abe and Breshawn caught up to Jidon, and stopped short trying to catch their breath. They were stunned. Jidon stood frozen in time, yet still on his feet. It was not supposed to happen this way. They were the three musketeers, one for all and all for one, forever. Jidon's eyes dilated, all his muscles tensed as he continued to stand upright for several seconds.

Abe and Breshawn watched, as Jidon existed in slow motion. Finally, Jidon's knees gave way and he sank down, his butt sitting on the concrete walk. His back relaxed, as did his body. At last, he reclined backwards, where he would remain. Blood and brain tissue spread from the back of his head in a crimson ring on the sidewalk. Jidon was no more.

Chapter 20

At first, Breshawn was in denial. He stared at his cousin who lay dead on the ground. Jidon's dilated eyes were open, vacantly staring at the smoky, darkened sky as if watching the aurora borealis display. Jidon saw nothing. Breshawn saw Jidon's executioner, fleeing and disappearing into the smoke. Pursuit would be futile. Breshawn had another reason to hate white people. One of them killed his cousin.

At first, he refused to accept the death of Jidon. Death and injury happened to other people but never to his friends or family. Breshawn crouched down, resting his knees on the asphalt. He grasped Jidon's bloody head with both hands, put his face down close to his dead cousin and started crying.

"Ah, man, it wasn't worth it, man. Don't die on me; don't die on me, Bro. I loves you, Jidon. Man, you're a brother to me." He looked up into the smoke-filled sky, trying to communicate with a God whom he had ignored most of his life.

"Ah, Jesus in Heaven, why did you let this happen? Ah, fuck, goddamn, Mary, Mother of God, shit."

Breshawn's hands, which were holding his dead cousin's head, were dripping with Jidon's blood. He bowed his head and offered a silent prayer and tears for another dead black man without a future. His prayer was futile. From all the pictures he had seen, Breshawn knew God was white.

Abe reached down, helping Breshawn to his feet. "Come on, Bro, we can't do anything for him now. The fires are coming this way, we have to go . . . or we're going to die. Move your ass, man!" As Abe was speaking, a Shell Gasoline truck exploded a quarter of a mile away. When Breshawn stood up, the shock wave from the blast knocked both of them to the street, just beyond Jidon's body.

The flames traveling from the tanker truck hit three Cuban boys running down the street, each with a case of cigarettes. They dropped their flaming cargo and continued to flee, blazing from head to foot, reacting as the two black kids did earlier. Fire was trailing from their backs, resembling the exhaust of a jet airplane. They dropped to the ground in unison, continuing to scream and roll in a feeble attempt to put out the flames. They died.

Breshawn got back on his feet and helped Abe up from the concrete. He was full of grief, wondering what to tell Jidon's mom about the loss of her son. "Abe, can we go back to Jidon's place? I have to see my Auntie Beulah, and see if she be all right, man. I have to tell her about Jidon. That's what blood has to do, Bro." He hesitated before adding; "This be the worst goddamn day of my life, man. Huh, can we go Bro?"

"Sure, whatever, but we have to move quickly if you know what I mean. The smoke is getting thick and it's too dangerous for us to stay here." Abe stopped and turned back once more, looking at his late friend Jidon, and spoke his own prayer. "You are at peace, my friend. May God, whoever he may be, guide you, forgive your sins, and give you the peace this life never did. Amen."

Breshawn pretended not to hear Abe's prayer. He already prayed to the white God who continued to ignore him. Jidon was still dead. He would remain dead. Both of them turned to retrace their steps back towards the apartment complex. Before leaving, Abe recovered Jidon's flashlight from the ground next to his body. The burning buildings provided the light they needed to get away from the madness surrounding them. He put the flashlight into his rear pocket for later.

The journey back to the apartment was uneventful. The farther they got from the inner city, the less carnage was taking place. They were inconspicuous, avoiding everyone they walked past on the street. The cars parked in the apartment parking lot complex when they started their journey had not moved. The old man was still sitting in his car, his eyes open but he was not moving. The old woman was gone. Abe and Breshawn never saw her again. If the old man were lucky, he already passed away. He was not lucky. Breshawn saw that the old man turned his head in their direction as he and Abe ran past his car. On the other hand, perhaps the darkness played tricks with his mind. Sometimes nature demands pain and suffering before claiming one in death. In this instance, Elijah would just quietly pass away before morning.

The apartment house was still intact. Thieves and rioters were more interested in looting the stores than low-rent apartments. Breshawn and Abe entered the building. It was dark, so eerily dark inside. Breshawn briefly turned on the flashlight, looking up and down the hallways, but saw no one. They found their way back to Jidon's apartment. They unlocked the door and entered the living room, closing and locking it behind them. Jidon's mom, Beulah Gibbons is not here.

It was quiet, unlike the rioting in the streets. Abe fetched a candle, lit it, dropping some of the wax on a bowl. He placed the candle in the wax long enough for it to solidify and sat the bowl on the kitchen table. The faint light illuminated the room to move around, but not enough to show people outside the apartment someone was here.

Breshawn brought back a six-pack of Budweiser from the fridge. He popped the pull-tab of one of the beer cans and chugged down the amber liquid. Abe did likewise. They consumed all six cans of beer in a half hour. Neither man spoke, dealing with their grief in silence. They took turns sleeping, apprehensive about intruders and arsonists who could set the apartment building on fire. Beulah Gibbons never returned home.

As the morning sun shined into the smoke stained apartment windows, Breshawn woke up. His head hurt. He could count his heartbeats in his skull as his arteries pulsed blood into his brain. He got up, opened the refrigerator, bringing back and finishing off a warm can of diet pop. After answering the call of nature, Breshawn glanced out the window overlooking the parking lot. Smoke was visible above the city. He could see flames leaping and dancing from the tops of buildings east of the apartment complex. If the wind had been from the east, the apartment complex in all likelihood would have burned during the nighttime. Debris was scattered over the apartment house lawn. The dead body of a young woman with her skirt pulled above her waist was lying in the parking lot. In all likelihood, she was raped and murdered; not necessarily in that order.

The old man's car remained, but he was unseen. His body could be lying in the seat. Breshawn would never know, nor at this point did he care. He could never imagine his beautiful city of Orlando, the home of theme parks, live entertainment, and excellent restaurants would be destroyed. He closed his eyes, while rubbing the back of his neck trying to get rid of a headache.

"Brother, what does it look like out there?" Abe asked as he sat up from where he had slept on the living room carpet. "I dozed off when dawn came. It was quiet enough, so I had to get some rest."

"Looks bad, Abe. Don't know what's to do, but it's time to leave this place. I know it for sure, I do. Jidon's mamma, she ain't a coming home. I'm going to do one last favor for Jidon. I'm going to go down to where she be working and see if I can find her. Got to tell her about Jidon, for sure I do, he being my blood cousin and all."

"I understand, Breshawn, yes I do. You know, I'm going to leave Orlando, go somewhere else, and get a new life. Now is the time to do it. You know what I mean? I'm going downstairs, open the door, and go outside. If I can get safely out of this city, I plan to start walking west, following highway 4 towards Tampa. Somehow, someway, I will turn south, maybe on highway 17 or 27. Then maybe I'll go all the way to the Keys. I always wanted to see Key West, and all those bridges. You know, I was told babes lie under the underpasses of Interstate 75, bare assed naked during spring break. Key West could be burned and pillaged, just like Orlando is. However, what the hell; one cannot turn back the clock. It's like my granddaddy once told me. "Abe," he said. "Some things in this world you must prevent from happening, cuz once they do, you can't take-em back." He said, "It's like this here pound of sausage I'm a frying up for breakfast, once it is all ground up, you can never turn it back into a pig." That's what he told me, Breshawn. You know what I mean?"

Breshawn continued to rub the back of his neck as he replied: "Life's like this, Abe. Jest one crisis after another. Jest when you believe it's getting better, shit happens again. You know Abe, with everything all screwed up, we have to do what we have to do. I know it now. I'll miss you Bro."

Breshawn knew they would split up and go their way. Life is this way. You have friends for a while, then circumstances change and they disappear. The old life was gone. First, Breshawn would try to find Jidon's mamma, then he too would leave the city. Breshawn knew one must always stand by one's blood, and Jidon was his blood. He would find his Auntie Beulah. Breshawn had no choice. He had to tell Auntie Beulah what happened to Jidon.

Breshawn entered the bathroom. He tried to wash his hands but found no water flowing from the faucet. Looking in the mirror, his hair was a mess. His clothes were wrinkled and dirty from the fires of the night before. His body had experienced too much tension, too many drugs and booze during the last six months. His eyes were bloodshot. If he didn't change his lifestyle, it wouldn't matter whether he was in Orlando or another city. He would be dead. Breshawn left the bathroom, no longer wanting to see his reflection.

Abe came from the kitchen and said, "There is nothing to eat, Breshawn, but I'm hungry. You know, the way I see it, we had better get out of this apartment building before someone torches it. I'm going to find some of Jidon's clothes and get out of these stinking rags. It may sound cold, but he won't need them anymore."

"Good idea, Abe. Me too. I'm wearing the same rags you guys put on me yesterday when I pissed mine. You're right, with Jidon gone, don't matter which ones we take. But this time, I'm going to put on some underwear."

Both men changed their clothes, throwing their old ones in the trashcan. They left the apartment, locking the door and heading down the stairway. There was nobody in the hallways. They left the building for the last time. Breshawn and Abe stood together in the parking lot where their adventure had begun. They stopped for a moment. Abe turned and hugged Breshawn, Breshawn returning the affection to his companion.

"Loves you, Bro."

Abe nodded and replied to his friend. "You take care, my brother. I don't know, perhaps someday our paths will cross again. You know just about where I'm going, so after you take care of your family business; make your own journey. Don't stay here in Orlando. Only bad shit will happen if you do. You've been a good friend to me, Breshawn. You and Jidon were my real soul brothers, you know. Although I'm not real blood, I feel we are blood. Give your Auntie Beulah a big hug for me too, if you find her."

"Sure will do that, I will. I'll miss you, Abe. I don't plan to stay here, I don't. I plan to head south after I find my Auntie."

Without saying more, Abe turned and began walking toward the west. Breshawn watched his friend disappear behind the apartment house. He glanced at the ground, before raising his head, looking into the smoky sky. The morning sunshine beamed through the haze with a reddish brown color. It was beautiful, yet it was blemished. Breshawn wondered what might have happened at Walt Disney World, Universal Studios, and the other theme parks. Breshawn had never visited any of them. He should have visited the parks a long time ago. They probably no longer existed. Life was frail and finite; one must grasp the moment, for tomorrow is uncertain and not guaranteed.

His hands fumbled around in his pockets. He shifted his weight from one foot to the other. Nervousness was a trait he was born with. To stop his fidgeting, Breshawn started walking towards downtown. His destination was Grove's Investment Management Company, the employer of Auntie Beulah. He had to tell her about Jidon. It would break her heart. She was blood, and blood counts.

Chapter 21

JAMES AND ROXANNE

W hile Abe, Jidon and Breshawn were smoking their crack cocaine in Orlando, Roxanne and James Miller, a young married couple in their early twenties are taking a late afternoon stroll sixty miles southwest of Orlando in a retirement mobile home park near Lakeland, Florida.

The afternoon temperature is 92 degrees. A slight southerly breeze brought some comfort to Roxanne and James as they strolled on the blacktop roadway through the park where they live. It was an easy way to get exercise. Four times around the small trailer park and they walked one mile. There are ten residents living in six occupied homes. With another twenty homes unoccupied, it would not be long before the park owner would be bankrupt and the units moved to other mobile home parks or to the salvage yard. The park was built for retired folks to spend their remaining days in comfort, but since it is near bankruptcy, Roxanne and James were welcomed as residents. Thirty years ago, when the retirement park opened, it thrived with activity. As the years increased, so did the ages of the residents. Some of them died while others moved back north to the homes of their children or assisted living centers. The children and grandchildren who inherited the homes sold them for small amounts of money, or left them to the owner of the park to rent or resell. Some units were rented to cover the park owner's expenses while others remained vacant. The revenues from the lot rent dropped, as did the conditions of the homes.

Other than pedestrians, today's only road traffic was the United States Postal Jeep. The carrier brought advertisements and a few bills, which she deposited in the postal boxes found alongside the Park clubhouse. Sometimes the carrier delivered mail ordered prescriptions directly to the homes. Most of the senior citizens saved money by ordering their needed medications rather than making purchases at the local pharmacy.

The few remaining residents went shopping during the first of the month when their social security and pension check statements arrived. The residents would make a quick drive to the bank to withdraw their money, and then spend a couple of hours shopping at the local Wal-Mart store before going back home. They stocked up on groceries and sundry items, which would last for a couple of weeks. Another trip before the end of the month completed most of their traveling. It was a never-ending cycle. For most of them, the only time they left their homes was to buy items or visit their doctors. However, seniors enjoyed living in seclusion. They formed their own community, took care of one another, and became a family. The retirement park community provided them with companionship during their last years of life.

Roxanne and James held hands like newlywed as they walked the blacktop roadway. They passed a tangerine tree, loaded with fruit weighing the lower branches to the ground. A tangerine had fallen from the tree and lay next to the roadway. Roxanne reached to pick up, but James jerked her away from it. "Do not touch, they are not ours," he said without smiling. They continued walking, passing wax begonias, daylilies, and flowering hydrangeas. Life was good.

"James?" Roxanne spoke, trying to get her husband's attention.

James did not reply. She turned her head toward him, but James continued staring forward, ignoring her. "James, let's pick up our mail on our last round; perhaps I'll get a letter from my mom and dad. I haven't heard from them in two weeks, and frankly, I'm worried."

"No, problem," replied James in a businesslike monotone. He did not break stride, continuing to stare ahead. He felt Roxanne squeeze his hand as an "okay," but did not respond by squeezing hers back, ignoring her subtle love signal. As the head of his house, James Miller had made the decision, no other action was necessary.

They completed their fifth rotation around Twisted Palms Mobile Home Park, three more to go. James attention focused on an old man cutting grass around a likewise older home. Probably the old man's home, he thought, not wanting to share his thoughts with Roxanne.

The old man cut grass as if living in a world of slow motion, never missing a stroke with his old Sears lawn mower. Forward three steps, and then back two. Forward three steps and then back two, resembling a mechanical robot using creep mode. James had heard the jerking of the pull rope and the machine starting to run after passing the old man's house on the last trip around the park. For James, it disturbed the tranquil silence and shattered the inner mantra he repeated in his mind during these walks. To him, this distraction disturbed an important time of mediation and contemplation. It was a time when James spiritually became one with God, letting the Holy Spirit stimulate his soul to appreciate the beauty of nature around him. The damn lawn mower disturbed his holy meditation about spiritual matters. The noise of the lawn mower disturbed God. James was not pleased.

The old man noticed the young couple as they walked in front of his home. It was unusual to have anyone under the age of seventy living in the park. The old man pulled his mower back for another cut; he hesitated and slowly raised his right hand, removed his baseball cap, exposing his baldhead and giving the couple a tired wave.

James could see the fellow was smoking a cigar, which he could smell far across the mobile home park. Cigars were evil. They smelled unpleasant and polluted God's air. Smoking cigarettes were also evil, destroying the body, which is the Temple of the Lord. It was against the holy will of Jehovah for one to smoke. Cigars smelled like burning dog turds. The old man will smell like cigars when he burns in Hell, thought James.

James let go of Roxanne's hand and returned a brief but insincere wave back to the man. He watched as the old one replaced his cap before resuming his slow repetitive movement, three steps forward, and two steps back. The old man seemed content to exercise patience. However, God judges actions, not patience.

"Hey there!"

A large rotund woman with hair curlers, wearing a blue smock dress, hollered at them from inside her Florida room. She stepped closer to the screen, coming into full view, getting the full attention of James and Roxanne.

"Don't forget folks, we have a potluck dinner scheduled a week from today at the Clubhouse! You know, as park residents you're welcome to attend the gathering. Hey, by the way, I'm Nancy Harrington, John's wife. You've met John haven't you? Everyone knows John!"

James would have ignored her, but Roxanne stopped walking. "Hi, Nancy. Nice to meet you. I'm Roxanne and this is my husband, Elder James Miller. No, I'm sorry, but I don't know your husband. We appreciate your invitation to the potluck dinner, right James?"

"Yes, of course" replied James with a frown. "How do you do, Mrs. Harrington?"

"Your wife called you Elder James? Are you a preacher man or something?" Nancy asked.

This was the invitation James needed to start evangelizing. "Yes, Mrs. Harrington. I am an Elder in **"God's Publisher's and Preachers"** church. I am sure some of our people have called on your home with our message of salvation." He stopped talking and waited, hoping for the correct response so he could proselytize to the woman. The ministering game had its rules and once it began, it could continue indefinitely, that is, if it followed a predictable pattern with the proper responses.

"Sure, I've heard about your religion and always invite your people in to share a cup of coffee with me while they give me sermons. You know, I believe you people do a fine work. I must tell you something. You know, because of your members' religious enthusiasm, it convinced me to return to the Catholic Church where I was a member. John and I didn't go to church for years, yet your people showed me that Christianity in my life is important. I was baptized a Catholic, you know. Did I tell you? Now, I never miss Mass. John doesn't go every week, but I do." Nancy was proud of her faith, and happy to share hers with James.

The smile on James's face converted itself to a straight line. It was neither his goal nor the goal of **"God's Publishers and Preachers"** to chase people back to pagan idol worshipping churches; it was his goal to recruit new members for **"God's Publishers."** He was trained to defeat the best of argumentative objections, countering with; "You know, Madam . . ."

"Just call me Nancy, never have been a Madam, and with this old fat body, I would starve to death if I were one. Although, picturing it, there might be some advantages to being a madam for an old lady!" She chuckled at her levity.

"Well Nancy, do you know when you pray to Mary and the other saints in your church, you are worshipping the statues?" James voice became louder, almost shouting with the authority granted to him by his church. "It is image worship! In the Book of Numbers chapter 20, God condemns image worship. Don't you read your Bible? If you have the time, I can show you the Biblical truth, so you could make the effort to save your life and that of your husband. For your Catholic church is in bondage to Satan. You know, Nancy, when Armageddon comes, the Lord God Jehovah will murder all who disobey him." James gestured wildly with both arms, extending them from his body outwardly with fast movement. "He will sweep across the surface of the Earth, choosing who will be worthy of everlasting life and destroying the rest with his mighty sword and Angelic armies led by his commander, Jesus Christ. You cannot worship statues and God too." He waited for an answer.

Roxanne smiled nervously, putting her hand on James's shoulder. "James, perhaps we should continue our walk," she said.

"Well," replied Nancy, "whatever you might believe, is all right with me. Besides, I don't want to discuss religion, I just want you and your lovely wife to share a meal with us at our potluck dinner next week. We gather in the Clubhouse once a month. Just bring a dish to pass and your own eating ware. At our age, we do our own dishes. Even my husband, John washes ours every other day. He also does half the laundry!" The smile wrinkles in Nancy's face grew even tighter as she talked to the young couple.

James glared at Nancy but did not speak. Roxanne moved her hand from his shoulder, once more grasping his hand in hers. There was no reason to continue this conversation. James painfully tightened his grip on Roxanne's hand and started to pull her away. He must get Roxanne away from the wicked Catholic woman.

Roxanne didn't budge. Once more she spoke. "Thank you, Nancy for the invitation. We'll consider the potluck dinner, but it's unlikely we'll be there, unless, you would allow James to give a half hour sermon after the meal."

"Sorry, we don't allow any Clubhouse religious discussions, but just remember you are more than welcome to. . . "

They could no longer hear Nancy's voice as James turned his back, forcing Roxanne to start walking quickly away from Nancy Harrington. They passed two more empty homes before coming to the clubhouse.

"James, won't you reconsider and go to the potluck dinner? It would be a good time to become acquainted with the other people in the park. Maybe if the residents got to know us better, they would be more willing to listen to your message of salvation. Please, can't we go?"

James jerked on her hand, squeezing it until it hurt. "No, and don't ask me again. The subject is closed. Aren't you going to get the mail?" James asked.

"I thought we were going to stroll eight times around the park this afternoon, James. I'll get it on our last round, okay?"

"I will make all decisions in this family. Next time, you ask me how long we will walk and I will tell you what our plans are. Do not always assume we follow a routine. Now, if you have your key to our mailbox, use it." James raised his left hand and stared at his watch. He got Roxanne's attention and began tapping on the crystal with his fingernail, suggesting that she was wasting time.

Roxanne opened their mailbox. It contained a pizza advertisement and a letter offering a Visa credit card at the amazing annual interest rate of 18%. There was no letter from her parents. She deposited the junk mail in a yellow plastic trash container sitting next to the mailboxes.

"There is nothing important James, just advertisements. I hope my folks are all right. You know, I haven't heard from them for two weeks."

James scowled at his wife; displaying irritation. "Do not worry about them, I have told you. They are not important. Did not Jesus leave his father and mother and go into the ministry? Did not the Lord say you are to leave your father and your mother and lose your brothers and sisters? Our calling has priority over our relatives. Now, forget about your parents and decide what you are going to fix for supper, woman. I will grill the hamburgers we bought yesterday before the meat gets too old. You know our refrigerator is a piece of junk and does not stay as cold as it should. You can fix us a salad. Move faster woman, I'm hungry."

Roxanne started to reply but stopped when a man slowly approached them, walking with a blue metal a cane for support.

Arthritis had taken its vengeance on the man's humped back and body. His knobby fingers are frozen at 30-degree angles from his hand. Between two of those fingers he clutched his mailbox key. The man squinted through rheumy eyes until he found the mailbox with his lot number stamped on it. He attempted inserting the key, trying to focus through his cataract eyes. With a second try, he succeeded and slowly opened the box. Seeing the young couple, he left his key in the lock and extended his right hand towards them.

"I'm John Harrington."

"Hello, Mr. Harrington. I'm Elder James."

James gingerly grasped the man's extended hand. It disgusted him to touch the stranger. Once more James shook hands with someone he knew would be a waste of time trying to convert into a true believer. Except for Roxanne, James hated touching other people. His grip was quick, limp, and pulled away from Mr. Harrington before the ritual was completed. James watched John Harrington cringe with pain, but said nothing.

Wiping his hand on his pants leg, James uttered. "Your wife is waiting for you at home, Mr. Harrington, so you better get going." James turned away, clutching Roxanne's hand, pulling her towards their home. James knew that Roxanne would not object to anything he commanded. It was not her place to speak.

*****

"Nice meeting you too." John Harrington replied sarcastically. He finished retrieving his own pizza advertisements from his mailbox and threw them away. John twisted the key, locking the box. Painfully, he put his keys back into his pocket. John rubbed his throbbing fingers and staggered slowly back toward his home. He continued a rhythmic taping of his cane on the asphalt pavement matching each painful step. John had hopes of eventually having his left hip joint replaced, but until it happened, the stinging pain continued radiating down his leg with every painful step. John had intended to rest his arthritic body on the Clubhouse bench beside the mailboxes. He enjoyed examining and smelling the flowers growing alongside the Clubhouse. He wondered why Nancy needed him. There was no time to rest, now. He hoped Nancy is okay. He would hurry the best that he could to get home.

Chapter 22

When James and Roxanne arrived home, it was time to fix supper. Roxanne prepared a salad while James set up the old rusted propane gas grill sitting in his driveway to fry hamburgers. This was the extent of his contribution towards cooking any meal. Roxanne formed the meat into patties and carried them outside out to her husband. She watched James light the gas and toss the burgers on the grill.

James's eyes caught a movement down the street. The old man who had been mowing his lawn was walking toward James. He is following a small dog on a leash.

"Hello! I'm MacArthur Gunderson. You can just call me "Mac" as everyone does around here. Saw you and your lady friend while I was cutting my grass a bit ago. This here's my dog, Buffy. Buffy, say hi to the nice man." Buffy ignored James, sniffing the air and focusing her attention on the cooking hamburgers.

"Course she can't talk," Mac continued, "but she's my best friend. I sometimes take Buffy for a walk around the park. She's getting old, you know." He slowly bent down and lovingly rubbed his ten-pound Yorkshire terrier on her head. Mac gingerly stood back up. "I had another Yorkie named Becky, but she died a couple years ago." A sad expression spread over Mac's face.

James cared nothing about the old man's history. He never liked dogs, especially small ankle biters like the one sniffing his pant leg. He hoped it would not crap on his lawn. He despised the smell of dog poop and hated stepping in it. Maybe the old man was smoking a dried dog turd earlier when they watched him cutting the grass. Dog piss killed grass. Since James was just renting this home, he cared less about dead grass. So let the dog piss everywhere if it wanted to do so. Dog crap was another matter. A preacher sporting a chunk of dog shit on his shoes rarely recruited new converts into his church. James thought about kicking the dog in the ass with his foot, but controlled himself.

James was getting impatient while listening to the old man speak. He continued to nod his head before deciding he didn't have time to waste with the old fart. Before the old man could say more, James spoke:

"I am Elder James Miller. My lady friend, as you referred to her, is my wife, NOT my lady friend. Her name is Roxanne Miller." He hesitated before speaking loudly. "Sir, WE DO NOT LIVE IN SIN as you implied."

James eyes squinted as his hand slammed his spatula on the storage rack beside the grill. He stood with his hands on his hips. James was proud of his staunch religious moral standards and did not appreciate the old man implying Roxanne was his mistress by calling her his "lady friend."

The old man ignored James' anger. "Ah, I'm glad to meet you, Mr. Miller. Can I call you James? You can call me Mac, everyone in the park does. I didn't mean Mrs. Miller wasn't your wife. I was just being polite. You know how our modern society is nowadays. I apologize if you took offense."

"If you don't mind, I prefer being called, 'Elder James' instead of Mr. Miller. We are missionaries of **"God's Publishers and Preachers"** church." James smiled, lifting his chin and expanding his chest in pride. James knew if he were Pastor James or Father James, he would receive more respect. For some reason, people never respected his "Elder" designation which was the highest appellation given to ministers of his church. He knew the old man was a sinner, remembering the man's smelly cigar. James regarded every sinner as either a potential convert or enemy. Time would tell which one this old man would be.

"Okay, I'll call you anything you want me to, young man. I just had to introduce myself and tell you that I've amassed a whole passel of tools over my long life. If you want to borrow any of them, er, uh, Elder James, you're more than welcome to do so. Just come down and help yourself. If my shed is unlocked, just go inside and see if what you need is there. I have extras of several of my tools, so don't worry about using one. Hell, everyone in the Park uses my stuff."

"Thank you, Mr. Gunderson, but I never borrow anything. It is not Scriptural you know. Each man must provide for his own, with his own, sir. Therefore, you said you have doubles of some tools. Let me ask you; is life better for having two of something? If you wish to make a gift of a tool to me, I would gladly accept it. Otherwise, I cannot borrow anything."

Mac picked up a small twig from the ground and started cleaning one of his yellowed fingernails as James flipped his hamburgers. The old man's demeanor changed, as he began speaking with a voice as slow as he moved:

"Your argument about owning doubles of my tools could open a discussion of Zen, but I won't go there. My life is good the way it is. The world is not perfect, my young friend. Some people can't afford the many tools I have, so I share them. I do not give them away, even if I have extras. We should help one another. I just thought I would make a friendly offer. If you change your mind, just help yourself."

"Mac, you are correct, the world is far from perfect, but did you know it will soon be perfect, with no death, no sickness, and all will shine forth the glory of our God? Have you not studied the Holy Scriptures?"

"Well, Elder James, let me put it this way. I know all about religion. I'm more familiar with your beliefs than you'll ever know. I know you believe idealism shall someday fill the planet. We live in a skeptical world, one that I've tried to make a little better during my long lifetime. Love is what each of us can contribute to making it better. Your utopian vision of a perfect world is far beyond the reality of how human friendship works. The perfect world which you envision is just a fantasy, and it just ain't going to happen."

James was surprised by the old man's keenness of mind. He would not allow the topic to fade without countering with his faith. A sense of outrage overwhelmed him. He would not be intimidated. "MacArthur or Gunderson or whatever your name is; I am sustained by faith, which is my idealism." James smiled with spiritual victory, assuming the old man would leave.

"Many people have faith, young man. Nevertheless, your faith can more than comfort your life; it can consume you like dry weeds in a forest fire. Faith is accepting as fact; something you know probably is not true. Here is a fact for you young man. Your hamburgers are burning."

"Time to go home, old man," James shouted." Take your damn dog home with you before it craps on my lawn." James stared angrily toward Mac. Smoke from the grill invaded his nostrils, signaling a burned dinner. "Damn the distraction," he said under his breath as he slid his flipper under each patty and turned it over. When James turned towards the road, he realized the old man and his dog had vanished. The dog left no turds in his lawn, none that he could see or smell anyways. How dare anyone question his faith! James had God on his side. The old man and his dog were already dead as far as James was concerned.

James put the hamburgers on a clean plate with the burned side down. He would never allow Roxanne to see anything he did wrong. It was not her position in life to criticize him. Turning off the gas grill, he carried the hamburger plate inside the house. He forgot the confrontation with the old man. Roxanne could clean the grill later after it had cooled. It wasn't his job to clean up.

*****

Mac was almost home when he reached down and picked up Buffy, cradling her in his left arm. He carried Buffy the rest of the way. "Buffy, remind me never to speak to that son of a bitch again." He lifted his dog up to his face, giving her head a kiss. Mac reached into his shirt pocket and retrieved a cigar. After putting it in his mouth, he decided not to light it, but just hold the cigar in his lips the rest of the way home. He would smoke it later in his screen room while drinking a couple cans of beer.

Chapter 23

Roxanne told James she was tired so she went to bed early. Soon, the power failure would happen. When one lives in central Florida, power outages are common occurrences but usually not a major problem. Sometimes outages would take place because too many air-conditioners were running. At other times, it was severe thunderstorms during the spring and summer months which disrupted the electricity. The evening temperature would gradually drop off from the low 90's to the high 60's before morning. It was unusually hot for November, but sometimes the winter cool down doesn't happen in Florida until mid-December. This was one of those years.

Six months earlier, James and Roxanne had rented the singlewide, thirty year-old Palm Harbor mobile home in the small trailer park just south of Lakeland. The rental price convinced James to sign a year's lease. Randolph Jennings, the owner of Twisted Palms Retirement Park was happy to see the full-time couple become residents. After all, twelve months of income is much better than the four or five months he received from snowbirds coming to Florida for the winter months. Twisted Palms Mobile Home Park was located at the end of a long driveway, a half-mile from a seldom-used blacktop road, which made it isolated from population centers. This isolationism was the primary reason the park was almost abandoned. Most of the Snowbirds preferred to stay at condominiums and apartment complexes or retirement mobile home parks near large cities, tourist sites, and golf courses.

Twisted Palms Retirement Park is small, consisting of twenty-six units. There are several empty homes available for this year's group of snowbirds, who often did not start heading south until late November. A couple of residents had died during the summer, leaving their homes unoccupied. Other than James and Roxanne's rented unit, there were five units rented by full-time residents. Those occupants seldom left the Park and associated with current residents who were their own geriatric group. There is little chance of more than a couple of rentals this late in the season, and no chance of full occupancy.

There is limited social interaction among the residents but so far, James and Roxanne had not joined in. No children could live in the park. Not being contemporaries of the older residents, the Millers avoided social contact. Occasionally they would exchange a short "hello" while getting the mail at the community mailbox site as they did with John Harrington. It is unlikely that Twisted Palms Retirement Park will remain in business after this season. The current revenue did not cover the cost of the taxes, mortgage and insurance. If Randolph Jennings did not find a buyer for the property, he would file bankruptcy.

The park had a small clubhouse, the size of a four-stall garage, where the seniors would meet and play cards every Friday evening, share potluck dinners, and sometimes have Christmas and New Year's parties. James considered card playing a sin. He and Roxanne would never play cards. James knew God would make the seniors pay dearly for their card playing sin when they arrived for their final judgment at the Pearly Gates. Seniors were already knocking at those gates, so they had little time to mend their aberrant ways and become righteous. James would offer a daily prayer for all evil ones to reform and join his church. It was up to God to send them to James. Obviously, God did not covet the residents living in the retirement park because none of them have asked him to teach them the way of the Lord.

Roxanne had met James at a church assembly when she was seventeen years-old and he was twenty-two. They had a platonic friendship at church events and Roxanne fell in love with him. They married after a limited one-year courtship. It seemed the right thing to do.

Both were strong believers in **"God's Prophets and Publishers"** church. Baptized church members are forbidden to marry or date someone outside the bonds of their beliefs. When Roxanne found a sexy man who was enthusiastic about God, she found her mate. He was six-foot tall, with short-cropped blond hair, clean-shaven, and slightly underweight. She found him religiously attractive and physically desirable. The church did not allow premarital sex. Roxanne and James consummated their marriage after their wedding and reception. It was only after sexually bonding and becoming one flesh, she felt righteously married to James, both under the eyes of God and with the Holy blessing of the church. Within six months, James was ordained as an Elder of the Church.

James was as taken with Roxanne as she was with him. To find God and the petite redheaded young woman of his dreams was an assurance that the Lord was blessing the union. James was going to be a special minister of the faith. His anticipation of her petting and fondling him after their wedding was almost more than he could wait for. Time could not pass quickly enough from the wedding and onward through the formality of their reception until he climbed into bed with his bride. He expected more from their first experience, but realized God may have been holding something back from their sexual encounter to teach him humbleness. Perhaps the Almighty was sending him a message his sexual wants were not supposed to take priority over his spiritual responsibilities. Yet, he loved Roxanne. Five minutes later, the consummation of the marriage was complete.

The church taught James that his wife was inferior to him. He believed she was unable to be independently viable without his family headship and guidance. Before getting married, James told Roxanne she had to be submissive to him at all times to honor the

Lord. She accepted his husbandly leadership, never questioning his God given authority. Roxanne consented to the rules of "***God's Prophets and Publishers***." It was her place in life to serve James, who served God.

Ever since he was a child, James suffered from insomnia. After the couple moved to Florida, he would often awaken during the night and stare at the revolving ceiling fan in the dim light of their bedroom. Sometimes James would roll over onto his right side, reach beside his bed and retrieve the earphone plugged into his radio, which was sitting on the nightstand. He would put the earphone into his ear and listen to far distant AM stations. By morning, he could give Roxanne a brief summation of the news and weather that occurred overnight in various parts of the country. One night he went to sleep listening to his ancient Zenith Trans-Oceanic radio. Unconsciously, he rolled over on his left side with the earphone still jammed deeply in his ear, pulling the radio off the nightstand onto his head. Ten minutes later, after getting his bloody nose to quit dripping, James went back to bed, but slept little. Roxanne thought it was funny, but quit laughing when James screamed at her to show submission to his headship. After the experience, James was careful to put the earphone loosely in his ear so it would fall out if he dozed off and rolled over in bed.

When James did sleep, he dreamed about church matters. As he was sleeping, Jesus was giving him divine instructions about what he must do when Armageddon came. It would be James' responsibility to provide instructions for those who would survive the coming Battle of Armageddon and help bring the Earth back into a paradise similar to the original Garden of Eden. James was to become a King, anointed by God, to rule over the State of Florida.

When morning came, his dreams would fade away. It would disturb James to have forgotten details of the messages from Jesus. He prayed for the attributes of Joseph, to be able to remember and interpret the divine dream messages. He knew he was to serve as a King for God. James also knew it would be soon.

It had been more than five decades since the suicide of James's distant cousin, Nathaniel Wilford Miller. The incident was still a forbidden topic, both by the church and his family. It had been an embarrassing moment in the history of the Miller family when Nathaniel committed the ultimate sin, of suicide. Unlike his long dead heretical cousin, James refused to ignore his personal calling from God. He would always remain faithful to God and his Faithful and Discreet Slave, the Governing Body leaders at church headquarters in Brooklyn, New York.

"God's Prophets and Publishers" was one of many millenarian groups that evolved out of the Adventist movement during the nineteenth century. Many such groups faded away and disappeared after their prophesied dates predicting the "Great Tribulation" and the "Battle of Armageddon" came and went, without anything of significance happening. **"God's Prophets and Publishers"** had the same predictions, but blamed the congregational members for misinterpreting their prophecies when nothing out of the ordinary occurred. After each failed event, the church would lose some members. Shortly afterwards, the predicted event was forgotten and the Church would prosper and grow by using constant indoctrination and love bombing techniques.

The church had an answer for everything, social rules, political rules, personal conduct rules, and special vocabulary words that helped identify true followers of the faith. *"God's Publishers"* put great importance in defining the family responsibilities of the male and female members. An iron hand of discipline was required and administered without condemnation by parents to command their children. Physical discipline was mandatory. A large yellow sign was posted in the church bathrooms, saying; "Spare The Rod and Spoil The Child." It was the place where parents of unruly children often administered physical discipline when they misbehaved during services.

The church taught that the husband is the head of his house, and most men loved the role. Thirty-five years after the death of Nathaniel, his late cousin's elderly mom and dad introduced James's parents into the church and conducted a home book study with them. Young James sat quietly in his chair, convinced beyond any doubt ***"God's Publishers"*** had the "truth." Although never learning all the details, he was told Cousin Nathaniel had lacked faith, was egocentric and did not consider the demands of God to be more important than his selfish desires. Cousin Nathaniel was a terrible sinner who failed to remain "steadfast and strong" in faith and to God. James learned from the mistakes of his cousin. The family no longer spoke Nathaniel's name. The memory of the long dead teenager was fading because such a sinful life must be forgotten. James's parents presented Nathaniel as an example of an evil heretic, as a warning to remain faithful within the church. James knew he was different. Unlike Nathaniel, he would be loyal to God and the church.

A psychiatrist had written and commercially published an analytical thesis about Nathaniel. The book contained selections quoted from Nathaniel's journal after the teenager committed suicide. However, that book was banned by **"God's Prophets and Publishers"** Governing Body. "It's considered apostate information," they stated. "Anyone who reads the book would be challenging God's laws," and could be excommunicated from the church. This would never happen to him. No sir! James was faithful, unquestioning, and never entertained doubts.

When he was sixteen years old, James stole several copies of the "Nathaniel" thesis out of the city library and burned them. He never read the thesis himself, but justified his actions by saying he was protecting his associate believers. James did not consider himself a thief, but rather as a holy man who could break civil laws to protect believers. James's calling came from God. Who could resist that calling of God? Halleluiah! Praise Jesus, Amen. Praise God! Amen. Praise the almighty Jehovah! Yes, Lord! Amen! Amen! Amen!

It was almost dark when Roxanne went to bed. Before joining her, James read a chapter from the Book of Matthew and offered a prayer to God. The sun was going down, so James flicked on the kitchen light switch so he could see to read. Nothing happened. The power was out. Could the power outage be a Holy sign? James brought back a Coleman gasoline lantern from his utility shed. Hurricanes were a seasonal threat to Florida. It was wise to keep alternate ways of providing light, some basic food supplies, and drinking water for such occasions. The owner of the house had left the lantern for such an emergency. The fall hurricane season was over, therefore most of the emergency food James and Roxanne had purchased and stored was already gone.

James picked up the lantern, shaking it to make sure there was enough fuel. He pumped the plunger several times to provide pressure to the gasoline, raised the mantle and touched a match to the fabric. The fuel ignited and glowed with a bright, white light. He lowered the mantle, carried the lantern into the kitchen, and sat it on the table. James placed his Bible in front of the lantern. He opened the refrigerator, moved aside a water jug and retrieved a bottle of kosher grape wine, the only alcoholic beverage allowed by "***God's Publishers.***" Jesus Christ and his Apostles shared grape wine at the last supper in the Jerusalem loft more than two thousand years ago. To James, it was a communion with Jesus to drink what represented the Lord's blood while reading his Holy Bible. He bought the kosher grape wine by the case.

James opened the bottle, pouring himself a glassful. He placed the wine bottle alongside the lantern. James said a short prayer, opened his Bible and began reading the Sermon on the Mount from the Book of Matthew. The words of Jesus inspired him. Two hours later, he had finished consuming the entire bottle of wine and completed reading the Book of Matthew. It was more communion than he intended, but now he was tired.

With the wine gone, James stood up, bowed his head over the good book, and closed the evening with another short prayer. On finishing, he closed the valve controlling the fuel of his Coleman lantern, and out went the light. He set the lantern in the middle of the table. James stood up and went into the bedroom. He removed his shirt, stripped to his boxer shorts and crawled under the sheet beside Roxanne. She was fast asleep, lying on her left side with her back towards him. James was too sleepy to perform his sexual duty tonight. Roxanne would have to wait until another time for him to carry out his husbandly obligation. He would not bother to wake her. The wine caused James to fall asleep right away.

Chapter 24

JAMES PROPHETICAL DREAM

James began to dream. It was one of those dreams where you are not sure you are dreaming or if it is realism. His mysterious dreaming was an integration of the mystical, combined with his religiously trained conscious into cognitive mental imagery. A total coherence of the real and unreal, so interwoven it was the same. Strange thoughts sprang from deep in the mind of James. He heard a voice, coming from the Holy Spirit. It lingered within the hidden areas of his mind, underlying and guiding his mystical religious faith. The voice was speaking to James from deep inside his id. It was real. The voice sounded the same as his.

All I have are memories. Memories of what, I do not know. I know I am lying in bed, but I do not feel Roxanne next to me. She was my companion when I went to sleep. Is she still beside me? This is a strange place. It is damp and my body is sore and stiff. Everything is dark. It is cold, so very cold. How can it be cold in Florida? It is so dark. Not a beam of light penetrates the void. I cannot remember such blackness, utter blackness. There is no smell, no touch, no conversation, nothing. Am I asleep or is this real?

The blood of Jesus Christ continued to manipulate James' brain. The intensity of the dream world took over his psyche, clouding cognitive awareness to the point where James was no longer master. The Holy Spirit became the controller. James knew God was giving him a vision.

I'm nothing but thoughts and memories. I do not remember the physical world. Am I in Heaven? If I died, would I still exist? If I exist, am I alive? On the other hand, do I live? Are my thoughts real or is this an illusion? I believe I am still asleep, but I am not sure. I cannot feel the presence of my wife. I hear no sound, except the hidden voice of the Holy Spirit in my mind speaking confusing thoughts to me. Oh, that voice seems so lonely!

I am trying to move my toes, but nothing is happening. I feel a blanket on my body; I must still be in my bed. However, it feels neither warm nor cold. It is just there. My back feels pressed into the mattress. I raise my knees a small distance upwards before touching something solid and cold. How can my covers be solid? I know that I covered myself with a sheet, nothing more. This is not a sheet. I extend my legs and try to move them sideways. There is nothing around me but a solid capsule encompassing my body like a mother's womb. I feel socks on my feet but no shoes. Did I go to bed with socks on? Why would I? I never do. I remember wearing only my underwear.

My hands are on my chest. I will try to move my fingers. I am not sure if anything moved. Is there feeling in my hands? Can I move them while I am sleeping? I am not sure. There is something smooth like a starched shirt under one of my hands. I try to move my index finger. It moved. I feel a button under my fingernail. I am moving my fingers.

I am clothed. How did I get dressed? My fingers are sliding along the button. I must be wearing a dress shirt, yet I am cold, so very cold. I moved my right hand a couple of inches but my elbow touch something solid. I will try my left hand. I feel movement, but oh, ever so slowly. I will bring my hand to my face. Do I have a face? There is no light.

Maybe I am having an out-of-body experience. Instead, could it be a near death experience? Perhaps it is sleep paralysis. I do not know. I may be awake. However, perhaps I am asleep or in the

Spirit. My mouth is dry and my breathing is ever so slow. Could the Lord's wine have poisoned me? The air is stale, but I recognize the faint stink of flowers. The air smells of lilacs. Something is changing. On the other hand, is it?

My hand has reached my chin. It feels ever so cold. My mouth is dry. I cannot open my lips. I touch my nose and my eyes. My eyes are open. It is so dark, so quiet. Is it always this dark in our bedroom? Where am I? I feel something cold on my lips. It is my watch. I always wear my watch to bed. Am I still in bed? I was in bed. I must be in bed. I must bring my other hand up to my face. Slowly, ever so slowly, I'm moving my right hand toward my chin. It is almost there. I touched my chin, touched my mouth, and tried to put my fingers into my parched lips. This cannot be a dream, so it must be real.

My mouth is so dry, but I can manage to get it open a small way. I try to speak but only a high-pitched sound comes out. Roxanne, oh my dear Roxanne, please wake me if this is a dream! The sound of my voice scared me. Can my voice be real when I am dreaming; or did I dream that I spoke? My voice terrifies me. I cannot move. In a fleeting moment, it seems as if hours passed, so I must again try to move.

My right hand touches my left and I can feel my wristwatch. It feels different from my mechanical watch. How did I get this watch? Where is my old mechanical watch? I would give anything to hear the tick, tick, ticking sound of it running. Even Roxanne's snoring would give me comfort, if I were asleep. Of course, I must be sleeping.

There are buttons on my watch. If it is electric, then one of the buttons when pushed will emit a neon light, which will illuminate the watch face. Can I find the button? Oh, time moves so slowly. Has a century passed? Has a millennium passed? I know it has been seconds, but it seems years. My mind is going. I cannot stand it anymore. I must find the button. I only need a sliver of light, to either awaken me or take away the darkness. The watch face is cold to the touch. The smoothness of the glass top gives me comfort. My body is twitching and tingling as my foot does when it goes to sleep and begins to reawaken. My wedding ring is gone. Did I have it on when I went to bed, or did I go to bed? What is the Lord trying to tell me?

I must find the light button on my watch. I try to lift my head, but it feels extremely heavy. I manage to raise my head, not far, just a little ways. My finger found the button on my watch. I am pushing it. Nothing happens. My finger finds another button, and I push it. A warm green glow shines from my watch face like a laser. The light has blinded me. For a fleeting moment, I see a little Indian girl, smiling and holding a multi-colored stone in her hand. The vision disappears, as the light gains intensity. Am I supposed to go into the light? Who was the little Indian girl? My eyes adjust to the warm glow and I see in horror that I am covered with a satin blanket. I can turn my wrist enough to shine the light both to my left and to my right. I cannot see Roxanne. Where is she?

There is a rubber seal on my right side and hinges to my left side. In utter madness, I shine the light above my head. There, embossed in a bronze plate is my name, the date of my birth and date of my death. I scream, scream, scream, and scream! My voice is stronger and resounding in the enclosed area. Why doesn't Roxanne hear me and wake me up? Is she ignoring my screams? Can Roxanne not be the person whom I believe her to be? Why won't she help me?

I let go of my watch and I am engulfed by total darkness. In desperation, I reach into my pocket and find a pocketknife. Why do I have a pocketknife? I do not know. With deepening panic, I cannot open it. My fingers are shaking; my fingernails are digging holes in my hands. I feel droplets of blood flowing down my fists. I must relax. I cannot relax. What is this message from God? What is the almighty Jehovah trying to tell me? I know this is prophesy being sent to me and I must not forget what is happening. Remember, remember, and remember.

I must relax. I cannot panic. I will panic, because there is nothing left of my domain. My knife is open and I am trying to pry open the box. Nothing is happening. I scream again, my voice is loud and piercing. I hear sounds outside my coffin. It sounds like dirt falling. I cannot stand it. I am going mad. I am mad. The world is gone. My knife is open and I scream again as I scrape it back and forth along the seal. My mind no longer ponders my existence. There is nothing but panic and darkness, so I begin screaming and scream again. I will never be able to open this enclosure with just a damn pocketknife. I scream, scream, and scream. What is the Lord trying to tell me?

Suddenly my lid opens. The light is so intensive; there is someone before me. It must be Satan. I must be in Hell. Therefore, it was not a message from Jehovah after all. On the other hand, is God still communicating it to me? I must remember, remember, remember. . ."

With all the strength I can find, I rise and plunge my knife into Satan's throat. Blood squirts from Satan over me. I pull back my knife and get ready to plunge it again. Satan appears to be Roxanne. Satan is Roxanne. Roxanne is Satan. I do not understand. One of Satan/Roxanne's demons is standing beside her and the demon swings a shovel at my face. It connects with so much force my teeth break into many pieces. Once more, darkness engulfs me. It is getting dark. All I have are memories. Memories are fading . . . but I must remember, remember, and remember."

"James! James, what's wrong? You were screaming!" Roxanne was shaking her husband, propelling him out of his nightmare. "James?"

James sat up in bed, noticeably trembling; his body was wet with perspiration. He opened his eyes, staring at Roxanne in the darkness. He took several seconds to gather his wits before speaking.

"I am fine, go back to sleep woman." He would not share his dream with her. He tried to analyze the message from God. Was it a warning about Roxanne? Was there symbolism in his entrapment inside a box with no way out? Who was the little Indian girl holding the stone? Why did he see so little of her? She faded as if she was fleeing from him. He would not forget the Holy Spirit's prophesy.

James continued to lie in bed, trying to interpret his spiritual dream. However, glorious sleep engulfed him once more. This time there was no dreaming. Sleep did not last long; only an hour passed before he awoke in darkness.

James turned on his radio, forgetting there was no electricity. Angrily, he rotated the knob back to the off position. After a half-hour passed, he got out of bed to go to the bathroom. James picked up a penlight flashlight from his nightstand next to the shortwave radio. He flicked the flashlight switch and shook it a couple of times before it came to life, projecting a narrow beam of light. Why did the flashlight work and the power failed? Maybe it was the will of God, thought James. He did not consider the simplicity of a battery heating the filament in the bulb.

That is what happens when you drop it on the floor too many times, thought James. Once the light became consistent, he slipped on his shoes. He never enjoyed walking barefoot. James entered the bathroom and closed the door. He sat the flashlight on the sink, allowing the light to shine toward the medicine cabinet mirror so it would reflect throughout the room.

After flushing the toilet, James did not bother to wash his hands. He picked up his flashlight and left the room, walking through the short hallway into the kitchen. He poured himself a glass of water from the gallon bottle from the old General Electric refrigerator, downing it in a few short gulps. It seemed strange to peep inside the fridge and see no light. The seals on the old porcelain chipped refrigerator had dried out several years ago, allowing heat to seep into the storage compartment. By morning, it would be room temperature. James returned the water bottle to the shelf and closed the door. Maybe the electricity would turn back on.

The tap water in many parts of Florida is neither the purest nor the best tasting, so Roxanne bought ten one-gallon jugs of purified spring water from Brown's Grocery store, always refrigerating one to get it cold. The remaining nine jugs were stored in a cabinet under the kitchen sink. After the first purchase, they could refill the empty jugs for twenty-five cents each from a Glacier Water refill machine. It saved them money. Money was scarce. It is not easy being a missionary of God. A preacher's needs and essentials are the same as other working people, but the income is much smaller and donations are few.

There was a practical reason for buying filtered water instead of just drinking tap water. The water flowing from the faucet smelled like sulfur. James compared it to the smell of a dog's fart after eating cheap dog food. Bottled water is the best. It tasted good, looked clear, and did not stink. The filtered water had a slight metallic tinge, but he considered the taste flavorful. James said it gave the water "personality." Overall, it was far superior to the dog fart stuff. When he and Roxanne first rented the mobile home, they tried to drink the tap water coming from the Park storage tank. After putting up with two weeks of diarrhea, James decided from then on, he would take better care of his health. He was willing to pay the 25 cents a gallon for bottled water. The water didn't bother Roxanne, but whatever pleased James rules all.

James put down the empty glass, opened his patio door and left the house, entering the porch. The locals called this a "Florida room." If it was an expensive porch, they called it the "Lanai". Wealth does have its own arrogance, thought James. To him, it was just a porch. A fiberglass screen enclosed the Florida room. Occasionally a chameleon would find its way into the room and live there, feeding on crawling insects to sustain its life. The room had an aluminum roof, which made a horrible racket during the summer rainstorms. At first, James enjoyed sitting there during a thunderstorm, having all his senses dulled by the loud clatter of raindrops on the roof. The amusement faded and now he preferred to go inside his home during storms and sit at the kitchen table, reading his Bible.

A soft night breeze was blowing through the screened room, stirring up a definite odor of mildew. A Palmetto bug was eating some potato chips on the floor, where James had spilled them from his supper plate. The bug scampered away from James' footsteps, running past his feet and sneaking into the house. Several more Palmetto bugs fled under a stack of newspapers occupying the corner of the Florida room. Florida had respect for the fifty million year-old insect species, calling it a Palmetto bug instead of a cockroach. Florida also is the home of billions of stinging fire ants, termites, black widow spiders, brown recluse spiders, wasps, snakes and lizards. The small lizards eat the termites and ants, the snakes eat the lizards, and so on. Overall, nature kept her balance in this semi-tropical State. All life sustained and propagated more life.

During the summer and fall months, the arid smell of mildew permeated the air as it did this night. The stale, recognizable pungent odor would creep up after a rainstorm or several days of high humidity and linger on clothing, furniture, and tools. It could hang in the air for months and cling to buildings, leaving a nasty green residue on homes and roofs.

James turned off his flashlight and sat on one of the plastic chairs in his Florida room. He looked out the screen into the front yard. The Florida room was where he and Roxanne read the Bible with potential religious converts, who visited them once a week for a study of the Scriptures. The screen allowed neighbors to see their study. James thought it gave a witness of his holiness to all who ventured past their house during the service. After their visitors left, he would sit in silence, offering prayers to God for the recruits, until he was sure they had made it safely to their homes. He was glad the mobile home park owner bought and provided porch furniture made of plastic. The plastic table and chairs were easy to clean; some bleach, a rag, and hosing them down with water made the furniture appear new. He made Roxanne clean them before every Bible study. It was her responsibility as a homemaker and his wife. It was his responsibility to make sure she did her work.

Sometimes, you know something is different in your environment. It was this realization, which caused James to notice an eerie glow shimmering on the queen palm tree in his front yard. Impulsively he realized it was not the palm tree glowing, but the sky behind it. His religiously trained mind entertained thoughts of the story of Moses and the burning bush. What was this; could it be another sign from God? Was his dream prophecy reaching fulfillment tonight? It was time to go outside and investigate this strange development. James never locked his Florida room screen door. He always kept a second Bible on the porch table. God and his Bible would protect his furniture and home from any potential thief. James didn't need locks. He had the Lord God. James pushed back his chair, stood and moved toward the outside door.

His hand turned the doorknob and he exited the Florida room, walking down the concrete block steps onto the driveway. As he inched beyond the queen palm tree, James raised his eyes toward the night sky. He saw the most amazing heavenly display presented during his life! The sky was full of gently dancing and waving energy patterns. It was unlike anything he had seen, including his native birthplace of Anchorage, Alaska where he lived the first ten years of his life. His dad worked for Standard Oil on a pipeline construction project. When the job was completed, the family moved to Michigan. At first James was dumbstruck, amazed, and in veneration looking at the Florida sky. Those emotions changed into a prayer. He dropped to his knees, put his hands together and prayed.

"Thank you God for your sign! Thank you for your prophetic dream you sent me this night, my Heavenly Father. I shall heed your dream warning and serve you with my life. I, James Miller am your humble servant and your lowly slave, Lord. Praise God, Amen."

James stood up and started running back across his yard, toward the Florida room. It was important to awaken Roxanne and share this most important event in the history of humanity with her. This was an exciting time, the time they had been prophesying about and awaiting since becoming members of "***God's Publishers***". Armageddon was coming! Yes, Lord Jesus! James's time of personal anointing as King of Florida was near.

In his hast back into his home, James tripped over their plastic pink flamingo ornament near the edge of his driveway. He fell at once, hitting his face on the ground. More embarrassed than hurt; he arose and flicked off the dirt and whatever night bugs or spiders that might be clinging to his body. He was still only wearing his underwear. His red colored Hanes boxer briefs resembled shorts in the dark.

James decided to slow down and be careful. Once back in his Florida room, James opened the sliding glass patio door and stepped into the dark living room. With his first step, he smashed the Palmetto bug that earlier entered and stopped in the middle of the floor. It stuck to the bottom of his shoe, to be scraped off with his next hurried step toward the bedroom. He stopped, shaking his penlight into life, directing its beam down the short hallway. He resumed walking and entered the bedroom.

Roxanne was sleeping under a rose-colored sheet, a gift from her mom and dad at their wedding reception. To James, it appeared to be a satin blanket. James blinked his eyes and the sheet was there as it always had been. He thought he smelled the feint odor of lilacs. As had the image of the satin blanket, the scent disappeared.

A lock of hair is lying across Roxanne's left eye and James could see beads of perspiration on her forehead. She is beautiful, thought James. "Roxanne, Roxanne, Roxanne, get up! It is a sign from God, you have to see it Roxanne! Get out of bed. Hurry up! Come with me because our deliverance is near! Quickly, do not waste time, please go outside with me."

In his excitement, James pulled back the sheet, exposing Roxanne's bare legs. Her nightgown had crept up beyond her hips disclosing her naked buttocks. He hesitated, staring at her nakedness before continuing to shake her shoulders with both of his hands.

Chapter 25

After Roxanne and James married, they decided their calling in life was to become church missionaries serving where no *"God's Publishers"* congregation existed. James penned a letter to the home office in Brooklyn, New York requesting an assignment. Shortly afterwards, the young couple received their commission to go to central Florida as missionaries. According to the words of their church Governing Body, "the need is great in central Florida." Their calling was to serve near Fort Mead. After their honeymoon, James and Roxanne said good-bye to their respective parents in Michigan, packed their seven-year-old Chevy sedan with what few belongings they owned and drove to Florida.

The newlywed couple decided before their marriage that it would be wrong for them to have children because Armageddon was so close. Their church Elders said it was important they spend whatever days remaining until Armageddon starting a new church and recruiting members for it. If they did not do so, they would be guilty of selfishness and bloodguilt with the Great Tribulation being so near.

The time to save individuals from God's wrath was short. Who could question the mighty Lord God? Jonah did, and it almost killed him. Rather than reproduce and bear children, their calling was to save those people already born. The calling of the Lord far outweighed the carnal demands of reproduction. James had gotten a vasectomy two months before their wedding. There would be no children, at least not by him. The Scriptures warned; "Woe, to those giving suck in those days." Roxanne and James Miller would obey

God rather than their desires to be parents. However, James hated little kids anyway.

During six months of missionary work in Florida, they recruited two more families as potential members of the movement. Those recruits studied "***God's Publishers***" books with James and Roxanne every Wednesday evening. This Bible Study would teach converts how to become true believers. After completing six months of extensive indoctrination, the potential converts could be eligible for baptism. Conversion must be mentally complete before the physical expression of compliance by public baptism in water. Once baptized, there could be no turning back by the convert. God hates people who do not obey the Elders of "***Gods Prophets and Publishers***." Anyone who left the movement was a heretic. Those people were punished by banishment and shunning by the church Elders and all members. James' cousin Nathanial was such a heretic.

Chapter 26

Roxanne's eyelids snapped open. She sat up bed, looking at her husband. "Huh, what's going on? Is there something wrong? Were you having a nightmare again? Why are you using the flashlight? Isn't the electricity on? James, what is it? Please, you are frightening me."

She was alternating between the twilight reality of sleep and wakefulness. She was in the mysterious void of recognizing the real world but not fully awake. Her anxiety stimulated her body to full wakefulness.

James sat down on the bed next to Roxanne, grabbing her left hand, gently squeezing it. "It's happening! God is giving us a sign in the heavens. Check it out! You have to see this, you really do! Hurry." Even before completing the last sentence, he stood up and jerking her hand, almost pulling her out of bed.

"Don't pull on my arm James. It hurts. Give me a second to put on my robe and slippers, okay?" Roxanne reached under her side of the bed and felt around for the large four-cell, Eveready flashlight she always kept there. After finding it, she flicked it on and sat it on her nightstand. She crawled out of bed. She stood up, self-consciously pulling her nightgown back down where it belonged. She grabbed her robe from the dresser, wrapping it around her and buttoning it.

She reached under the bed, getting her pink bunny slippers. They were a gift from her dad when James and she entered the ministry service. She shined the flashlight on each slipper, giving them a quick shake but found nothing in them. With all the insect creatures in Florida, she would not put them on without checking to see if some critter had taken up residence inside. After putting on her slippers, Roxanne sat back down on the side of the bed, rubbing her eyes.

"I'm ready; now tell me what is going on, James?"

"My time had arrived, Roxanne, it is amazing! I had a vision and a sign from God telling me our redemption is near! I must show you this, so you will believe."

While she had been getting dressed, James slipped into his trousers. He bent down on one knee in front of her, grasping her hands as he remained in a kneeling position. "Come outside and you will see the presence of the Lord God." He was shouting with excitement. James did not wait for his wife. He let go of Roxanne and stood up, walking hurriedly out of the bedroom toward the Florida room. He was overwhelmed with enthusiasm. Nothing else mattered. He turned, to make sure Roxanne was following him. She was.

Roxanne exited the Florida room behind James, stepping onto the front yard, closing the screen door behind her. She was standing at the edge of the queen palm tree. Dew was forming on the grass because of the high humidity. Her bunny slippers were getting damp but she did not mind. The cosmos dominated her total attention. She searched beyond the long umbrella shape of the Queen Palm's leaves into the sky.

The night sky featured no clouds, but resembled a huge colorful screensaver on a computer monitor. Colorful patches of light were flashing, contracting and expanding throughout the heavens. The display obscured most of the stars. Only the full moon exceeded it in brightness. The pulsating radiant light mesmerized Roxanne into a tranquil alpha state. Roxanne never saw anything to compare with the beauty displayed in the night sky. She slowly bent down to her knees, placing them into the damp grass. She lowered her head while raising her hands skyward, saying, "Praise God, our deliverance has arrived at last. Oh, James, the Great Tribulation is here!"

Roxanne closed her eyes for a moment of silence. Opening her eyes, she felt she was becoming part of the anomaly above her. Tears began gently dripping down her cheeks and cascading onto her robe. She was smiling, crying and trembling with joy at seeing the glory of God. James took his wife's hand in his, knowing their deliverance into a perfect society on Earth was about to happen.

James told Roxanne to bring two chairs from their Florida room and put them on the front lawn. They sat down and viewed God's glorious display as it flashed across the night sky. The plastic pink flamingo was broken beyond repair, so James pulled it out of the ground and tossed it into his neighbor's yard. Nobody lived there anyway. The couple continued viewing the sky.

After two hours, it was time to retreat into the house and meditate about the prophetic sign to discover what they must do. Roxanne sat at the kitchen table with James facing her. James turned his smaller flashlight toward himself, shining the light into his face. It cast a strange shadow, giving his eyes huge dark circles, as if he were in a 1940's cheap horror film. He lifted his face towards the ceiling of their home and spoke a long verbal prayer to his God. A loud "AAAAAA-MEN LORD" completed his prayer. Roxanne followed her husband's manner but did not repeat the prayer aloud. As a woman, Roxanne could never pray aloud if a man was present. She could close the prayer with her husband by saying a loud "AMEN," which she did. Both began waiting for God.

Nothing happened. God was quiet, or perhaps preoccupied with creating the heavenly phenomena. There would be no more sleeping tonight. A few minutes later, Roxanne opened the warming refrigerator, retrieving a quart bottle of diet soda. She poured a large glass for James and a smaller one for herself. She *opened* the freezer, but the ice trays had melted. There would be no more ice. The warming soda would have to quench their thirst. James resumed his praying. Roxanne remained quiet.

Chapter 27

During their Bible studies with new converts, James warned them of an impending spiritual event. "Now, when you see signs in the Heavens, you know the Great Tribulation is near. When this happens, my dear brothers and sisters in God, arise and come to our home. As the Israelites were told to "Flee to the mountains," I tell you to flee to our home. Here we shall gather and await the great battle which will end all wickedness on our planet." James always repeated this mantra at the end of each Wednesday Bible study. The students smiled.

James knew the converts would take heed in awe and respect, knowing these were not his words, but spoken through his body by God himself. Like James, the brother of Christ, who was the leader of the first century Christians in Jerusalem after Jesus was murdered, James Miller was the modern antitype. It was time to assume the leadership role of his namesake. He was about be given a Kingship with its leadership responsibilities. Elder James would soon have the royal title of "King James." His Kingdom would be the State of Florida.

The couple continued to sit at the kitchen table the rest of the night, pondering God, the Bible, and the prominent heavenly sign. The Florida morning came as a silent whisper, until the birds began to sing in the huge oak trees surrounding Twisted Palms Retirement Park. A tired James arose from his chair.

"Roxanne, please prepare for our guests, who may begin arriving sometime today. Prepare the way, for today is the beginning when God shall bless us and kick Satan's ass all the way to Hell!"

James picked up his Bible and began reading from the book of Revelation. He must be prepared to lead the "little flock" of converts.

First the Great Tribulation would appear, then the Battle of Armageddon, followed by the long awaited resurrection of the dead. It would be his responsibility to teach everyone THE WAY of righteousness and the goodness of *"**God's Prophets and Publishers**.*"

Chapter 28

Roxanne was trying to do her housework. She was exhausted and stressed due to the lack of sleep. She would have appreciated going back to bed for at least a few more hours, but it was obvious James did not intend to let her do so. She examined the contents of the refrigerator and found nothing but a couple of grapefruit, six oranges, and several bottles of diet cola and another jug of Abram's Kosher Grape Wine sitting alongside the bottled water. Everything was warm. There were four more cases of Abram's Kosher Grape wine in the closet. The wine would give them some calories and a few headaches, but at least it was something to drink.

Roxanne had faith in God, but she still realized humankind does not exist without good food and clean water. If God was going to provide the necessities of life, then He better start rolling in his royal "meals-on-wheels" chariot and supply them with something to eat. She walked over to her food storage cupboard. The door itself was a dirty white with smudged fingerprints around the stained brass knob. She opened the door. Looking inside the cupboard, Roxanne found a box of Saltine crackers, some cheese curls, the leftover potato chips from yesterday's supper and two boxes of cornflakes. Roxanne knew the cornflakes wouldn't taste good covered with grape wine or water. Not much to fill the growing hunger pains in her stomach, much less to feed a small flock of believers, who James thought were already on the way. The second shelf sported two cans of green beans, five cans of condensed soup, and some taco mix with four cans of Tuna Fish and six boxes of macaroni and cheese. A more serious matter for the moment was the lack of freshwater. They had two more gallons of drinking water stored under the sink and nothing with which to flush the toilet. Seven empty gallon jugs sat with the two full ones.

A can of Campbell's condensed chicken noodle soup, diluted with water, served with a tube of the saltine crackers was eaten for lunch. Roxanne and James both took afternoon naps, followed by an orange and grapefruit each for supper. They woke up just as darkness was falling. There was no time to waste, Roxanne and James returned to the front yard awaiting more signs from God. They were not disappointed.

Once more, the two of them sat together on the lawn, experiencing the beauty of the celestial night. God was presenting his message to the world. The electricity remained off. Four hours later, Roxanne and James went to bed. James performed his husbandly sexual duty. As Roxanne got up to go to the bathroom, James went to sleep.

The next morning, more problems appeared. The bathroom was beginning to smell. The morning before, the tap water had slowed to a trickle and stopped running. The five hundred gallon holding tank supplying the water to the Park was empty, with no more forthcoming.

There was a build-up of urine in the toilet bowl. It was emitting an unpleasant ammonia smell. Roxanne's anxiousness increased when she thought about the impending sanitary problems. Even the smelly dog fart tap water would be welcome after being without it for two days. Roxanne realized it would have been to their advantage to fill the empty water jugs from the faucet yesterday morning while it still flowed. It was too late. She had hoped the power would be on by now. Sanitation is becoming a major problem. The normal everyday convinces, often taken for granted, are sorely missed. Without the electric fans to circulate the hot Florida air, home temperatures became almost unbearable. Opening the windows brought some relief, but still, this was Florida, and when the sun is shining, it is hot.

Abnormality was becoming the normalcy of the day. Another evening and night came. James and Roxanne resumed sitting in their plastic chairs in the front yard, James bent down placing his knees on the ground, giving homage to the LORD while looking at the awesome aurora borealis display. The extreme beauty of the Heavenly event would impress the most skeptical religious person. Roxanne always accompanied him, following the husbandly lead of James, bowing as he did in front of the display, but praying in silence. Everything went well until she placed her knees in a fire anthill. She jumped up, started squirming and dancing wildly from the insects' painful attack.

"James, James, what is it? My whole body is stinging, what is it?" She yelled.

James said, "You are smitten with the spirit!" He began jumping up and down, raising his arms above his head, shaking his hands to the sky, praying boisterously to his unseen God. "Praise Jehovah, hallelujah, hallelujah, I beseech you Lord and thank you for this glorious sign!"

"Sign my ass; I am being eaten by something, James! Help me!"

James turned on his flashlight, directing it at Roxanne. On closer inspection, he saw fire ants crawling on her body. He slapped at them, squashing their bodies against her flesh. Once all the insects were gone, James spoke with a stern voice. "WOMAN, NEVER MOCK THE LORD." After a long silence, he again watched at the night sky, ignoring his tormented wife.

The next morning, Roxanne saw red puss filled spots on her legs, breasts and private areas. They itched. Her feet are swollen because of the poison flowing in her blood. She found a box of antihistamine tablets and started taking two tablets every four hours. The medicine helped reduce the allergens and swelling. The itching intensified during the daytime, when the hot Florida sun caused her to perspire. Scratching increased the infection, drawing blood from the worst sores, collecting blotches of brownish red under her fingernails. Without bathwater to soak away the corruption, she is wretched.

Chapter 29

James was not helping her pain. He continued spending most of the day sitting at the dining room table, reading the Bible, drinking wine, and taking notes in his spiral three-ring notebook. His unkempt hair and dirty clothes exhibited the look of a homeless street person. He had not shaved since the first night of the Heavenly sign nor would he shave again. James decided to grow a full beard, similar to that of Moses and Jesus. Like Roxanne, he needed a shower but since the first century Christians only occasionally bathed, to James it was another identifying mark of his faith in God. He would not worry about his body being clean, because his inner soul was attaining perfection.

It had been four days since the power went out. There was no visit from their potential *"God's Preachers and Publishers"* converts. James and Roxanne seemingly were alone. They had not walked around the park since the holy sign appeared the first night. There were no mail deliveries or any motor vehicles running. James tried to start his old Chevy sedan, but it wouldn't run. The retirement park was quiet. James continued to spend much of his waking hours sitting at the dining room table, reading his Bible, trying to interpret the "End World" prophecies. He too, was getting restless, but for a different reason. James was impatient for his Kingship to begin.

In the early part of the afternoon, James rested his ballpoint pen on his notebook and focused his attention on Roxanne. She was lying down on the couch. There was no time for relaxation.

"Roxanne, my people will arrive tomorrow morning. I know the reason they are not yet here. It is as our beloved Lord was dead for three days in the grave. Three days as dead, and the fourth day shall awaken and begin their journey here. Prepare the way for our guests."

Roxanne rolled over and watched James from the couch, resting her head upon a pillow. She was not in the mood for a sermon. Roxanne breathed deeply, sighed; raising her head, she spoke sharply: "Okay, James. What would you have me do? We're getting low on food and there is one gallon of water left. My ass itches because I need a bath. My ant bites are infected, the house stinks, and we have a gallon of piss and some shit floating in the toilet. Speak up, James, you're God's messenger; give me an answer, your Holy Kingship."

She arose from the couch, stood and put her hands on her hips, glaring at her husband without smiling. She dared to question James' God given authority. Roxanne had spoken with contemptuousness in her voice to her husband. She had sinned.

James' reaction was unexpected. He slammed his hands against the tabletop, causing his Bible to leap up and fall back in place. "Get behind me Satan!" He shouted. "May the Lord of Heaven forgive you for your lack of faith, woman. I beseech you to be in subjugation to your husband as the Lord God himself has put me in charge of you! Do you understand?"

Chapter 30

James watched in silence as Roxanne disappeared. He quickly forgot her, returned to the kitchen table and sat down. Returning to spiritual matters, he bowed his head in silent prayer and with the same motion, raised his arms, holding his Bible up toward the ceiling. After the prayer, he put the Bible down, closed his eyes and spoke aloud: "Lord, direct me to your ways. Tell me, your most humble and faithful servant, what to do. Guide my hand into your Holy Book and direct my eyes to your commands."

James placed the Bible squarely in front of him and closed his eyes. His left hand grasped the book's cover and he began thumbing the pages with his right hand. The room was silent, except for the turning of the pages. Once more, he smelled the faint odor of lilacs. It is a sign from the Holy Spirit. James allowed God to guide his hands through the Bible. His fingers stopped in the second chapter of Revelation. Only when he felt confident this was where God directed him, did he dare to open his eyes. James read aloud:

"Just the same, holdfast what you have until I come. And to him that conquers and observes my deeds down to the end I will give authority over the nations, and he shall shepherd the people with an iron rod so they will be broken to pieces like clay vessels, the same as I have received from my father, and I will give him the morning star. Let the one who has an ear hear what the sprit says to the congregations."

Therefore, it was true! The Lord was putting James in charge of the earthly reclamation! Yes, it had to be so! How fitting it was for him to witness the heavenly signs. Yes, the Lord was guiding him through his Holy Spirit. The smell of lilacs grew stronger.

The morning star mentioned in the Book of Revelation must be the aurora borealis viewed the last few nights. The clay vessels are his neighbors and his potential Bible study converts. They had to be broken into pieces, and molded into the shape of holiness. God would give James the authority over the nations. His kingship would begin establishing leadership over the residents of the trailer park. Once completed, his next domain would be the State of Florida. Who knows, maybe God would put James in charge of ruling the United States, even the Earth alongside Jesus Christ himself!

It disturbed James to see Roxanne defying his authority and leadership. She was the weaker vessel. Roxanne was putting herself in opposition to God's hierarchy. Potentially, she was the anti-Christ. Perhaps the prophetic dream given to him by God was coming true. Yes, he remembered God telling him in his prophetic dream that Roxanne was Satan. James didn't want to believe it. Could this be true? He would know soon enough. James would no longer question his God. The memory of the little Indian girl holding the stone faded forever from his mind.

James continued examining the Scriptures and mulling over their interpretation. Was it Roxanne's goal to defeat and corrupt the holy church of God? Nothing would prevent James's Kingship. There would be no so-called rapture as many fundamentalist religions taught, because God's Kingdom was about to be set up on Earth, not in Heaven. James would do everything to ensure it would happen the way God directed him. He knew God respected him more than the weaker vessel Roxanne, for she was a woman, not worthy of having a personal relationship through God, except through James.

A movement in the living room caught his attention. James saw a small ghostly image resembling a fog mass hovering and expanding just above the broken television. Within the mass, he saw red eyes staring at him. To James, it was an Angel of God. It could be the Almighty himself! He rejoiced at the new sign. At last, James' eyes were open. He knew what he had to do. The smell of lilacs was everywhere.

Chapter 31

Roxanne walked quickly down the blacktop road toward George and Ruby's home. She hesitated for a moment, listening to the birds singing in the upper branches of a huge water oak tree. A group of crows flew above the tree cawing warnings to other bird species to leave the area. This was their territory. Perchance it was the way of all life. If a blue jay or crow approached, the other birds fled in fear. Roxanne did not want to be a crow or blue jay. She smiled. James would be a perfect crow. Roxanne stopped for a moment, looking far into the sky to watch a group of osprey as they drifted with the wind currents. The osprey circled, gathering altitude, gliding higher without flexing their long outstretched wings.

Roxanne's thoughts drifted to her past. She remembered walking on the road, just south of the retirement park when she came to an abandoned phosphate pit. It was a large area of water covering at least 40 acres, surrounded by an artificial dike about 100 feet high. The water was pumped out of the reservoir to a working phosphate strip mine about eight miles north of the pit. The water would wash the phosphate from the gravel before it was pumped back into the pit. The solid waste would settle to the bottom of the pit, so the process could begin again.

Roxanne remembered walking past the "No Trespassing" sign on the gate and climbing to the top of the dike, intending to observe the ducks, alligators and other wildlife inhabiting the area. It was a beautiful sunny Florida morning. A few clouds were floating above the horizon. A slight breeze moved across Roxanne's body evaporating the perspiration from her face. She recalled walking a short way along the dyke before seeing two alligators at the water's edge, lying in the sun. The alligators scurried into the water. Roxanne took no chances, knowing the creatures could outrun a human for a short distance on land. Although the alligator was a relic dating to the early days of life on Planet Earth, Roxanne knew it could never be a friend or pet. She would give it the respect it deserved as one of the remaining reptiles who had ruled the swamps for millions of years.

Roxanne resumed strolling along the top of the dike, when she saw an alligator over twelve felt long. The reptile showed no fear, ignoring her. She turned, followed a path away from the reptile. It would be pleasant to live as the alligator did, lying in the sun with no natural enemies. No cares or worries for this creature. Roxanne admired the reptile. She envied its quiet solitude.

Roxanne remembered seeing an osprey pluck a fish out of the water two hundred feet from the alligator. The osprey was seeking a meal, not intending to be one. The osprey gained altitude and flew to a group of cypress trees standing about a hundred yards east of the phosphate pit. One of the ancient five-hundred year-old trees served as a rookery for the birds. Roxanne recalled the osprey carrying the fish in its beak, circling the trees before landing upon one of the four nests. The nests were almost three feet across, built with leaves, sticks, and reinforced with bits of trash. Unlike many species of birds, the Ospreys kept their nests for years. Roxanne watched the Osprey tear apart the fish with its talons and feed it to her two offspring who swallowed it. Her babies were no longer chicks but juveniles, large enough that their mother did not have to swallow the fish and regurgitate it to feed them. Roxanne remembered feeling kinship with nature while eavesdropping on the ospreys' home like a peeping Tom.

Since the day at the phosphate pit, Roxanne often thought about how dedicated the female osprey was to her offspring. How she nurtured them, fed them, and someday she would free them from her nest. This is the parenting practiced by nature, and to

Roxanne, it was beautiful. She remembered turning around and facing a security officer. The officer asked her to leave the property for her own protection and safety. Roxanne remembered walking back to the highway, leaving the haven of wildlife.

Roxanne yearned to be an osprey, even more so than an alligator. She could drift along in life, have babies, and let nature take it course. It was the natural order of life, unlike her married life with James. Roxanne never told James about her trespassing experience. He would not have approved.

Roxanne quit daydreaming and considered her present circumstances. Could the ospreys circling above her be an omen? Perhaps they were a sign from God, telling her she could drift along in life without worries, or, perhaps they were just birds doing what birds do. If anything was an absolute, it was the fact she was not living like the osprey.

Roxanne continued walking toward George and Ruby's home. She hesitated, hearing the mockingbirds singing in the oak trees. She loved the mockingbirds' large variety of songs. Not long ago, she noticed some of the mockingbirds mimicked ringing cell phones. For this, she felt sorry about the harmful effects modern technology had on nature.

The afternoon sky was gathering a few wispy clouds. Roxanne's imagination went wild. One of the cloud images was Buddha, while the other was the image of Jesus. The two clouds were side by side, but merged into one. The single cloud metamorphosed into the likeness of a little girl with a bird flying towards her hand. The form of the little girl rotated with the winds, looking down towards Roxanne. A few moments later the little girl with bird in hand cloud drifted upwards, disappearing as it reached a higher altitude. As Roxanne continued to stare at the vacant spot, a dove appeared seemingly from nowhere, flying towards Roxanne then disappeared out of sight. Was everything she was seeing a sign from God, or was it her imagination? Could God indwell within her sentient consciousness? Perhaps this is where God exists. Maybe the deities recognized by Buddhism and Christianity were all the same substance. Could the image of the little girl be herself when she was a child? Roxanne was beginning to believe the only quantifiable transcendence was her self-awareness. Shocked and astonished about her thoughts, she again forced herself to stop daydreaming.

Roxanne walked up the driveway of George and Ruby Long's home. All Roxanne knew about them was their names from the Retirement Park's directory. George Long carved plywood into images of sunflowers and hummingbirds. George also made miniature windmills, one of which decorated his and Ruby's yard. Roxanne knew Ruby spent her time making beautiful Afghans and quilts which was one of her hobbies listed in the same Directory. Roxanne remembered seeing pictures of George and Ruby's craftworks on the clubhouse walls, the one time she had walked through the building.

It was obvious nobody was home at the Long's home, because the window blinds were closed. With the day so warm, she knew the windows would be open if anyone was there. Roxanne suspected the couple might have gone to the Middle School public shelter, located a few miles down the road. Polk County had earmarked the school building for emergencies during the annual hurricane season. A mobile home was the least secure place for residents during a storm. Perhaps some of the senior citizens left for the shelter because of the power failure. After knocking several times on the Long's front door and not getting an answer, Roxanne left, resuming her journey down the quiet street. The story was the same at Nancy and John Harrington's home.

Further, down the street she stopped at Oscar Sparks who lost his wife to cancer. He shared his home with his sister Beverly, who had moved there to take care of him. Beverly fed wild birds, keeping four feeders alongside her carport. The feeders were empty; it was enough evidence for Roxanne to continue walking. She didn't bother to knock on their door.

The last home on the street was where the old man lived. The same old man who visited their home a few days ago and argued with James while he cooked hamburgers. MacArthur Gunderson lived in a blue, singlewide home needing some repair. The shingled roof was in dire need of replacement. The huge water oak tree next to his home had dropped residue and tree sap on its roof for many years. The residue provided nourishment for mildew. The result was a layer of green growing on the shingles. The roof didn't leak, but it wouldn't be long before it would start seeping water into the wall boards, attracting carpenter ants who would feast on the wood and make tunnels in the studs.

Mac was 90 years-old but mentally alert. After his confrontation with James, Roxanne felt uncomfortable about visiting him. She apprehensively trudged up the stairs to his Florida room door and entered it. She knocked on the patio door leading into the old man's house. It was so quiet inside Roxanne figured the old man had gone to the Middle School with the others. She waited, not planning to knock on the door again if there was no answer.

"WHAT THE HELL DO YOU WANT?" MacArthur shouted from inside the building. "Don't just stand there, open the door and come inside, because I sure the hell ain't coming out to open it for you. You ain't got a broken arm do you?"

The loudness of the man's voice startled Roxanne so much that she almost wet herself. Her only companion for the last few days was James. She waited for a moment for her terror to subside. Regaining her composure, Roxanne opened the door and entered the home without responding to the old man. It took a moment for her eyes to adjust to the contrasted darkness inside the home. The white window blinds, now yellowed with age, were swaying gently as a slight breeze blew through the open screened windows. Roxanne recognized the pungent smell of stale cigar smoke permeating the air. Other than needing new window blinds, the inside the home seemed in good order. The interior was in stark contrast to the outside. Roxanne noticed the old man was a good housekeeper, considering he lived alone. She believed a man needed a woman to do the domestic housekeeping work for a man's home to be clean. According to the teachings of her church, this is God's duty for women. The old man's house was organized. The first object catching Roxanne's attention was Mr. Gunderson's dog.

With a loud voice, the old man said; "Hey, don't just stand there, have a seat and rest for a while. You're the first company I've had in ages. Say hello to ol' Buffy dog, so she can get to know you. She ain't seen anyone else in this house in a longtime."

Roxanne responded to what the old man said with a bobbing of her head. She reached over to the small dog, which lay reclining on an old stuffed chair. Buffy wagged her bobbed tail as Roxanne began patting the animal's head.

"Hi Buffy girl! How are you? Huh? Good girl. Gosh, I wish I had a dog." The touch of Buffy relieved her fears. If only humans could accept love as easily as this pet. It only took a pat on the head and a compliment to relax both her and Buffy.

Roxanne stood up, keeping her eyes on the dog before turning her attention to the old man sitting on a lounge chair in front of her. "Mr. Gunderson, I'm Roxanne Miller. Do you remember me? Are you all right?"

"Oh, hell yes, I remember you. I'm not mentally feeble you know. You're the pretty little gal living down the street with, oh, whatshisname; Elder something or another, aren't you? Of course, I know you. I spoke with your husband in front of your home while he burned hamburgers on the grill a few days ago." He hesitated. "Boy, that guy is a piece of work. Glad you didn't bring him with you." After a short silence he continued, "Hey, gal, just call me Mac."

"Thank you Mac. Please, just call me Roxanne." Roxanne stood nervously in front of the old man, glancing at Buffy dog, not knowing what to do next. She thought about extending her hand to Mac, but didn't do so.

"You're already in my house Roxanne, so as I said when you came in, just have a seat. Just don't sit on Buffy's chair. The corner chair is hers, the rest of them in the house are mine. Hell, gal, I ain't had company since I don't know when. The other old buzzards and their wives ask me to go with them to the Middle School three days ago. Hell, I've spent the last twenty years here and ain't a running off to no goddamn school building and be catered to like those old farts. Besides, I learned by living life, not studying stuff in school . . . Hey, that was a joke, you know."

Mac hesitated for a moment, seemingly expecting a smile or a comment out of the young woman in front of him. "Ah, forget my weird sense of humor. You look exhausted and thirsty to me. Would you like to have a glass of water?" There ain't any ice and it's as warm as piss, but there is plenty of bottled water if you would like some."

Roxanne was embarrassed by Mac's language, but his hospitality and the circumstances excused his lack of grammatical graces. She had waved her hand to him a couple of other times as he slowly walked past her house. She never told James. Roxanne realized she keep many events in her life from her husband. Mac always seemed busy at one thing or another with his continuous slow motion movements.

Roxanne sat down on the couch, leaving the chair for Buffy. A closer observation of the man in front of her showed he did not weigh much over 130 pounds. Mac always needed a shave. Physically, he appeared to have the strength and tenacity of a much younger man trapped in an old body. "I would appreciate a drink of water, Mac. Thanks for offering."

"Well girl, then you just get up and get it yourself. I ain't serving anybody anything anymore. The glasses are in the cupboard to the left of the sink. Get a clean one, not the one sitting at the back of the sink, that one is mine."

"Thanks," said Roxanne as she got up and went into the kitchen. She found the kitchen neat and orderly. She expected as much after seeing the living room. Over all, she would grade him high on cleanliness. She always wished James helped her more around the house, but she knew it would never happen. Roxanne opened the cupboard and got a glass, filling it with water from a plastic gallon jug sitting on the counter.

"Would you like a glass of water too, Mac?"

"Nah, I have about ten cases of beer still in my shed, which I've been a tapping into since the power went out. Did you know people in Europe rarely drink cold beer? It always tastes best when served at room temperature. I learned that when I was serving the armed forces in Korea. The beer was as hot as the babes in Korea back in those days, uh, that was before I got married, you know."

Roxanne, with glass in hand came back into the living room and sat back down on the sofa. She took a long gulp, following up by drinking half of the clear liquid. "Can I hold Buffy while we talk?" Roxanne asked.

"Sure, she ain't ever chomped anyone yet. Pick her up easy though, she is getting a mite frail, as she grows older. What makes you visit this old man anyways? Do you know what caused all this power outage? I haven't heard a goddamn word about it myself. It doesn't matter much. There I go again, just after I promised myself not to be long-winded with you. If I talk too much, just remember, I told you I don't get many visitors, so bear with me!"

Roxanne picked up Buffy and took her back to the couch. As the old man spoke, she held the dog on her lap, rubbing its neck and ears. Once more, the loving touch of the dog calmed her nervousness and helped frame her thoughts into words making sense. She felt awkward.

"I take it you are not fond of my husband?"

"Ah hell, you remember me chatting with him. You were standing in your Florida room when I offered him access to my tool shed. Yup, he sure is a piece of work, that one. He acts too stupid to know how to use my tools if he did borrow anything. Sorry, I don't intend to offend you but, I cannot understand what you see in that guy. But then, it ain't any of my business."

"I know you're not here so we could have a conversation about your husband. In addition, you had better not be here to convert me to your religion. If recruiting me is your reason, this is going to be a mighty short visit."

Just as she was starting to relax, Mac's words sent a wave of nervousness through Roxanne's body. She knew it was necessary to explain why James sent her around the park to speak with everyone. She didn't wish to offend Mac, yet she couldn't avoid the reason she was here. She had to do as James told her. Her anxiety caused her voice to change pitch, making the conversation sound unnatural.

"I don't know any more than you do about the power outage, Mac. Have you looked at the night sky the last two days? James believes the nighttime aurora borealis display has something to do with the lack of electricity. He says it means God has intervened in the affairs of man and this is the beginning of the Great Tribulation prophesied in the Book of Revelation."

She squirmed, waiting for a reply or condemnation. Would Mac understand? She hoped so. Most of all, she did not wish to alienate the man who seemed rational.

Mac watched the young woman in front of him. A slow smile began to build across his aged face. "You got to be kidding me, gal! Hell, I heard that doom and gloom horseshit during World War 2, during the Korean War, then during the 70's when the Jehovah's Witnesses were preaching their year of 1975 Armageddon prophecies. I heard it again during the Gulf war. Who can forget the doomsayers making the rounds during the so-called Y2K scare? Just before the end of the millennium, all those crazy preachers were saying the Rapture was going to happen at the stroke of midnight when they dropped that goddamn ball in the center of Times Square. There was the "Heaven's Gate" group of men who were so whacko they cut off their own balls to prevent sexual desire. Hell, without balls, it was no wonder they killed themselves! You probably remember Harold Camping who had the

Family Radio broadcasting outfit. Hell, he predicted the end of the world for May 21, 2011 and when it didn't happen, he predicted it again to happen on October 21, 2011. Nothing happened again!" Mac began to laugh so hard that he had to wipe the tears from his eyes before he could continue speaking.

"Now you say that your husband has expressed more of this crazy stuff. You know, my second wife believed all those crazy preachers. Yes, a right regular believer she was. She even gave some of my hard-earned money to those bullshitters. You know, one evening I went with her to a Pentecostal tent meeting held in a vacant lot just outside town. The first half hour was enjoyable. There was music, singing, and all that fun stuff. Then the whole place turned into an insane asylum. People started jumping up and down and talking crazy. One woman was wiggling on the floor like a rattlesnake I killed one time behind this house. I began to laugh so hard at all of them, it embarrassed my wife." He laughed, reminiscing.

"My wife, she got mad and never invited me to go with her again. She died about fifteen years ago. I didn't have a preacher send her on her way. I just had a private funeral for a few of her friends and me. Hell, most of her close friends and family members had died over the years anyways. There were ten of us there to say good-bye" For a moment, his face became sober and his manner reflected inner sadness.

"I'm sorry, Roxanne. I didn't mean to get off on a tangent, sounding like a rambling old man remembering his past. Anyways, what were you saying about your husband?"

Roxanne was thinking about what Mac had just said. She had watched people in churches being "smitten by the Spirit" but she never experienced it herself, although James thought it happened to her while they watched the sky last night. The fire ant stings still hurt. Her curiosity about Mac's experiences forced her to continue the conversation with the old man.

"He prefers to be called Elder Miller. That is the title bestowed on him by our church."

"Yup, that is what he called himself, he did." Mac replied sarcastically.

"But, getting back to what you were saying, Mac, what do you believe causes the speaking in tongues and those spiritual feelings people in churches are experiencing?" Perhaps if he gave her a rational explanation, it would help her better understand James's fanaticism.

"Ah, gal, there is a simple answer. It was nothing but mass hysteria caused by that Pentecostal preacher man who was just screaming and jumping up and down like a lunatic in front of the congregation. I believe it was a subtle case of mass hypnotism, which is contagious among fanatical fundamentalists. You see, I studied Christianity for a while, besides doing cult religion research for a time, trying to see why my wife would give those assholes so much of my money."

Doubts began growing stronger in Roxanne's mind. Perhaps the old man had a greater insight into living than James did. Could it be possible that Mac's amassed wisdom throughout his long lifetime exceeded those of her church and preachers? She knew James had sent her to gather all the neighbors together and since Mac was the only person still here, she must ask him to join them. She knew what his answer would be. However, Roxanne had to obey her husband.

"Mac, James sent me out to notify our neighbors about his anointing as God's prophet. He said all of you are to bring your remaining food and water supplies to the Clubhouse tomorrow evening after 6 PM, and everyone should be there. He said God would protect any Park residents if you were with us. Will you be there with us?" In her heart, she knew Mac thought she was loony.

Chapter 32

Mac raised his hand and rubbed his chin, deeply staring into the eyes of the young woman sitting in front of him. She reminded him of his late daughter who was killed in the passenger jet, which crashed near Pittsburgh on the famous eleventh day of September 2001. He tried not to laugh at Roxanne's tenacity to ask him such a silly question. He wanted to gather her in his arms and give Roxanne a hug as he would his daughter if she were still alive. Roxanne was not his daughter, but his fatherly instinct was to protect her. James had hijacked her mind as much as the damn terrorists had hijacked the airplane.

"Roxanne, I know conditions are confusing for you. I will try to be serious, because I feel badly because you are so involved with your church. Please forgive my sarcasm and strange humor. I apologize for not being more respectful to you. There is a serious side to me. Please listen with an open mind."

Without waiting for her to answer he continued; "You're torn between loyalty to your husband, loyalty to your religious beliefs, and loyalty to your God. I'm sure you appreciate my honesty. I will give you a gallon of water to take with you, but I will not go to the Clubhouse. The only way I can tell you what I'm about to say is to be blunt. Please don't take it the wrong way. Frankly, my dear young woman, your husband is irrational. I hope you understand what I'm saying and consider what I'm telling you. The way I see it, all you need for daily living is logic and universal love towards all. Forget all the religious bullshit. Forget all the end of the world crap and the so-called Heavenly signs you spoke about. All this stuff is just nonsense. Sometimes, Roxanne, events such as the aurora borealis just happen. Shit happens, as the old saying goes. Sometimes we don't understand why a happenstance such as losing all electrical power occurs, but there is a logical reason for it. Like it or not, we are all bound by the laws of physics and nature, not by providence."

"I don't know what has happened to our world Roxanne, but I do know there is a logical - not a religious explanation. I believe whatever happened; it was Earth-wide and not just something local. Hell, when I was a kid we didn't have good communication about world events. After what happened a few days ago, it's not much different now from what it was eighty years ago. I don't know what the hell happened, but I do know we'll survive it. Whatever happened, we must accept it, bond as one big family, and not put more into the causes than occurred. It is neither religion nor your God that will bring us together. It is our love for others which will bring closure."

"You know, Roxanne, ol' God has been non-communicative with us for over 2,000 years. I doubt James has more insight into God's mind then my little ol' Buffy dog here. My money would be on my dog if I had a choice. You know, ol' Buffy here is my best and constant companion since my wife died. She sleeps on my bed and never demands anything but food and love." Mac hesitated for a moment, to both catch his breath and let Roxanne concentrate about what he was saying.

"I'm sorry; sometimes my old mind wanders a bit. Roxanne, your husband James is insane. Close your heart to your emotional connection to him and think logically and objectively. If you weren't his wife, would you consider your husband's actions rational?" The old man stopped his long monologue, tired and waiting for Roxanne to answer.

"I never thought about what you're saying, Mac. Rational? Probably not. But, I am not supposed to question his husbandly authority." She bowed her head toward her lap, fidgeting with her hands as the old man resumed speaking.

"Now pay attention, Roxanne gal. If you feel James isn't rational, then it's time to make some hard decisions about your life. Protect yourself. For Christ's sake, young woman, move on with your life. Dump this nut and find yourself a good man. You can get married again and have some babies. Afterwards, live each day of your life to the fullest, because I can tell you, the years pass by much too quickly."

Mac watched as Roxanne lowered her eyes, trying to hide the tears flowing from them. He saw the dirty clothes she was wearing and watched as she continually intertwine her fingers nervously. She picked up Buffy and held the dog as she would a child.

Mac gave the young woman time to ponder what he told her. He stood up, went into his kitchen, getting a warm can of beer. After pulling the tab, he drank half of it. He wiped his lips with his left wrist, and drank the remaining liquid. It tasted good and the small amount of alcohol started to relax him. If there is a God, thought Mac, he drinks beer. Mac left Roxanne alone with her thoughts while he enjoyed his drink. She needed a moment of privacy.

Chapter 33

Roxanne appreciated the old man leaving her alone for a short while. She collected her emotions before thinking about her appearance. She looked and felt like a bag lady. She smelled as if she had crawled out of a dumpster. Roxanne was thankful Mac said nothing about her appearance.

Some of her thinking reverted to ideas taught to her by "**God's Publishers and Prophets**" church. The old man did not understand the divine guidance given to James. On the other hand, maybe Mac was right. Perhaps James was screwy and needed mental help. She loved her husband. At least, she thought she loved him. She tried to be in subjugation to his husbandly authority. In her heart, Roxanne knew something was wrong. Not one of their converts had joined them after signs presented themselves in all their Godly glory in the night sky.

Mac returned to the living area and sat back down in his chair. "Can I convince you into a drinking a beer with me? It will relax you."

"No, thank you. I can't drink beer Mac. We are allowed to drink kosher grape wine but no other alcoholic beverages. I appreciate your debate with me and I'll consider what you said. Even if you don't want to go to the Clubhouse tomorrow, I wish you would go. However, I know that's out of the question. If you need me to help you with anything, please let me know. I mean it, Mac."

"Roxanne, I appreciate your kindness. As I said, go and take a gallon of water with you. Maybe it will calm that ding-dong husband of yours. I can see he popped you a good one in your face. You know, gal, you've got one hell of a goddamn shiner around your left eye."

"James didn't hit me; I fell over the plastic flamingo in our yard while we were watching the Heavenly signs last night." Roxanne realized that Mac knew she was lying.

"Let me say this and take it for what it is worth, Roxanne. Don't let the bastard hit you again. You don't have to defend him; I know what spousal abuse is and I can recognize it immediately. My advice is to leave the fucker as soon as you can."

"Don't worry, Mac. I will be all right."

"Roxanne, before you go home, if you want to clean up a bit just feel free to use my shower. He smiled a bit; knowing the idea would interest her.

"Do you remember seeing the fifty gallon plastic barrel I have sitting just under my downspout out back? You may not have noticed it, but I keep the roof gutter above it clean all year around. There is a purpose for it. The barrel catches rainwater. My daddy taught me how to do it when I was a young boy. I use the water to put on my plants during the dry season. There is plenty of water there. You can draw a bucket full and use it to wash up in my shower. The shower stall drain still works. I have a dozen bottles of bleach in my shed. Just pour yourself a cup of bleach and put it in the rainwater barrel. There is an old broom handle leaning against the back of my shed. Use it to stir the bleach into the water. The chlorine will kill any bacteria or critters in the barrel. The choice is yours, so decide before you run out of time here."

"You don't mind?" Roxanne had a strong desire to enjoy a small bit of comfort. "I'll clean up your shower and bathroom before I leave. I won't be long because James will be furious at me if I don't return soon."

"Ah, just grab a pail from under my sink over there, gal. Then go fill it up and use it. There is a drain valve on the side of the rain barrel. Use that to draw the water. Just be sure to close the valve when you finish. I can't afford to have the remaining water drip out."

Roxanne did not wait for another invitation. She stood up, gathered a bucket from under the sink and went outside. She poured a cup of bleach into the rain barrel, stirring it up. The water turned from a slight green color into a milky blue. A few dead bugs floated on the surface but they did not bother her. The bleach removed the slight musty smell of mold, replacing it with the odor of pine-scented Clorox. Roxanne filled a bucket from the valve, and hurried back inside the house. She entered Mac's small bathroom, got undressed, dropping her clothes on the floor at her feet. She stepped into the shower.

First, she splashed water on her body and soaped herself all over. She used the remaining water to rinse herself. She remembered her dad telling her a longtime ago, "that is the way they did it in the military to conserve water." It felt good to be clean again. She exited the stall and dried herself with a towel hanging on the rack next to the toilet. She wiped down the shower stall with the same towel. She wished she didn't have to put on her dirty clothes, but there was no choice.

Chapter 34

Roxanne was walking up the driveway to her home. James was no longer sitting at the table, nor was he reading his Bible. He sat on one of the plastic chairs in the Florida room waiting for her return. As Roxanne entered the screen room, she knew something was wrong. James eyes were oval shaped, wide open and not blinking. He stared at her. She felt the hairs rising on the back of her neck, and fear gripping her. It was as if a surgeon had inserted his gloved hand in her open chest cavity and began squeezing her heart, cutting of the blood supply.

"Where the hell have you been, woman? Where are my people and where are the supplies?" James stared at her, waiting for a response.

"I was able to get one gallon of filtered water. I was lucky to get that, James." Roxanne's hands starting trembling.

"Just one bottle of water, huh. Did you not hear me, woman? Where are the people? Where are the other provisions I requested? The Lord spoke to me while you were gone. He is all knowing, all-powerful. The Lord was watching you, to see if you were going to remain a loyal servant of his. DID YOU HEAR WHAT I SAID? The Lord God himself spoke to me through my Bible, while you were gone!" James was shouting, screaming. Beads of perspiration were forming on his forehead, dripping down into eyebrows. His eyes squinted, still not blinking. James' face tightened and his body is trembling with wrath. Droplets of saliva spewed forth into Roxanne's face from James' mouth as he continues speaking:

"The Lord told me you are an evil spawn of Satan, a whore of Babylon, and your number is 666. Where did you get the water bottle, woman?"

"James, honey, I got it from the old man down the street. You met him a few days ago. His name is Mac, you know, the man we saw cutting his grass. He is the man with the little dog. He gave it to me to give to you. Please don't be upset."

James' eyelids turned to slits, responding to the information she gave him. "Woman, the old man is of the devil himself! Do you hear me? Do you not see it? Only evil lives as long as he has."

"James, you don't know what you're saying. Think about what your alleging, honey, and how you're acting." She waited for a reply. Roxanne's body was trembling with fear. Perspiration was flowing from her armpits down onto her shirt.

It was as if James was deaf. Before she could say anything more, James arose from his chair and stood in front of her, staring into Roxanne's eyes. Roxanne heard his words, but what she saw while looking deep into his soul was an absence of conscience. She saw fear, fear of what he had become and fear manifested as James himself.

"You smell different, wife. Your hair is wet, you are clean, but your soul is as dirty as the clothes you wear on your body. Did you fuck him for the water? Huh, did you fuck the old man? What else did you do, huh?"

Roxanne faltered and her voice grew shaky. "James, for God's sake, he is at least eighty or ninety years-old. Please, you are my husband and I care about you, but you are frightening me with your words. Mac gave me some water from his rain barrel and let me wash in his shower, and gave me a gallon of drinking water, nothing more."

Roxanne slowly extended her right hand towards James. She put her fingers on his left cheek, caressing it gently while trying to keep her composure. "James, there is no one except you, me, and Mac in the retirement park. Everyone has gone to the shelter at the Middle School building. You know the one they use for hurricane warnings. Mac . . ."

James did not wait for her to complete the sentence. Instead of replying, he began hitting her in the mouth with both fists. Blood splattered on his hands and sleeves from her broken lip. Roxanne had not prepared herself for violence. James knocked her backwards over the plastic table and she landed on the concrete floor of the Florida room. Roxanne tried to sit up but could not. She slid her butt back on the floor until her back rested against the wall, sitting without moving. If there were any demons here, they had to be inside James. Tears were flowing down Roxanne's face. She tried not to let James see her fear.

"You know the Bible woman. When a Jewish woman was guilty of adultery, she was taken outside the city and stoned to death. Why should you be treated differently?"

"This is not Israel, James. Didn't Jesus forgive the harlot? Honey, you are the only man in my life and I have never broken our marriage vows. You must believe me."

Chapter 35

James searched the ceiling scanning every corner. After a moment, he found the apparition. It appeared and hovered just above Roxanne's head. Again, the Holy Spirit carried with it the strong aroma of lilacs, smelling like funeral flowers. He remembered the same smell from his prophetic dream. The Spirit hovered away from Roxanne, drifting to the center of the room, just below the ceiling. Its wings expanded and stretched from its body.

"It's another sign from you, my Lord," James spoke to the translucent image, not visible to Roxanne. James knew as the head of his family, Roxanne could not communicate or see the Messenger of God. The specter did not move. It sent its commands telepathically. At last, James was getting divine guidance and his Kingship. James stood as a bronze statue, unmoving except for his lips, which spoke: "Yes, Lord. Yes, Lord. I will punish her. She is the evil one, I know. Yes, your holy will is my command."

James pointed his finger at Roxanne. The phantom nodded its head in approval. It drew its wings in and tucked them behind its shoulders.

James saw blood dripping down the front of Roxanne's chin, flowing onto her exposed breasts, peeping through her torn blouse. It sexually excited James to see her this way. The color of her blood almost matched her red hair. Red is the color of anger. He should have recognized this feature about Roxanne before getting married. Yet, the violence and her appearance caused him to be fully stimulated, and it bothered him.

He tried blocking the evil sexual thoughts from his mind. They had to be coming from the "Evil One" with whom he was about to battle, perhaps from Roxanne herself. James reached down, grabbing Roxanne's left hand. Using the strength of the Biblical Samson, he dragged her across the floor of the room, scraping the backs of Roxanne's feet on the concrete. He continued pulling her through the patio door, sliding her body across the dead palmetto bug, into the kitchen. James Miller was insane.

James grabbed Roxanne's shoulders tightly with both hands. She tried to get away, but was not strong enough to force him to release his grip. With a mighty shove, he picked her up and threw her on the linoleum floor. Roxanne struggled to get up, but there wasn't time. The assault resumed.

James reached behind the broken Sony television. He pulled on the electrical cord, jerking it out of the wall socket. With a couple more strong yanks, it pulled free from the back of the television set. Yes indeed, God was in command! The Lord gave James strength and wisdom. The spirit apparition followed him into the house. It hovered above the kitchen table, looming above his Bible as it did over the Ark of the Covenant back in the days of King Solomon. James' house is the Temple of God in Florida. The kitchen was the Holy of Holies.

Judgment time was here. The Lord had revealed the evil Roxanne as the anti-Christ. It was time to finish this business. James drew back his foot and kicked Roxanne in the kidneys, causing her to roll on her stomach. Imitating a lion from the days of Samson, James flung his body on Roxanne, planting his right knee against her neck, and pulling her left arm behind her back. Grabbing her wrists, James pulled her hands together, binding them with the electric cord, leaving about three feet of the wire hanging free.

"You can't stop me, Satan!" Spittle flew from his mouth. He pulled her up off the floor, dragging Roxanne's battered body back out of the house and into the Florida room. Scrape marks appeared on her knees as he dragged her over the metal casing of the patio door. Blood seeped through the cuts, leaving a small crimson trail behind her body. He pulled Roxanne out the screen door, dragging her onto the front yard.

James used the remaining portion of the electric cord to tie Roxanne to the queen palm tree where they first witnessed the Heavenly signs. Once again, Roxanne was sitting in the fire ant mound. Hundreds of the vile creatures were crawling up her legs. The attacking ants sent out a signal and they started biting her in unison. The feast was on. Blood continued flowing down her chin. Her legs and body were stinging from the fire ants and scrapes. Roxanne was desperate. Her voice, no longer calm, shouted back: "James, please. Look at me . . . I am your wife. Please . . . remember I love you. Please, remember why we came here, James. Don't you know what you're doing to me? You have to stop!" She was screaming.

For a moment, James stopped. What was happening? Why was Roxanne bleeding? As quickly as those thoughts had entered his mind, they fled. He recalled his vision from God, who told him in his dream that Roxanne would try to kill him by burying him alive. She was trying to do it by not bringing people to him and proclaiming James as King. She is the anti-Christ, the whore of Babylon, the Harlot riding on the back of the Wild Beast of Revelation. The Holy Spirit was in command.

James once more saw the Specter. It had followed them from the house and levitated into the massive leaves of the queen palm tree. The Specter was watching, witnessing, and preparing to report to the Almighty.

Cognitive reality faded. James smiled at Roxanne. There would be good news for the Specter to report to God. Let the Specter watch and report. Somewhere behind him, James heard the voice the Lord, not in his mind, but in his ears!

Turning around, James saw the Angel of God approaching him in the flesh! He was coming to anoint James into his Earthly

Kingship. A mighty scepter was in his hands. "Halleluiah, praise the Lord!" James shouted.

*****

Mac had been sitting in his living room, reading one of his favorite books, "Centennial" by James Michener. The history of the United States intrigued Mac, especially because he lived long enough to experience part of it himself. He closed the book, setting it on the coffee table, laying his reading glasses on top of it. Suppertime was near, time to prepare something for him and to feed Buffy. From his open window, the old man heard Roxanne screaming from down the street. Mac left his house and shuffled back to his storage shed. Once there, he opened the door, stepped inside and brought back a shovel. Using his slow-motion gait, Mac started walking toward the screams.

Chapter 36

The messenger of God with his mighty scepter in his hands stood before James. The apparition no longer had ghostly properties, but was as fleshly as James was. It stood before him as the Angels did before Lot, before the destruction of Sodom and Gomorrah. This was the final sign. With a loud voice, the Angel spoke to James:

"WHAT THE HELL IS GOING ON HERE?"

"She is the anti-Christ, the spawn of Satan. She is your enemy, my Lord."

James' eyes were transfixed. He mouthed words without changing facial expression. His bottom jaw made a motion as if it were independent of his other features. It was the only perceptive movement of his face as he spoke. It was as if he was a wooden puppet, and God was pulling the strings. James was seeing, but not seeing. He was hearing, but not hearing.

*****

"You must have shit for brains, bud. . . Elder James or whatever the fuck you call yourself. That's Roxanne your wife tied to the goddamn tree. Let her go."

Mac had no fear of this man. After living ninety years, whatever life he had left was a bonus. He knew old people usually died long, drawn out deaths because of their strong fortitude. Better to die quickly at the hands of a lunatic than cancer. However, Mac did fear for the man's poor wife.

Mac was silent. If he moved too quickly, which he no longer could do anyways, or made any sudden actions without forethought, he could further endanger Roxanne who remained tied to the tree. Being a lifelong man of peace, Mac had hopes of verbally defusing the situation. James thought Mac was an Angel of God. Perhaps he could use the delusion to defuse the confrontation.

"Mr. Miller. . . James. . . I mean Elder Miller. You are a good servant, but have you considered that any idea or doctrine is not so strong or powerful that it shouldn't be tested by doubt?" Mac did not expect an answer, and none was given. He would try using James's own religious orthodoxy against him. Mac thought for a moment, and continued:

"Perhaps doubt strengthens faith, did you ever consider this idea, young man? Mac hesitated again, hoping the man in front of him was at least partly grasping what he was saying. Perhaps James's mind was already past comprehending corporeality. For the moment, James was no longer threatening Roxanne. When religion is the problem, Mac hoped, it could also be the solution.

James listened to the Angel, saying nothing.

"Let her go, Elder James. Your pretty little gal loves you, which is all that matters." Mac waited, hoping this final plea would settle the crisis. Was this working? Did the man understand anything at all?

Mac was tired. His life had been long; the days ahead would be short but not happy ones. Already the old man was feeling fatigue. Mac was gripping the old wooden shovel handle. His yellowed fingernails dug into the wood. The tool was now serving as a cane for support. For Mac it served as a walking stick, to James, it was a scepter.

"Let your wife go, last chance." The old man said.

*****

James turned away, paying little attention to the Angel standing before him. He felt the apparition drift from the top of the queen palm tree and felt the wrapping of its wings around his body like a mother protecting a child. The Specter was telling the truth, not the Angel standing before him. James looked Heavenward and spoke: "Lord, I have served you faithfully. I have followed your Holy Spirit, and believed all the doctrines you taught me. Roxanne is no longer a believer, my Lord. She questions. She must be punished.

Without further consideration, James turned away from the old man, walking over to the edge of his house. He bent down and removed one of the bricks from the skirting below the mobile home. He stood up and started walking towards Roxanne, who was crying hysterically. She slid her back tightly against the trunk of the tree.

Roxanne frantically pulled at the wire behind her, trying to get free. Her feeble efforts caused the wire to draw tighter on her wrists, cutting off circulation. Her hands were getting numb. Fire ants continued crawling up her torso, attacking her stomach and breasts, seeking the sweet flesh hidden under her blood-covered blouse.

James stood in front of Roxanne and raised the brick above his head. In the manner of Moses who raised his staff above his head before parting the Red Sea, James cried out:

"In the name of Jehovah I punish ye your sins, woman. Ye shall be stoned, then ye stand before the judgment throne of the . . ."

Before he could say more, before he could crush Roxanne's skull with the brick, James felt the front of his face being compacted with Mac's shovel. He felt his teeth break and his nose rupture as the broken cartilage impelled deep into his brain.

Darkness invaded the daylight, as the normal din of the physical world around him grew silent. James's life played in his mind; memories flowed forward from his youth as if they were on fast playback, viewed and deleted. His last thoughts were of his prophetic dream. Ironically, James was going to die the same way he died when he tried to escape from the coffin in his dream. God's prophecy came true.

James sank to his knees, dropping the brick on the ground. It fell harmlessly between his wobbly feet. The Angel was no longer a messenger of God, but resembled the old man who lived down the street.

He spoke one word; "Roxanne" James died.

Chapter 37

Mac sat down on the blacktop road. He never thought about killing anyone. The idea of him taking a life was beyond the absurd. He hung his head. For the first time since his wife died, he sat down and cried.

"Mac," Roxanne spoke gently to the broken old man. "It's okay. Just untie me. You saved my life."

Mac stood up, turning away from James who lay in a spreading pool of blood. Some movement was perceptible in James' body, but it was just part of the dying process. The old man walked slowly over to Roxanne. Reaching behind her, he untied the wire. Roxanne's wrists were bleeding and her hands have a sickly blue color. After freeing Roxanne, Mac took her hands and rubbed them the best he could with his, getting the circulation back. He helped her remove the stinging insects invading her clothing and wounds.

Roxanne laid her head on the old man's shoulder and cried. She cried for herself, and Mac. She grieved for James. Roxanne turned away from James and walked with Mac back to his house.

Mac entered the kitchen, opened the door next to his refrigerator and took out a bottle of Black Velvet Whiskey. He drank two quick shots, poured another and gave it to Roxanne who was sitting on the couch. Roxanne for the first time in her life drank bourbon whiskey. She coughed once, but the alcohol began doing its job. Mac poured another shot of bourbon and she drank it. Only then was she able to discuss what happened.

Mac pulled a chair across the room, setting it in front of Roxanne. He sat down, reached forward and grasped her hands. "God, I'm sorry, Roxanne. I didn't know what else to do. I didn't mean to kill him, but I thought your husband was going to murder you for sure." Tears were flowing down his weathered and wrinkled cheeks. "That's the worst thing I've ever done in my whole life."

"You saved my life, Mac. I know it. I know James would have killed me. He lost his perception of reality the night of the signs. I saw it, but I didn't accept what was taking place until you spoke with me earlier today. I still thought there was hope for James when I went back home. I loved him, I did."

"What do you want to do, gal?" Mac wiped his face with the back of his shirtsleeve, dampening it with some of his tears. "Do you have any ideas?"

"I don't know. Maybe, maybe you and I can go to the Middle School emergency shelter and stay there. The other people from our park could be there. My family is too far away and I have no way to contact them. I can't tell them what happened. They would never understand."

"Whatever you say is all right with me. I feel so goddamn bad right now. If you weren't here, I would drink a case a beer and stay pissy-assed drunk for a week."

"Would you mind helping me with James?" Roxanne asked.

"Of course, we can't leave him there. I have a heavy canvas paint tarp out in my shed. Let's get it and use it to wrap him up. I'll lock his body in my shed. I have insecticide to put around the building until we can report this to the police. That is, if we still have cops."

"Okay. . . God, Mac, I wish we didn't have to do this. I wish I never heard of religion. I wish I would have had a normal life and babies, I wish. . ." She was crying again. Her grief would be long, and no doubt affect the rest of her life.

Mac starred at Roxanne. She was in no emotional condition to help him with James' body. "You just stay here. I'll take care of James myself. Don't watch what I'm doing. Just wash yourself and put some hydrocortisone on those damn fire ant bites. I have hydrocortisone cream in my bathroom medicine cabinet. Don't take any pills after drinking the whiskey. I might have some medicine you can take later. We're going to be leaving this place in a while."

The old man stood up. He bent forward, hearing his spine crack and gave Roxanne a squeeze of her shoulder. Mac backed up and turned away. Roxanne watched him leave the house, heading toward his shed before going where James lay dead under the queen palm tree.

Chapter 38

It was not an easy task for the old man to wrap up the body of James in the paint tarp. Mac took his time, knowing his physical limits. It took a half hour to drag the tarp into the storage shed, and then sprinkle dry insecticide over the tarp and the floor. He tossed the rest of the insecticide around the building. Mac sat down twice to rest. During his long lifetime, exhaustion had never mastered him as it was doing now. He breathed deeply and exhaled in long wheezing gasps. Time was his enemy. Living is good, but witnessing death removed much good from the experience of being.

When the gruesome task was completed, Mac reached into his shirt pocket and got a Dominican Hand Rolled cigar. After biting off the drawing end, he used his Bic lighter to ignite the cigar. He took several puffs before walking back to his house. The rich cigar smoke relaxed him, giving him a sense of tranquility.

On returning home, Mac found Roxanne sitting in the living room looking despondent. She had washed herself, but cleaning the outside would never serve to repair the internal damage to her psychological well-being. She sat on the living room couch leaning forward, with her head in her hands. Mac watched as she grieved.

"Hey gal, everything was taken care of. To be honest, I haven't the energy to go anywhere this afternoon. If you don't mind, let's just pack some stuff to take with us and leave early tomorrow morning. I just don't believe I could make the trip now."

Mac was more than physically exhausted. The events of the day played heavily on his mind. Could this James Miller be . . .? Probably not. Nevertheless, the old man needed rest, or he might be joining Elder Miller in the shed, covered with insecticide.

Roxanne did not hesitate. She nodded her head in approval, and began planning what items to take with her. Mac knew that keeping her busy would be the best therapy considering what happened.

Chapter 39

Mac accompanied Roxanne to her house where she gathered a few necessities. As she exited to go back to Mac's home, she knew this part of her life was over. She never would live in the trailer park again.

Later that night, Roxanne reclined on Mac's couch, trying to sleep, but sleep would not happen. Although her body was painfully exhausted, her mind continued to rehash the day's happenings. Roxanne sat up and turned on the flashlight Mac left for her on the table. She directed the beam around the floor of the room. Mac had deliberately left a table lamp turned on so she would know if the electricity were restored. The power was still off. Roxanne heard the patter of feet as Buffy bounded into the living room from Mac's bedroom. The dog leaped up and landed upon the couch, climbing on Roxanne and reclined on her chest, staring at Roxanne's eyes.

"Quiet, Buffy, please don't wake Mac." Roxanne picked Buffy up, cradling the dog in her arms. "I know what you want, Buffy. Be quiet and I will take you out with me."

Roxanne quietly left the house, not wanting to disturb Mac. Once outside, she put Buffy down in the grass and watched as the dog urinated. Roxanne picked Buffy up after she finished. Roxanne looked up at the night sky. The aurora borealis continued to flash and dance, but not with the intensity of the first night. The event no longer gave her a sense of religious piety. It told her this would be a time of despair, and hopelessness. The night was lonely without James; it would take time for her to adjust.

Buffy squirmed in her arms and emitted a low growl. Roxanne focused her attention down the street toward her own home. The queen palm tree was a dark silhouette. The broken plastic flamingo remained in her neighbor's yard. James and Roxanne's house was dark, almost invisible from where she stood.

Suddenly she froze. Roxanne thought she saw a ghostly light. It drifted from the top of the queen palm tree down to the fire anthill at its base, then float back upward. There was a faint smell of lilacs in the air. She replayed in her mind what James had done to her, as if it was happening again. As the ghostly light faded so did the mental images, disappearing into infinity. Buffy stopped growling. The light was gone; maybe it had never been there to begin with.

A few minutes later, Roxanne went back inside Mac's house and lay on the couch. Unconsciously, she put her hand on the back of Buffy and drew her close, clinging to the creature as if it protected her.

Buffy curled up with the woman long enough for Roxanne to doze off. The dog jumped down to the carpet and left the room, heading back to where Mac was sleeping. Buffy jumped up on Mac's bed, closed her eyes and joined him in sleep. She belonged with her master. Without knowing what she did, the dog had served to renew Roxanne's will to live.

Chapter 40

Mac was up before daylight. He took Buffy outside for her morning constitutional, and brought her back inside the house. This was a routine he had practiced every day for the last ten years. After feeding his pet, Mac packed some necessities, including a six-pack of beer to take to the school shelter. When the backpack could hold no more, he packed another one with items Roxanne might need, including the items she brought from her home.

Mac hid his remaining stash of beer in the crawl space underneath his mobile home, covering it with some pieces of plastic privacy lattice left over when the home was assembled on its lot many years ago. He carefully replaced the stacked bricks. Nothing looked disturbed. Mac did not intend to stay at the Middle School shelter, but he wouldn't tell Roxanne his plans. If world conditions were as bad as he assumed, Mac would return home and stay. He belonged nowhere else, nor did he wish to die under a stranger's watchful eyes. This was his domain, his castle, and it would serve him until his death. Mac would not be alone. Buffy would be his companion.

If there were no police or emergency people available when he returned, Mac planned to dig a grave and bury James. This is the least he could do; otherwise, the hot Florida weather would not be kind to a dead human wrapped in canvas covered with insecticide. Mac was too old to grieve what he did. All his mourning was over after he hid James' body. His remaining time on Earth was too short for such trivialities as extended sorrow. He would grieve for the living, particularly for Roxanne.

Not only did Roxanne remind Mac of his late daughter, she also brought back memories of a young woman named Brenda, whom he had known years before. Thankfully, Brenda never was a member of a cult. Brenda loved a young man who was a member of the **"God's Publishers and Preachers."** It had been several years since Brenda had written a letter to Mac. He did attend her graduation ceremony from Michigan State University. A few years later, Mac was told Brenda earned her Doctorate degree in child psychology. Brenda never married. Although Brenda eventually retired and moved to California, Mac wished she was here to share her experiences with Roxanne.

Mac had worries about Roxanne's future. He hoped she would someday recover from what happened to her husband James. She needed closure and a normal life. That is, if there was any normal life to be experienced with no electrical power.

Chapter 41

It was a cool morning. Roxanne awoke at daylight to see Mac getting ready to go to the Middle School shelter. She watched as he inspected the backpacks. There was no reason to stay in Twisted Palms Retirement Park.

Roxanne entered the bathroom, fixing herself up the best she could. She dabbed some blush makeup over the black eye and tried to cover up the bruises and cut lip. The rest of her body hurt, but she would heal in time. Depression and guilt churned deep into her soul. Was it something she had done which caused James to break down? Could it be the result of an inferiority complex, because she did not go to college and was not skilled in anything except serving **"God's Publishers and Preachers**?" Roxanne felt terrible. Perhaps Nathaniel Miller had felt this way when he committed suicide years ago. She was the image of despair, worried about the future. Roxanne tried to close her mind to the thinking process.

Sometimes, she thought, thinking itself can be the problem. Oh, for the blessed solitude of shutting off the little voice in her head, which continuously spoke to her as if she were someone else. She left the bathroom. Roxanne's thoughts continued to annoy her.

Roxanne sat at the kitchen table, resting her elbows on the chipped surface and covered her face with both hands. She felt a gentle touch on her shoulder. Looking back, she peered into the eyes of the kindly old man who had saved her life.

Mac gave her a sympathetic smile, while squeezing her shoulders with both of his wrinkled, weathered hands. "Don't worry, young woman. Just give yourself time, forgive yourself, and start to love yourself. Your life will be better, you'll see. Trust the old man here. I have seen all sides of humanity, most of which are not good. You can find some beauty in life, if you seek it out. Let yourself see the good, ignore the bad, and trust your feelings." Mac raised his hands from Roxanne's shoulder, and patted her back several times. He grasped her right hand, encouraging her to stand up from the chair. "Let's go. There's nothing left for you here."

Roxanne wore a pair of shorts and a remaining wrinkled blouse she had taken from her trailer. She needed to look her best when they reached the Middle School. She put her knapsack on her back, and began walking ahead of the old man. They left James and the trailer park, far behind.

Buffy sauntered alongside her master. After a half mile, Roxanne reached down, picked up Buffy and began to carry her. The dog felt good in her arms, comforting her strained nerves. Someday, she thought, I may just get me a little dog and live alone with her. Buffy licked Roxanne's face.

"Dogs can sense love," Roxanne said aloud, as she smiled for the first time today. She didn't know how correct she was about the mysterious benevolence of dogs and other pets.

Mac smiled, but didn't reply.

It was a four-mile journey to the Middle School shelter from the trailer park. It seemed to take forever for Roxanne because Mac sauntered, using one consistently slow speed. They made an odd-looking couple, the grandfatherly old man contrasted with her beauty of youth. Roxanne's hair was a mess and her clothing was tattered, stained, and wrinkled. Mac's clothing was clean and groomed. Some of the cuts on Roxanne's face, made by James's fist, began showing through her makeup. The scores of insect bites, continued to torment her. Less than a mile from the trailer park stains of perspiration in the shape of footballs marked the underarms of Roxanne's blouse and Mac's shirt.

After going two miles, they approached an impressive banyan tree. It covered an acre of ground, dropping new roots from its huge branches, seeking out moisture and phosphate in the ground for nourishment. The banyan tree resembled several umbrellas all grouped, offering shade from the Florida sun.

Roxanne noticed the old man was tired. "Mac, let's sit here for a while in the shade of the banyan tree and take a break."

"I thought you would never ask. This will give ol' Buffy a chance to sit for a spell too. Besides, we're in no hurry. It sure is abnormally hot for this time of the year."

They sat on the ground and Mac reached into his backpack bringing out a beer. He popped the top open, handing the can to Roxanne. She took it. He reached into the pack and got one for himself.

"Thanks, Mac. Can I ask you a question? I'm curious how you know so much about human nature and religion. Were you a minister at one time?"

Mac hesitated. Before answering her, Roxanne watched the old man take a water bottle from his backpack. Cupping his left hand, he poured some water into it for Buffy. The dog quickly lapped up the water. Mack continued giving her water until she drank no more. He put the bottle back in his backpack.

"Well, I usually don't share with others what my career was before I retired. However, you deserve an answer, Roxanne. At one time, I was a Clinical Psychiatrist. I retired about twenty years ago. Not because I grew too old to practice, but because I perceived the world was just about beyond repair. Now, let me ask you something. Was James related to Nathaniel Miller?"

Roxanne was shocked. She felt her heart begin to pound as adrenalin shot into her bloodstream. Could it be? Could Mac be the author of the manuscript found on anti-cult sites on the internet? Is that why he knew so much about her beliefs? She hesitated, then replied; "You wrote the manuscript,* didn't you, Mac?"

"Yup, I did write a medical treatise about Nathaniel, but it was a long time ago, Roxanne. A few years later, some asshole hacked our Psychiatric hospital computer records and distributed some of them to a hacker in Sweden. I found that about twenty years ago, my report about Nathaniel was all over the goddamn internet. Thank God that I used my initials on the treatise instead of my name. The Miller family filed a confidentially breaching lawsuit, but they could not win without a defendant. No hacker was ever found so no action was taken. I didn't put your names with Nathaniel's because of so many Miller families in this country."

"I read your treatise Mac, but I couldn't tell anyone, especially my husband. Your treatise is banned by the church. You know, I felt sorry for Nathaniel. He was a third cousin of James. James family still used Nathaniel as an example of evil conduct."

"Nathaniel's death broke my heart. It happened many years ago, but it had a profound effect on my career. I wrote my treatise to clear the experience from my mind and move on with my life. In addition, a record had to be recorded for the hospital about all the patients and their diagnosis for future treatment. Hell, I wrote that fifty years ago, I surprised they found it and posted it on the internet. I suspect the Psychiatric hospital transferred all their records to a mainframe computer. I might have been able to help Nathaniel if he had been an adult, but as long as he was under the control of his parents, there was little any psychiatrist could do. Most of the people who get involved in cults are beyond hope. I could not stand dealing with them anymore. Adults are not the true victims, it's the children raised within controlling cults who suffer."

"Mac, was I brainwashed?"

"To be honest with you gal, no; that never happened."

His reply was not what she expected to hear. It would be easier if she could put the blame for her actions on a cause, which she could use to absolve herself of guilt. Roxanne looked towards the ground, frowned, then asked; "If not, then what was it?"

"Well," Before continuing, Mac took another drink. "Consider this. Every day of our lives, you and I are emotionally manipulated, and persuaded to perform actions by controlling people. It is the way of our American free enterprise system. You are asked to buy what you do not need, eat food that is not good for you and donate money to organizations that do not tell you how your currency is used. You are taught to hate what the news and political media ask you to detest, to vote for candidates you don't know, and to worship an invisible God who has not communicated with human beings for twenty centuries."

Roxanne remained quiet and took a long drink from her beer can, while waiting for Mac to continue.

"Now consider what I'm about to tell you, Roxanne. Advertisers on television, in magazines, and everywhere spend millions of dollars to manipulate you. Once they saturate you with their suggestions, they incubate within your mind and eventually you accept them as your own ideas. Advertisers and religions would not do so unless it was a successful venture. You and I, because it is our human nature, not because someone forces us to do their bidding, accept their persuasion. It is because the action of persuasion evolves into conformity, which gives us personal contentment. It's also a comfortable way for us to adjust to the rest of society by following others. If we feel accepted, we feel loved. So, quit blaming yourself for whatever happened with James. You are not perfect, I cannot make you perfect, nor can you accept guilt for your actions that weren't intentionally planned to hurt others. Only when people like James cross the line between sanity and insanity, can one readily see the horrendous effects of such conditioning. You know Roxanne, it took me a long time to forgive myself for what happened to Nathaniel, but you can move beyond this event in your life. I did."

Mac finished. He drank the rest of his beer, returning the can to the knapsack. He took Roxanne's empty can and did the same with it.

"Roxanne, just live your life, love others, and forget about the past. That's all I am going to say. Let's go."

"Thank you Mac. This means more to me than you realize." She stood, picked up Buffy and started walking, leaving the precious shade of the banyan tree behind them.

*(For more information about **"God's Prophets and Publishers"** read **"Nathaniel Wilford's Journal"** The treatise found at the end of our story)

Chapter 42

Roxanne and Mac saw nobody until they were about a mile from the shelter. Two men approached them, carrying shotguns. Mac stopped walking and Roxanne stood by him. She served more as his protector than protected. She continued to hold Buffy in her arms.

"STAND WHERE YOU ARE," the larger of the two men shouted as he raised his shotgun. He directed it over their heads, not at their bodies.

"Identify yourselves and tell us where you're going," said the second man who was black.

Roxanne stood still. Wasn't it enough to escape the abuses of James? Would she suffer more at the hands of these strangers? The two men were far more than Mac could hope to overcome. She did not wait for Mac to speak.

"I'm Roxanne Miller and this is MacArthur Gunderson, one of my neighbors. We both live in Twisted Palms Retirement Park, which is a couple of miles down the road.

"Where are you going?" The black man asked.

"We're heading to the Middle School shelter, which was set up for hurricanes and as a refuge for people from our mobile home park. Some of our neighbors probably are at the shelter. Mac said it was time we should join them. We have some food we can share with others. That is, if we're welcome."

"Yup, food," interjected Mac, "but I'm keeping my cigars and beer."

"I'm Abraham Washington Jefferson, replied the young black man as he lowered his gun. Don't ask me about my name, just call me

Abe. I arrived here a couple of days ago, myself. The people from the shelter befriended me so I'm helping them. I left Orlando the next day after the power went out, stole a bicycle, rode down Highway 4 before taking the side roads, and headed south. I was going to Key West, but ended here instead. I see no reason you couldn't join us. We patrol this area because of civil disturbances throughout Florida. Orlando was burning before I left. The city is all gone by now. A friend of mine was murdered the first night of the power outage. I try to keep those memories deep in my unconsciousness, but they haunt me almost daily. From your appearance, I can see you two have been through hell."

"Hey, cute dog," said the other man who was of Spanish descent. He was stocky, around 50 years old and several inches shorter than Abe. He lowered his shotgun.

"I'm Martin Cabarra. I teach, or rather taught computer science at the school. All my computer expertise is now useless. I'm sure my story can wait. You're welcome to go to the school. We have food and cots set up in classrooms. We have a limited supply of freshwater. We must require you to share all your belongings with us and we'll share ours with you."

Abe spoke before Roxanne and Mac could reply. "I sure could use a beer." He reached for the old man's backpack.

Mac jerked away from him, reiterating what he said earlier. "Nope, neither my beer nor my cigars, or I will just turn around and head back home."

"Okay, you don't have to share your beer and cigars at the shelter. But, do you mind just sharing one beer with me?" Mac nodded his head and reached into the backpack. He removed two cans of warm beer, and gave one to Abe.

"I suppose you want one too?" Mac asked Martin, hoping he would refuse.

"Nope, you wouldn't happen to have a Diet Coke in there would you? I thought you wouldn't have. I gave up alcohol a longtime ago, my friend."

Mac smiled, pulled the tab on his own beer can and started drinking his second one today.

"Well, young woman, are you and your friend ready to go with us?" Martin asked.

"Thanks for helping us. Please call me Roxanne. Of course, I appreciate what you men are doing for us. I'm ready to leave anytime. Buffy, would sure like to get someplace where she could lie down too."

"Sounds good to me, what are we waiting for?" Mac finished his beer in a couple of long gulps. He put the empty can back into the backpack, joining the two empty cans he and Roxanne had earlier. "Let's go."

"Abe, I will go with Mac and Roxanne to the school. Do you mind staying here and patrolling? I'll be back as soon as I can."

"No problem, Martin. I made it here from Orlando by myself and this is easy. Take your time."

"Okay, just hang in there, be back soon."

Martin motioned for Roxanne and Mac to follow him. "Let's go. The sun will be getting hotter as it rises higher in the sky. If you stay in the sun much longer, you will get more exhausted."

Roxanne walked next to Mac, still carrying Buffy. Both followed Martin. An hour later, she could see the school shelter ahead of them. There is nobody outside, but Roxanne knew she would find friendships inside the building. Her life would change.

"I have four kids," said Martin. "Two were in college when all this happened. The other two are married and have their own families. I'm concerned about my son and daughter who are attending Ohio State University. But, at least I know they are looking out for each other."

Roxanne could see love in the man's face. She wished her father could have shown as much love. To Roxanne, the past must now be a memory. It was time to recreate herself into someone different.

"I am sure they will be all right, sir."

"Please, just call me Martin. Heck, my friends gave me the nickname of Taco when I used to be into C.B. radios. Then a friend of mine showed me his computer system. That's when the Taco name slowly disappeared. The world of computers put my old radios into storage. Now this power outage has put my computers into retirement. Maybe it is time to break out the old radios and see if they might still work. Can't do anything much without electricity though. I'll probably just leave them on the shelf, and put my computers there with them." He opened the front door of the school and all three entered the building.

There would be no time for Roxanne to mourn the loss of her husband James. From this moment on, it would be a time of renewal, a beginning where she would never allow herself to second-guess what had been her past life.

Mac stepped into the building behind her. He took Buffy from Roxanne's arms, sitting down on the first chair he found. "Roxanne, I'll only be staying with you tonight. Tomorrow, ol' Buffy and I will be a heading back home."

"Please, please don't leave me here, Mac." She pleaded, but she expected him to go home anyway.

"Nope, my home is back in the Retirement Park with ol' Buffy. Besides," he spoke quietly. "There's an important project for me to take care of, I'm sure you know what I'm talking about."

The subtle message got through to Roxanne. Even if James was a cruel person and a victim of his own inadequacies, he deserved a burial. Mac would do it. The rest of the world would never know how or why James died. It was the time to bury the past in the ground with James' body.

"I will miss you, Mac. Mac, I love you," she said.

The old man reached over to her, gathered her in his arms, saying; "I love you like a daughter, Roxanne. Go, find your way and forget the past."

Chapter 43

THE ELEVATOR

Beulah Gibbons packed her cleaning supplies onto a four-wheeled stainless steel cart and began pushing it down the corridor. She had worked for Grove's Investment Management Company for ten years. Beulah's job was not managing stocks and bonds, but cleaning toilets, floors, emptying wastebaskets, and scraping chewing gum off the checkered black and white ceramic tile floors.

Beulah's wages paid for groceries and covered the cost of her cheap apartment in Orlando. Her twenty-year-old son, Jidon lived with her. Jidon sporadically gave his mom money to help with the household expenses. Beulah never asked where her son's money came from. Money does not have a conscience. She learned this lesson from watching Grove's investment brokers manipulating their clients and taking money for advice that was wrong half the time. She was a quiet observer of the happenings within the corporation. Nobody noticed the housekeeper listening to conversations while she emptied the trashcans and swept the floor. Beulah ascertained the motive of the investment brokers was to make money for themselves, not their clients. They pretended to their customers to be honest but in reality, were mostly self-serving. Unlike the stockbrokers, Beulah never tried to impress nor take advantage of anyone. At least being a housekeeper at Grove's was honest work. Whatever the other employees did was none of her business. Groves paid her to clean the floors, not to be the conscience of the investment brokers.

The only difference Beulah saw between Groves and her son was the firm could legally steal clients' funds, whereas her son might steal on the sly, if that is how he obtained money. She thought Jidon might be selling drugs. With all her heart, Beulah hoped she was wrong. He was her only child. She protected him when he was growing up but those years were behind her and Jidon was a man. Jidon's lifestyle often contrasted Beulah's strict moral code but she refused to ignore the responsibilities of being his mother.

Wilber Grove, the personnel manager who owned 51% of the company, offered to set Beulah up with a 401k retirement investment program when she began her career ten years ago as a housekeeper at the firm. "Mrs. Gibbons," he said with his elbow on the desk and his left hand supporting his clean-shaven chin, "We'll add a ten-percent stock contribution to every dollar you invest with us in our company. Your 401K plan will be exempt from Federal and State income taxes until you reach age 59 ½, and then you'll have a tidy nest egg to supplement your Social Security when you retire." He cocked his head sideways, sporting the same silly grin he presented to his investment clients. This time his sales speech was wasted.

For a moment, Beulah did not say anything. It was laughable, knowing there was no possibility of any excess funds finding their way into her meager paycheck. Although she was laughing inside, her face remained sober. She used the same face when she found out that her ex-husband Darnell had picked up a case of the clap after messing with a prostitute. A black person often learns to laugh internally, it would be wrong to betray her inner feelings to people who did not deserve this knowledge.

Again, Beulah thought about Darnell, remembering him standing and straining at the toilet, trying to take a piss with his pipe plugged with infection. It served the bastard well after the way he treated her during their marriage. She felt blessed she never caught a sexually transmitted disease from him. Beulah knew Darnell screwed around on her during their marriage. Darnell thought he was the top cock on the block, but as in matters of honor, his philandering caught up with him. Every time she needed an internal smile, she thought about what a nice job Mother Gonorrhea had done on him. She divorced the bastard.

"Well, Mrs. Gibbons, what's your decision regarding our retirement plan? Can we sign you up? Mrs. Gibbons are you all right?"

"Sorry Mr. Grove, I had some other things on my mind. Thanks be to you anyways, but now I needs all my monies and can't afford to invest right now."

"Well, if you change your mind Mrs. Gibbons, just come into my office anytime and I will sign you up. We keep all the forms available here for our employees. Regardless, you will continue to get your one share of stock for every three months of employment while you work for us. You will receive the stock when you retire." He smiled his shit-eating grin as the light from an overhead fixture reflected off his balding head into her face.

"Thank you, Mr. Grove, I sure do appreciate the offer, I does and I appreciates the stocks you gives me, I do." With those words, she left his office. It was time to go home and tell Jidon about her new job and prepare to report for work the following Monday.

Jidon was four years-old when Beulah gave his daddy Darrell the old heave-ho. After the divorce, the finances were not much worse than during the marriage. The only difference was Darrell no longer took her money to party with his bitches. Even though the court had ordered him to pay a measly $40.00 a week for child support, he never paid one cent. She didn't expect he would, but it sure could have helped with their son's expenses. Darnell never supported her financially during their marriage. Beulah had no reason to expect him to do so after the divorce. Within a year of their divorce, Darnell Gibbons disappeared. He could be alive in another city, dead or in jail. Beulah hoped Darnell was dead.

Beulah could not invest anything for retirement now or ever. As long as she had the necessities for life each day, tomorrow mattered not to her. She figured the company knew this and offered the retirement program to placate local work laws and the Janitorial Union Local 2440. She was proud to be a dues paying member.

Groves Investment Company flaunted its 401K plan to potential clients, telling them how successful the investment firm was. "All employees," they claimed in their television and newspaper advertising, "are part owners of the company." The price of each share of Groves Investment stock had never exceeded ten dollars. At most, she would accumulate 40 dollars of Groves Investment stock in her 401k retirement program a year. What riches it would give her during her retirement years, she said mockingly to herself.

Whenever Beulah overheard the sales pitch to potential investors, she thought about the employees of Enron and other companies who either folded into oblivion or became bankrupt. Employee's company stock often became worthless, not suitable for toilet paper. Grove's had clients investing in stocks, bonds, gold, real estate and derivatives. All investments were far beyond Beulah Gibbons knowledge. Many investment offers sounded like schemes designed to take money from the poor working slob, who didn't have the expertise to know their funds were at risk. Beulah did overhear how the derivative market was a downfall of the banking system in 2008 and that was several year ago. Someone said the influence of the Federal Reserve dumping money into the American economy caused the stock market to climb once more to record highs. Derivatives, what is a derivative? It sounded more like diarrhea to Beulah, and she knew diarrhea was not pleasant, nothing but worthless crap. When Beulah worked, the money she earned would be for her son and herself. She did not need derivatives or diarrhea for that matter.

Regardless of the policies of her employer, Beulah was satisfied to work hard and do a good job. She believed that whatever one does in life, he or she should do it with the intension pf being the best. If one is a hamburger flipper, he or she should become an expert. Of course, this same theory would support the premise that anyone who wanted to be a thief should be the best crook and thief according to his or her abilities. In that regard, Beulah believed all investment brokers were successful. Beulah tried to be an honest woman.

Over the years, she gained weight and broadened across the hips. With her added girth, Beulah resembled a Detroit Lions fullback in stature. Although her body was big, her heart was bigger. Beulah had compassion for everyone who deserved it. Beulah was content to play life as it confronted her. She loved life. She loved her son most of all. No matter what Jidon did, he was her legacy for the future. Only Jidon could carry memories of her for many years after she died.

Beulah reached the end of the hallway and stood waiting for the elevator. Because she is paid by the hour and not the job, it mattered not if the elevator was prompt or took forever to stop at her floor. With an energetic effort, she had finished cleaning the offices on the fourteenth floor and it was time to go down to the lobby and start there. It was 5:30 PM, the Stock Exchange bell has rung, and the market is closed until tomorrow. Grove's customers already left the building and the lobby would need mopping. It was her last job before going home.

Beulah's biggest complaint was the cigarette butts that clients and employees slung on the floor throughout the building. Although ashtrays were everywhere, people only occasionally used them. It wouldn't be long before smoking would be banned in public buildings. Beulah looked forward to that day.

Yesterday, she watched with disgust as one of the building custodians standing in the lobby, put one finger against the side his nose, cocked his head away from the public and blew a huge gob of snot on her clean floor. She dipped her mop in her galvanized pail and quickly pulled it out, slopping water on his trousers. Beulah gave the custodian a disgusted look as she swabbed up the blood stained slime deposited on the tile floor. She should not have to do the job twice. As a fellow union member, the custodian should have respect for himself. He turned silently away, probably too embarrassed and afraid to say anything to her, thought Beulah.

Every morning, it was Beulah's primary responsibility to clean the bathrooms. If there was anything she disliked about her job, it was toilet duty. After first checking to see if the toilet stalls were empty, Beulah would hang a CLOSED sign on each bathroom door and spray pine scented room deodorizer into each one. She would go into the hallway and wait for the air to be more breathable. She entered and cleaned the facilities, mopping the floors and sanitizing the stalls.

You can tell a lot about them peoples from their toilet habits, thought Beulah. She always found soiled toilet paper on the floor in the stalls, and piss on the seats where the men were too lazy to lift them before taking a leak. I bet they don't do this at home, she thought. There were as many paper hand towels on the ceramic tiled floor as what went into the trash basket. It disgusted Beulah to find the liquid soap containers almost full, in both the men's and the women's bathroom. People only wash their hands if someone else be in the bathroom at the same time. Even then, they seldom used hand soap. A man's voice behind her interrupted Beulah's thoughts. The elevator still had not arrived.

"Hello, Beulah."

Beulah raised her eyes to see Michael Foster standing next to her. Michael was a tall 45-year-old white man with salt and pepper hair. He wore an off-the-shelf, cheap Sears's business suit, which needed a trip to the dry cleaners. Polyester had been out of style for years, but Michael Foster's budget didn't allow him to buy expensive clothing. His necktie resembled a Rush Limbaugh reject. However, Michael did look physically fit.

Alongside Michael was Jennifer Smith, his secretary. Jennifer stood fidgeting with her fingernails. Her blond hair flaunted her haughty personality. Jennifer squirmed as if her shoes were a size too small. On seeing Beulah, Jennifer raised her chin and did a little sniff of her nostrils. The flaring motion sent a signal to Beulah, suggesting Miss Smith didn't approve of Mr. Foster's acknowledging Beulah's presence.

Beulah returned Michael's greeting, with a soft, low voice. "Hello Mr. Foster. The elevator sure be slow today. Did you have a good day, sir?"

"Hell, no. I got a client that . . . you wouldn't understand, no, it has not been a good day."

"Sorry you has a bad day, Mr. Foster. I shore is sorry." Beulah added "and good day to you too, Miss Smith." Beulah had caught Jennifer's eye language, and refused to be insulted.

Jennifer saw Beulah's eye contact and turned her head away, snubbing the housekeeper, before muttering in a low voice "Hello Beulah."

Beulah continued; "when the door opens, Mr. Foster, please let me put my cart in first, so I don't accidentally spill some of this here nasty water in these here buckets on you and Miss Smith. Just wait a second and I'll shove it all the way to the corner at the back of the elevator."

"Yeah, okay we'll wait. I can't leave the building for another half-hour anyway." Michael frowned impatiently while shifting his body out of Beulah's way as the elevator door opened.

Beulah stepped in front of them, carefully pushing the cart over the crack between the floor and the elevator. The cart bumped, splashing the dirty water in the buckets, but none spilled over the sides onto the floor. She watched Michael Foster step back and let Jennifer stride into the elevator ahead of him. Mr. Foster brushed his hands along the back of Miss Smith's rear end as she stepped forward. Beulah thought, I bet you touch her ass more often than you touch your wife's ass. Beulah kept her thoughts to herself.

Michael stepped toward the control panel, pushing the LOBBY button. The elevator's door closed. The cage jerked and began descending. The elevator traveled for a short time and distance. Suddenly, with a heavy jerking motion, it came to a screeching halt. The automatic emergency brakes engaged as the electricity shut down. Beulah's cart jerked and slid sideways, splashing some of the filthy water in one of the galvanized buckets on Jennifer's dress. The emergency battery powered light hanging on the wall came on.

"Ah, shit!" Jennifer angrily blurted to no one in particular.

"Now my dress is ruined. Why did you put so much water in those buckets, Beulah? Damn it, nothing is going right for me." Jennifer's voice expressed her disgust.

Michael reached over to Beulah's cart, ripping a couple sheets of paper toweling from a roll lying there, handing them to Jennifer. "Here, use these. Just blot it up, don't rub it."

Jennifer angrily snatched the paper from Michael and blotted off her dress. The towel absorbed the water but left residual stains on the hemline. She wadded up the towels and threw them into a small trash container hanging on the backside of Beulah's cart.

Chapter 44

Michael, stepped up to the elevator's control consol, raised his left hand and rubbed his chin, considering what action to take. The panel was old with red diode lights to identify the floor numbers on a black background. All the lights were out. He looked up at the floor identification strip above the door. None of the floor indicator lights was lit. It was impossible to tell where they were when the elevator stopped. If he remembered correctly, they would be somewhere between the eleventh and tenth floors, but Michael could not be sure. He always took it for granted when one gets on the elevator it is the destination, not the journey, which is important. This was the same way he lived his life.

The battery powered emergency lantern hanging at the back corner of the elevator produced an eerie yellowish light. It reflected throughout the chamber giving it an aura of mystery.

Michael removed his hand from his chin, using it to lean against the wall. He turned toward his companions and began speaking, first softly then amplifying his voice. "This has been the worst goddamn day of my life. I need a vacation, away from here, away from elevators, investors, and my life." He hesitated, calming himself before continuing. "We could be stuck here for a while, ladies."

Jennifer reached towards a small door panel next to the control panel in front of Michael. She turned the knob and opened an access door hiding the emergency telephone. "I had to use one of these several years ago when a lift I was riding in got stuck between floors while I was in London. My parents paid my way to the United

Kingdom after my high school graduation. I bet you didn't know they call elevators "lifts" in England, did you Michael."

"Shut-up, Jennifer" snapped Michael. Michael grabbed the phone from her hand and pushed the EMERGENCY button found in the middle of the cradle. Holding the receiver to his ear, he heard nothing. He jerked the receiver, banging it against the elevator wall a couple of times before pushing the button again. There was nothing but silence. Finally, no longer controlling his temper, Michael gave the cord a yank and pulled it out of the wall. "Not a goddamn thing works in here." Michael shouted at Jennifer. "Maybe you would be better off back in England, since your so damn smart about everything in Europe. Your parents should have left your ass there."

"Well, what a mature reaction by you, Michael. You know, the telephone might have worked if you waited longer. The telephone won't work now, will it hero? I see you're quick on the trigger in more than one-way, huh, Mike."

Michael raised the cordless telephone receiver as if to hit Jennifer. He stopped and threw it onto the floor, shattering the plastic earpiece. The elevator became quiet.

Chapter 45

Beulah moved sundry items off the top shelf of on her cart and planted her huge rear end on top of it. She shook her head in disgust at the bickering couple. Beulah crossed her arms defensively, tucking her hands in her armpits under her large breasts. "You might's as well just relax; it may be some time before this here thing is fixed." She said.

Beulah endured several major crises during her lifetime. It was difficult listening to the whining of people who never grew up in the ghetto, never lived in utter poverty, and never had to struggle to get food. Hell, she never finished high school much less earned a Business Administration college degree like Michael Foster.

Beulah tried to evaluate the woman trapped with her. Jennifer Smith took pride in her appearance and good looks. Beulah suspected Jennifer had a weekly visit to the hairdresser. Beulah did her own hair. Jennifer's fingernails were trimmed and polished. Beulah's hands were chapped with broken nail because of her cleaning job. Beulah didn't own nail polish. Beulah decided it was best to remain quiet and not to speak with her companions. She knew the way Mr. Foster and Jennifer were going at it, Michael would not be getting any pussy from her tonight. She smiled at the thought, once more thinking about Darnell.

The argument between Michael and Jennifer ended almost as quickly as it had begun. Fifteen minutes later, Michael broke the silence. "Well, might as well get comfortable. You will excuse me people, but I'm going to sit on the floor. Join me if you like. There's only one seat in the house, and Beulah already sitting on the cart."

*****

Michael took off his shoes and put them next to where he sat. The simple comfort was enough to relax him. His behavior mellowed, indicating his accepting the malfunction of the elevator as another of the day's failures. Michael's wife Cindy was likely fixing dinner for their kids, expecting him to arrive home shortly with a shitty smile on his face. Michael didn't care if he went home. The kids got on his nerves and Cindy would complain about the grocery store prices. The subject would get back to money again, how he made too little and she spent too much. Cindy worked part time as a real estate salesperson, but hardly made enough commissions to pay for the kids' private schooling. There was no reason the damn kids could not go to public schools, but if the discussion came up, another argument would start. What a shitty life.

Jennifer watched Michael slide his back down the wall and sit with his legs extended out on the floor. Following his example, Jennifer removed her shoes, kicking them off her feet.

"Beulah, would you PLEASE give me some paper towels from your cart, so I can at least have something CLEAN to sit on? Otherwise, you can to do your job and wash the floor for us. Michael can sit in dirt, he looks natural there, but I won't do it."

"I will please you, Missy Jennifer, sure I's will. Here, lets me gets you them towels and makes a place for you to sit. Yessum, sho will."

Jennifer didn't wait for Beulah to comply. She stood back up and reached behind the huge woman, retrieving the roll of paper towels. Jennifer tore off a few sheets, folded them into a small mat, which she placed beside Michael. She pulled her dress up to keep it off the floor and sat down. Jennifer's eyes turned towards the floor, then the walls.

"You can't look me in the eyes, can you Miss Smith." Beulah said.

"Beulah, I'm embarrassed and sorry for the way I spoke to you. Really I am. It has been a long day, and I will not try to excuse my bad manners, so could you please forgive me? I mean it, please? God, I'm so sorry. You don't deserve disrespect from me or anyone."

The black woman hesitated before grasping Jennifer's hand. "No need to apologize, but I appreciate hearing you say it. Oh yes, I do forgives you though." She squeezed the extended hand and released it. Once more, Beulah smiled.

For a longtime, it was quiet. They settled into a routine of waiting, not realizing this was the beginning of a long stay between floors. Tension was replaced with complacency. Each person sat quietly, planning what he or she would do after work tonight.

Chapter 46

Michael would go home, stopping on the way to fill his Ford sedan with gas. He would complain to Cindy for fixing dinner too early and he would have to eat another cold supper. It would be better to go on the offensive before she had a chance to accuse him of being late because he was screwing around on her again, which he often did. Michael planned to break off his relationship with Jennifer, but this wasn't going to be the day he would tell her. She was getting stale, comparable to his twenty-year-old marriage. It was time to move along. He would make some excuse to put Jennifer back into the secretarial pool, and hire a new secretary. In a few weeks, Jennifer would find herself in another stockbroker's motel room. As long as she was attractive, there would be stockbrokers who would enjoy taking care of Jennifer.

Time moves slowly when there is nothing to do. Michael was impatient. "Beulah, IT HAS BEEN SEVEN HOURS NOW, WHERE IN HELL ARE OUR MAINTENANCE PEOPLE?

"Don't ask me, replied Beulah. "Do I look like I run this here place? Mr. Foster, you is getting on my nerves, you is."

Michael Foster knew he wouldn't get an answer, so he turned his attention to Jennifer. "Jenny, if you're tired you can move closer to me and rest your head on my shoulder. I don't mind,"

Jennifer glared back at the man sitting next to her, slapping his hand while it was creeping toward her back. "Mike, you pay attention. If you reach over and feel my ass one more time, I am going to take one of Beulah's mops and jam it up yours. Do you understand me?"

Michael was sweating; the air was hot and stuffy. The closeness of Jennifer's body was still exciting him, even though he planned to dump her. With nothing to do, a little touchy-feely of her body would break the monotony of being trapped with nothing to do. He scooted closer, until his hips were gently touching hers. "I'll remember what you said after we get out of here, Jenny. Just keep it up."

Jennifer yelled; "Yeah, that's something you can't do very well." She jerked her body farther away from him, looking the other way.

Michael decided to ignore what she said. Nevertheless, it was a lesson to remember. Bad luck often brings out the true nature of the individuals involved.

"Does anyone notice anything different in here?" Jennifer asked.

"It's darker," said Michael. "The light from the battery-powered emergency lantern is getting dim. Soon it will be pitch black in here."

"I can see it's getting darker, I'm not stupid Michael. I know what it is, I smell cigarette smoke. It's you isn't it, Mike? Goddamnit, Mike put out your cigarette. What are you doing?"

Jennifer, I'm hungry and when I'm hungry, I smoke. Here, baby, have a drag."

"You're an asshole. I'm an adult, not your fucking baby. You know I don't smoke."

Michael screamed back in her face, blowing smoke into her hair. "Don't get your ovaries in an uproar, BABY. If I want to smoke, I'll smoke. You can shut up."

Jennifer slapped the cigarette out of Michael's mouth. "Don't you understand anything? The air is getting bad in here. If the power is out, then the air circulation pumps are not working. The smell of your damn cigarette is stinking up this place. Mike, you will have my resignation as soon as we get out of here. Then you can play grab ass with Beulah if you like, or better yet, just go play with yourself."

Beulah laughed aloud. "Gee, Missy, you takes life much too seriously! You is right about one thing, it's getting very stuffy in here. One more thing, Missy, I sure as hell don't need him to be a pestering me, I don't. Go play with yourself, I sure likes that one I does!"

Michael said no more. He retreated into a corner of the elevator away from the two women.

Beulah regained her composure and wiped a couple of laugh tears from her eyes. She grasped the sides of her cleaning cart, stood up then joined Michael and Jennifer by sitting on the floor. She occupied the last vacant corner of the elevator in front of her cleaning cart away from the bickering couple.

Blessed silence filled the cage once more. Michael leaned against the wall and loosened his shirt, giving him a slovenly appearance. His head began to bob up and down while he fought drowsiness. In a short while, he lost the battle and went to sleep. A few short hours later, he woke up to the sound of Beulah voice.

"I hurt. I can't breathe. It's cold in here. I am freezing, isn't you two cold?

Beulah was shivering and perspiring at the same time. The light from the lantern continued to grow weaker. Squinting through the dimness of the chamber, Michael could see something was wrong with the housekeeper. Beulah's dark face was ashen. Her flowered blouse saturated with perspiration, her body gently trembling. Beulah's hand moved up near her left breast where she rubbed her chest.

"Oh shit," blurted out Jennifer. "She is having a goddamn heart attack. Beulah, do you have any medication? Are you taking any prescriptions?"

"No, I'm as healthy as a horse."

"Mike, what can we do for her?"

"How the hell do I know? Do I look like a frigging doctor? What do you expect of me? All I know is what I read on the internet some time ago. The message said if a person is having a heart attack; he or she should breathe very fast and cough. It is supposed to keep the heart going or something. Try breathing in and out very fast, Beulah. Cough if you can. Please try to do it, Beulah." Michael moved over, sitting next to her.

"I tried to do like you say, but I can't. It can't be my heart; I never had any problems my whole life." The huge woman straightened out her legs, rearranged her dress and continued to sit propped upright against the wall. "Maybe I can take a nap and feel better in a little while." Beulah laid her head back against the wall, closing her eyes.

Michael looked at Jennifer and shook his head, but said nothing. Jennifer responded to Michael by thrusting up her closed fist, sticking her middle finger in front of his face.

"Yeah Jennifer," said Michael with a sarcastic smile, "You're a mature person, but yours is the best offer I've had today. Do you want to do it right here, right now?"

"Go to Hell, Michael."

A short time later, Jennifer stood up and began examining Beulah's work cart.

"What are you looking for?" Michael asks.

"I'm getting hungry. I thought Beulah might have a lunch bag but I can't find one."

"Hah, I bet you were planning on stealing her lunch weren't you? There's nothing here, I already looked. Just go sit back down, out of my way."

"If there's anything consistent about you, Mike, it's you're a goddamn loser. I've been meaning to ask you Mike, how is your wife?"

"If you don't shut up, I'm going to knock all your teeth out, including the bridgework I helped pay for. You didn't act like this when you were screwing me to get those pay raises, did you Jennifer? You faked screaming and moaning so much, I thought you were trying out for a part in a porno film. Well, you don't have to fake it anymore Jenny, so just SHUT THE HELL UP. Let me tell you something else, you make my wife look mighty good."

Michael crouched back into his corner of the elevator as far away from Jennifer as he could get. The chamber became quiet. Once more, Michael went to sleep, so did Jennifer. It was hard to know if Beulah was sleeping or in a labored coma. The sounds of Beulah's erratic breathing bounced off the walls of the elevator.

Michael woke up. It was dark. The emergency lantern's battery had given off its last light. He could hear Jennifer and Beulah breathing slowly, both of them still sleeping. Michael thought about his life. His thoughts wandered to his wife, whom he never appreciated enough. Lastly, he thought about many mistakes he made over the years, both with his family and employment. Sure, the affair with Jenny served his biological needs, as did the other women who shared intimacies with him during the last several years. The only reason keeping him married was his son and daughter. Not that he loved them so much that he could not bear to leave them. Michael did not want to pay child support. The old saying was true; it is cheaper to keep her.

As an investment adviser, Michael was average, making a few dollars for some clients and losing money for others. His salary was not dependent on his clients' success. Profit for the broker is dependent on the buying and selling, not the prosperity of the procedure. Michael picked good investments, but his timing was poor. He convinced his clients to invest in Japanese funds, just before the devaluating of the yen. He pulled the money out and invested his clients' money in the bond market. The bonds protected their capital, so his clients decided not to risk the money in other securities. Without buying and selling, Michael's income didn't increase.

Jennifer had respected Michael when she became his secretary, identifying his powerful ego and aloofness as a stockbroker and manliness. Michael played the flirt game. Two weeks after she was hired, the game of touchy-feely started secretly in his office before progressing to Jennifer's apartment. It wasn't long before Michael spent every Wednesday's lunch hour draining his body of fluids with Jennifer instead eating food.

Chapter 47

Jennifer awoke, her eyes squinting to see in the darkness. "What the hell, it's dark in here." She said.

"Personally, I like the darkness, Jenny, but if you'll wait a second, I'll find my cigarette lighter." Michael reached into his left trousers pocket and retrieved the gold lighter, which years ago, had been a gift from his wife. He could feel the "Love, Cindy" engraving on it with his thumb as he snapped open the lid and flicked the striker. A small flame replaced the slight smell of lighter fluid. Michael used the light to find the paper towels on Beulah's cart. He ripped off a sheet from the roll. He twisted the paper into a narrow cone shape, so it would burn slowly. After lighting the paper, Michael closed his lighter and put it back in his pocket. Peering through the subdued light, he saw Beulah sitting on the floor. She was awake and staring at him and Jennifer.

"I'm feeling better now, maybe I just needed some rest. I have to get home to Jidon, I bets he be worried about me now."

"Who is Jidon? Is he the man you're living with?" Michael asked.

"That's the problem with you white folks, Mr. Foster. You always tells me about your kids, but you never ask about my family. Does you thinks I have affairs like you? I ain't living with no man."

Michael turned his head, retrieving his cigarette lighter. Opening and closing the cap, repeatedly with a loud snap. "Ah, shit" he said.

"Beulah, I don't have anyone at all, not after today," replied Jennifer. "Please forgive me for never asking you about your family. I admit to being insensitive when it comes to the feelings of others, Beulah. Please tell me, who is Jidon?"

"Why he be my son! He's twenty years old now. I raised him after me and my husband Darnell Gibbons, broke up. Darnell carried on like Mr. Foster here, except he never kept a job. I divorced the son-of-a-bitch to be sure. I had the responsibility to raise our son Jidon. He better off without his worthless daddy. I love Jidon with all my heart. He is my flesh and blood and he loves his mamma too, he does."

"Okay," said Michael. "You have a kid, big deal, I have two of them. Does it make me special? Hell no! Kids are a pain in the ass. They are God's retribution against a man for having sex with a woman."

"That is what I means about some of you white folks, Mr. Foster. You take us for granted and you don't care about our feelings and lives. Shit, you don't care about your own children. I bet your wife and kids would be better off without you. If your family is not important to you, I know you don't fancy knowing anything about me does you, Mr. Foster? I know you believe you are better than I am. All you want from me is to empty your wastebasket, clean your office floor, and for me to make sure you don't run out of ass wipe in the shithouse. If I were your wife, I would kick your ass out as I did my Darnell. You ain't worth the bloody snot spots I cleans up off the lobby floor, you ain't."

"Beulah, I'll make sure you get fired when we get out of here." Michael said under his breath.

"No, you won't," replied Jennifer. "I'll deny she said anything to you Michael."

Michael didn't reply. How did this stupid conversation start? He didn't give a rats ass about Beulah's son. Michael's head throbbed as he curbed his growing anger. He knew if he continued to argue; there was the possibility of agitating Beulah into a full-blown heart attack. He didn't want rescuers finding Beulah dead on the elevator floor. Jennifer would tell everyone it was his fault. Michael decided the only way out of the conversation would be by changing the subject.

"I'm glad you're no longer in pain, Beulah. Please understand when I tell you I have no desire to talk about your son, or my family. We have a more pressing matter. The way I figure it, we've been stuck in this damn box for over 24 hours. The air stinks. I'm uncomfortable because my colon is full and my stomach is empty. Like both of you, I'm tired of pissing in the cleaning bucket on Beulah's cart. It's time we tried to get out of this elevator ourselves. By now, I can assure you our elevator repair people are no longer in the building. Does everyone agree with me?"

Beulah's fists remained clenched in anger.

Michael knew if Beulah's son were here, he would beat the shit out of him or maybe rip out his throat. He watched as the housekeeper continued to have labored breathing and held her hand to her chest.

Jenny slid closer to Beulah, putting her hand on the woman's forearm, trying to calm down the woman's growing anger. "I would be proud to meet your son when we get out of here, Beulah." Jennifer said.

"Enough of this shitty conversation," yelled Michael. His head was hurting; his eyes felt like they would burst from his skull. What little patience he had, was gone. "Now you ladies shut up for a minute and hear me out, because I don't like repeating myself. I'm asking you one more time; isn't it time we try to get out of here ourselves?"

"No shit, Sherlock, finally figured that out, huh Mike."

"Jenny, quit your badmouthing me and help. I don't need your attitude."

The light from the burning paper towel was diminishing. Michael dropped burning embers into the water bucket just as the flames approached his fingertips. The pungent smell of burned paper drifted around the trapped passengers. The cell plunged into darkness.

"Crap. There goes our light. It doesn't matter. We don't need a light for this. I remember seeing what looked like a maintenance access door just above our heads in the ceiling. I'm going to roll

Beulah's work cart into the middle of the elevator and climb up on it. Jenny, hold the cart so it doesn't roll once I have it in place. I will climb on the cart and try to open the access door."

"Yeah, Mike, whatever. Maybe I'll just shove you off the damn cart, instead of holding it."

"Jenny, I'm going to only say this one time: When you get out of here, you can do anything you goddamn please. Right now, just do what I tell you. If you don't help me, I'll do it myself. When I get out of here you can be assured I will close the door and your ass will stay here."

The darkness prevented Michael from seeing the hate he knew was on Jennifer's face as she helped roll the cart to the center of the cage. Michael put his shoes back on to stabilize his balance before climbing on Beulah's cart. He put his left foot on the bottom shelf, which would serve as a step. With both hands grasping the side, Michael carefully climbed on top. He stood erect and reached up towards what he figured was the access door. He did not tell the women he was afraid of heights. His wife Cindy used their ladder to clean all the outside windows at home. No way in hell would he get on a ladder. His fear of heights was the main reason he didn't suggest trying the access door earlier. Michael was trembling, thankful the women couldn't see him. He carefully reached above his head and touched the ceiling. Groping his hand back and forth, he touched the access door. His head continued to throb.

Michael found the release lever and gave the door a push. The door did not move. He pushed harder. Still nothing happened. Perhaps he needed to pull, rather than push the door. He reversed actions and violently pulled. Again, nothing happened. At last, he flexed his knees and rising quickly, shoving the door with all his strength. The door did not move, but the cart did. Michael slipped off the top and came down, landing on the floor of the cage.

"I'm going to kill you, Jenny. You did that on purpose, didn't you! Huh, didn't you!"

"I can't see you Mike, but if you move any closer to me, I'll knock you through the wall of the elevator with this mop handle. To answer your accusation, no, I didn't move the cart. Don't be stupid. I want out of here as badly as you do. You caused the cart to move by doing whatever you did up there." A few seconds passed, tempers cooled.

"Michael, if you calm down, why don't you light up another piece of paper towel? You could put it in the empty pail Beulah has in the other side of her cart. It will give us some light and free your hands. At least you will see what you're doing and not accuse me of anything. We could keep the fire going by dropping more paper onto the pail and use the other piss bucket to put out the fire if it starts to get out of control.

Michael didn't reply.

Beulah stood up. She was unsteady on her feet, but some of her chest pain had subsided. "Here is the empty pail and paper towels. If you lights it up, Mr. Foster, I will add some paper to it as it burns down. I'll hold my cart if you wants to climb on it again. Maybe the both of us can keep it steady for you. Why didn't you get the hatch open?"

"That's a dumb question. I don't know. How would I know, Beulah? I'm trying the best I can. I want to get the hell out of here. I'll tell you this, Beulah; If Jenny doesn't shut her goddamn mouth I might try to beat the hatch open with her head."

Michael rolled a small piece of paper towel, repeating his earlier act with the lighter and the paper cone ignited. He dropped the flaming cone into the empty pail. The light reflected onto the emergency hatch. Michael surmised the hatch was locked from the topside. The hatch cover was designed for repairs to be done from the outside, not for access from the inside of the cage. Once more, Michael climbed onto the cart. It had to open; it was their only chance of escape.

"Jenny, hand me a mop."

Holding the cart with one hand, Jennifer handed Michael a mop handle, carefully avoiding the wet, nasty working end.

Michael took it. Using his best effort to keep his balance, he jabbed the handle several times into the hatch. It only moved about a quarter of an inch. It was either a lock or a hasp with a snap clip holding it secure from the top of the elevator cage. Whatever it was, Michael was not going to move it or break it with a mop handle.

Smoke from the burning paper was filling the cage and the light from the flickering flame was fading. Michael once more climbed off the cart, picked up the burning pail and dumped the contents into the pail of liquid. With a hissing sound, the fire went out. They were in darkness. Escape from the elevator cage was futile; they would have to wait until the maintenance people could free them. It would be a long wait.

Beulah sat down on the floor, resting her back against the wall. "The pain is feeling heavy in my chest and going up into my neck," she said. "But, I be alright, I will."

Although the fire was out, smoke continued to permeate the air. The trio could not see smoke, but they could smell its odor. The sir should have cleared by now.

Beulah's voice broke the silence. "The floor of this here elevator is starting to get real warm. I can feel's it on my butt."

The smoke had the stench of burned plastic, fabric, and other strange odors. Michael realized what was happening. "Hey, the goddamn building's on fire!"

Flickers of light were visible around the cracks in the elevator door, shooting like lasers up the wall. Light was beginning to illuminate the drifting smoke inside the cage. The trio could see wisps of soot particulates drifting from the elevator's air vent, rising towards the ceiling.

Jennifer began to whirl her head back and forth and start screaming. "Oh shit, we're going to die. Oh shit, we're going to die. Oh shit, we're going to die. Oh shit, we're going to die." She repeated the sentence faster and faster like the mantra of a Mystic at prayer.

Michael stood up, realizing Jenny was correct. Most likely, they were going to die. "Get out of the way, you idiot." Michael screamed as he shoved Jennifer against the wall. "Beulah, HELP ME! Grab the back of this cart. We'll slam it against the elevator door. Maybe it will spring open for us. Give it hell; throw your weight behind it, woman!"

Beulah stood up, getting behind the cart. She and Michael grasped it and with a mighty shove, slammed the cleaning cart into the elevator door. Other than creating a loud noise, nothing happened. They shoved it again, same results. Beulah reached with all her strength and one more time, gave it the push of her life. The door remained closed.

As Beulah looked back toward Michael, her eyes began to glaze over. Her feet started to slip forward and her hands dropped towards her side. Beulah's butt slipped along the wall, resting on the warm floor of the elevator cage. Her head tipped forward before finally coming to a final rest on her right shoulder. Beulah Breshawn was dead.

The trapdoor at the top of the cage opened. A disheveled young black man shined a flashlight down into the chamber.

"Auntie Beulah, Auntie Beulah, is you here?"

Jennifer's mantra stopped and her voice exploded back to the real world. "For God's sake, get us out of the hellhole, mister! Please, please help us!"

"Get the fuck out of my way, Jenny," shouted Michael, as he started climbing onto the cart.

Breshawn's flashlight beam focused on Beulah, who was glassy-eyed with her head resting on her shoulder. He saw she was dead.

"Oh God, Oh God, Auntie Beulah, what have they done to you? First, Jidon dies and now you are gone."

"WHAT THE HELL DID YOU DO TO HER?" He screamed, looking from Michael to Jennifer.

"Nothing, she had a heart attack, and if you don't help us out of here we're going to be fried!" Michael yelled back at him.

"Don't you know the goddamn building is on fire? There is no time to waste. Are you going to help us or not? If not, get out of my way." Michael yelled.

"Sure, I know the building is on fire. Listen asshole, you ain't coming up here yet," said Breshawn. "Let the lady get up first, and then I will help you."

Michael was desperate. Panic is contagious and spreads like a cold virus in a school bus after the first day of classes. He had to get Jennifer out in a hurry, or perhaps the bastard looking at him from the access door might decide to close the escape hatch and lock it. He had no choice. Michael stopped climbing on the cart, turning toward Jennifer.

"Jenny, I'll hold the cart and you climb out of here. Move your ass."

She started to climb up on it, but not fast enough for Michael. He put his hand on her butt, giving it a mighty shove upward. She said nothing about what he did.

Chapter 48

Breshawn hesitated, continuing to gaze at his dead aunt's body. Now both members of his beloved family were gone. Beulah would soon burn up like her son Jidon, who was cremated by the exploding gasoline truck. His thoughts wandered to Abe, who might be dead or lost somewhere west of Orlando. What would he do? Where would he go? With his family and friends all gone, who would befriend him? Breshawn reached down into the elevator and grasped Jennifer's extended hand. He was helping white people, whom he hated and despised. Would this torture never end?

"Hang on to me and I'll pull you up."

Jennifer smiled with joy. She reached up, grabbed Breshawn's muscular hand with a firm grasp of her own. Breshawn slipped his hand lower and grasped her wrist. He pulled the woman off the cart and to the top of the elevator cage.

Jennifer stood there, grasping the greasy cables for support. Breshawn gave her his flashlight. "Shine the light down into the elevator and I will help your friend. But first, I'm going down there." Breshawn grasped the side of the hatch opening and lowered himself into the cage. Michael stepped aside, looking scared.

Breshawn stooped down and silently looked at his Auntie Beulah. He put his fingers alongside her throat, trying to find a pulse. There appeared to be no damage to her body, so they were correct, she most likely died of a heart attack. Breshawn would not leave the elevator, until he made sure the white people had not killed her.

The smoke from the building fire was increasing around the elevator cage, filling up the shaft like a wood burning stove's chimney. The white man was right. If they did not get out of there soon the smoke would kill them just prior to the fire cremating their bodies.

Breshawn yelled at Michael; "Get back, I'm going out first and then I will help you. Don't say anything or you will stay here." Breshawn stepped on the top of the cart and pulled himself out with little effort. "Your turn, you better hurry if you don't want to fry."

Michael climbed onto the cart, jumped up and grasped the edge of the hatch door opening with his hands. He pulled himself out, ignoring the extended hand of Breshawn. Michael glared at Jennifer who shined the light in his eyes.

"If you don't take your light out of my face, I am going to take it away from you and use it to smash your head in, bitch."

Breshawn had gained access to the elevator shaft from the 12th floor opening. He pried the elevator door open on the fifteenth floor where he heard voices and commotion coming from the stalled cage somewhere below the twelfth floor. He ran down the adjacent stairway for three levels and pried the door open before climbing down on the cage and opening the access door into the elevator. With the building burning, this was the last place he intended to search for Aunt Beulah. Already, Breshawn had made up a story, how Jidon was killed trying to help a woman who was on fire during the gasoline truck explosion. He wouldn't have to lie. Auntie Beulah would never know her son died. God, he wished he had some crack. What would Abe do if he were here? Abe was not here. Breshawn was alone. He found his Auntie, but it was too late.

Breshawn knew if he did not leave the building soon, he would never get out. The bank building next door was blazing when he had entered the investment firm. The flames must have spread to Groves. He didn't intend to spend much time trying to save two strangers, especially the man to whom he was speaking. If they didn't save his auntie, the man and woman probably contributed to her death.

"Before opening your mouth again asshole, and I mean do not speak to the lady or me, listen to me. To begin with, I hate white people. Therefore, shut your mouth or I won't help you. God, don't you know what trouble you be in? I don't care if you live or not. So, you honky bastard, you had better be nice to me or I will throw your ass back into that box, lock this hatch and you can just sit there and fry. I'm strong enough to do what I say."

Michael said nothing.

The white man reminded Breshawn of Mr. Watson. All white men reminded him of Mr. Watson. Breshawn's world was changing, but it was still a world controlled by white people. He would not let anger destroy his chances of living.

Breshawn watched as Michael found where he forced the 12th floor elevator door open to gain access to the elevator cables. Michael leaned the top part of his torso over the opening and grasped the sides of the doorway. With a small push with his feet, he left the top of the cage. His momentum carried him out of the shaft and into the hallway.

Michael looked down into the shaft at Jennifer and his rescuer. He knew the stories Jennifer would tell everyone after getting out. First, she would tell his co-workers, and then she would tell his wife Cindy. She would tell them he caused Beulah to die. Michael would not allow it to happen. He shut the elevator door, trapping Breshawn and Jennifer on top of the cage.

"Good-bye, Jenny. Give my regards to Beulah; in a few minutes, you will be with her in hell." Michael's own survival and reputation was important to him, nothing more. Michael disappeared.

Chapter 49

"I will kill you, honky," screamed Breshawn.

Jenny was so surprised when Michael left; she almost dropped the flashlight, which they needed if there was any hope of getting out. The smoke was dispelling the oxygen, contaminating the air. She is starting to cough. Mucus was forming in her nose and beginning to flow into her throat, gagging her. Her eyes are tearing from the smoke particles.

"What is the matter with that guy, lady? Is he nuts? Doesn't he know I saved him? Don't you fret; all these doors can be released from the inside, not like those in the elevator cage. I'll take care of that honky prick when we get out. He'll be a dead motherfucker."

Breshawn reached up, grasping the release handle bar where Jennifer was shining the flashlight and pulled. The door opened. He climbed off the top of the elevator cage and into the hallway. Breshawn crouched down, grabbed Jennifer around both wrists, lifting her up and out of the elevator shaft. She was free.

"Follow me," he said. Breshawn started down the hallway with Jennifer alongside him. The flashlight disclosed the stairway sign. They opened the door, entering it. It would be a long ways to the main floor and time was against them. Breshawn and Jennifer picked up speed and dashed through the hallways. The smoke was getting thicker. It was time to leave the building.

The walls alongside the stairwell were beginning to crack from the heat. Smoke is coming out of the openings. Jennifer was not running well after her long inactivity. Her feet hurt and her legs were stiff and slow. As they rounded the third floor, Breshawn grabbed her arm, stopping her.

"I didn't come in this way. We have to go into the third floor area itself, to get out of here. I came into the building using that fire escape at the other end of the corridor. The stairway is locked with steel bars at the lobby floor entrance. The security guards must have padlocked it when they left."

Jennifer said nothing, but followed his lead. She was mentally numb. After leaving the stairway, she followed Breshawn until coming to an open window. A view of the city greeted them. She saw several other building on fire. It would not be long before Orlando, Florida would be no more.

Breshawn turned, looking behind him, but saw nothing. He suspected the white man continued down the stairs and if he did, then he was trapped. They wouldn't go searching for the asshole. The building itself would take care of him. If perchance the man survived and Breshawn saw him again, he would pop a cap into his head. No one screwed with Breshawn, especially a honky.

Jenny stepped through the window to the catwalk. Breshawn followed her. The metal rusted catwalk ladder led down the outside the building to the street. The pair climbed down the ladder and stood on the sidewalk. They had escaped.

The morning sun had risen, but as obscured by smoke from the numerous fires burning throughout Orlando. Everything looked worse than it did from the third story window. There are dead bodies scattered along the sidewalk and into the street. This must be the end of civilization.

Jennifer looked at Breshawn and he looked at her. They glanced at Grove's Investment Building as the fire began jumping out of the windows. Glass exploded outward because of the intense heat, falling like missiles from the upper floors, plummeting towards the concrete sidewalk. They had to get away from here or risk being impaled by glass or debris and then bleeding to death.

Michael was nowhere to be seen. He was probably dead, trapped somewhere between the third floor and the first floor lobby.

Breshawn grasped Jennifer's arm, pulling her away from the falling glass and debris. They began running together down the street, away from the city.

Breshawn suddenly stopped and looked back. "Goodbye Auntie Beulah, sorry about Jidon. You will be with him now. I'm sorry I couldn't find you before you passed on. I tried. I really did try. I will be a good person. I'll survive. Maybe I'll help rebuild this world. Forgive me, Auntie Beulah for not finding you in time."

Jennifer took his arm. The large black man was crying. She also cried. They both turned away from Grove's Investment Management Company, and resumed walking toward the edge of the city.

"I never got to thank you. I'm Jennifer Smith." She said while giving him a hug.

"I'm Breshawn Racheed. Enough talking, let's get the hell out-a-here."

They would try to survive. The couple disappeared as they traveled through the streets, out of the burning City of Orlando.

Chapter 50

CLAY WHEELER

C lay's thoughts haunted him as his eyes turned away from home towards the highway. He would not look back. Every journey once begun, must continue until completed. The long stroll down his driveway seemed different from the many times he traveled it before. The narrow driveway reminded Clay of the "B" horror films he watched on Saturday night television when he was a child. He remembered seeing movie films where an actor was walking down a hallway, only to see it get larger, longer, and seemingly extend into infinity. His driveway was the endless hallway. Time appeared to stand still. The unknown causes of the power outage bothered him. Was he wasting his time and putting his family in jeopardy by leaving them? He did not understand what compelled him to go. It was as if his journey was predestined by providence rather than free will. Clay is beginning a journey into enlightenment, perhaps to his foreordained future. His Indian blood taught him to be the protector, provider, and leader of his family. He was no longer Clay the plumber but was Clay the Huichol Indian Brave evolving into a Shaman, searching for answers. He is making a pilgrimage, seeking knowledge about both himself and why the world seemed strange.

Clay would miss the loving companionship of Maggie and his children. Most of all, he would miss the security of his family unit. The Michigan weather conditions are making the traveling slow.

The forest is lonely for a man walking by himself. Clay knew he was not alone. Life was everywhere. The trees were alive, providing food for insects and homes for birds. Animals and rodents were moving silently through the forest, foraging for food and shelter. Clay remembered Great Grandmother Clay Bird Spirit saying the forest had its own conscience much like humans. Clay felt inner cognizance as if nature was drawing itself into him. Walking alone through the forest provided Clay with feelings of love, much as he felt for Maggie when they were dating. He belongs to the forest as much as his ancestors did long ago. Clay craved freedom, as did his ancestors. The woodland needed humanity to be interdependent with all life forms. Clay believed if one followed the old ways of simplicity, that man would once more have balance with nature. Life would be good.

With one side of the equation, Clay loved indoor plumbing and electricity to power his pumps and light up his house. He also loved the simplicity and functionality of the hand pump on the well he had driven in their backyard, which was not dependent on electricity. The other side of the equation was Clay's hatred of television advertising, loud stereos, automobile horns, and the demands of society to become financially indebted to the business world. To Clay, financial debt was a form of slavery. He would work hard to pay off the loan for his house. In ten years, Clay planned to be debt free and working only for his family. He did not know it, but his debts were already gone.

Clay longed for the days of Thunder Eagle. Those were the times when one worried about the necessities of life, rather than luxuries. There was no reason to worry about upgrading a computer system every three years because a faster processor with a larger hard drive was available. Clay realized in some ways, the past was not always good. There were no antibiotics, decongestants, or pills to cure anything. Plagues and disease would ravage towns and communities. You could often tell how old a person was by counting how many teeth he or she still had and subtract from the number fifty. Poor dental hygiene and care was the norm, not the exception in the old days. On the other hand, the forest required no one to go into debt. His Indian ancestors lived on the land, lived with nature, and never needed a deed to prove ownership. If humans respected nature, it could be the best of times. It depressed Clay to know humans are too self-serving and selfish to become one with nature.

In the old days, nature was still pure, without synthetic pollution. Mother Earth provided clean food from the Michigan forestlands. She provided deer meat and wild berries to preserve and eat during the long snowy winters. When one worked, it was for himself, not for the benefit of an employer. There were no monotonous assembly line jobs, which could drive a worker to take drugs, drink too much alcohol, and use anti-depressant prescriptions. Clay's goal when moving to northern Michigan was to incorporate the good from today's industrial revolution into a commune with nature.

Clay was not paying attention where he was walking. He stumbled and almost fell, tripping over a fallen branch in the driveway. The knapsack went flying off his back. He picked it up, brushing off some fallen leaves and plant seeds that clung to it as hitchhikers hoping be rooted elsewhere in the forest.

"God, I have to quit this damn daydreaming before I break my neck." He said aloud to no one. The forest was listening. Clay felt physically weak, which was different from the strength he usually enjoyed.

After regaining his footing, Clay repositioned his backpack, drawing the straps tighter across his waist. As he resumed walking down the driveway, his mind once more drifted back into history. He loved thinking about the past. It is as if his mind is a revolving doorway. He could enter the past and leave it at will.

His memories about his family history were making the journey easier. He ignored his trepidation about what might be at the end of his travels. The information about why the electricity failed was important, but so was the journey itself. Clay's feet developed their own rhythm, guiding him to the highway as those of horses a hundred years ago. A team of horses knew the path home while pulling a sleigh through the deep snows of Michigan. A horse pulling a milk wagon knew which houses to stop at, so the milkman could leave bottles of milk and cream on the porch. The forest and instinct were guiding him. Clay was no longer master of his destiny. He was a student of nature.

Uneasiness and foreboding caused Clay to begin shielding his body from possible view of others. He was skirting behind the trees along the sides of his driveway until he found himself standing on the gravel shoulder of Highway 2. Once more, he looked north and south, but there was nothing to see. The road seemed as empty as it did the last couple of days. Clay peered into the sky, but still heard no sounds of aircraft. He shivered as chills radiated throughout his body, knowing he should be feeling warmth from the walking exercise. Could anxiety be causing the chills? On the other hand, could it be something else?

The damn silence disturbed him the most. A dove flew out of the brush near his feet. A shot of adrenalin entered Clay's heart causing it to skip several beats before shifting into overdrive, heightening his senses. Clay had not expected the noise. He watched the dove disappearing among the maple trees. There was no reason to be afraid of them. Doves symbolized peace and tranquility. A few years back, Michigan began allowing hunters to shoot them. Clay would never kill a dove. He damned the legislators when they passed the law, wrote letters of protest to several newspapers and his State Representative who ignored his appeal, the law remained.

"Ah Hell, this is stupid, there's nothing to be afraid of," he said aloud. This time he did not bother to see if Skully and Fox Mulder were spying on him. He meandered inconspicuously walking north along the edge of the highway.

Clay raised his face, looking upwards at the cloudy sky, observing the falling snowflakes. His face tingled as small icy particles landed and melted on contact, chilling his cheeks. Precipitation often fell from the sky during the late fall season in Michigan. From experience, Clay knew the light snow would last for a few minutes and quit, resuming later.

Numerous clouds were gathering over the tree line. The wind was gusty from the west, shifting to the south. If the temperature dropped a few degrees, Clay expected an accumulation of snow. He wouldn't mind walking in snow, it would be more pleasant than rain. Clay figured the closest house was two miles down the road, a small summertime jaunt. It would take much longer to get there with the cold weather and the bulky clothes he is wearing. His heartbeat returned to its normal rhythm but the chill remained. He wiped the wet snow from his face with his sleeve, sneezed twice and continued staggering down highway 2.

The world around him reminded Clay of the parallel worlds in one of Steven King's novels. Clay considered King one of the great horror writers of all-time. Steven King was able to inspire an entire new generation of fictional writers who began writing horror stories. His favorite book by King was "The Stand" which he considered a classic among the doom and gloom "end of civilization" literary genre novels. Clay also enjoyed reading "Swan" by Robert McCammon, another story about the end of civilization. Perhaps the world is experiencing a similar event, which would affect humanity forever. Both books relied on a higher power to bring a resolution to the crisis. Maybe humanity needed more faith and less reliance on science. Yet faith and religion caused most of the humankind's wars. Hah, Clay began to laugh at his circular reasoning.

God, he wished it were summertime again. His warm weather addiction was listening to Detroit Tiger baseball games on the radio. Nowadays, most of the games are played at night. Clay enjoyed spending his evenings sitting in the family den with the windows open and a fan blowing toward him. His ears would be listening to the Tiger play-by-play on his radio. Sometimes Clay drifted to sleep while listening, only to get up later, go upstairs, and climb into bed. Maggie did not mind his worship of baseball. After all, he wasn't an alcoholic, didn't hang around bars in town after work, and always came home to his family.

Baseball: This is the first relaxing thought Clay had since leaving his family. Thunder Eagle and Great Grandpa Wheeler were history, but baseball was forever. Baseball is a game of chess played on a field with a ball, bat, cap, spiked shoes, and four men dressed in blue to judge when the rules are broken. Hotdogs, peanuts, and beer with a frozen tub of the strange lemon stuff, eaten with a wooden spoon by breaking and scraping it off in small frozen chunks, was as important as the game itself. It was all part of the game's experience at a professional baseball stadium.

Yes sir, that's the life. That's living. Fans have the freedom to cheer their team, eat hotdogs with their families and drink an occasional expensive glass of beer. Most fans dreamed about catching a foul ball to keep as a souvenir. Although he saw few baseball games in person, Clay preferred going to night games, which were much cooler than sitting in the hot sun during day games.

As Clay continued daydreaming, he thought about his days as a boy when he carried a 9-volt transistor radio in his shirt pocket and listened to Ernie Harwell and Ray Lane call the play-by-play of the Detroit Tigers. Sometimes local sponsors of little league baseball teams would charter a bus and pay for bleacher seats for kids who couldn't afford to attend a professional baseball game. One of Clay's fondest memories was riding a chartered bus to Detroit and watching Kirk Gibson hit a home run at the old Tiger Stadium ballpark.

If conditions returned to normal, Clay would take Maggie and the kids to a Tigers game at Detroit's Comerica Park next summer. Perhaps someday his kids would like baseball as much as he did. Clay Wheeler was relaxed and at peace.

So far, his walking had been uneventful except for being startled by the dove. Clay suspected it would continue this way. The clouds were thinning out. The sun had risen about thirty degrees into the southeastern sky. There was plenty of daylight left. The snowy mist had stopped.

His thoughts about baseball faded. It was time to meditate about what may have happened to Planet Earth. He wished his good friend S.T. was here to discuss the issue with him. S.T. loved to discuss philosophy, ethics, morality, physics, and concepts of time and space. S.T. enjoyed studying the many religions of the world. Similar to Steven Hawking, who searched for the "Theory of Everything," S.T. thought he found the answer of God, and corporal existence.

S.T. was not a nominal, fundamentalist Christian believer. Instead, he claimed to be a Mystic, believing in an all-encompassing multi-dimensional Mind continuously projecting all matter into existence. S.T. said it was a continuous process, not one with a beginning or end. He believed one's inner consciousness could touch the God force. Unlike many fundamentalists, S.T. believed the Ultimate Mind was without substance and didn't occupy a physical location in the cosmos. He believed the entire world and universe was an illusion, constantly projected from the Ultimate Mind.

Clay's thoughts wandered to a conversation he had with S.T. a few years ago. "You told me how much you enjoyed the movie "Matrix," S.T. said. "Our existence is the same. We are much like a program, a dream, not produced by us, but one continuously experienced by the Ultimate Mind source, with the eventual goal of perfection for humans gained through several reincarnated lifetimes."

Clay often wished he had asked if S.T. had seen the movie, "Groundhog Day" which presented an idea of completeness by learning from mistakes, until one's lessons on life results in perfection. Only when the main character of the movie lived the day, transforming his life into good, could he move on to another day.

S.T., on the other hand, believed time travel could be possible and events could change, but we would never know the change because of experiencing one time line. This was a funky concept for

Clay, but many new truths and facts, once weird and strange to others based on theoretical speculation eventually proved true. S.T. believed he was in contact with the Ultimate Mind, but Clay was skeptical about his claim.

To Clay, faith was love and compassion, based on one's ability to deal with the challenges that cognitive existence presented to him as he journeyed his path of life towards his inevitable death. Faith is his love for Maggie and their children. He wished S.T. could be with him now, as an adviser and friend. Besides, the conversation would help pass the time. He remembered S.T. telling him the Ultimate Mind was real regardless of what Clay thought or believed, and his belief or non-believing didn't matter.

In many ways, it sounded similar to what his Great Grandmother Clay Bird Spirit had told him about his Huichol Shaman beliefs. Clay decided all faith concepts came from the same source, but it is humankind's attempt to understand and analyze the source, which is corrupted. Most humans would argue and sometimes kill to defend the honor of their God. They believe my God could kick your God's ass. Since my God is not here to do it, I will do it for him and kick your ass. Clay hated religion. Nevertheless, right now, Clay was walking in the woodland church, integrating and melding with the forest, learning the lesson it was teaching him.

Clay's thoughts metamorphosed from the metaphysical world into concern for Maggie and his children. Sometimes he thought too much. Drops of moisture were flowing from his nose. Clay wiped it with his red handkerchief, stuffing the damp rag into his coat pocket.

The road curved to the east. Alongside the highway, lying upside down in the ditch was a red Ford pickup truck. Clay could see the cab was underwater. If anyone had been in it, he or she would be dead. There was no reason to get into the water to examine the cab. It would only serve to get him wet and colder. No one could have survived.

Clay had no idea why the truck rolled into the ditch. Did the engine fail because of the power failure, causing the driver to panic and crash? Could this be the reason he found no running vehicles on the road or aircraft cruising the sky? The red Ford truck, plus the failure of his Clay's Chevy truck to start, gave him the evidence he needed to realize the power failure was more serious than he first surmised. The sight of the ditched pick-up truck brought renewed thoughts about Maggie and the kids. Just in front of the truck, a huge deer sporting a twelve-point rack of horns bounded across the road. The sight of the magnificent animal startled Clay back to reality.

"If I see you next deer hunting season" he said out loud to the fleeing buck; "you will be in my freezer. "Clay dabbed his nose with the sleeve of his coat.

Clay stood still too long. He was getting cold. He resumed marching, leaving the overturned pick-up truck behind. The deer continued running, eventually stopping in a small grove of poplars and finally hiding behind a group of large red sumac bushes growing abundantly under the oak trees. The beautiful creature raised its head and Clay saw the deer staring at him. It was as if the creature were analyzing Clay as much as he was studying the animal himself. The huge buck sniffed the air and snorted. It looked towards Clay and bounded off disappearing into the trees. Strangely, it was as if the creature had never been there. Not a leaf or branch on the ground was disturbed, as the deer traveled through the woods into infinity. Clay heard no sounds of its hoofs or rustling of the underbrush as the animal moved through the trees. It was as if the deer drifted atop the ground, not touching the underbrush, floating as if it were in another dimension. Could this deer be the one Kaya Bird had seen? If so, why didn't he see the deer when she did?

With all the precautions he took, it had taken Clay an hour to travel the one-mile from his home to his present location. He began staring at the gravel alongside the highway while continuing his journey. The sky darkened up. Clouds were forming and amassing in the western sky. A few drops of cold rain began falling on the west side of the road, making its way to the other side where Clay was walking. He could hear the raindrops spatter around him pounding the few remaining tree leaves. There was no way to protect his body from the impending rainstorm. Water dripped from the bill of his cap, dampening his coat. He lowered his head, keeping the rain out of his eyes.

Clay thought of the times when as a boy he lived a mile from school. Back in those days, the only public transportation in his school district was his two feet or his English Racer bicycle. He rode the bicycle to school until it was stolen from the bike rack at Coolidge Elementary School. The thief had broken his safety lock and left it on the ground before taking the bicycle. One week later, the police recovered his English Racer, but after the incident, Clay seldom had the courage to ride it to school again. From then on, Clay remembered locking his bicycle even when it was stored in his dad's garage, although he knew it was safe there. The lock only inconvenienced him, not the thief who would have little problem breaking it. Clay had few toys when he was a child and they had been precious to him. No one would steal from him again.

The sky was getting darker as the clouds gathered. The slight breeze gave way to a colder wind. Lightning is flashing out of a large bank of clouds rolling toward him from the northwest. Clay realized a cold front was moving in. This is an Arctic blast blowing out of northwestern Canada, crossing Lake Superior, and rolling across Michigan on its journey toward the eastern part of the United States. Clay did not want to experience this storm. Thunder boomed its angry voice and it began to rain harder.

Thunder is intense and loud in the woodlands, away from buildings, which often muffles the rumbling sound in cities. With the lightning so pronounced, Clay knew it would not be safe to seek shelter from the storm by standing under the trees. He decided to take the less pleasant route, going down the center of Michigan Highway 2.

The rain was cold and merciless. His coat absorbed water, getting him wet and chilled. Instead of just a couple of hours, it seemed days had passed since he left Maggie and the kids. He regretted leaving his family, cursing Mother Nature under his breath for making him miserable. She was a constant observer and intent to play this weather game with him. Clay's Indian blood renewed its memories with the forest. His quest must be completed. Damn the rain, thought Clay, damn Mother Nature to Hell. She would not defeat him. His goal was to find out why the world seemed strange and unusual.

Clay started shivering as his body temperature dropped. His clothing was drenched. Hypothermia began affecting his vision and stamina. Although he had traveled only two miles, the physical activity failed to keep his body warm. If Clay were to survive out here alone, it would be necessary to seek shelter. Looking around, Clay saw what he thought was a house sitting about a quarter mile east of the highway. Leading up to the house there appeared to be a long unused driveway, overrun by weeds and undergrowth in its two-track ruts. It resembled more of a firebreak than a driveway. The tracks appeared to be made by wagon wheels rather than tire tracks. Impossible, he thought, but he followed the path anyway. The highway disappeared behind him.

The volume of rain fluctuated between a sprinkle and drenching, but it was too late for Clay. His clothes and his underwear were soaked with rainwater. He felt chilled to his inner soul. The lightning and thunder stopped, but the rainfall suddenly became intense. A figure jumped out of the woods and into the pathway in front of him. Again, it was his friend, the twelve-point buck. Clay stopped.

Clay knew from his deer hunting experiences it was unusual to see the same deer twice in one day. He only remembered it happening one other time, and it was while he was crouching in a deer blind, hidden from view years ago.

"Hey, bud, maybe I'll show mercy on you next fall if you continue to follow me like a puppy dog." He said aloud. His voice should have scared the buck, but the creature did not move. This is not normal.

If he were living in Thunder Eagle's day, the deer sign would be recognized as Clay's totem. Three times it has been seen, twice by Clay and once by little Kaya Bird. The deer would be Clay's guide from the animal world. The deer didn't move. It turned in Clay's direction and pawed the ground twice. The wondrous creature raised its head, sporting huge antlers with pride. The animal bobbed his rack as if saluting, before bolting off towards the west. Clay remembered what Kaya Bird had told him about the deer she saw. How could she have known? What more did she know? Clay knew that deer move into swamps during storms to find protection from the elements. The buck was telling Clay to seek shelter. Seek shelter. Seek shelter.

The pathway into the woods toward the house was unusual. Squirrels, which were not present before Clay saw the deer, lined up along each side of the pathway, as if they were giving honor to royalty as Clay traversed the footpath. He watched two snowshoe rabbits as they stood facing the path from each side. When Clay reached where they were sitting, both ran off in opposite directions, stopping about two hundred feet away. The rabbits resumed their posture, watching Clay. In all his days of hunting game, Clay had never had such an experience.

The pathway ended in front of a log house, located on a small hill. It was common in northern Michigan areas for people to build log structures; it was an attempt to get back to their early rustic American heritage, or to smell the pleasant cedar fragrance inside their homes. Whatever the reason, the structure in front of Clay was beautiful. It looked new, but it also looked ancient, as if it had been there since the early 1800's. The corners of the home were interlocked with notched logs, with gaps filled with cement. The roof was made of timbers, covered with hand hewn cedar shingles, shaved to fit closely and overlapping to keep the rain out. The roof offered strong protection against the ice and snow accumulation which often occurred in northern Michigan.

Clay hesitated and stopped walking. He gripped his coat tighter but it failed to give added warmth. His hands are wet and stiff from the cold. Clay removed his soggy gloves and began rubbing his hands and fingers together attempting to increase blood circulation to warm them. His fingers remained a sickish blue color without much feeling. Clay's shivering intensified as small droplets of liquid continuously dripped out of his nose. They joined the rainwater running down his face, over his lips, dropping off his chin. Clay needed a place to recuperate and get warm. The deer had led him to the cabin.

Clay knocked on the front door. The sounds echoed back to him. Strangely, the reverberations sounded as if they traveled much farther than the small building could acoustically allow. He thought nothing of it, because sounds behave differently in the wilderness. Clay dismissed the strangeness as slightly odd, like the behavior of the animals alongside the pathway leading to the door of the cabin. Nobody came to the door.

"Hello, HEY IS anybody here?" he shouted. – "Hello, I'm your neighbor to the south. Please, please," Clay pleaded, "if anyone is here, open the door. I'm sick and I need help!" There was silence. He turned the brass door handle, but found it locked. Clay could not look inside, as there were no windows along the front of the building. Clay turned and began walking towards the back of the cabin. He trampled through the overgrown vines next to the cabin and came to a window.

Clay was desperate to get protection from the storm. As an outdoorsman, he knew the dangers of hypothermia, and the danger was closing in on him. He peered into the window. The glass itself was old. Clay could see the mark in the middle of the pane where it had been hand blown. The windowpane and casing is worth much money, he guessed. It was strange to find such a valued windowpane in a Michigan cabin, unless the cabin was ancient. It was commonplace during the 18th and 19th centuries to find hand blown glass windows, but he never saw one except at Greenfield Village in Dearborn, Michigan when he was a child. Clay enjoyed seeing the home of Thomas Edison and the replica of the factory where Henry Ford build his first automobiles. Clay toured the homes of Robert Frost and Noah Webster. Most fascinating was touring the laboratory of Thomas Edison which was relocated to the park from Fort Myers, Florida. Clay remembered seeing where the first working light bulb was created. Instead of creating a light bulb, Clay was taking a journey seeking to find why they no longer cast light.

The window hung by two old-fashioned brass hinges fastened to the building. Clay tried to pull the window open. The frame hesitated, and then moved. He had to be careful; it would be sinful to break the precious glass. Someone either had not locked the window, or had overlooked it when securing the building. On the other hand, perhaps the window was unlocked so someone could gain access without destroying it. Better to be forced open than to be broken. Clay carefully pulled opened the treasured glass and repeated his initial shout:

"Hello! I'm Clay Wheeler. I'm your neighbor. Hey, is anyone here? I need help!"

The only reply heard by Clay was the wind whistling as it traveled through the forest. Inside the cabin, there was silence. The only sound was the echo of his voice, which seemed to travel a long distance before echoing back to him. Clay felt uncomfortable about what he was going to do, but he had traveled too far and was sick. Trying to return to Maggie and the kids would be stupid, and most likely deadly.

Clay climbed through the window opening, entered the cabin, and closed the window. He felt dizzy. His eyes blurred. He felt faint, as if a strange force held his mind and body in its control. He slowly took a few steps and came upon an old oak chair covered with a canvas tarp. Clay sat down on the chair. Water was dripping from his coat onto the floor. He lowered his head down between his legs for a couple of moments. His head quit buzzing.

Clay waited for his eyes to stop watering before raising his head. The walls of the oil polished cedar in the living area were old. The cabin had a small kitchen area, with knotty pine cupboards. He saw no running water or well pump. On one side of the room stood a double bed without a headboard, covered with a white comforter. An old pine dresser stood beside the bed. Upon the dresser was a woman's silver musical jewelry box. The box was as old as the hand blown glass window. Clay opened the box, found it empty, except for a ballerina that sprung from inside and stood vertically on one toe. A short chorus of the "Dance of the Sugar Plum Fairies" played. Clay carefully pushed down the ballerina and replaced the lid. The box became quiet. Once more Clay removed the lid, listening to the soothing sound of the mechanical music while watching the ballerina rotate. Strangely, the spring, if it was spring driven, never ran down. He closed the lid and put the box back on the dresser. Other than the lonely ballerina, the dresser was empty.

A sheet of brown canvas hung from a rope fastened across the ceiling of the cabin, separating the bed from the living area. Clay had no reason to pull the canvas shut. In old times, when parents wanted some privacy from their children during the nighttime, the canvas would be closed. The pine floors had worn areas in the cabin's traffic area.

Clay reckoned someone who lived in Flint, Grand Rapids, or another large metropolitan Michigan town used this building as a hunting shack. Michigan has many automobile workers who purchased land for deer hunting and other recreational activities near the Upper Peninsula. They often built cabins where they would spend two weeks out of the year, hunting deer and bear, drinking, and bonding with their male friends after a hard year's work in the factories. The cabins served another purpose too. During the summer months, the hunters brought their wives and children to the cabins for a two-week vacation to get away from the busy city life.

Some vacationers would drag a small boat behind their vehicles and use it to go fishing in one of the area's many inland lakes. Change was necessary for the mental health of an assembly line automobile worker. It was necessary to relieve the stress caused by such monotonous and repetitious employment. Families looked forward to getting away from the cities and heading to northern Michigan for a vacation. Nobody respected the automobile worker. He or she was damned for making a good wage, following union rules and accused of getting a paycheck for not working. Nobody saw the many carcinogens the autoworker breathed and touched every working day. The summer vacation and deer hunting somehow helped the autoworker to keep going to work every day.

Clay sat in the chair and visually examined the inside of the cabin. In one corner, he saw a small wood-burning stove. The stove vented out through the roof, with a small draught control facing the front, controlled by a hinge and adjustable with a small weight at the back of it. A small pile of split dried oak planks was sitting about five feet to the left, in a wooden retaining box. The cabin was clean. Where was the dust? Except on the floor, there was no dust. This is not normal. He did not allow this to trouble him. Most importantly, the cabin provided Clay with shelter from the freezing rain and wind.

Why am I so cold? He thought. Clay never felt this cold while working during the winter months on plumbing jobs. Normally he was immune to the cold. He shivered and felt physically weak. His body tried to retch, but nothing came up. Clay arose from the chair, walking to the wood heater. A two-foot stack of old magazines was next to the unit.

Clay spoke aloud; "You got to be kidding, a stack of *New World Watchers* magazines published by *God's Publishers and*

Prophets. Hell, I wonder who brought this crap here. I suppose they work for starting fires, not much good for anything else." The sound of his voice took away some anxiety.

Clay gathered six or seven of the magazines. He tore them apart and wadded them up into paper balls. He stuffed them into the heater. Clay removed his hunting knife from its sheath and gently cut some slivers of wood from one of the oak kindling. He placed them on the paper. He used his knife to slice off some larger strips of oak then stacked them in the form of a teepee above the paper and slivers. Reaching into his coat pocket, he retrieved a waterproof match container he carried for emergencies. He used one of the matches to ignite the paper. The magazines were damp from the humidity, but with a little coaxing and blowing air on them, they ignited into a warm dancing fire. He wadded up and tossed several more magazines into the fire on top of his wood strips. Once the wood was burning, Clay would add larger pieces of kindling.

The wood burned and a feint smell of burning oak permeated the air. Some steam sizzled out of the wood pores. The snapping and popping of the fire was a pleasant sound to his ears. Ten minutes later, Clay added two larger sticks of wood to the glowing embers. The cabin began to get warm.

The successful fire brought back memories of a story he read during childhood. Of all those childhood stories, "To Build a Fire" by Jack London was his favorite. Only in London's story, the hero was not successful and froze to death.

It was strange how Clay's childhood reading influenced his lifestyle and philosophy of life. He loved reading John Steinbeck. His favorite story by Steinbeck was "The Grapes of Wrath." The story told Clay that regardless of adversity, one deals with it and moves one. He especially enjoyed "The Illustrated Sherlock Holmes Treasury" by Arthur Conan Doyle. The stories, first published in STRAND MAGAZINE 1901-1905, taught Clay the importance of using deductive reasoning. When problems arose for Clay, he would ask himself; how would Sherlock Holmes work it out? Clay loved to read all literature, from pulp fiction, to horror, and historical biographies. His favorite book was "Gone with the Wind," by Margaret Mitchell. Clay loved the movie, but the book taught him more about the problems facing the United States during the Civil War. Clay found very few books about Indian history in the Americas. What was primarily available was a history of conquest of the Indian Tribes by the white settlers.

Clay knew Thunder Eagle could not read. His Great Grandmother Clay Bird Spirit also was illiterate, yet they survived using logic, tribal stories, and common sense. Much history was lost when a recorded record of the Huichol Nation was never written.

The cabin was getting warmer. Clay took off his wet clothing. He opened two green metal folding chairs that seemed out of place, sitting them next to the heater. He draped his wet clothes on the backs of the chairs so they would dry by morning. He wiped his nose. Clay crunched up his face and sneezed, followed by another wipe of his nose. He picked up a couple of more sticks of firewood and tossed into the heater.

Although it was mid-afternoon and the cabin was warm, the fire did little to draw the cold from his body. Clay stumbled to the bed, pulled back the comforter and the old hand sewed quilts exposing the sheets. He removed and shook the comforter, but nothing fell on the floor. Spreading the comforter back on the bed, Clay slipped inside, pulling the covers up to his neck. He rolled on his side, laying his head on his arms for a makeshift pillow. Clay might share the cabin with several mice running on the floor, but he did not care. He needed rest. Maybe he would feel better in a couple of hours. Slowly the heat from his body was contained in the comforter and the shivering stopped.

Clay did not know when he went to sleep, but the process happened. His was a restless sleep. He dreamed about his childhood and his Uncle Ty, who always befriended him more as a son than a nephew. He dreamed about fishing for bluegills in a small twelve-foot aluminum rowboat on Pine Lake. It was early morning in June and the fog was lifting from the lake as they put their fishing equipment in the boat.

There was no fancy equipment for Uncle Ty! No sir, just two twelve-foot bamboo cane poles strung with monofilament line holding a wooden pencil bobber and double hooks with sinkers. Clay pushed the boat off from the shoreline, getting one foot in the water as he jumped into the bow and gingerly kept his balance. He sat on the seat in front of Uncle Ty Wheeler, grasped the oars and began rowing the boat to their secret fishing hole. Uncle Ty whispered directions as Clay centered the boat two hundred feet from shore, lining it up about one hundred feet east of a huge weeping willow tree standing at the edge of the shoreline. They were careful not to speak aloud or make noise, which could scare away the fish.

Clay stopped rowing, reached over and carefully dropped the anchor into the water. The rope snaked twenty feet straight down before lodging in the mucky bottom. Clay tied the end of the rope to his oarlock. Fishing would begin.

"I can smell em, lad. Can't you smell them bluegills, boy? They're out there, we're a going to get a mess of em today. Yup, gonna get a whole bunch of em. Remember boy, if they ain't the length of my hand from my wrist to the tip of my middle finger, just throw em back. Let em grow, we'll catch em later."

Clay lifted his bamboo-fishing pole into the air, swinging the hooks toward him for baiting. On one hook, he placed a cricket, careful to hide the point of the hook. The other hook was baited with a square of fresh shrimp. Uncle Ty smiled as they both threw out their lines and watched the bobbers float to the top of the water. The monofilament line disappeared under the surface, both invisible to the anglers and the fish.

Clay could smell the fresh air while watching the fog lifting from the lakeshore. A mallard duck flew among the cattails, rising quickly away from the anglers. The rising sun brought morning breezes, causing a slight ripple on the water, moving the fishing bobbers enough to make the submerged bait look alive.

Clay's bobber disappeared. He raised his cane pole quickly, careful to set the hook in the mouth of his first catch. Sometimes he would catch two bluegills at time. At other times, Uncle Ty would do the same. They both had the same equipment, but young Clay always marveled at how Uncle Ty could catch more fish than him. After a couple of hours, they would bring the boat back to the dock, tie it up, and clean the fish for dinner.

Aunt Donna who was Uncle Ty's wife, would fry the bluegills up in a skillet and the feast would begin. He loved his Uncle Ty, and felt regret because he never told him he loved him before the man passed away due to a massive heart attack. Clay's fishing dream faded into oblivion, waiting to be conjured up again some future night.

Clay dreamed of Maggie, Eric, Joey, and little Kaya Bird. What is wrong with little Kaya? Kaya is staring out the window of his house, standing as if she is a statue. She appears to be in a trance, covered with perspiration. Kaya Bird seemed not to be aware of her mom or brothers. It is as if her mind is occupied with other matters. Kaya Bird must be looking for her daddy, but could not find him. The dream about his family terrified Clay.

"Maggie, Maggie, Maggie, help me!" Clay screamed. His yelling woke him up. It was morning. He had slept much longer than intended. Maggie was not here. Clay was alone. He missed his dream catcher. One pleasant dream and one filled with apprehension. Yes, if only he had brought his dream catcher there would be no nightmares.

The fire was almost out, but his clothes were dry and the cabin was still warm. Clay sat up in bed. Speaking aloud, he said; "Are dreams real or is what I consider reality a dream? Perhaps S.T is right." Once more, he missed his mystical friend.

He sensed his dreams might be a warning for the future, or a memory of the past. Long ago Clay realized there are two worlds, one of conscious reasoning and the other a world of dreams. He entered the dream world for enlightenment. Perhaps he was passing through alternate realities, allowing him to see the future and the past. Clay rubbed the back of his neck, slowly getting out of bed, leaving his dreams for another time.

The dream about Kaya depressed Clay. His family was depending on him. Clay felt better than he did when arriving at the cabin yesterday, but he was sick. Maybe his illness was induced by apprehension, but whatever the cause, his strength was declining. The mucus from his nose is still flowing and his throat is sore and tender. A fit of coughing caused Clay to hold his chest with his hands, fighting for breath until his lungs relaxed and stopped their spasms.

Clay climbed back in bed, pulling the comforter up to his chin. He rested until long after daylight. Finally, he got up and dressed. The rain had stopped falling during the night. The cabin was getting much cooler, but Clay did not throw more logs on the fire. The flames must be extinguished and cold to the touch before he would leave the cabin.

Clay sat at the table and opened one of his cans of Vienna sausages, consuming them with a half dozen Saltine crackers. He was thankful that Maggie had covered this eventuality and packed some supplies for him. After eating, he twisted a cap off a water bottle. The water tasted good.

Before leaving the cabin, Clay took care to clean up whatever he disturbed. He found a pencil and wrote a note on a piece of scrap paper, thanking the owner of the cabin and leaving his name and address so they could contact him for expenses or charges for his stay. Life is not good without honesty, he thought. He felt bad about entering the cabin without permission, but sometimes one's survival is worth taking risks. Clay put on his coat, hat and gloves. He left the cabin through the window as he had entered it. If he used the door, he would not be able to lock it from the outside. The window remained unlocked; perhaps another stranger who sought shelter someday would open it again.

The weather was about the same as yesterday morning. Partly cloudy, some westerly winds with the temperature about 40 degrees. It would warm up a bit today, but not enough for Clay to feel the difference. He started the quarter mile journey back to Highway 2. A black squirrel was eating an acorn on the pathway. It saw Clay and scampered up an oak tree. There it watched as Clay passed below on the way to the road. Once the human was gone, the squirrel disappeared.

The highway was still empty. Clay looked south toward his home. He could not go home yet. He turned his back, putting his home behind him and began trudging north on the shoulder of Highway 2. He never looked back at the cabin where he had stayed the night. There was no other choice but to continue his journey.

Alongside the road, he saw several pop cans, broken beer bottles, and assorted McDonald's restaurant bags. Uncaring drivers and passengers threw the items out of car and truck windows. Further, down the highway he could see a small two-track firebreak running off the road to the west. Even from the highway, Clay could see where people used a small clearing as a dump. There was a threadbare couch, a broken washing machine, a busted 27-inch RCA television set, and three old mattresses among the dead grass and sumac bushes. Teenage girls and boys found the mattresses handy during summer sexual escapades. They would build a campfire, drink beer, smoke dope and use the mattresses before climbing into their sleeping bags for the night. Some people uncaringly refused to recycle goods no longer needed. Other than the mattresses, the rest of the trash served no useful purpose. The beauty of the woodlands was spoiled by ugliness.

Clay looked at the dumpsite and shook his head from side to side. "Shame on you people. You dishonor America and yourselves. Recycle; don't trash the home of the forest creatures." Clay's ancestors never polluted the forest. Clay did not have time to consider this further. He would report the trash dump to the Michigan Department of Natural Resources next spring when the weather would be warmer. Clay continued walking north down the highway.

It was not long before he began to feel worse than he did yesterday. Clay could see the sun between the occasional breaks in the clouds. He pulled his coat tighter around his neck, hoping to keep warmth next to his body. It did not help. He is getting colder and shivering. The wind pulsed like a mild whisper tiptoeing across the landscape. The breeze caressed Clay, making him feel colder, letting him know that nature was in control.

"I feel like shit," he said aloud with only the animals and Mother Nature to hear him. Clay removed one glove and unbuttoning his coat, put his hand inside shirt and felt his chest. It was wet with perspiration. Clay put the palm of his hand against his forehead. He was burning up with fever. His nose was no longer dripping but plugged with mucus. No longer could he be in denial, it was not allergies causing his misery, Clay was sick. His nasal congestion felt as if a cement truck had backed up, aimed its trough up his nose and shot a full load of concrete inside it. When Clay was twelve years old, his nose was broken by a softball thrown by his dad. He missed it with his outfielder's glove as the ball sailed to him, but he was successful blocking it with the bridge of his nose. He remembered the trip to a hospital emergency room, where the doctor stuffed his nose full of cotton gauze to stop the bleeding. Today, it was worse. There was no gauze to remove to restore his capacity to breathe.

Clay's eyes itched and burned. His body is shivering so badly, he assumed his under shorts would fall off if his trousers were not preventing it. Confusion overruled rational thought as the sickness took control.

Clay is disoriented and walking without thought. His body was traveling as if on cruise control. Instinct guided him through the trees, with occasional glances at the fleeting sun. His ears were aware of the sounds of woodland wildlife, as he took step after step after step. After sneezing some of the cement out of his nose, Clay smelled the pine needles and the arid smell of rotting vegetation. The smells disappeared as his head plugged back up. Those moments of free breathing were sporadic and temporary.

Lucidity returned with shocking suddenness. Where was the highway? Clay had walked toward the sun following Sol's track as it moved toward the evening sky in the west. The highway was gone. He felt water in his boots. Clay looked down and realized he was crossing a small flowing stream, meandering through the forest. How did he get here? The flowing water seeped through his boots, stinging his feet with its coldness. Clay was lost.

"Where is my water?" He said aloud. Reaching inside his backpack, he removed one of the two remaining twenty-ounce Sam's Club plastic bottles. He twisted off the cap, tipped it over his lips and drank. A couple of minutes later he vomited the water onto the green moss covering the knoll where he stood. Clay retched, until there was nothing left to spew on the ground.

It brought back memories of the time he was lost with his dad while deer hunting at age fourteen. It was late November and snow was on the ground. Clay and his dad hiked for about four hours, before they crossed their own tracks in the snow. A check of his dad's wrist compass resulted in finding the problem. Dad had put the compass over his Timex watch. The steel watchcase caused the needle to point in the wrong direction. Therefore, no matter which way he turned, it was north. After removing the compass and holding it in his hands, his dad guided both of them out of the woods.

Clay was lost again, but this time he had no compass. He could occasionally see the sun through the clouds. This would provide him an inaccurate compass by observing its movement across the sky. If he headed north, he would be paralleling the highway and could travel several miles without crossing a road. If he followed the sun, which had already crossed its zenith, he could end in Antler Valley, a huge deer hunting area covering many square miles of wilderness, void of humanity. He opted to head north, keeping the late afternoon sun over his left shoulder. Clay tried to compensate for the Sun's more southerly location because of the late fall season.

The sun, his most faithful compass was stating to disappear, dropping below his vision among the tall trees. It would be dark in about forty-five minutes or so. Clay had stopped shivering, but he knew it was important to find shelter for protection from the weather. Although Clay thought he must be close to a road or two-track firebreak, there was no time to find it. He looked for shelter. Clay realized he should have returned to his home and family after spending the night in the cabin. It was too late. He no longer knew where he was.

In a small grove of maple trees, Clay found a small deer blind, which was built by an archery deer hunter before the October 1st start of deer season. This would at least offer some temporary shelter. The hunter had built it by stacking dead logs, brush, and twigs against three maple trees forming a triangle. It made a good camouflage hideout for hunting. The deer blind could provide him with some protection but it would be cold. If he could reinforce the deer blind and make it larger before it became dark, Clay had a chance to survive.

Tears formed in his eyes, but again he refused to let his emotions follow the temptations of his eyes. God, he missed Maggie and the kids, would he ever see them again?

Clay pulled his hunting knife out of its sheath and cut branches off a red pine tree, stacking them next to the deer blind. He hacked on some larger boughs, removing some of the smaller branches to use for interweaving the larger ones together, forming a windbreak to provide protection and block the rain if it returned. It took only moments to complete the task. He stored his knife back into the sheath, locking it place. He was thankful for having the foresight to bring it with him.

Clay entered the blind. He curled up in a fetal position, pulling the smaller pine branches over the top of him. He was shivering again. Removing the top of his last bottle of water, Clay sipped it as if it was the finest bourbon whiskey. Clay hoped that drinking small sips of water would prevent the nausea he experienced earlier.

The Michigan sky clouds up before dusk and darkness arrives quickly. A slight cold rain was falling, enough to sprinkle some water droplets on the pine branches covering the deer blind. However, not enough rain to get Clay wet. As the darkness consumes the daylight, so the sounds of the woods emerge with the scampering of nocturnal creatures. A strange world emerges, one of scampering feet of raccoons, skunks, woodchucks and other creatures. Clay listened to the movement in the brush around him, as something scurried across his encampment. Animals and forest creatures would not hurt him; it was part of Clay's ancestral heritage to live in the forest and be part of the woodlands.

It was not long before Clay entered a cold, restive sleep. Before going to sleep, his eyes betrayed his body. He cried. He knew he could freeze and die while sleeping. He cried for his family, not himself. Clay had been stupid to leave them at home.

The sleep masked the cold air as Clay dreamed about an old man in a tropical climate. A younger woman and man were standing next to him. The woman was screaming and the old man was trying to comfort her. Clay dreamed there was a sinkhole in the old man's yard, and the young man was slipping into it. The young man yelled; "Help me, help me, help me."

The old man reached to help him, but the young man kept pulling his hands out of the old man's reach. He continued to slip deeper into the hole. The old man stood up and spoke to the young man. "Sometimes," the old man said, "you can only help yourself." The young man disappeared and the hole closed.

The dream faded. Clay began dreaming that he was driving a taxicab. A man opened the door, climbed into the backseat and yelled, "Take me where it is safe!" Clay started driving off, stopped, and looked into the mirror to see his passenger. "How can I take you where it is safe when I don't know where I am?" A closer look at his passenger revealed his own face on the person sitting in the back seat. He was dreaming of himself.

Infection was rampant in Clay as his body began shivering and sweating at the same time. His clothing was damp from his perspiration and the sporadic rain. Once more, Clay lost his sense of reality.

He reached over to put his arm around Maggie in his bed. She was not there. Where did she go? "Where are my kids?" All cognitive awareness of the carnal world left him. Clay was delirious. He was preparing to die. However, death would not come. The mystical dream world of his ancestors was controlling his inner consciousness.

Clay was with Thunder Eagle, in a sweat lodge. All the leaders of his Huichol tribe were sitting in a circle within the lodge. Clay was to be the Shaman successor to Thunder Eagle. It was an important time for the tribe. Thunder Eagle was seeking a vision. A flickering light radiated from the buffalo dung and wild grass campfire. Within the fire were several large sacred stones. Naked warriors sat with their legs crossed almost touching one another staring into the flames. Each man sat with his open hands resting upside down on their knees, fingers together in the shape of a cup. A large clay jug of water sat beside each warrior. Each warrior would pour water on the rocks, causing the steam to rise, raising the Sweat Lodge's temperature. Thunder Eagle held three brightly painted dream disks he had drawn from a previous vision. As shaman, only Thunder Eagle was allowed to touch them. He waved the disks first to the sky, then towards the four corners of the Earth. Once the task was completed, he put them on the ground in front of the fire. There were no other disks. A Dream Catcher was hanging behind Thunder Eagle, from which he had removed the disks for the ceremony. He would reattach the disks later. Clay recognized the dream catcher as the same one given to him by Grandma Clay Bird Spirit long ago.

This was Clay's first sweat lodge experience. To Clay, it is a real event, whether in his flesh or in his spirit, it mattered not. Clay felt perspiration break from his forehead, and his naked body covered with sweat. Thunder Eagle handed Clay two peyote buttons, obtained from the tops of a peyote cactus seven days before the ceremony.

Clay poured a jar of water onto the rocks. The steam boiled off causing a thick fog to form inside the hut. He opened his mouth and chewed a peyote button, keeping one for later. His grandfather chewed three buttons that he had kept for himself.

The salt from Clay's steamed body caused his eyes to sting, blurring his vision as perspiration dripped from his forehead. Both Thunder Eagle and his apprentice Shaman would see a vision, if the Great Spirit were receptive to their request.

Clay's carnal body squirmed and tossed around in the deer blind where he was shivering from the cold. His dream journey continued while he experienced REM sleep. The dream world assumed full reality. He was leaving a carnal existence and entering the inner world, where the spirits would share their knowledge; teaching him the ways of his ancestors. He chanted with the leaders, as the sweat lodge continued becoming warmer, filled with cloudy steam rolling off the heated rocks. Clay reached for his second peyote button, put it in his mouth and chewed it. His head and body became weightless. His eyes continued to roll around in their orbital sockets, searching, looking, and seeking.

Clay reached for his water jug and poured its remaining contents on the rocks. A mass of steam arose, almost burning him. One rock cracked from the water, the explosion reverberating throughout the lodge. This is a good sign. It was the sign he was seeking. Clay's head dropped down with his chin resting on his chest. He was becoming the tribe's Shaman.

As Clay's body slept in the physical world, his brain produced alpha waves. He found his spirit traveling in a deep strange forest. His tribe knew nothing about these new trees, because in Mexico where they lived, there were no forests like this one. He journeyed far, and the Great Spirit was with him.

Clay was running through the woods. He was a male deer, huge in stature with the markings of kingship on his head. The huge rack was his crown. Clay realized the male deer was to be his totem, not temporarily but forever. The deer was his animal guide, his protector, and his mentor. It would always serve as his teacher. Clay saw himself as part of nature, as the deer was also part of him. All of nature was one and he was one with nature.

Clay loved being the deer. He was elated to run, jump and smell the forest woodlands. His sensitive deer nose picked up the scent of man. He stopped running and began studying the sick man walking through the rain and underbrush. He decided to guide the man, serving as his protector. The portal between the worlds opened, the buck and the stranger passed through the opening to find a cabin on the other side. It was to be a cabin of refuge.

Clay woke from his dream. He knew who and where he was. He was no longer perspiring in the Sweat Lodge; but was damp and cold, curled up tightly trying to stay warm. The deer blind could shield him from the biting wind and occasional sprinkle of rain accompanied by snow, but would not warm him. Did his deer totem travel from the past, or was it he who traveled back into yesteryear?

Again, Clay missed his Dream Catcher. Perhaps there was truth to what his Great Grandmother Clay Bird Spirit had tried to teach him about Indian folklore. This dream was not a premonition of the future, but it was an explanation of what had already occurred. He went back to sleep, this time his sleep was not broken by visions.

Chapter 51

Dave Stoneman was seventeen years old. With the power failure and school buses not running, he missed going to school. Dave's grades were above normal but not extraordinary, although his track skills were. He was a runner and outdoorsman, like many young men living in northern Michigan. Dave ran with the high school track team and had placed second to Reynard Beckman by a scant three seconds in the mile run. This would be Dave's last year of high school. Dave had already signed up to attend Grand Valley State University near Grand Rapids, assisted by a fifty-percent track scholarship. The rest of his tuition would be paid through student loans. Dave would miss his parents and living in northern Michigan. To get a good education, it would be necessary to attend the University, but he would visit his parents during spring break next year and between semesters. Dave knew his future needed the sacrifice of living in a large city for a few years. This was today's plan, but often tomorrow brings a different destiny. Unknown to Dave, the massive power failure would change his life's plans, as it would for the rest of Earth's population. He would never attend college.

With nothing to do, no way to go to school, Dave decided to go poaching for deer behind his dad's house. Like secluded people, Dave and his parents raised vegetables and had some stored for the winter. With the freezer not working, his family was out of meat. Many isolated people in Michigan poached deer. Most of the local Game Wardens looked the other way when residents hunted out of season. They concentrated on catching poachers who came from the southern parts of Michigan into their north woods. If deer were hunted illegally, it would be us locals who would do it, not outsiders. Rifle hunting season wouldn't open until November 15th. Dave's family needed meat and his chances were better using a rifle, not his bow and arrows.

For local residents, poaching fulfilled two purposes, one to protect the farmers' crops from the deer and secondly, to provide meat for their tables. A few hungry deer could eat several hundred dollars' worth of corn from a field and strip an apple tree.

Dave planned to go hunting behind the old single-wire barbed fence at the edge of the ravine behind his house. The wire separated his dad's property from land owned by the State of Michigan, designated for hunters, hikers, and anglers.

The house was located a half mile off Jeanette Road, which crossed Highway 2. During the legal deer season, Dave would be out of the house before daylight, hiding in his deer blind, waiting to kill the first buck daring to cross his path after sunrise. Today was not different, except he would kill either a buck or doe for meat, unless the doe had a late season fawn with her. Dave got out of bed at six A.M., using a flashlight to find his way to the kitchen. After lighting a candle, he returned to his bedroom and put on his hunting clothes. He preferred using his 60# pull Darton compound bow with three tip razor broad heads. Today, Dave opened his dad's gun cabinet, took out his Remington 30:06 and a handful of 180-grain hollow point shells. The gun was a semi-automatic, the most popular hunting rifle used in Michigan.

It was necessary to make sure his boots and clothing were clean before going into the woods. Deer can smell human scent from a long way off. Dave's breakfast consisted of a cup of coffee and a roll. He fried no eggs today. The smell of eggs was another scent the deer picked up from a man's body. Although a hearty breakfast of bacon and eggs sounded tasty, he knew if he consumed them, it would be a waste of time to go hunting.

After exiting his dad's home, Dave sprinkled a few drops of female deer urine on the tops of each boot. This was the secret of good hunting, according to Michigan Outdoors magazine. He always purchased a couple of bottles of the stuff from Bob Johnson's Sporting Goods store just before hunting season.

Dave's mom frowned on the smell of deer piss on the carpet. She did not approve of him using his money to buy bottles of animal urine. During the summer growing season, Dave's dad purchased bottles of Coyote urine to spray around the edge of their small vegetable garden. This kept the rabbits from eating the beans, carrots, and lettuce. They never told Dave's mom what the product contained, just telling her it was animal repellent. Critters such as rabbits, a potential meal for coyotes, would recognize the urine smell and stay out of the garden. A Michigan teenage boy considered his first deer hunting experience to be an initiation ritual into manhood. Most northern Michigan high schools authorized a couple excused days from classes for a boy to go deer hunting with his father every year. More so in northern Michigan than in the southern parts of the State where the large cities and most of the population lived. The northern Michigan school felt it helped bond a son to his father. The sport was not limited to boys, but fewer girls and women hunted than men did.

Dave compromised with his mom by leaving his boots outside the house after hunting, with the intention of washing them off if he did not hunt in the evening. The scent of female deer urine would mask his human smell and attract male deer. He put the stuff on his boots to create a false trail, hoping the male deer would smell it and follow him, intending to find a doe waiting to breed. The trail would lead to Dave, a big mistake for any buck wanting to get laid.

Like many good deer hunters, Dave preferred to walk slow and stalk his prey on the way to his hunting spot where he would sit and wait for a buck to walk in front of him. He trained himself to walk slowly and deliberately, moving as if he were a mime. It was important to put his feet down gently, not making more noise than necessary. If he felt a twig under his descending boot, he would stop and place his foot in another area to prevent the noise of a breaking twig. Dave picked up each foot, raising it above the dormant undergrowth and quietly placing it back down, making slow forward progress.

The sun was starting to show itself above the edge of the southeastern horizon as Dave left the fence line behind his dad's property. The hidden mysteries of the darkness gave way to revealing ghostly silhouettes. Dave intended to check some scrapings a buck had left on a tree yesterday. The tree was about fifty yards from the fence. A female deer would urinate on the ground near some trees. The male, finding the scent of the female, would scrape the trees with his horns, piss on her piss, and hope that she would return for mating purposes. When the male deer returned, he would find a bullet instead of sex, if Dave got there before the doe.

Dave saw some fresh deer tracks disturbing the morning dew and started following them. A huge buck, one with an enormous rack, likely made the tracks. He could determine this from the size of the prints and the heavy imprint into the wet grass. A large dear left heavy four-toe prints, whereas a fawn or doe only showed the front toes, not those located higher up on the deer's feet. The tracks led through the wild grass and the green moss undergrowth covering the ground. The first morning sound came from a woodpecker hammering for bugs in a nearby fallen rotted elm tree. All the squirrels were hiding. They would stay hidden until later when the sun came out.

As he was following the tracks, Dave saw that they led to the deer blind he had built and used during archery season. From two hundred feet away, the blind looked disturbed, somehow different. He decided to investigate.

There could be a bear hiding in the blind. Bears are common in upper part of the lower peninsula of Michigan. Black bears are not harmful to humans, unless molested by them. Even then, under normal circumstances they flee rather than engage in a confrontation. Dave's senses became fine-tuned and his heart started racing. There is nothing better than hunting to get one's adrenalin flowing. He would peek into the blind and if a bear was there, not disturb it. He had no desire to kill a bear nor eat its meat, which was full of marbled fat, unlike the lean meat of venison.

The wind whispered ghostly sounds as it traveled through the trees. As Dave crept closer, the forest was waking up. He listened to chickadees singing, joining the woodpecker. There was a distant crow involved in a loud verbal territorial dispute with another species of bird. The last leaves of a silver maple tree drifted down in front of Dave as he stepped forward. Dave reached the deer blind. He had not made a sound. Gently, oh, so very gently he parted some of the pine branches, hoping not to disturb a bear if one was inside it. The branches moved. A hand and arm reached outside towards him.

"Holy Jesus in Heaven!" Shouted Dave. "God, man, you scarred the Hell out of me!"

A pathetic looking man lay shivering among the branches. The man had a muscular build and was around fifteen years Dave's senior. At once, Dave could tell the man was not a hunter sitting in his blind, but seemed delirious and appeared sick.

"Joey? Eric? Is that you?" The stranger asked. "Just let me be. Let me go." He reclined into the pine branches and started pulling one of the larger pieces back over him.

"Mister, quit screwing around and get up. Do you want to die here? If you don't move, you will get your wish and die." David said.

Dave took a couple of deep breaths to compose himself. "Hey, guy, something is wrong with you. What are you doing out here? Are you nuts? I can't believe you're alive. Damn you look bad. Let me give you a hand and I'll take you to our house. My dad and mom can take care of you. Mister, you're a lot bigger than me. You're going to have to help me. I'll help you stand up, and you can lean on me. We are only about a quarter mile from my home."

Before reaching for the stranger, Dave removed the four shot clip from the rifle, putting the ammunition into his left jacket pocket. Dave opened the breach of his rifle and removed the shell from the chamber. He expanded the sling on the gun before hanging the rifle on his left shoulder. This man's life was more important than killing a deer.

"I'm Dave Stoneman." The young man said.

"I'm Clay Wheeler. I live somewhere south of here, with my wife and kids."

"Grab my arm, Mr. Wheeler; I'll get you back to my house."

Clay supported himself against Dave. Abruptly turning his head, he sneezed downwind a couple of times and coughed, hacking up a spot of blood with gobs of yellow mucus. He spit the liquid onto the mossy ground. "Sorry," replied Clay. "Maggie and the kids are, are, are, I don't know, my mind seems all fogged in. I'm freezing."

"Just call me Dave, but I doubt you will remember who I am. Lean against this tree and let me get you something to help you walk."

Dave reached over and broke off a branch about two inches in diameter and three feet long from a fallen tree. He stripped it clean of twigs and leaves before handing it to Clay.

"Use this as a walking stick to help yourself. Just grasp it with your right hand and I will support your left side. You have to help me, sir. I cannot get you home by myself, you're too damn big. Let's get going if you want to live."

"You must be suffering from hypothermia besides having one bad cold or flu bug," said Dave. The pair reached the fence line and made their way through a small grove of huge White Pine trees toward Dave's home.

Chapter 52

Ten minutes later, Clay looked at the world through dazed eyes, seeing the brown colored exterior door of a house. The house was upwards of fifty years old, but someone had installed white vinyl siding over the original cedar shakes. Clay was aware of someone with him, but it was as if he was dreaming. Everything is strange. He drifts in a twilight world between reality and something in the past. He continues to feel both hot and cold at the same time. His companion opened the door and held it with his left shoulder, banging his rifle butt against the screen as they struggled to get inside. After entering the house, Clay sat down on an old stuffed living room chair. It was warm here.

"What the heck is going on, Dave?" Glen Stoneman put down the book he was reading, stood and hurried over to his son, looking at the man who collapsed onto a chair. "Who is he? Where is he from? What happened? Are you all right, son?"

"ANNA, HEY Anna" Glen hollered. "ANNA, please bring a cup of hot tea in here with you. Where did you find him, Dave?"

"He was laying in my old deer blind at the end of our fence row, dad. I thought a black bear might be sleeping in there, so I decided to check it out. When this man reached his hand out from under some pine branches, I swear dad, he scared the hell out of me."

"I hope your finding him won't bring us bad luck, son." Glen scowled.

Dave stooped down, resting his butt on one foot and lying his elbow on his knee. He grasped the stranger's boots, unzipped them, and pulled them off.

"Dad, do you mind helping me with his coat?"

Glen was far ahead of his son, beginning to remove the man's wool jacket. The coat was damp and stained from the dirty moss and branches where Clay had slept.

Clay was hardly aware of what was going on. "I'm Clay Wheeler. I live, I live, I live down on highway 2. Where am I? What is the matter with me? Where are Maggie and the kids? God, I feel sick." He started to tremble and shiver. Once his jacket was removed, Clay sat back, closed his eyes and said nothing more. He continued to alternate in and out of consciousness.

"Don't worry Mr. Wheeler." Turning towards Dave, Glen continued; "You might have saved his life, son. This man is sick. I don't believe he understands anything we are saying. I sure don't need his goddamn problems, whatever they are. Only a crazy man will sleep in the woods at night. Holy Christ." Glen shook his head and made a growling sound. "He is talking about other people. You didn't see anyone else near the hunting blind did you?"

"No, the man is confused. As far as I could see, he was alone, Dad."

"Now son, you know by bringing him here, we will be exposed to whatever disease he has. You know I don't need to get sick. I'm getting away from him, so you and your Mom take him into the spare bedroom. I don't want him contaminating the living room."

Dave helped the stranger out of his clothes. Moments later, Anna entered the room, carrying a hot teapot with one hand and a china cup in the other. Anna put the teapot on the oak nightstand, carefully setting the cup on the nightstand.

"David, this man is very sick. Pull back the covers on the bed. Let's get him into bed. I'll make him drink this cup of hot tea which may help warm him. He has a real high fever. He needs liquids in his body to fight the infection. Poor soul, I don't know how he survived out in the cold last night. He knew how to take care of himself or he would be dead. He could have frozen or choked to death in his sleep. The man is a survivor and we'll do what we can to keep him alive."

Clay felt better once he was undressed and in bed. He sat up and sipped the warm liquid, although he didn't know how he got here. He remembered the shock of seeing a face staring at him in the deer blind, then seeing an older man and woman. The blank areas of his memory were many, without coherence, as if someone edited a film of his life while leaving certain details on the cutting room floor. Clay was living by his ancestral survival instinct. He sipped the tea continuing to shiver image faded from Clay's thoughts.

Chapter 53

Anna asked Dave, "Did this man tell you his name and what he was doing alone in the woods?"

"He said his name was Clay Wheeler, that's all I know, Mom."

"That's not much Dave, but I'm sure he will tell us more tomorrow. Let's leave him for the night. She took her son's arm, leading him out of the bedroom so Clay could sleep.

The Michigan weather was consistent. It was another cool, damp morning. Frost covered the tree branches and leaves. Snow continued to fall to the ground during the night. Before daybreak, Dave got out of bed, and went deer hunting.

Just before noon, Anna heard Dave return, without any meat. Earlier she had looked in on her uninvited guest. His body showed no signs of frostbite, which could have been disastrous without the ability to get the man to a hospital. However, not everything was good.

Anna recognized the symptoms of pneumonia and Clay Wheeler had them. During the night, they heard him cough hard enough to lob millions of airborne viruses or bacteria, whatever version of the disease he had, all through his bedroom. Before her family got out of bed, Anna arose early and sprayed the cabin with Lysol disinfectant, hoping it would kill any contaminants Mr. Wheeler was propelling everywhere with his coughing and sneezing.

Chapter 54

Glen was depressed. He was supposed to stay away from crowds to avoid exposure to diseases. Now, for Christ's sake, he had a sick man staying in his house, living under his roof. If Glen wanted to be around people, his family would still be living in Lansing, Michigan not isolated in the woodlands. Fate had kicked him in the ass many times during his life; with the stranger sleeping in his house, Glen could feel fates' boot once more bouncing off his rear end. Glen slowly shook his head in dismay and strolled into his radio shack. Glen would love to go hunting with his son, but three plugged arteries, replaced by a coronary by-pass operation three years ago limited his activities.

Glen was an amateur radio operator. For many years, he enjoyed listening to police agencies on scanners. However, his scanners were useless since moving to northern Michigan. Scanners are only good for receiving short distance communication in or near cities, not for wilderness living. Most government agencies currently use digital communication, not compatible with Glen's analog scanners. His most valued radios were his collection of old short-wave receivers and four old transceivers. Most of his equipment predated modern solid-state radios and are powered by a large assortment of batteries charged by a windmill generator sitting alongside his house. He made the windmill charger himself out of a generator taken out of his '55' Chevy and a small airplane propeller. God, Glen wished he had kept the Chevy, with the generator intact. Who would have known the '55' Chevy would eventually become valued as an antique? Providence plays unusual games with people. The non-solid state generator still worked as it contained a simple core winding with carbon brushes picking up electricity from the armature as it rotated in the wind. Once he combined it with an old voltage regulator, also taken from the Chevy, it was enough to charge the batteries connected to his ham radio equipment. Glen's batteries are connected in series to raise the voltage. A converter was used to change the batteries output from direct current to alternating current in order to produce 110 volts AC current and power his radios.

Glen had scanned the lower frequency radio bands two days ago, hearing a ham operator. The signal was weak and his batteries were getting low, so he did not try to communicate with the operator. Glen could not understand what was being said, because of the low signal strength. Glen turned off his transceiver so his batteries would not get too drained and no longer be rechargeable. The deep cycle batteries were old. He bought them from a friend of his who took the batteries out of two golf carts, replacing them with new deep cycle batteries. They still worked, but their best working days had been on the golf course. Glen never considered buying new batteries with his limited social security income, nor did he expect to rely on the batteries as his only source of electrical power for his radio equipment.

Glen powered his transceiver back up, and locked into the frequency where he had heard a voice two days ago. The voice was back with a stronger signal. Glen's concentration was interrupted as Dave burst into the house, closing the door hard behind him. No deer today, otherwise his son would have shouted his success.

"Dave," hollered Glen. "Come in the radio room with me and listen to this. I hear something on the 11-meter band."

"Be there in a minute, Dad." Dave threw his hunting coat on the back of a chair and leaned his rifle against the corner of the kitchen wall, next to the back door. He grabbed a Michigan delicious apple from the pantry, wiped it off on his shirtsleeve and took a bite, carrying the apple with him into his dad's radio room. Dave opened a folding chair and sat next to his dad, who was tuning the radio.

"Have patience, son" said Glen who was talking more to himself than Dave. "I'm having trouble pulling the signal out. The damn batteries are only running on 70% amperage."

"I hear a voice on the radio, but I can't make out what the operator is saying. I heard him say something about his old tube type radios but I could not understand more. I'm going trim the antenna and see if we can contact him."

Glen turned a potentiometer on his old Hallicrafter's receiver/transceiver unit, to increase the audio gain. He followed by tweaking the notch filter to narrow the frequency hoping to filter out some of the background noise. The quality and clarity of the sound increased.

"Ah, to hell with F.C.C. protocol," said Glen as he disgustedly keyed the microphone. "Skip land. Skip land. Skip land. This is 1136 in Michigan getting back to you. This here is the Hobo, ten-four. You got a copy on this here, breaker?" There was no reply.

"Ah shit, nothing yet." He keyed the microphone again. "CQ, CQ, CQ, CQ, DX." Then he repeated his often-used CB handle of "Hobo". "Can you read me? --Copy?"

The radio continued to crackle, with an occasional voice breaking through the static. "I suppose the propagation is not good, son. I better turn the radio off, let the generator recharge the batteries and try later. I'll leave it tuned to this frequency and try tonight after it gets dark. Propagation conditions will be better after the sun goes down."

A frustrated Glen turned off the radio. He flipped a mechanical gear to engage the drive belt from the windmill to the generator, so the batteries would at least regain some of their lost charge before nightfall. There was no sound, but a low voltage indicator bulb showed a flickering orange glow just above his bench, assuring Glen the batteries were charging. He shoved his chair back, put his feet on the radio desk. He was deep in thought and for the moment, ignoring his son.

Dave broke the silence. "I'm bored, dad."

Dave was fidgeting with the chair where he was sitting. Glen figured Dave missed his girlfriends and school.

"No problem Dave, I can fix your boredom for you, yes sir. Just go help your mom in the kitchen. Help her cook supper, which is almost a full-time job for her since we lost electricity." replied Glen, with a sarcastic smile

"Yeah, thanks, dad. That's what I wanted to do. Yeah. I won't have time to help because I'm going hunting again this evening." Without giving his dad an opportunity to reply, Dave stood up, pushing back his chair.

"Dad, if you can hook-up the radio to the batteries, why can't you do it with my computer? It'll run on low voltage, you know. I could play "Civilization" or Hoyle card games, or at least do something."

"I tried to use your computer yesterday, Dave. Nothing happened. Your computer wouldn't turn on. I couldn't get the picture on the monitor to light up, everything was dead. I tried to use the 5000-watt generator to power it, but it would not run either. Damn that generator, I bought it just to use in times like this and it will not start. I will take the damn thing back to Lowe's once this crisis is over. It was supposed to have a five-year warranty. I don't understand why my old tube radios will work and solid-state equipment like your computer and the gasoline powered generator will not. I am worried about what is going on. It doesn't make sense." Glen rested his elbow on the desk, holding his head in his hand. "Hey, are you going to help your mom or not?"

"Okay, I'm out of here." Dave threw the apple core into the wastebasket beside Glen's chair and stomped out of the room.

Glen felt sorry for his son, remembering how he felt at age seventeen. It is the age when you feel you're a man, are treated like a child and apprehensive about your future. Those were the years Glen wished he could live again to correct mistakes in his life. However, he had a good wife, a loving son, and was still alive. His plan to have a huge bank account and drive a new pickup truck changed when the damn heart attack screwed up his future. With his working days cut short; he applied for Social Security disability income and retired.

Glen pushed back his chair, stood up and left the radio room. Glen's favorite movie was "The Butterfly Effect." The movie was about traveling back in time to change events in one's life, altering present circumstances. If Glen could do so, he would exercise more to prevent the heart attack. He would run for public office to change a system of government, which was broken. Instead, he was living with a meager income in a cabin. Sure, there could be grandchildren someday, but Glen only thought short-term, knowing how frail his health was. His thoughts were for his wife and son, not himself.

Before going to bed, Glen peaked in the bedroom at Mr. Wheeler, who was either sleeping or semi-comatose. One way or another, Glen didn't give a damn. Why couldn't someone besides Dave find this man? Fate had plugged up Glen's arteries requiring a by-pass operation. Once more, fate threatening him with whatever disease Mr. Wheeler brought in his house. Glen's chin dropped to his chest and he slowly swung his head back and forth. How could Dave and Anna survive if he got sick or died? If only he could go back in time and change the present. Only the future can be changed, but what happens today is dependent on a flawed past for Glen.

Glen left the stranger's bedroom and slowly entered the bathroom, closing the door behind him. He took great care to wash his hands every time he was exposed to his guest. He poured Witch Hazel on his hands. Witch Hazel was amazing stuff to Glen. He used it for after-shave, insect bites, and hair tonic. Besides, it was cheap and Glen refused to pay for expensive smelly stuff to splash on his face and hair. Perhaps it would prevent him from getting sick. His last task was squirting a gob of hand sanitizer on his fingers, rubbing it into his hands. One could not be too careful.

Evening came. Anna and Glen had a limited amount of food but a good supply of kerosene and lamps. She had collected antique lamps and until now, the only purpose they served was the exquisite display on a shelf in her dining room. The wicks were good and if they limited the lamps use, Glen had enough fuel to last for ages. Burning kerosene permeated the house with an unpleasant smell. Yet, Anna did not mind the odor. Whatever pleased Glen pleased her.

Dave failed to get a deer again. After Mr. Wheeler woke up, Dave helped him into the bathroom. The man was still incoherent, but at least he knew enough to use the toilet.

It was dark and two kerosene lamps glowed with a flickering yellow light. Anna used one and Glen carried the other throughout the house. Anna looked in on Mr. Wheeler. He was awake but still not coherent. She left the bedroom and returned with another cup of hot tea, which Clay drank. A few minutes later, she returned with some of chicken broth in a cup.

Clay drank part of it, hacked out some nasty looking substance from his lungs, drank more broth and lay down. His sinuses were plugged, but beginning to drain. Anna put a full box of tissues next to his bed and inserted a plastic bag into the wastebasket beside the nightstand for him. Shortly afterwards, Clay was sleeping.

Glen Stoneman heated the family's house with a large wood burner stove located between the living room and the dining area. This is a common practice in older Michigan homes without forced air furnaces. Dave would cut up dead trees found in the woods during summer. This provided enough firewood to last through the winter, without using expensive fuel oil or liquid propane gas for heating, which Glen could not afford. For heat to circulate in his home, it was important to leave the inside doors of the house partially open. Glen made sure his unwanted guest's door was open a few inches, double-checking to make sure Anna had not opened it more than necessary. Glen was determined to keep whatever germ or sickness the man has confined to his bedroom. So far, he had managed to keep his anger controlled and not complain about the man's presence.

Glen entered his radio room and sat down in a chair. He hesitated, before turning on his transceiver. The batteries were not charged much more than when he turned the unit off six hours earlier. The wind outside was not blowing enough to spin the old generator to collect a quick charge. It would be futile to attempt communication tonight with low amperage. Glen stood up, pushed back his chair and took his lamp, making his way to his bedroom.

The bedroom was cool. Glen did not bother to put on his pajamas, but pulled off his shirt, dropped his pants to the floor and climbed into bed next to Anna, leaving his socks and underwear on. He was tired. Sleep came quickly.

The next day was a repeat of the one before. Glen decided to let the batteries continue to charge a second day, perhaps longer if necessary, hoping to get them back to maximum working capacity before turning on his transceiver radio again.

Their unwanted guest - at least this was what Glen considered him, remained confined to his sick room. Anna found a bottle of aspirin tablets, although they smelled old and vinegary, started giving them to Mr. Wheeler, hoping his fever would go down. The aspirin did its job.

Another day, another night passed. It had been four days since Clay arrived at Glen's and Anna's home. Anna got up before her husband and son, put on her robe and slippers and entered Clay's room.

Clay was awake. "Where am I?" "What am I doing here? I'm soaking wet. How long have I been here? Who are you?" Clay looked confused, but at least he was lucid.

"Well, I guess we'll have this conversation again. We have been through this a few times before, but you don't remember. I'm Anna Stoneman. My son, David found you in his old deer blind behind the house. You either have a bad case of the flu or pneumonia, or both. I'm no doctor, but I have managed to keep my family well for many years. I had doubts about your surviving when David brought you here, but you're going to make it. My husband, Glen is in the living room, you haven't seen much of him, nor are you likely to do so. He's not fond of guests."

"Where are Maggie and the kids?"

"Was someone else with you? David said you were alone. Oh Lord, I hope we didn't leave anyone else out there!"

"NO, no," replied Clay. "Maggie is my wife; Joey, Eric and Kaya are our children. I left them back in our house on the highway before taking off. Being concerned for the safety and comfort of my family, I was trying to find out why we lost our electricity and no cars were running or airplanes flying. That's why I was hiking down the highway. I got sick and disoriented. If it wasn't for your son and family, I would be frozen dead in the snow somewhere."

Anna looked relieved after finding out Clay was alone in the woods. "Thank God. I assume your family members are still okay." Anna was standing at the side of his bed, looking at Clay. She touched his forehead with the back of her hand.

"That's enough talking for now. It appears your fever broke during the night and you have perspired on everything. I'll get you a pair of Glen's pajamas, I'm sure it will not make him happy, but you can wear them. I'll bring you a washbasin full of water and you can wash up and change. Lordy, your bed is wetter than a baby's diaper! You will need some fresh sheets. Before you make your bed, I'll get a pan of water and be back in a bit." Anna turned and retreated out of the bedroom, closing the door behind her.

Clay threw the bed covers back, careful to keep his body covered by the sheet and sat up in the bed. Turning, he rested his weight on his arms as he waited for Anna.

A few minutes later, Anna entered the room carrying a small basin of cool water and a blue washcloth with matching towel draped across her arm. She sat the pan and bar of Dial soap on the nightstand next to Clay.

"Don't have any hot water, but here's some that's not as cold as when comes out of our artesian well. We keep a bucket of water sitting beside the wood burner. It gets none too warm, but the chill is gone. Go ahead, wash up and change your clothes. Here are some clean sheets, so if you can change your bed, just put the dirty ones in a pile. I'll get them later. Don't be shy; you don't have anything special to be seen anyhow." She smiled.

"Thank you" replied Clay. He sat up in bed, dragging his fingers through his hair before rubbing the back of his neck. Anna left his room.

*****

It troubled Clay to be dependent on strangers. He was giddy as he swung his legs to the side of the bed and sat up. The room was spinning, at first he did not know if he would sit up, throw up, or fall off the bed. He lowered his head for a moment until the world stabilized. Clay reached over and began using the pan of water. He had no business here, yet, destiny saved his life, putting him with this family for a purpose. Clay washed his face, splashing water on his long straight black hair, pulling it back out of his eyes. In his life, Clay had never been dependent on anyone; perhaps this was another lesson to teach him humbleness, to honor his Indian heritage and himself. After cleaning up, Clay made his bed and went peacefully to sleep for the first time in days.

Chapter 55

Just as daylight approached, Glen woke up and crawled out of bed, careful not to awaken Anna. A few moments later, he left their bedroom and gathered a couple of pieces of firewood from the pile stored away from the wood burner. Opening the door of the unit, he tossed the kindling inside. It would take a few minutes before it ignited by drawing fire off the glowing coals at the bottom of the chamber. Although David had cut the wood for the winter, Glen helped him by using a manual hydraulic wood splitter to section the logs for proper size. Splitting the wood made it burn cleaner and more efficient. His heart doctor allowed him to use the splitter, but Dave did the rest of the work. Glen didn't know what he would do when his son left for college. Dave said he would still spend the summers at home and cut enough firewood for his mom and dad. However, in a few years, Dave would have a family and his own responsibilities. The day would arrive when he and Anna would relocate closer to doctors and shopping centers. Glen hoped it would be years from now. Anna was a strong woman and could extend the years they lived in the woods by doing most of the work. It hurt Glen to know Anna would be taking care of him, rather than he taking care of her during their senior years.

Glen took a teakettle, filled it with water and put it on the wood stove to heat. He looked at Clay's bedroom, and shook his head. This fool, who was crawling with microbes, interrupted his isolation and health by sleeping in the damn deer blind. Nothing worked in Glen's favor

Forty minutes later, the water began to boil. Glen sat down at the kitchen table and poured the steaming liquid into his cup, while scooping in a teaspoon of instant coffee. Just as he was adding dry creamer and sugar in the cup, he heard a noise behind him.

Clay opened his bedroom door and walked slowly into the dining area. He stopped, looked over at his benefactor and continued into the room, sitting down at the table with Glen. "Thank you for taking care of me. Please, just call me Clay." He reached out his hand.

"WHAT THE HELL ARE YOU DOING? For Christ's sake, get back into the bedroom and stay there a few more days. Man, I have a heart condition, and I don't want to catch whatever the hell virus that kicked your ass. Maybe we would be better off if Dave had left you to freeze in the woods." Glen was seething.

Clay withdrew his hand. "I'm sorry. I understand what you're saying. Please forgive me. I have a wife and three kids down the road. I was trying to find out what happened to our electricity when I got sick. Just give me a couple of days to recover and I'll leave your home."

Glen slid his chair back, stood and moved away from Clay. "Okay, okay. Sorry to be so blunt, but hell man, I can't get sick. I'm Glen Stoneman, told you my name several times, but you don't remember. I might get some information about the power problem and when I do, you will know. In the meantime, get back in your bedroom. I have an old transceiver short-wave radio, which is working, so I'll try to get information tonight when transmitting and receiving conditions are right. So far, I haven't been successful. Don't take too much offense in what I'm telling you, but please GET THE HELL OUT OF HERE AND GO BACK INTO THE BEDROOM. I don't want to shake your hand. I don't want to touch you. Don't you get it? This conversation is over."

Clay seemed perplexed. "No problem. I'm sorry. Please accept my apology." Clay stood up, left the table and walked back into the bedroom.

Chapter 56

A nna had overheard the confrontation between Clay and her husband from her bedroom. Knowing Glen's problems, her sympathies were with her husband. She put on a bathrobe and strolled to Clay's bedroom. He sat on a chair next to the bed.

"Don't be too hard on my husband," Anna said in a low voice. "He is a good man. When breakfast is ready, I'll bring you a tray so you can eat."

Anna brought Clay his breakfast. Anna gathered the soiled bedding from the floor in the bedroom, and carried them into the laundry room. Anna put the soiled linens in the laundry tub, added a half-cup of bleach, some liquid Tide, and watched as the water slowly filled the tub from their artesian well. It took almost ten minutes to fill, but at least they had water without electricity. She would hang the bedding outside to dry, that is, if it did not snow or rain the rest of the day. At least the bedding would be sanitary.

Anna's husband Glen had found the artesian well when he pounded his shallow well pipe into the ground. The water had low natural pressure, but needed assistance with an electric pump to provide normal volume for household use. With the electricity out, it was a simple task to bypass the pump. Toilet and sinks still worked, but more slowly. They had an unlimited supply of flowing freshwater.

*****

Although Clay was feeling better, he continued to cough until he thought he would burst the blood vessels in his eyeballs. Perhaps Glen was right. Clay's survival could result in the sickness and death of someone else. The Great Spirit, or God, or the mystical Ultimate Mind played some strange games when it came to fate. He hacked and coughed again, this time spewing up spots of blood. Clay felt like shit.

Clay dozed off, but his sleep was restless because of the severe coughing. His nose was draining gobs of snot, both down his throat and into the paper tissues. The continual coughing was clearing his lungs. He would live. Glen had made the correct decision when he ordered Clay to stay in the bedroom.

Evening came; Anna brought Clay a bowl of warm chicken broth. It was the best tasting broth he had eaten. The chicken broth contained some potatoes, celery and sliced carrots. Anna also added onions, and some whole grain rice. Clay consumed the soup, only to puke it back up an hour later. Nevertheless, he did feel better. Some of soup must have remained to nourish his body.

An hour later, Anna brought him in a few old Popular Mechanics magazines, which he read between coughing and sleeping sessions. By dusk, he was sleeping.

Chapter 57

The following morning found Dave going hunting again, this time he was successful. It was close to noon when Dave returned with a dead snowshoe rabbit. "Hey, Dad, check this one out! I got it with my second shot. I killed one of your pumpkins with the first one. This critter was chewing on one of the smaller pumpkins. I wanted to show it to you before I dressed the rabbit out. We're going to have fresh rabbit meat! Yeah!"

"Nice job son, but take the dead rabbit outside before your mom sees it. You know, if you show it to her, she won't eat it, and I'll have to cook it."

"Okay, sure you don't want to gut it out yourself?"

Glen scrunched his eyebrows and spoke with a serious look in his eyes; "Get out of here before I boot you out, son."

Dave smiled. He took the rabbit outside, after retrieving a pan from the kitchen to put in.

Suppertime came. Anna made rabbit stew. Clay ate a small portion. This time he kept the food in his stomach.

As darkness arrived, the kerosene lamps again burned, but not for long. Dave went to bed shortly after dark planning to hunt tomorrow morning. Fifteen minutes later, his mom also retired after taking care of Clay's needs. Once more, Glen stayed up, hoping to contact someone while using his transceiver.

Glen sat in his recliner and trimmed his lamp wick to provide a minimum of light using little fuel. He was always conservative in his lifestyle, including turning off lights when not needed and buying only what was necessary. He made some exceptions for hobbies and pleasure. Before long, his eyes gently closed and his head rested against the back of his chair with the lamp still burning.

A raccoon interrupted his sleep when it tipped over the trashcan outside the house. Living in the woods had disadvantages. Raccoons in the trash were one of them. However, Glen preferred the raccoons to the black bears that sometimes pawed the side of his house at night. It was difficult for Glen to get used to the darkness at night because the house was located among the woods, with trees blocking off the stars and moonlight. Sometimes the quiet nighttime was disturbed by the sounds of wandering bears, skunks, and other nocturnal creatures. Glen considered getting a large dog for protection, which would have been a good idea with a stranger sleeping in his spare bedroom. Yes sir, after Clay Wheeler left and his life got back to normal, Glen would get a dog. A cat would be good to keep away field mice, but Glen hated cats. Glen's greatest fear was the apprehension created by the isolation. Although he knew his fears were unfounded, they always lurked as a hidden cancer lurks in one's body before eruption into a full-blown disease. Glen glanced at his old mechanical Timex watch and found it was almost 11 P.M.

"Damn" he said aloud to himself. "I wasted lamp fuel for the last three hours. Crap." He brought his lamp with him, turning down the wick to a small glow before strolling over to his transceiver. A click sounded as he turned on the radio.

The soft, green glow of the analog dial of the old Hallicrafters radio shined eerily in near darkness. The tubes began to heat up and emitted an orange reflection on the wall behind the unit. It is comforting for Glen to sit and play with an old tube-type radio. The heated smell emanating from the hot tubes and capacitors brought back memories of his childhood when he used to sit listening to the old RCA radio receiver his mom owned. The audio emitting from tube radios sounded differently than modern transistor units. Old radios did not have perfect pitch with filtered digital sound. If the capacitors weakened, the sounds included a permeating background humming from the speaker. Glen could always hear the white noise, which is the background static caused by the entire spectrum of all matter pulsating through the universe. Modern radios filtered out the noise. Yet, it was consoling and nostalgic for Glen to use his old equipment. Perhaps today's world was too perfect, too determined to remove all flaws in everything.

To stabilize the frequency drift occurring in older tube type radios, Glen let the Hallicrafters warm up for ten minutes. The continuing glow cast on the wall from the flickering tubes forced ghostly memories from his childhood. Glen could almost hear the *Jack Benny Show*, *Amos N' Andy*, and *The Lone Ranger* replaying in his mind. To Glen, it felt as if visitors from yesteryear were sharing the radio room with him. The nostalgia relaxed him, giving Glen the peace and tranquility missing from everyday living.

His hobby had originated many years ago on the eleven-meter band, which was nothing more than Citizen Band radio frequencies. When he still lived in Grand Rapids, Michigan, Glen decided to build a huge Citizens Band antenna. He installed an illegal linear amplifier in his radio room to increase the transmitting signal. Before long, he was communicating with people from all over the world. That is, until the FCC caught him using 1000 watts of power. The output of his equipment far exceeded the legal limits of four watts. It was good-bye linear amplifier, good-bye illegal radio, and good-bye hobby until he moved into the woods away from populated areas. He would not have been caught while living in the city either, except when he keyed his microphone; his voice was received by everyone who lived within a quarter mile of his house, both on television sets and on landline telephones. If his neighbors had just gone to him and discussed the matter, he would have used antenna filters to clean up his broadcast signal. Nevertheless, Glen knew he was in violation of the law. What the hell, the past was the past - this is now. Deep in the Michigan woodlands, there was no one to complain. He went back to the love of his life, illegal radio broadcasting. He worked the dials, surfing the eleven-meter band. If anyone was broadcasting, this is where Glen expected to find him or her.

Glen decided to switch to single sideband where lower power units could broadcast much farther using the same amount of electricity. He would not use his linear amplifier because it would kill his batteries in about five minutes. Instead, he cranked up his radio to its maximum of 100 watts for ham radio operators. That would have to do. It still exceeded the FCC's maximum 4 watts limits for the eleven-meter band, but since the Hallicrafters is designed for ham radio communications and not Citizens Band, it had more power. Glen didn't have a ham radio operator's license.

Glen continued to receive white noise static. Occasionally he could hear a Morse code signal, but reading Morse code was far beyond his expertise.

"CQ- CQ- CQ- CQ- this is Washington State calling the central and east coast, does anyone copy?" A signal burst from his radio startling Glen.

"Better turn down the volume or everyone will be awake." Glen said aloud while cranking it lower. He often spoke to himself, if he had a dog he could say he was conversing with it. Yes, he must get a dog.

CQ- CQ- CQ- CQ- this is Washington State calling the central and east coast, does anyone copy?"

The voice sounded again, drifting in and out. The operator is adjusting his beams to cover most of the east coast. Glen thought as he grasped his microphone and squeezed the send button.

"Got a copy, Washington State, here in upper Michigan for sure! Ten-four. This here be the Hobo, ol' 11-36 back at you."

"We copy you, 11-36. Big ten-four. Got a ten-pounder reading on you. Over."

Glen felt his heart race as he replied to the welcome sound. "Ten four, Washington. Glen Stoneman here. Just call me Hobo. Forget the FCC protocol, hell I don't have a license anyways."

"Hello, Hobo. This is Doctor Henry Kovak. I am a retired astrophysics professor. Just call me Doc. I'm also an amateur ham radio operator. You must be living in an isolated area, because the cities are either burning, or rioting. Ten-four."

"Copy that Doc. My family and I live in the forests of northern Michigan. I have a system of batteries charged with a homebuilt windmill generator. None of my newer radios work, just some of my antique tube-type equipment function, which I restored several years ago. Do you have any idea what caused the electrical outage? You are the only person I've talked to since the power went off. I had no idea the cities were having problems. It sounds bad. Over."

It took several seconds before the voice returned to Glen's receiver.

"Ten-four there, Mr. Hobo. You have similar equipment to me. I'm using an old Johnson radio, vintage 1951. I assume you have no idea what happened, so I will fill you in before our signal drifts off somewhere else. I got the information I'm giving you by eavesdropping on a military radio transmission just before the power failed all over the world. I hope others with working radios are listening in, so he or she can learn what happened, even if they cannot broadcast to us. Here is what I know:

A huge solar flare burst from the sun. It caused an immense wave of electromagnetic radiation. Planet Earth was in the direct path of the solar pulse energy. The solar storm's electromagnetic wave was too strong for our solid-state devices to withstand. The electro-magnetic pulse caused by the blast destroyed all solid-state electronics. The old tub and resistor/capacitors radios and equipment tolerate higher magnetic forces and voltages. That is why our radios still work. This is the simple and short explanation of what happened. Over."

Glen lowered his eyes to the microphone. It was almost a full minute before he replied. "Ah shit. Copy that Doc. I know enough about electronics to believe what you are telling me. It was always a possibility this event could happen, but we ignored it. So now, civilization is screwed, huh." He hesitated, not knowing what to say. This was a larger problem than he imagined. His world was gone. Perhaps there is some hope. "Have you heard anything about the military or government, Doc?" Without waiting for Doc to answer him, Glen continued with anger. "I'm going to load my goddamn guns when I get off this radio and protect my wife and son. Over."

"Hey, Mr. Hobo quit talking stupid. It's not the time to panic. Paranoia and hysteria is the major problem right now. There is excessive ignorance, violence and panic everywhere, at least this is what I learned by talking with several ham radio operators in Europe and South America. Humans, over the last seventy years have forgotten how to depend on one another because they spent more hours staring at the goddamn television than socializing. People don't know how to live in a world without electric power. Ten-four."

"Ten-four there Doc. I guess I'm not ready for such a change myself. Pisses me off big time, it does. Over."

"Don't feel bad, Mr. Hobo. Yours was my first reaction too. Now back to your question. Some of the military and government agencies are still functioning. However, they are limited due to the lack of working equipment to depend upon. The military should have kept a few horses for transportation instead of building all those goddamn tanks."

"I was told a few old coal powered electrical generation plants are attempting to come back on line. It will take months because they must bypass all the burned-out solid-state controllers and voltage regulators. It requires the generating plants installing old magnetic relays with silver contacts. I hope they have some old electronics components stored in warehouses, otherwise it won't happen. If some power plants do manage to start working, they will only provide limited amperage. There is no way to provide coal to the plants so they will shortly run out of fuel. It looks to me like we'll be living as people did back around the beginning of the twentieth century. Over."

"So, we're finally fucked, huh." Glen let go of his microphone key and mulled over the conversation.

Doctor Kovak broke the silence. "Yours is a common reaction, Mr. Hobo. Remember, you control your destiny, my friend. Be careful not to be involved in the paranoia gripping the world. Just protect yourself and your family. For Christ's sake, don't panic. I heard there are disasters around the Earth. There are nuclear power plant meltdowns in a several European nations and also in China and Japan. Be thankful you are isolated and not near a major city. Rioters have burned most of the cities, after stealing merchandise they can no longer use. Death is everywhere; disease will be the next killer of humankind. Just bond with your neighbors and get your family and friends to establish a local community for protection and the necessities of life. Do you remember the communes of the 1960's? Communal living is a good idea for our new world. Over."

Static started to mask the radio's signal. It would not be long before Glen would lose the signal's propagation, ending the conversation.

"Ten-four there, Doc. I'm losing your signal. Will you be on the radio again?"

"Try again any day on this frequency at 2300 hours UTC time. (More static) A few radio operators are trying to communicate information and set up a network. I have an extensive system of batteries and established several communications during the last couple of days. (Static) So, feel free to take note of this frequency. A few radio operators may stay on stand-by here. Over."

Glen noticed the meter telling him his batteries had dropped to 55% charge. "Okay, doc. I will try to contact you again, but my batteries and generator are not the best. Therefore, communication from me will be sporadic. Over."

The ghostly voice faded in and out once more. "Copy that Mr. Hobo. Picture --- word 'commune' Mr. Hobo. You could begin to live --- --- Amish who probably are dealing with the power outage better --- the rest of us ---. Best --- luck -- you --- yours. This --- Doctor Henry Novak, ---."

Glen double clicked his own microphone sending a carrier signal, ending the transmission. He sat for a moment and continued to look at the orange glow reflecting from the back of his transceiver. He turned the knob controlling the wick on his lamp and the room got brighter. Glen turned off his radio, switched on his battery-charging windmill and carried the lamp into the kitchen. Darkness followed him.

Glen's hand reached above the refrigerator and grasped the neck of a pint bottle of Southern Comfort whiskey. He poured some of the amber liquid into a juice glass, lifted it up and took a big gulp. The whiskey burned into his tongue and down his throat on its journey to his bloodstream. Glen put the cap back on the bottle and went to check the wood in the heater, carrying the bottle and his glass with him. He sat down on his recliner, and stared at the fire in his wood stove. The flames danced and popped as they always did. Only Glen and his perception of the world were different.

Life would not be easy. The world had changed so swiftly it was as if modern history had never happened. Civilization had taken a backward step of at least one hundred years. With all the radiation from the nuclear power plants getting into the atmosphere humankind would never fully recover.

Glen raised his left hand, grasping the front of his thinning gray hair with his fist, momentarily holding it then began running his fingers to the back of his head. It was a mannerism first recognized by his wife shortly after they were married which identified stress and anger in his life. He tried to stop, but never broke the habit. He poured and drank another shot of whiskey.

Glen placed the glass on the table alongside the bottle and blew out the lamp. It would do no good to get intoxicated tonight. He stood up from the recliner and ambled into the bedroom, joining Anna in bed. There was nothing to gain by sharing what he learned with anyone until tomorrow. Glen snuggled up to Anna, his eyes gradually closed, waiting for sleep. The closeness of her body gave him comfort. Glen slept.

The next morning was a mirror image of those preceding it. The routine was getting to be a wearisome habit. Clay was getting better, but still confined to his room. Glen shared what he learned about the power outage with his wife and son. He carefully opened Clay's bedroom door and told he what he knew.

"Damn this sickness. I better get back to Maggie and the kids." Clay said before covering his mouth and coughing into a tissue. "I have the answer to what happened, so it's time for me to go home and prepare my family for whatever may befall us. I see no reason to stay here."

"Sure, good idea, uh huh," replied Glen. "Go and share your snotty nose and bad lungs with your family and get them sick. You've already exposed mine. You should have never left your family to begin with."

"Hey, you know it wasn't my choice to be here. Your son should have left me to die in the woods. My ancestors died in honor when Great Spirit called for them." Clay angrily replied.

"Don't get your balls in a tizzy. I know nothing about your heritage, except you're here and we are here. You should stay here with us for a couple of weeks. By then you should be well enough to go home. I only ask you to be careful so my family doesn't get whatever shit disease you have. In a couple of weeks, most of our supplies will be gone."

"I'm sorry to be an imposition on you." Clay replied sarcastically. "I didn't get sick on purpose."

Glen lowered his head, speaking softly. "I'm sorry, Mr. Wheeler. May I call you Clay? Just call me Glen." Not waiting for a reply, Glen continued. "I'm dejected to see all my dreams turning into nightmares. My son's future looks bleak, my health problems limit what I can do for my family, and the world is flushed down into the toilet. I didn't mean to take it out on you. I apologize. What are your plans?" Glen asked.

"As soon as I feel better, I'll leave and return to my family. What about yourself, Glen?"

"I haven't decided any course of action yet. As I said, our supplies are getting low. Maybe I'll take Dave and Anna and we'll walk north. We might find people who have extra food. On the other hand, if Dave shoots a deer or two, we could stay here longer. Hell, I don't know what to do, but doing nothing isn't the answer."

"Glen, why don't you just come with me? You can bring your family and any important items you need for survival. We could all share my house. I have a big home and it would be safer if we were together. That is, if you can get over being such an asshole to me."

Glen looked at Clay, realizing the last statement was meant as humor. He began considering the logic behind the man's offer. With his own future and longevity dubious, it would be best for Anna and Dave to be with someone else. If he died, it would be important for them to have security; and they deserved something from Clay for saving his life.

"Let me consider it, okay?" Glen replied.

"Take your time making the decision. I suggest you discuss this with your wife and son before deciding to leave your home. Their opinions are important."

"I'll talk with them. Thanks for making such a generous offer, Clay."

Glen turned his back to Clay, leaving the room. As usual, he entered his bathroom and washed his hands. There was no need to take any chances. Clay said he was an asshole. Joke or not, Glen did not give a shit. He reached up, opened the bathroom cabinet, and took out the bottle of witch hazel. After sprinkling the liquid on his hands and rubbing them briskly, he went back into the living area of the house.

It took another week before Clay recovered from his respiratory infection. Two weeks later, Glen and his family decided to go with Clay to his home.

Anna packed the medical supplies. Glen and Dave gathered their remaining food supplies and put them into backpacks. Glen took precautions to hide his radios so they wouldn't be stolen or destroyed while they were gone. They were too heavy to carry. Without the batteries, they would be of no use. So far, he had logged six different radio operators throughout the country and gained considerable knowledge about what was happening, at least in the United States. Two of the operators had picked up signals from what they thought was Russia and Germany, but not speaking the language, only a few words were understood. The details of what caused the electrical failure were the same from everyone. Glen discovered there was strength in isolated population communities, anarchy within the cities, and large areas of the country continued to burn. Fires, disease and death had desolated major cities including New York, Chicago, Detroit and Atlanta. Millions of people were dead. Another billion people would die throughout the world before the long winter months were completed in the northern hemisphere. The advantage seemed to be in countries considered Third World, who never progressed technologically and electronically, as did the industrial nations. Glen was depressed. If it were not for his wife and son, he would eat his shotgun.

"Dad, are you ready?" David asked. His gloved hands grasped the 30-06 Remington rifle he elected to carry with him. He had about sixty shells, five of which were loaded in the semi-automatic rifle, and four more in a spare clip ready to be loaded if necessary. He placed the remaining shells in a plastic bag deep in his backpack. "Hey Dad, we've got to get going, you know."

Glen nodded his head. It was time to leave home. Just before departure, Glen let the fire in the wood burner die out. Dave scooped out the ashes and emptied them into the compost bin behind the house. Everyone worked together and hid what food they could not carry. The last chore was turning off the main feed from the artesian well.

Chapter 58

The journey back to Clay's driveway was not eventful except in a mystical way. There were no deer, so Dave would not fire his rifle. The buck, which was Clay's companion during his first journey, was gone. In his mind, he knew the deer might not have been real, at least in the carnal world. If the buck reappeared, he would prevent any harm to it. On the other hand, perhaps the buck was immortal or a specter. One way or another, Clay had no desire to find out. Above all else, Clay would honor his ancestors. Clay's ancestors never had electrical powered luxuries, but they survived.

Maybe the deer truly was Clay's totem, his animal guide with its large eyes, huge rack and brown sleek hair. Whether imaginary or real, whether in this reality or another, Clay knew what he had seen and experienced. In Michigan, the deer was king; it outnumbered both the black bear population and the elk introduced in State of Michigan by the DNR to create another hunting season. It was not to preserve the elk as a species, but to provide income for Michigan by selling more hunting licenses through a lottery. Clay decided he would never hunt deer again. Someday, he would tell his sons and Kaya Bird the story of Thunder Eagle and the cabin he found in the woods. His stories would be added to those told to Clay by his great grandmother, long ago.

One did not need to eat venison. There are other foods to eat, vegetables and fruits could just as well sustain life. Perhaps all life was holy. Living in the north woods, bonding with nature during this harrowing experience caused change in Clay's spiritual perception. He saw hidden messages within nature and life. Maybe the deer he saw in the woods was himself and its twin antlers could represent his twin sons. Perhaps it was the spirit of Thunder Eagle, traveling though time, examining the legacy of his descendants. On the other hand, perhaps it was just a deer watching him walk through the woodlands. Clay preferred to accept the mystical apparition than a carnal reality.

All life was precious since the magnetic pulse had destroyed modern civilization. Could this experience for humanity be a rebirth of the human spirit, forcing humankind to become dependent on one's self and one's neighbor? Could it be nature's way of forcing human beings to live in honor and simplicity? Whatever it was, Clay was content to move with the fluid flow of time. He was accepting his new life and deleting the old one as if it never existed. Clay believed most persons would adapt to a new way of life, each viewing the experience as it affected him or her. Those who refused to adapt would not survive.

*****

As he walked, Glen felt remorse for the way he reacted to Clay's presence in his house. Glen was disappointed and had counted on living his life in a normal linear flow of time and events. He expected his son would go to college. It would not happen. He expected to enjoy his radio hobby and live in comfort, relishing his solitude during the few years he had left. It would not happen. His heart bypass operation had revealed his vulnerability to illness and happenstance. It was a major shock to realize his best years were behind him, and his future depended on adapting to changing circumstances. Anna was strong. Glen's primary concern was for Dave. He was young enough to accept a new life, but also smart enough to know his future was going to be more difficult than planned.

Glen was concerned about possible radiation contamination from nuclear plant meltdowns. By now, he realized his family already could be exposed to some radiation. Every creature on the planet would be affected. Radiation poisoning is a long-term problem. More pressing for him was making plans for his family to survive this winter.

Glen thought about the numerous cancers the radiation would cause. He considered it a real probability that many genetic defects and mutations would result in shorter life span for young people. Before the solar pulse they expected to live extended and prosperous lives, especially with current medical advances. Many of those advances were wiped out in a single blast of a solar pulse from the sun. These were no longer normal conditions.

Glen was worried about his wife, Anna. Dave would take care of his mom if he died. Wouldn't he? Wouldn't he? Glen realized his anxiety could eventually kill him. Glen began to sing in a low voice, a song he remembered from his past. It was a Harry Chapin song, one which played often in his mind as he walked or sat alone in his radio room.

He first hummed the tune then began singing. "Remember when the music, came from wooden boxes strung with silver wire, and as we sang the words, it would set our minds on fire, we believed in things, and so we'd sing . . . . . I dreamed that something's coming, and it's not just in the wind. . . . . We had dreams to live and we had hopes to give, a gift the future gave . . . . .and so we would sleep, we had dreams to keep. "

Glen had not paid enough attention to the 70's generation while living it during his youth. Glen missed his chance to be part of those years of rebellion and social change. Before he realized it, those years were gone. He relived them through folk music. Yes, he wished he had been to Woodstock, listened to Dylan, and all the entertainers, while wearing a dirty pair of cut off blue jeans and drinking bottle after bottle of beer. Glen hated war, loved freedom, and valued his own virtues above whatever society told him what should be precious to him.

*****

Dave loved his dad, and emulated him in many ways. He was worried about his father although he knew the man was strong. Even the strongest of people are vulnerable. He continued to listen to the words as his dad sang. Some of the verses were missing, but it was the emotion emanating from his dad, which energized him. He felt compassion for his dad, but at the same time, felt honored to be the son of a man of principle.

Dave traveled alongside his mom, with Clay taking the lead. He had listened to folk songs many times during his youth with his parents while sitting in the living room with the phonograph playing softly next to the bookcase. The music and life of Harry Chapin had inspired and influenced who his father was.

Dave had good feelings about Clay. In some ways, the man was a younger version of his own father. He decided to work with Clay so that they would survive. It would be best to stay with the Wheeler family until the spring thaws came in Michigan. There was uncertainty about the direction of civilization. He knew changes would be necessary to encourage people to begin trusting and help one another, or humanity would not survive. When the springtime came, Dave would seek out other neighbors and see if they would cooperate and organize. Working together, they could grow vegetables and other foodstuffs next summer. By coordinating their efforts, they could produce enough for all to survive through the next and future winters.

Dave's love of the outdoors and hunting would grow stronger in later years. Spring would bring a rebirth, and perhaps he could find someone to love and share his intimate dreams. Someday, Dave would get married and have a family, one he could protect as Clay did his.

Chapter 59

Suddenly Clay froze. Glen, Anna and Dave also stopped. Glen stopped singing, wondering what bothered Clay. Clay thought, could this be the place - where he spent the night in the cabin? The terrain looked similar, yet it didn't. Clay was positive this was where he left the highway and found the cabin where he stayed the night. It looked as if there was a path here ages ago, on the other hand, it could be just a deer trail.

"Glen," Clay said, "Would you and your family wait here for a moment? I'll be right back. I have to do something, and I must do it alone."

Glen looked puzzled, but refused to question Clay's motives. "Don't be too long, okay Clay?"

"I won't be," replied Clay as he started into the woods. He traveled three hundred feet west of the highway before he knew the cabin was not there. It was a strange feeling, as if he did not belong here, never belonged here. He turned and started back to the road. A huge buck jumped across his path, running full speed around him and into the Cedar trees. It could have been the same buck Clay saw when he was sick.

Clay stopped, stood for a moment of silent meditation with his eyes closed. When he opened them, he thought he saw the cabin again, but it was a fleeting image, disappearing as quickly as it came. It had to be an illusion.

The deer was standing where he thought the cabin had stood. It lowered its head, rubbed its antlers on a small birch sapling, and raised its head. Again the buck lowered his head, raised it as if saluting Clay. It turned and bounded into the brush. The sound of the running deer suddenly stopped as the animal appeared to morph itself into the forest, vanishing. Clay's mind filled with confusion. There were no thoughts and words available to translate this mystical experience into rational ideas. He knew this was sacred ground. Clay turned and retraced his steps towards the road, not daring to look back. He soon found himself back with his companions.

"What did you see? Glen asked.

"Nothing, just memories, just memories, my friends."

Dave looked at Clay, but quickly forgot about the matter. They resumed walking. Yet, Dave could have sworn Clay's body almost glowed when he arrived back with the group.

"Dave, would you do me a favor?" Clay asked.

"Sure, what is it?"

"Whenever you go deer hunting out here, if you see a twelve-point buck, would you please, please promise me you will NEVER kill it? Do not ask me why, but I have a reason. Just promise me as a friend would, you will never kill it. Okay?"

"Well," Dave hesitated, "I guess. Okay, I promise. You know, it would be a shame if I did let a big one get away, but for you -- and I trust you have good reason, I promise never to shoot it. You can count on me, Clay."

"Thanks. Someday, I might tell you my reason. I hope you understand."

"No problems, we have our secrets," replied Dave.

It was not long before they arrived where Clay had found the overturned truck. The mystery of the truck remained. The water in the ditch had risen and covered most of the bed leaving only the rear axle visible. The occupant or occupants could be still inside the cab, dead. The ditch would soon freeze, preserving its hidden cargo until springtime. The group stopped to view the vehicle but did not investigate it further. After a passing glance, they continued on their way. Sometimes there are no answers.

Clay was surprised when he came to his driveway. Little had changed, except it began to snow. He figured Glen and his family lived about ten miles from his home. He had not realized that he had walked so far. He had wandered a long ways the day after he leaving the mysterious cabin, meandering through the swamps and woodlands until Dave found him in the deer blind. Clay dropped the supplies he was carrying and started running down his long driveway toward his home, leaving his companions behind.

"What's going on?" Dave asked his father.

"Just let him go, son. Clay needs a private moment with his family, and then we will go ahead. Some moments are not meant to be shared."

Glen stopped walking. Anna put her arm around her husband, leaning her head against his shoulder. She grasped his hand and held it tightly. Ten minutes later, they started following Clay's footprints in the snow.

Chapter 60

E ric saw his dad running toward their home.

"MOM, it's DAD, it's DAD!"

Joey was behind the house when Eric hollered. He began running around the house, fell in the wet snow, got up and joined his brother by jumping on his dad, embracing him.

Clay, with tears in his eyes, hugged both of his sons, went down on his knees and held them close. "Is your mom alright boys? Is Kaya Bird all right? I love you guys," he said.

Joey broke away, hollering back, "I'm getting Mom right now!"

"Don't worry, Dad," replied, Eric, "we took good care of Mom. Kaya is well too. We missed you. What happened? You look like you lost weight, Dad." Eric looked at his dad's thin face as if expecting an answer, but none was forthcoming.

"You'll hear all about it later, Eric. Let's go see your Mom and my baby girl." Clay held his son's hand and started walking up to the porch. Clay opened the door. He was home.

Afterword

Eight months later, the survivors of the solar pulse began to establish communities. Some of these were good, while some were not so good. For most people, there were no major political leaders or countries. It was back to living as people did during feudalism. Some people, like Clay Wheeler and his group were beginning to thrive because of their ingenuity and ability to adapt to the changing lifestyle.

Roxanne never saw Mac again. She became a volunteer in the new social order established at the school refuge center, keeping herself busy to eradicate the memories of her dead husband James. She had no time for religion. Religious legalism had consumed too much of her life, destroying much of her individuality. Roxanne would never again allow fanaticism to take precedence over logical reasoning in her life. She was in control of her happiness.

Abraham Washington Jefferson, being a restless spirit, left the school refuge center and headed north intending to eventually travel west toward New Orleans, or see California.

Jennifer accompanied Breshawn to Cape Kennedy where William Hendricks, a onetime engineer who had worked on the space shuttle program befriended her. One month later, Jennifer married William in a civil ceremony.

After leaving Jennifer, Breshawn traveled south and took up residence with a group of Seminole Indians living on a reservation near Everglades National Park. At last, he was happy. There were no white men here.

Twenty years after the solar pulse, a cucumber shaped body of rock, one mile long began its decent into the atmosphere of the

Earth. Ice and debris from the surface of the cratered rock began to flake off and riffle though the atmosphere as fiery meteorites.

Breshawn was standing on a dock looking toward the eastern sky waiting for sunrise so he could go fishing in the Everglades with his Seminole Indian friends. He felt accepted by people who were neither white nor black. His Indian companions could relate to his livelong suffering and discrimination. At last he was happy and at peace. Many of the memories of his drug use and adventure with Jidon and Abe back in Beulah's apartment were forgotten. Breshawn married a Seminole Indian woman and was the proud father of three daughters. The old life was gone.

It was a beautiful morning, not many mosquitoes were buzzing the swampland. Breshawn had hopes of netting many fish. A few stars were still visible in the sky. A hint of amber light was starting to streak from the sun as it started to rise above the edge of the horizon. As Breshawn was looking toward the eastern sky, many meteorites appeared. A much larger object caught his eye just behind them. A huge fiery ball seemingly the size of the moon was racing across the heavens. It broke into two glowing parts; one continuing its westward journey and the other directed more to the southwest. Never in his life had Breshawn witnessed anything so beautiful. It reminded him of the aurora borealis display he saw back in Orlando, many years ago, before the fires of the city blocked out his view. It was "some remnant of the space station or other large artificial object that was entering the atmosphere," he said aloud to his wife who was helping him load his fishing boat.

The objects disappeared over the western horizon. Breshawn finished gathering his fishing gear, climbed into the boat and pushed off into the Everglades.

*****

Part of the asteroid continued its journey around the Earth and back towards the edge of the Solar System. The other half of the asteroid bounced off the atmosphere, circled the Earth once more before grasped by the planets' gravity. It struck the Pacific Ocean 800 miles east of Hawaii, sending untold amounts of water vapor into the atmosphere.

Within three days, the steam and water vapor caused by the impact vapor would cause the sky to darken and massive storms would hit the western part of the United States. The huge Tsunami caused by the impact would reach inland into California, Oregon, and Washington State, killing thousands of people who had survived the solar pulse.

The same morning the asteroid hit the Earth; Clay had awakened to find his Dream Catcher again on the floor. This time he left it there as an omen, knowing it was a sign from Thunder Eagle and something terrible was once more going to happen. Unlike many years ago, his community was prepared for any eventually, artificial or by nature. Maybe it was time to hang the Dream Catcher in Kaya Bird's window. She was a beautiful 25 year-old woman with dark complexion and straight black hair crowning her head and reaching halfway down her back. Her ancestors would have been as proud of her as her father and mother are. Perhaps his Dream Catcher was telling Clay it was time to pass it on to Kaya Bird. Clay was still tired, so he went back to bed, cuddling up to Maggie. Once again, Clay dreamed.

Thunder Eagle came to him, bringing Clay visions of the deer. The deer turned towards Clay and one antler disappeared into the heavens while the other flew off into a huge body of water. The deer spoke:

"Clay, you will survive the last omen with your family. Remember the ways of your ancestors. Remember nature is precious. There are storms bearing down on you and your friends but be not afraid. Let Dave help you, let your family and friends help you, and rely on the wisdom of Maggie. Those who you love will survive. Kaya Bird will bring honor to you and humanity. She will carry the Dream Catcher long after you are gone. Kaya Bird has powers of which even you are not aware. She is Thunder Eagle, she is Clay Bird Spirit, and she is the deer that saved you. She is the good and bad of all, and all is part of her. Restore the land with the guidance of Kaya Bird in the ways of our ancestors. Kaya cannot change the past, but from the past one learns to make the future."

Clay woke up. He looked toward his window and was surprised to see his Dream Catcher back where it belonged. How did it get back there? He would remember this vision from the deer. He arose out of bed, removed the Dream Catcher from his window and walked out of the bedroom. He had to talk with his daughter. The Dream Catcher now belonged to Kaya Bird Wheeler.

THE END

NATHANIEL WILFORD MILLER'S JOURNAL:

FOR HOSPITAL RECORDS ONLY:
By M.G. - Psychiatrist

A couple years after beginning my practice as a clinical psychiatrist, I treated a young man who evolved from normal to abnormal. The illness of my client, Nathanial Miller was due to extreme religious orthodox fundamentalism. Some people believe religious orthodoxy has its benefits, and that Nathaniel's mental illness was caused by other societal problems. After reading Nathaniel's Journal, one will see how religion changed the personality of a normal boy, transforming him into a troubled young man.

Some individuals claim God "IS LOVE" and therefore whatever befalls humanity is under divine direction of the Almighty. Often religious affiliation, instead of being beneficial to individual growth and stability, becomes hurtful and damaging to the lives and mental health of individuals. If God is all knowing, all-powerful, and omnipresent, then humankind is nothing more than a preset program like a movie recorded on a DVD. Therefore, the program of human life is predetermined and there is nothing we do can change the ending. Perhaps God is a fable or a myth, or has little or no interest in humans. Another theory is, God is in control of the DVD and playing the disk as he programmed it. Whatever the answer is, we have insufficient data to analyze and understand God. We will see how religious membership and belief in a benevolent Creator affected the life of Nathaniel Wilford Miller.

Excerpts are quoted from Nathaniel's personal journal, exposing his innermost private thoughts. I counseled Nathaniel during a troubled time in his life and present this expose to warn others who may be victims of cult religions and fanatical fundamentalism. For personal reasons, I have requested my full name not be used.

To understand the complexity of the problems that caused mental depression in Nathaniel Wilford Miller, I will present direct quotes from his personal Journal, penned by Nathaniel's hand. Only one liberty was taken. I corrected the misspelled words written by Nathaniel in his journal and some of the grammar:

January 19, 1955

I am writing a record of my life! I am ten years old. My Grandpa Miller bought me a journal book with a small lock and key on it. Grandpa Miller said he had a journal when he was a boy. I would like to read Grandpa's journal someday. Grandpa Miller told me I can read parts of his journal when I get to be a grown up. He said it would tell me about my great grandparents. They are dead. I would like to know what life was like when Grandpa was a little boy like me. He told me life was simpler then. He didn't have a lot of toys, but had a dog named Daisy. I like dogs.

I have a Scottish terrier named Max. I feed Max every day. He likes table scraps so I give him what we do not eat. Max and I are pals. He likes meat. He is a little dog so he doesn't eat very much. Max likes to play with a ball. He will hit the ball back to me when I throw it to him. Max reminds me of a seal I saw at the circus last winter. I love Max. He could be a circus dog too.

I also have two guppies in a bowl. I keep the bowl clean. I feed my guppies. They like me.

I have a mother and dad. I do not have a brother or a sister. Mom says I am an only child. Mom and Dad's names are Frank and Mary Miller. My grandpa is Wilford Miller and my grandma is Lucy

Miller. I have Grandpa's first name as my middle name. Maybe that is why he gave me a journal. My birthday comes in two weeks. I like birthdays and Christmas. I got lots of stuff for Christmas. My favorite toy is a Roy Rogers's pistol and holster set. I have a cowboy hat. I would like to ride a horse someday. My second favorite toy is my baseball glove. Mickey Mantle autographed it. It is not his real autograph, but his name is stamped below where my thumb goes in the glove. I will have a birthday party in two weeks. My friends from school will be there. It will be lots of fun! I hope Brenda can come. I like Brenda, even if she is a girl. She goes to my school. Brenda Fox lives about a mile from me. I have known her my whole life. Brenda comes over and plays on my swing set with me. We used to dig holes in my sandbox with spoons. Brenda is lots of fun.

Mom said my guppies might have babies. She bought some seaweed to put in the bowl so guppy babies can hide after they are born. She said that mama and daddy guppies eat their babies if they do not hide after they come out of the mother fish. That is gross. I hope the baby guppies are not eaten. I am glad I am not a guppy.

Tomorrow is Friday. I have to go to school tomorrow. I really like school. I play with all the kids in my schoolroom. They like me because I am good at sports. They always pick me first to be on their softball teams. Some kids always are picked last. I feel sorry for them. That is not nice to always be picked last. I would feel hurt if I got picked last. I like weekends, because they are so much fun. Today a man and woman came to our house selling books. Mom invited them in. They talked about some church stuff for a couple of hours. It was so boring I went in my room and played cowboy and Indians by myself. Sometimes I wear my Davy Crocket coonskin cap when playing cowboys. When I came out to eat lunch, the man and woman were gone. I hope they do not come back. They looked mean. Mom has some of their books on the coffee table. I looked at one of the magazines. It said "God's Disciples and Publishers" print it.

February 4, 1955

Today is my birthday. Brenda came to my party and gave me a puzzle book. I am glad she came. Six other kids from school also were at my party. It was a real fun time. We played games. I won a Chinese finger puzzle. We had a birthday cake that Mom baked. She made my favorite, chocolate with vanilla icing. Everyone sang the song "Happy Birthday" to me. I blew out all the candles after making a wish. I was careful when blowing out the candles. I was at a party once when Timothy Johnson tried to blow out the candles on his cake and spit slobber all over the icing. It was gross. Timmy's mom would not let us eat any of that cake. His mom did not serve it to us. I guess Timmy got to eat the whole cake by himself. If I ate it, I would have puked. I did not tell anyone my wish but I hope my wish comes true. I want to be a professional baseball player when I grow up.

Everyone seemed real happy at my party. I am glad my birthday was not two days ago. That was Groundhog's Day. Everyone would tease me if I were born on Groundhog's Day. I am now eleven-years old. Two more years and I will be a teenager. I can hardly wait to be a teenager. I know it will be the best time of my life.

The church book salespeople came to the door during my party. Dad told them to come back some other time, because we were real busy right now. Then Mom talked with them. They left some more magazines with Mom. They said they would come back. They dress funny, like people do when they go to funerals. I hope they don't come back.

It is time to put my journal up and go to bed. I will dream about my party. I will never forget this day. It is the best day of my life.

April 17, 1955

I played soccer at school today. I was the goalkeeper. I blocked four different shots. All the kids think I am a good soccer player. I can run fast. Next week I will be playing softball. I will play in a league this summer. Last year I was the first baseman, but I want to be a catcher. A catcher gets lots of action and can control the game. Last year, my coach, Mr. Thornton said I had the best catching abilities of any player he ever coached. He said I should be behind the plate rather than a first baseman. He is really smart and knows a lot about baseball. I am learning a lot from him. I like Mr. Thornton. I hope he will be my coach again this year. Dad likes him too. Dad helped Mr. Thornton coach our team. Dad came to every game. I am glad Dad likes to watch me play. Dad plays catch with me almost every day after school. I enjoy that. Dad wants me to be a good ballplayer and says I have "great potential," whatever that means. I love my dad.

Those church people are coming every week to our house. They sit down at the table and read their books and ask goofy questions. Mom says they are having a Bible study. Mom makes me sit there with them while they read and talk about Bible stuff. At the last study, I got so bored I fell fast asleep with my head on the table. Mom bopped me on the head with a church magazine and I woke up. Everyone was staring at me. They never smile. Mom doesn't smile as much anymore either. The older woman who studies with Mom wears gobs of makeup. Her breath smells funny too. Dad just leaves the room while they are here. He watches Roy Rogers and Hopalong Cassidy movies on television while Mom is having her study. I would rather watch TV and sit with Dad than be with these church people. Dad said some religious training would be good for me. Parents are really funny about that stuff.

June 1, 1955

School is out for the summer. I start playing softball next week. The league has eight teams and it looks like I might be on the best team. Dad was going to help coach again this year but now he says he doesn't have time. Dad finally joined in the church people's study. Mom and Dad are going to church and that is taking up some of our time. Church stuff is really boring. We sit for an hour listening to someone talk about stuff I do not understand. Then we study the church magazine the people leave at our house. After church, Dad and Mom stay and talk. Everyone seems to surround us and treat us special. Dad said they are giving us an extra portion of love because we are new members. They do not hug but just shake hands with everyone. It is more fun after the sermon is over than sitting and listening to all that church stuff. I have no idea what they preach about. I brought a pack of peppermint gum to church last week. Dad saw me chewing a stick during the meeting; he took it from me and looked really mad. He will not let me take any hard candy to church either. I must just sit and stare at the minister. Sometimes I see people falling asleep. Mom won't let me sleep; she said the Elders sermons are important and I should be paying attention and not sleeping. I don't know what the Elders are talking about. Nobody smiles.

Mom says she wants to get baptized and become a full member of "God's Disciples and Publishers." Dad said he is not ready to do that yet, but he sure reads their church stuff. I asked Mom what "baptized" means. She said she would wear a bathing suit, get in a tank of water and the church people will stick her head under the water. She said she would no longer have any sins. I did not know my mom had any sins. What kind of sins is she talking about? It seems kinda silly to stick her head underwater to get rid of sins. She said by being baptized, she could find Jesus. I told her "I did not know that Jesus was lost!" She slapped me across the face. I think this is the first time Mom ever hit me. Things are not as much fun as they used to be around here. I do not want to get baptized.

July 3, 1955

I hit my first home run yesterday. We won by beating the Barlow Mini-Yanks by a score of 10 to 3. I was the catcher for the whole game. I saw Brenda on the edge of the field. She was watching the game. I like it when she watches me play. I think I play better when Brenda is watching me. I talked to her after the game. Brenda said she was going downtown to see the July 4th fireworks display tomorrow night and asked me if I would like to go with her and her parents. I told her sure, but I would have to ask my Mom and Dad first. Dad said we could not go to the fireworks this year. He said Independence Day is based on politics and that as a member of ***"God's Disciples and Publisher"*** we could not watch the fireworks. Dad said that all governments are evil and support Satan the Devil. He also said the fireworks represent war and we cannot be part of wars. I told him my teacher at school said we should celebrate Independence Day and be proud of our freedom. Dad did not smile as he told me I would be supporting wickedness to watch the fireworks display. Dad said I must not have paid attention at church when they taught us that stuff. He said from now on, he was going to ask me questions after church meetings. If I could not answer them, I would have to give up my softball league to study ***"God's Disciples"*** books. Why do my teachers tell me one thing about our government and my dad something else? I do not understand why he says our government is evil; we have many freedoms and lots of food and stuff to buy. In my history class, we studied about Hitler and Communism. Hitler and Communism are evil. But, we are not evil. It really bothers me to think about this stuff. I wish Dad would let me go to the fireworks with Brenda. My life has changed since my birthday party. I called Brenda and told her that I could not go. She sounded really disappointed. I am sad.

Dad got baptized last month. He said he is now the family head and we must all be in subjection to him. I do not know what subjection means, but I will look it up in the dictionary when I have time. Dad said he will have a home Bible study with Mom and me. Dad said a Bible Study with us would improve his standing in the church. That made me sad. I do not want to study the Bible all the time. I want to play softball.

September 4, 1955

School started today. We opened the day with a Bible scripture, then pledged to the flag and sang the National Anthem. Mom came to class with me to see our classroom. She watched everything we did and left at lunchtime. Mom was really, really mad when I got home from school! She yelled at me for a longtime. She told me that God would kill me for saluting the flag and singing the National Anthem. She said it was just like the Independence Day stuff. I was not to do any of it, because it would make Jehovah angry and my everlasting life would end up being everlasting death. I had not thought about that stuff. I am twelve-years old and things are becoming clearer to me every day. I did not know that you could make God so mad he would kill you. If God is perfect, how can he get mad? I hope Jehovah does not kill me for saluting the flag today. I feel guilty. I made God angry. Mom said I gave an act of worship to Satan by saying the flag salute. She said I should say a long prayer to Jehovah God asking forgiveness when I go to bed tonight. I even colored a flag on a piece of paper at school today and brought it home. After Mom told me about my sin, I tore it up and threw it in the wastebasket. I have committed a terrible sin against God. It bothers me real badly. I will not sleep very well tonight. I bet God hates me right now for being so bad.

I do not want to be murdered for being an evil kid, so I asked Mom what I should do at school about the flag salute. Mom told me to tell my teacher I no longer will salute the flag. I must leave the classroom while the other kids salute the flag and sing the National Anthem. I told Mom I did not want to tell my teacher about it. I asked Mom to write a note and explain it to Mrs. Strongbow, my teacher. Mrs. Strongbow is an American Indian, and she teaches us a lot of history and culture. Mom said it is my responsibility to talk to Mrs. Strongbow about this problem and my everlasting life was at stake. I had to tell Mrs. Strongbow that God only wanted worship for himself and any worship of an object like the Flag would mean I was worshipping Satan. Mom told me to tell Mrs. Strongbow the story about the "Three Hebrew Children," but I had no idea what she was talking about.

I did not know what to do. I was embarrassed to tell Mrs. Strongbow. It seemed silly to think the pledge to the flag is Satan worship. I am so scared. I do not want to go to school tomorrow. I do not want to tell Mrs. Strongbow this stuff. She might laugh at me, or make me do it anyways. What will I do if she won't let me stand in the hallway? What will I do if she laughs at me? If I stand in the hallway, will the other kids in my class laugh at me? I'm really, really scared. I don't know if I can do it. I wish that I did not have to go to school ever again. I am so scared.

September 5, 1955

I talked to Mrs. Strongbow today about the pledge and National Anthem. I was shaking all the time I was telling her. She was more understanding than I thought she would be. I thought she felt sorry for me. I could swear there were some small tears dripping from her eyes. She said I could just step out of the room into the school hallway every morning for a few minutes, then return. I thanked her. She told me she would not say anything about this matter to the other students in my class. I was very happy! I thanked her and felt much better. She told me a few years ago that she had another student who believed the same way as me. I asked her who that was, and she didn't say anything. I almost believe she may have been raised the same as me when she was a little girl. I feel better now.

October 1, 1955

I am having a real problem at school. Even though Mrs. Strongbow did not say anything to the other students why I leave the room, most of the kids now ask me why I do. One of my friends told me to go to the bathroom before I came to school in the morning and laughed. Some of them tease me. I don't like being teased. I told them I do go to the bathroom before school. They don't believe me. What else can I tell them?

I don't dare tell them the Pledge of Allegiance is evil and the National Anthem is a song that honors Satan. They would not like that. I am no longer talking to most of the students. I hardly talk to anybody at school. By avoiding them, there are fewer problems for me. I am becoming a non-person. I still see Brenda and she talks to me. She is a good friend. She is not in my classroom. She knows something is up because Brenda is real smart. She is pretty too. I think girls may be even smarter than us boys. Brenda is the smartest girl that I know.

November 16, 1955

Thanksgiving Day is coming up in two weeks. Dad told me I couldn't do any Turkey or Pilgrim drawings for our art class because I do not believe in celebrating Thanksgiving either. We usually just visit Aunt Katie, Mom's older sister, and eat turkey and watch the football games on TV Thanksgiving Day. I don't understand all this religious stuff anyways. Religion only seems to make your life miserable and less happy. Dad said we would not be going over to Aunt Katie's this year. He said we will stand downtown on a street corner handing out magazines printed by ***"God's Disciples and Publishers"*** on Thanksgiving Day. He said the end of the world is coming very soon. Dad said it is our responsibility to bring in new members to our church so God will not kill them when he destroys our human civilization. Dad said

God is going to kill everyone who is not a member of our church. The Elders of the church said the only way to salvation is by being a member of our church and giving out *"**God's Publishers**"* books and magazines. Dad wants to be a Deacon in the church. He said he could not be a Deacon unless his wife and I are in subjection to him and God. This time, I did look up the word "subjection." It has the same meaning as "helplessness" or "hopelessness" or "weakness." That did not sound good. It seems to mean Dad is in charge of everything and Mom and I are helpless without his guidance. Dad said God is the head of Jesus, and Jesus is the head of man, and man is the head of woman. As a kid, I am at the bottom of the list. It means Dad is just below Jesus in power. That scares me. Dad said I must be a publisher for him to become a Deacon. He told me a publisher is a member of *"**God's Disciples and Publishers**"* who goes from door-to-door and sells their stuff for four months in a row. We have to report to the church how many hours we sell stuff and what we sell to people. I told Dad that I would rather just celebrate Thanksgiving as we used to and not be a publisher. Dad said I had evil thoughts and smacked me on the ass. I don't think Dad loves me anymore. Life sure isn't fun like used to be.

December 1, 1955

Thanksgiving was boring. We stood on the street corner for three hours and I sold four magazines. It was cold standing outside. It started to snow and some of it got on my magazines. I was shivering the whole time we were there. My nose was getting stuffy, too.

I was embarrassed when a couple of my classmates came by and saw me standing on the street holding up the magazines. I pretended to look the other way and not see them, but I know they saw me. Maybe they will forget about it by Monday when I go back to school. But, I know they won't. They will ask me what I was doing downtown with those magazines. I will have to tell them all about our church and that stuff. I do not want to go to school Monday. Maybe I can pretend to be sick and Mom will let me stay home. Maybe I will really get sick and I can stay home. When I saw my classmates' downtown, I wanted to just run and hide my head in a trashcan.

December 5, 1955

We haven't bought any Christmas presents this year. Dad said Christmas is also a day when we honor Satan, but other churches are fooled into believing they are honoring Jesus. Dad said we would not have a Christmas tree, because it is evil. There will be no singing of Christmas carols at school or in our house. He told Aunt Katie not to get us gifts this year. I hope she gives me one anyway. We don't see much of her or Uncle RJ anymore. I liked to play with their son, my cousin Jimmy during softball season. He is a good softball player. Jimmy is my special friend because he is my cousin. He looks a little bit like me, but I am taller. I really miss Jimmy.

The kids, who saw me Thanksgiving Day on the street corner with the religious magazines, teased me again Tuesday. I started to tell them about how God was going to kill me if I did not give out ***"God's Disciples and Publishers"*** magazines, but I thought it would be better if I kept my mouth shut. I told them my parents made me do that stuff. They started to laugh and poked their fingers in my ribs and called me "Church boy, Church boy, Church boy." I turned away and looked toward the floor as I walked into our classroom. I think they thought we were selling the magazines to get some money. I hope they do not think we are poor. I have decided to speak to my classmates only if they speak to me. I hate school. I hate school. I hate school. I hate school. I hate school. I hate school. I hate school. I hate school.

December 27, 1955

Christmas is over. Aunt Katie did send me a present, but Mom and Dad made me give it back to her. I do not know what was in the box, but she looked sad when my parents asked her to go home. I was going to go next door to visit Mark and Roger Williams who are twins. They are one year younger than I am. They invited me to play with some of the toys they got for Christmas. Dad said those toys would be evil and I should stay away from non-believers. He said God only blesses true believers. Dad says we have the "truth" and that "truth" has set us free from the evils of the world. If we have the truth and God loves us so much, why do I feel so badly all the time? Much of my time is spent sitting in my bedroom reading books. I sneak down to the school library and check out lots of books about boats, ships, and stories written by Jack London. I read then on the sly, because my parents only want me to read stuff published for our church. Almost every night after Mom and Dad go to bed, I sneak out a book and read with my flashlight. I like being alone. No one teases me. I like reading the books of people who enjoyed having adventures in their lives. Jack London lived a lifestyle similar to the stories in his books. I would like to live in Alaska and the Yukon, alone with my dog Max. Maybe I would see Sergeant Preston and his sled dog King up there. I would love to mine gold, or just explore the mountains by myself. It would be fun to be in a cabin with snow all the way up to the roof for the entire winter. It would be just Max and me and nobody. I would bring enough books to read all winter long. I want to be alone, away from church people. My vocabulary is improving as I read novels. My real friends are dead authors. Sometimes I wish that I were dead.

Dad said I might not be able to play softball next summer because we will be going to an eight-day religious assembly in New York City. I want to play softball. What does God have against having fun? I must put this journal away for tonight and see what is happening in Jack London's story, the Sea Wolf. I like Wolf Larson who is the captain of the Sea Wolf. He can question life and get away with it. Wolf Larson has some good discussions with Hump about religion, life and death. Hump was a writer who was forced to work on the Sea Wolf ship when the ship he was riding on sank and one of the sailors on the Sea Wolf rescued him. I dream that I am Wolf Larson. Why couldn't I have been born as Jack London, or Wolf Larson?

Sometimes I don't feel as if I have a life of my own. I am becoming the property of our church, forced to accept the world is evil. I wish I could go to sleep and wake up when I am 21 years-old and living on my own.

February 4, 1956

Today is my birthday. I'm twelve years old. Nobody wished me a "happy birthday." Mom said it was just "another day" and told me to get my *"God's Disciples"* guidebook and read about pagan celebrations. I didn't know that I am a pagan. Dad told me to join the "Preaching School" which meets once every Wednesday evening at the church. I will be required to give ten-minute Bible talks. Dad said I would write my own talks and they must be good. He said I had better not embarrass him because I was not prepared to speak in front of the church. He told me it would be good if I got baptized at the next religious assembly. If I were baptized, it would be a credit to him and he could become a Deacon Study Conductor. He would have a weekly study meeting with about six *"God's Disciples"* families. Every Tuesday evening, we would go to a home where the leader would say a prayer and we would study one of our religion's books. Dad wants to be a Deacon real bad. He said it will give him respect in the church and people would look up to him. I don't want to get baptized, but he'll probably make me anyways. Maybe when they stick my head under the water I can find Jesus! If Mom were ever to read my journal, she would slap me again.

Mom and Dad never laugh at anything anymore. They said I was always supposed to be serious and act like an adult. I am just a kid, and I used to enjoy being just a kid.

But, this is my goddamn birthday. Dad and Mom don't love me anymore. All they talk about is their stupid dumb shit religion. If I ever disagree with what they say, I get a smack across the ass. I hate myself. I hate God. I hate religion. I hate my parents, and I hate school and everyone in the world. Why cannot everything be the way it was before those *"God's Disciples"* people knocked on our door?

March 22, 1956

Today is the first day of spring. This morning, I watched a robin pull a worm out of the ground. I wish I was a bird. Dad said that I would not have time to play soccer this spring. He said I could play a few softball games, but I can't join any league. I don't know what to do. The kids at school ignore me. I like being a non-person. Last week I saw an old movie on television about the "Invisible Man." It would be nice to be invisible, just going to school and sitting there and being invisible. I don't answer questions in class much anymore when the teacher asks them. I don't get my homework done either. I still read my novels. I think Mom found them in my closet, but she did not say anything about me reading them. I am glad she did not tell Dad.

I sat with Brenda during math class today. She is getting really pretty. She is starting to get boobs. Brenda is the only person I can talk with. I think she understands about our religion, but she is a non-denominational Christian, whatever that may be. We don't talk religion. Brenda sure is getting pretty. I feel real funny when I am around her.

April 23, 1956

Dad said they excommunicated a man at our church last Friday. He said the Elders caught Brother Bradshire smoking a cigarette. After they told him about the evils of tobacco, Brother Bradshire failed to repent his horrible sin. Elder Jacob Kostra saw Brother Bradshire smoking in his garage as he drove by to go to church. He reported it to the Presiding Elder who called a special meeting with Brother Bradshire at church. Dad said Brother Bradshire told them he tried to quit smoking several times, but couldn't. The Elders just kicked him out of the church. Mom and Dad said I could no longer speak to Brother Bradshire. They said if I saw him walking down the street to look the other way and pretend not to see him. I guess God really hates cigarettes. Dad said Jehovah would kill Brother Bradshire at the Battle of Armageddon if he did not repent and rejoin the church. Brother Bradshire must be a terrible and evil person to continue smoking even though he knows it is a terrible sin worthy of death. He doesn't look like a Satan worshipper. Mom told me not to talk with his sons, Jamie and Philip Bradshire who go to the same school as me. That will not be a problem; I don't speak to anyone anyways. My grades have dropped from A's and B's to C's. I don't care anymore. If I had a cigarette, maybe I could smoke it and the church would excommunicate me. I would like to light it up at the church. I would like to see the looks on their faces when I took a great big puff. I would inhale it so hard my face would turn bright red. I know that it would not happen because I am afraid of the Elders. I know Dad would kill me himself if he caught me smoking.

I talked to Mom and Dad about playing softball again. They told me I could play five games this summer, but no more. They said I should rethink my goal of becoming a professional baseball player. Dad said I should have a career as a Special Missionary for *"God's Disciples and Publishers."* Dad said it isn't important to go to college. He said the church would give me the training I need to be a good minister. Mom and Dad want me to work at the World

Headquarter of the church and help in their publishing plant. Dad said they pay workers four dollars a day. Dad said it would be like working with the Apostle Peter in the Jerusalem after the death of Jesus. Someday I could preach in a foreign country such as India. Becoming a missionary would show that I care about saving people who are not members of our church. Mom and Dad said they would be proud of me. I would rather be dead. I cannot imagine spending the rest of my life reading that shit and preaching to people. Why would I want to live in India? Mrs. Strongbow said India is a terrible place to live with its poverty and starvation. How could those people have money to buy *"God's Disciples and Publishers"* books and magazines? I wanted to tell Dad if I were back in the first century, I would murder Peter to stop all this religion bullshit. Instead, I just said; "Yes, yes, Dad. It would be nice to be a missionary." If I disagree with Mom or Dad about our church, my life would become intolerable.

I walked home from school today. I looked down at the sidewalk the entire way home. I counted the number of sidewalk blocks. I never look up anymore. I would rather look at concrete, and perhaps find some coins other people dropped. I never look people in the eyes anymore. I like looking at the ground. Maybe someone will hit me with a car and kill me.

I don't have real faith in God, so He doesn't like me. I swear and cuss at school. I feel free of the church when I say bad things. I hate my life.

June 10, 1956

Another school year has ended. I said good-bye to Brenda today. I felt a tear in my eye. Brenda is my only friend. My parents will not allow me to talk with her outside school anymore because Brenda's parents refused to talk with a couple of *"God's Disciples"* ministers who went to their house. Dad said Brenda and her parents are part of Satan's Organization. If I knew where Satan's Organization was located, I think it would be nice to be a member. If Satan allows birthday parties, Christmas, and other good things, he must be better than Jehovah. I must be careful, if my parents knew what I wrote in my Journal, they would burn it. Then, they would take me before an Elders' tribunal for counseling or excommunication. That would devastate my dad who is now an Elder himself. I care more about my dad and his feelings than he cares about me. He said he won't have time to coach softball again. He won't have time to come to my five games either. Dad said the time is short before Armageddon it is important for me to preach so others can join our church and be saved. Otherwise, Dad said, "There would be blood on your hands Nathaniel, for not saving some of Jehovah's children." I feel guilty for wanting to play softball and not save people.

August 22, 1956

School will start in two weeks. Who cares? I played my five softball games, and hit one home run. My coach wanted me to play full-time, but after talking to my dad, he didn't ask again. Dad started preaching to Coach Thornton telling him God was shortly going to kill everyone who was not one of *"God's Disciples Church,"* so there isn't time for Nathaniel to waste playing softball.

Coach Thornton turned his head and looked at me. He said; "Nathaniel, if you ever, ever need any help for any reason, please come and talk with me." I know Coach Thornton felt sorry for me. I was embarrassed at what Dad told him. I wanted to just crawl down a sewer hole and drown in a stinking pool of shit water. I hate my life. I like Coach Thornton. I wish he were my dad.

February 5, 1957

Happy birthday to me, happy birthday to me, happy birthday dear me, happy birthday to me. I was thirteen years old yesterday. Brenda walked home from school with me yesterday and wished me a happy birthday. I know she feels sorry for me. She didn't walk all the way to my house. She took a different way home when we were about a block away. Before saying good-bye to me, Brenda turned toward me, stood up on her toes and gave me a quick kiss on the cheek. She then smiled and wished me a "happy birthday, Nathan" and ran off. It was the best day of my life. When I got home, no one else mentioned my first day as a teenager. Dad told me it was time to study my Bible lesson. I made the mistake of telling him I did not want to do it. He took off his leather belt and smacked me on the ass three times. He said it was God's command to punish children when they talk back to their parents. Dad quoted some stupid scripture saying, "spare the rod and spoil the child." I guess God wants people to use belts on kids' asses. If God is going to kill 6 billion people in a mass genocide, then he doesn't care about the pain on my ass today. Dad is like God. Dad is cruel, and so is God. Sometimes I think Dad thinks he is God. I don't care anymore.

I'm going to go to bed, read a Todd Moran mystery story and dream about the birthday kiss Brenda placed on my cheek. Sometimes I dream I am a professional baseball player, breaking Babe Ruth's home run record. Sometimes I dream that I am riding a horse with Roy Rodgers and living in the Wild West. I would like to be living in the days where I would not worry about anything but my horse. I never saw Roy Rogers go to church. If I get married, I don't want any kids. I wouldn't want a kid to live my life. Tonight, I will dream about Brenda.

My life is only tolerable because of my dream world. When I am dreaming I can be anything or anybody. Sometimes I dream my dreams like a movie serial, with one sequence tonight and the next tomorrow night. Tonight I will be the greatest baseball pitcher in the world. Tomorrow, I will go into outer space like the movie; "From the Earth to the Moon."

Sometimes I dream about Armageddon. My dreams become nightmares. I wish that God would stay out of my dreams.

May 1, 1957

Brother Leonard Fine was killed in an automobile accident three days ago. We went to the funeral today. The Elder talked about how faithful Brother Fine had been as a full-time preacher for "**God's Disciples**." Brother Fine was a member of our church for 31 years. His wife died three years ago of breast cancer. I didn't know he had children. A woman who looked to be in her early 20's came to the funeral service. Dad said she was Brother Fine's only daughter. Dad said we could not speak to her because she was an apostate. I asked him what an apostate was. Dad said it was someone who quit our religion and believes something else. Mom said Brother Fine's daughter is an evil person because she told some people in our church that our doctrines were wrong. I looked at Brother Fine's daughter. She was standing by herself. A little girl stood beside her. Mom said Leonard Fine's daughter is named Linda. She was in a way named after her dad, Leonard. I looked at Linda and she was crying. No one walked over to her, nor did anyone offer her comfort. I felt bad for her. I know Linda probably loved her parents. No one else was crying. Linda and the little girl remained alone.

We left the funeral home and started to go to the cemetery. Dad saw that Linda and the little girl didn't have a ride, so he asked them to go with us. She gladly accepted. All the way to the cemetery, Dad and Mom didn't speak to her. She left our car and walked with her little girl to the graveside. Mom and Dad wouldn't walk with her. People moved away as she put a rose on her dad's casket. Dad whispered to Mom; "It's another pagan ritual."

Mom and Dad took Linda back to the funeral home. When we arrived, she got out of our car and said; "Thank you" and walked away. Mom did say, "You're welcome." I don't know how she got home from the funeral home. I felt bad for her. I never saw them again.

June 2, 1957

My Uncle Henry got married today. He and his bride are Catholics. At first Mom and Dad said we wouldn't go to the wedding. Henry wanted Dad be his Best Man, because they are brothers. Uncle Henry is ten years younger than my dad. Dad said we couldn't go into a Catholic Church because of all the statues inside. He explained that God hated people who worshipped images, and according to the *"God's Disciples,"* the Catholics were the worst offenders. He told me Satan loves Catholics because of their image worship. Mom said it didn't matter what kind of church they were going to get married in, if it was not one of ours, then it would be wrong to go inside the building. Dad and Mom did go to Uncle Henry's wedding reception. We sat alone. Dad and Mom only said a few words to Uncle Henry and his new bride, Aunt Marge, who is pretty. Uncle Henry seemed disappointed because we didn't go to the ceremony. I was hoping Dad would not go into a long speech about the evils of the Catholic Church. For once, I got my wish. Dad said nothing about religion to Uncle Henry. Dad and Mom didn't buy them a wedding gift. Instead, they gave Uncle Henry and Aunt Marge a year's gift subscription for our *"God's Disciples and Publishers"* most important magazine, titled "New World Watchers." I bet they will be thrilled to start receiving that piece of shit in the mail.

July 17, 1957

Our church assembly was held in Pittsburg this week. I was baptized. Dad said it would be recognized as a real act of faith and showed my confidence in "God's Disciples" for me to get baptized. I got baptized because I don't want to die. Dad said if I wasn't baptized, God would kill me with all the Catholics when Armageddon came. There was another reason. I knew Dad would beat my ass and make my life horrible if I didn't get baptized. My dreams about Armageddon are more frequent and bloodier. Maybe they will stop since I am baptized. I do not want to be killed by God. My baptism made my parents happy, God happy, and the church happy. Perhaps it was for the best, besides there is not much of a life for me outside the church, according to Dad.

October 23, 1957

Halloween is next week. Dad said it is another holiday to honor Satan. I wanted to go to Brenda's Halloween party but didn't ask Mom or Dad for permission. I knew they wouldn't let me go. I don't understand all this stupid crap. How can dressing up in a Donald Duck costume be evil? I think it would be more fun to be evil. I told Brenda that I couldn't go to her party. Her dad called my dad and asked if I could go. Dad told him about Satan worship and how Halloween is a day for devil worshippers. I know that Brenda's dad is not a devil worshipper. I hope he doesn't think my dad is nuts. Brenda promised to sneak some candy and give it to me the day after Halloween. I will like it.

November 4, 1957

Three years ago, Dad told me when I got old enough; he would take me on a deer-hunting trip. Today he said he no longer believed in hunting rabbits and squirrels or killing deer. He said the church teaches you cannot get all the blood out of the animals by shooting them, so we would not be able to eat the animals. Dad said eating blood was a serious offense and God would never forgive a blood eater. Dad and Mom won't buy chickens from the food market anymore. They said the slaughterhouse might not bleed them properly.

Yesterday, Dad drove to a farm out in the countryside where they sell live chickens. We watched as the farmer cut the heads of ten chickens, reached his hand inside their warm bodies and pulled out their guts. He dipped them in boiling water and plucked off all their feathers. One of the chickens ran across the yard after his head was cut off. Blood squirted out of the hole in its neck. Dad said it was necessary for us to watch this to know the chickens had been bled the right way. I threw up. Dad got mad at me.

When we got home, Mom fried up a chicken for supper. I looked at it and couldn't eat. Dad sent me to bed. I went to sleep and dreamed about chickens, blood and guts. My stomach hurts.

December 21, 1957

Christmas is near. Aunt Katie hasn't been invited to our home in a year. She called and asked us to her home, but Dad said he couldn't go because of his church responsibilities. I miss Aunt Katie. Mom said if we associated with Aunt Katie and Uncle RJ, our spirituality would be challenged. It is best not to see them at all. Mom said Satan would try every means to bring us into his evil organization. Mom said that Satan is using Aunt Katie to lure us out of the church.

School let out for Christmas vacation today. I will be bored for the next two weeks, but Dad said we would be spending a lot of time going from door-to-door preaching about the end of the world. Whoopee shit. We spend about 15 hours a month going from house-to-house, giving away and selling *"God's Disciples"* books and magazines. I have to write down the address where I sell stuff, go back in two weeks, and ask them how they liked reading the silly shit. I don't read the damn books myself, except when Dad forces me to read them for our meetings. It is more interesting to sit and watch a dog lick his privates than to read stupid religious shit.

I'm scared to talk to people. I don't like strangers, I don't like going from house-to-house, and I don't like God. Dad said that Jehovah is a father. He said that God has a son. He told me God had to let his son get killed so his own personal name "Jehovah" would be honored. Why would God let his son get killed? That was the dumbest thing I have heard in my life. God is a lot like my father. Would he let me die to get honored too? I have no doubt he would do so. I am sure Dad values his life more than he cares about mine.

January 5, 1958

I'm back in school after what seemed to be a short Christmas break. There is no happiness for me anymore, neither at home nor at school. I got to see Brenda again at school. Talking with Brenda, makes me feel good. Mrs. Strongbow told us about the possibility of a nuclear war with the Soviet Union. She said some people are building fallout shelters in case we go to war. Mrs. Strongbow said people with fallout shelters are putting guns inside to shoot anyone who may try to break in and steal their food if we go to war. If atom bombs are dropped, Mrs. Strongbow said people would live in those shelters for several months. I got to thinking what it would be like. After a while, the shelter would be full of shit! Ha ha ha ha ha ha ha.

Maybe what our church is teaching is true. Maybe the end of the world is coming. If the Russians send bombs over here, I will stand outside my house and be vaporized. I wouldn't have to spend several months in an old fallout shelter with Mom and Dad reading **"God's Publisher's"** books and standing up to my neck in shit.

January 14, 1958

Mom took me to the doctor today. I have a snotty nose. I've had a cold and sinus infection most of the winter. Since we started going from door-to-door a couple of years ago, I'm constantly sick during the winter months. I cough and hack, sometimes until my face turns as red as my ass does when Dad hits me with his belt. My doctor told Mom not to keep me outside for long in cold windy weather without wearing a cap and warm clothing. He said I should be wearing a scarf around my neck. He told her to have me stay warm and indoors until the sinus infection heals. I'm sure it's not going to happen.

Our churches Elders tell us we are more than just "fair-weather" Christians. We must preach the message about the end of the world both when we are well and sick. They called it "both in season and out of season." Nobody misses church meetings unless they are near death. I must shake hands with every man and boy at our church before each meeting. I probably get many of my sinus infections and colds from other people who go to church and blow their snot on a rag, then stick it in their rear pocket before shaking hands with me. Some of them even sneeze without covering their noses. I told Dad I didn't want to be sick. He said, "God would take care of me." I wish God would start protecting me, because I feel like I am going to suffocate from all the boogers in my head.

Feb. 4, 1958

Another birthday, another year, another day living in hell. Brenda sent me a birthday card. I managed to get it out of the mailbox before Mom and Dad got their mail. I know they would just throw it away if they had seen it. Today, I'm fourteen years old. My sinus infections are not much better. I just seem to get over one when I catch another virus. My right pocket is always wet with yellow slime on my handkerchief. I carry three handkerchiefs with me. I rotate them from one pocket to the next with the left hip pocket reserved to dry the worst wet one, which made its journey from my front to right rear pocket finding a final spot in the left hip pocket. After it dries enough, it makes it back to the front pocket where I start to use it again. It has completed a circle.

Dad said there would be no soccer playing this year for me. He said I could still play five games of softball if I did well at church. Dad volunteered me to cut the church grass and clean the bathrooms in the church building this summer. He said it would be good training for me because many of our church members become janitors after high school and are involved in cleaning businesses. Dad said I would be a good janitor. This means he would rather have me cleaning out shithouses and swishing toilets than playing professional baseball. I'm getting sick of this religious crap. Dad had me clean up the church bathroom room after a kid went in there and puked on the sink and wall. He said that God would give me an extra blessing for being such a good servant of His. Let God clean up the puke. After all it is his damn shithouse the kid puked in. Some of the little boys piss on the wall behind the toilet. It stinks. If God wants me to be a piss polisher, I will do it. I hate church. I hate Dad. I hate God. I just thought of something! If I start preaching when I am cleaning the bathroom, does that make me a shithouse prophet? Ha ha ha ha! Perhaps I should spit shine the porcelain God.

May 17, 1958

Dad said there would be a special announcement at our annual church assembly this summer in New York. I can hardly wait. It is a bullshit book we will have to dissect next year at church. Last year they published a book about the book of Revelations, the last book in the Bible. It is titled, ***"An In-depth Analysis of Revelations."*** It was the most convoluted collection of bullshit I had read in my life. According to them, everything in the Bible means something else.

Only *"God's Prophets and Publishers"* can interpret the real meaning in the Scriptures. The Elders say everything in Revelations was written for our last days and especially *"God's Prophets and Publishers."* Apparently, our religion is the only one God uses to spread the truth about Armageddon and the last days of mankind. According to Dad, if I do not agree with what they tell me to believe, it is just tough shit. Of course, I took what Dad said out of context. He didn't really say the word "shit," but "shit" is what he would have said if he was honest with me. I am beginning to talk more slang, as I get older. Of course, I only do this at school and write it in my journal. God's Disciples have my body but they cannot have my mind. I guess talking slang is just another part of growing up, or perhaps I do not give a goddamn about anything. If Dad and Mom knew I talked slang, they would beat the fucking hell out of me.

During summer vacation when school is over and all my classmates are having fun, I will be cleaning shithouses, wiping piss off walls, and sticking sanitary napkins in the Ladies' room dispenser. Most important of all, making sure there is enough ass wipe hanging in the church bathrooms. I thought about sprinkling some cayenne pepper on the shithouse toilet paper in the men's room. Perhaps one or two of the Elders could come out of there with their assholes on fire. My life is not worth living.

I started cutting the church grass last week. Dad would not let me use the gasoline lawn mower. He said the exercise of pushing the 20-inch rotary push mower would do me good. That is what I need, all the pollen propelled in the air by the lawn mower giving me more sinus infections. I told him I could get better exercise by playing softball, and Dad never cracked a smile. I guess God does not smile much either. I don't think God has a sense of humor. He is like my dad.

I considered getting some weed and grass killer and using it to write the word "Fuck" in the churchyard. When it killed the grass, everyone could see my message. But, like many other ideas; I think about them, but do not have the courage to do what I dream about. Without my dreams, my real life would be worthless and a void without thought.

June 4, 1958

I ran all the way home from school today. I like running and will do more of it. Besides, it is something I can do by myself. I don't have to be around people when I run. It would be nice to run every day. I love the feel of the breeze moving through my hair as I sprint down the sidewalk. Running clears my mind of the church, people, and life in general. I feel elated as I run faster and faster with nothing in my mind but the thought of getting somewhere quickly. The runner's rush feels good and I can watch the world just fly by. I try to run two miles a day. Running is a sport I can do alone. I like being alone, with nothing but my private thoughts. When I run, I can watch the world as if I were a television camera panning the horizon. People do not speak to runners, they only watch as they pass by. I run until my heart pounds in my chest like a judge's hammer during a court trial. My head gets hot and my legs and body ache. When I stop to catch my breath, I like hanging my head down toward the ground and putting my hands on my knees. Perhaps I will get lucky, have a heart attack and die. It would make my parents feel like martyrs at church and they would have a goddamn party after my funeral. I know Brenda would cry.

July 25, 1958

We packed our stuff to go to our annual assembly of ***"God's Disciples and Publishers"*** today. I get so sick of wearing a business suit and necktie. It is going to be 100 degrees this week in New York City and I will be wearing this goddamn polyester suit and nylon necktie. I will be sitting in the assembly stadium with the sun shining in my face while listening to some boring speaker and feeling sweat running down my back and into the crack of my ass. Dad said we show our respect for God by dressing properly for all the meetings. When I die, I hope they bury me naked with my ass pointing up at the whole world. It would show everyone the rash on my ass caused by all the sweaty assemblies. Maybe they will tie a nylon necktie around my waist and lay it across my butt, draping it down my ass.

July 28, 1958

I hid my journal in my suitcase. I feel freedom when I can put my thoughts on paper. Today we went to an all-day session at the assembly stadium. There were over 40,000 God's Disciples members sitting in the stands. It was impressive to look at all the people and see them watching the preaching sessions. We bought some hot dogs at the food stand. My hot dog was green inside so I could not eat it. There were some rumors going around that some of the people got sick from the food, but one of the announcement speakers said it was just a rumor and unfounded. I know he lied. I would like to stick the green hot dog that I bought down his goddamn throat and see if he got sick.

The main speaker today announced that Armageddon would be here in 1965 and the Earth would become a paradise full of *"God's Disciples and Publishers"*. It sounds like living in hell to me. I hope that I am one of those people God kills; it would be better than living for eternity serving the church. Dad and Mom were elated over the announcement. Dad said; "See Nathaniel, I told you that you would not need college. You will be living in a perfect world when you are twenty-one years old!"

I asked dad if God is going to kill Brenda. Dad said it would probably be that way. He said if someone does not become a member of our church, then God would judge him or her harshly. The speaker continued to tell stories about blood flowing to the heights of Chevrolet truck headlights and Jesus hacking bodies with a long white sword while riding on a white horse across the Heavens. He told us it would be our responsibility to clean up all the dead bodies after the great Battle of Armageddon. I will graduate from cleaning the church shithouses into cleaning up dead bodies. God, what a life I will have. It seems Jesus is willing to kill people as that farmer killed those ten chickens for us. It makes me sick to think about it. I still don't like eating chicken.

I wish I were back home and running across the field. I would run until by heart would pump enough blood into my brain to cause a hemorrhage and drop dead. There is nothing to look forward to anymore. No softball, no baseball, or anything else. I am waiting for a pissed off God to murder everyone so I can clean up his stinking bloody mess.

My dad said there is no reason for us to go to the dentist anymore. Dad said we would be getting perfect teeth in 1965, so the money would be better spent selling ***"God's Disciples"*** books and magazines.

The speaker told us it would not be a good to plan to get married. He said the time left before 1965 should be spent preparing for Armageddon by putting more hours into door-to-door preaching and delivering ***"God's Disciples"*** literature. He said all young men and teenagers should plan for a life of being full-time ministers for the church. Whoopee shit, what a fucking future to look forward to.

The speaker said; "if a young man has the opportunity to be a full-time minister and does not take it, he would be guilty of bloodguilt by God for not telling people about the beauty and love in our church membership." I can never do enough to please God or the church. I can never do enough to please my parents. But I'm a good shithouse cleaner. I'm going crazy.

August 27, 1958

Back to school next week. What a shitty summer. Dad said because the time was so short before Armageddon, I could no longer play softball. He called a gathering of the church Elders at our home to counsel me. They showed me Bible scriptures they said proved "bodily training does little." They talked to me about becoming a full-time minister of the gospel. I just agreed with everything they said, by saying, "Yes sir, yes sir." In my mind, I was saying; "Fuck you, fuck you, and fuck you."

Aunt Katie dropped by to say hello to Mom yesterday. She said Grandma and Grandpa Porter are not doing very well. They are Mom and Aunt Katie's mom and dad. Aunt Katie has decided to go over to Grandpa Potter's home and fix them meals twice a week. Mom said; "That's nice of you, but I will not have time to help you. We have our responsibilities with our meetings and church duties. Besides, Grandma and Grandma Potter told me I should never have gotten involved with *"God's Disciples"* and they rejected our beliefs. We cannot do much for them because when they rejected our church - they rejected God."

Aunt Katie replied "I am not a member of your church either. It seems to me your church should be preaching love and empathy for everyone, not just their own members."

"We believe in and teach love, but we can only support people who agree with our church doctrines. Everyone else, including relatives like our Mom and Dad, who refuse to believe our religion, is judged by God to be a member of Satan's organization. We cannot be around those people. They would be a bad influence on our spirituality and perhaps draw us out of the truth. Sorry, Katie, but this includes you."

"I am not evil!" Aunt Katie shouted. "Your church is evil. You treat our parents with contempt because of your stupid religion! Look what it is doing to your son. He is introverted, hardly speaks to anyone and is not the boy I knew three years ago! Where is your parental responsibility about Nathaniel and his needs?"

Mom told Aunt Katie to "leave our home and do not come back unless you want to study the Bible with us." Aunt Katie left and I went into my room, crawled under my bed and cried like a little kid.

January 1, 1959

Happy New Year. Bullshit. It is just another day to me uncertain and boring. Life is getting to be a drag. Dad and Mom continually make me go from door-to-door and sell the goddamn books and magazines we get from church. I don't feel I'm saving lives by selling stupid shit. Perhaps it would make good toilet paper. I tried it once, but it left ink on the back of my ass. It was kinda funny to look down and see "Published by the God's Disciples and Publishing Company" as a stained mirror image on the back of my ass. My life is nothing more than a mirror image of yesterday, the same today and tomorrow. Just once I would like to see my life backwards, like the mirror image on my ass. Ha ha ha ha ha ha ha ha ha ha ha!

I feel sorry for other kids who grow up in this religion. I suspect many of them must feel like I do. I cannot wait to get out on my own. I have much to look forward to. I'm the best polisher of toilet bowls in the congregation. I can scrape off dried turds from the bottom of the bowls with the best of them. Perhaps I can get a diploma with a picture of a shiny, polished toilet bowl on it to show to clients when I start a janitorial service.

My parents stopped the newspaper from coming to our door last year. They also stopped all magazine subscriptions except for of our church published crap. They said we must avoid the politics of the world, so we shouldn't read newspapers. The world was getting more evil every day, and Dad said it wouldn't be long before Jesus would be killing the evil people on our planet. I hope Jesus kills me too. I said this before. My life is like a bad television rerun. My nose is all plugged up again and I am hawking out big gobs of strange looking stuff out of my throat. Dad and Mom said not to worry about it because I would get perfect health when Armageddon comes in 1965. Meanwhile I am drowning in buckets of snot.

March 2, 1959

I did not write anything about my birthday this year. I am fifteen years old, and I believe my parents have no idea how old I am. It has not been a good winter. Max, my pet Yorkshire terrier died in February. He was only nine years old, but he had a bad heart from birth. Some thoroughbred dogs have unseen birth defects from inbreeding. We did not know Max had problems until he started coughing and hacking. The vet said fluid was gathering in Max's lungs and causing the wrenching and coughing. I woke up one morning to find Max on his side and dead in his doggy bed, which was at the foot of my own bed. I loved Max; in secret, I called him my "atheist pal." Dad said dogs never get a resurrection or have everlasting life. It seems God has no use for dogs and just watches them die off. I don't believe Dad or the church. If there is a God and he is kind, he should resurrect all the dogs and just nuke the people on Earth. I wish that I were a dog and could just eat and sleep, and never have to worry about religion or giving out stupid magazines and books to people who laugh at you.

I wanted to bury Max in the backyard and mark his grave. Dad said I would be giving too much importance to an animal, and thus it probably would be a sin. Instead, he forced me to put Max in a plastic bag, wrap it tight and fasten it with friction tape. Dad and Mom watched as they made me put Max in the garbage trashcan and sit it at the edge of our driveway to be picked up by Trash Management Haulers on Monday morning. I hate both my parents.

My guppies did have babies a few years ago. I ended up with almost 40 of them in one bowl. Brenda wanted them, so I gave her the bowl and enough food to last for months. She still has a couple of guppies; I suppose they are descendants of the originals I gave her. She put a light above the bowl and a castle in the colored gravel in the bed of the tank. Brenda told me the guppies sometimes hide in the castle and vanish. I wish I could hide from everyone, disappearing like a guppy in a fishbowl castle.

Life at home has not gotten any better. I wanted to buy an Elvis record album, but Mom said that his music promoted evil and his stage gyrations were encouraging sexual immorality. I like Elvis. Late at night, I turn on my radio beside my bed and often listen to the top ten rock n' roll songs. Sometimes I sing some of the songs as I run home from school. I have been getting much better with my running. I wish I could try out for the track team; I know I could win if I were running cross-country. I don't talk to Dad or Mom about soccer or softball anymore. The only sport I have left is my private world of running. I am keeping a record of the time it takes me to run two miles. But, I can only view it myself. This is my secret life. Without my secret life, there would be nothing to live for.

May 1, 1959

My dreams have become more intense as I get older. Lately I have been dreaming that I am trapped in a building and can never find the exit. I travel up the elevators, climb out on the building steel, and walk through the many corridors of the building. When I find a window and look out of it, I see darkness, with no real place to run. Sometimes I do get out of the building and begin to run. I run down the darkened streets, behind the houses and try to stay hidden from people who are in pursuit of me. I never get away. They always catch me and bring me back into the building. They are all dressed like *"God's Disciples and Publishers"* Elders. The dream repeats itself night after night. There seems to be no end to it.

July 12, 1959

Our annual *"God's Disciples and Publishers"* assembly is going to be in Pittsburgh this year. The assembly is going to be at the Pittsburg Pirates Baseball Stadium. I wish that I was going to a baseball game instead of the stupid church assembly. The program was the same old bullshit preached last year. The time is short, five and a half more years and Jesus will kick Satan's ass and all non-believers will be so happy that we will smile till the edges or our mouth touch one another on the back of our heads. I have taken what the speaker said out of context, but the real meaning is here.

They preached about the evils of rock and roll music. The speaker said the launch of space satellites is part of the "signs in the Heavens" that mark the end of the evil world. I like the space program. I dream about going up in a rocket and being alone with nothing and nobody to intimidate me. Perhaps someday human beings will put a man on the moon; I hope it will be me. But I know it won't be. The speaker talked about our evil government. He said the only good in this world can be found when one is associating with the members of *"God's Disciples and Publishers."* The speaker made a real hilarious comment today. He said; "We are the happiest people in the world." I laughed so hard inside my head I thought I was going to blow snot out of my plugged nose.

Dad and Mom never smile. They don't talk much without arguing. Dad bitches that he is the family head and expects the house to be cleaned before he gets home at night. Mom says she works outside the home too, and therefore he should be sharing all the work with him. Both of them bitch at me to hurry up and help straighten up the house so we can attend all the meetings. I wanted to go to a Minor League baseball game last week at a stadium in our town. Dad said it would be a meeting night and if we did go, people in our church would think we are "spiritually weak." Dad said we would be setting a bad example for others. I could give a flying monkey fuck what anybody thinks about me anymore. Mom said they always stand for the flag salute and sing the National Anthem at the ball games, and it would be honoring Satan. I am getting tired of hearing the same old shit. If we did go, Mom said it would be best to arrive late and not be part of anything honoring our country. We could pretend to be walking to our seat during the singing of the National Anthem. "But", I replied, "I would miss all the batting practice and autographs of the players."

Dad said getting autographs would be giving honor to the players and I could not ask for autographs if I did go. I don't have a goddamn chance of attending a professional baseball game, or play in one myself. Everything fun is evil. Everyday my life is getting worthless to me.

September 29, 1959

My school coach saw me running from school several times, when he was driving home after teaching all-day. He asked me if I would like to join the track team. Damn right I would! But I told him "no." I said our church does not allow us to play competitive sports and it would be honoring Satan if I ran and beat another schoolmate in a race. He looked at me sadly. I wanted to tell him the truth, I would like to join the team but if I did, my parents would stop all my running and accuse me trying to impress others with my athletic skills, then beat my ass with a belt.

Brenda walked home with me from school today. I don't run every day. She is becoming a good-looking girl. She is the only person that I talk to unless someone speaks to me first. I hate people. I was going from door-to-door preaching our bullshit religious crap last week when a man threatened me with a knife if I did not leave his house. The man told me to take my Bible literature and jam it up my ass so far that it would choke in my throat. When I told my dad and the Elders about this experience, they smiled and said; "See, aren't you glad that you have God's Kingdom! You can be happy knowing that you have the truth and God will condemn that man for his actions at Armageddon in five years." I wanted to take all our literature and do to the Elders what the man told me to do to myself.

I often think about what I am missing in my life when I go from door-to-door, dressed in a cheap polyester suit, and watching people live their lives as I talk to them about our religion. I saw a man watching television with his kids, eating out of a shared bowel of popcorn. He refused the literature. I saw a Mom come to the door with a baby hidden under a towel, breast-feeding her child. She refused the literature, too. I watch children play basketball, ride bikes, and play tag as I walk past them to the next house where I must tell the person living there how their lifestyle would be better if they joined my church and became a member of ***"God's Disciples and Publishers."*** I would walk up to some houses and knock quietly on the door. Knock so quietly that my fist hitting the door would sound like a leaf falling to the dew covered grass in the fall. By pretending to knock, I would be putting on a show for my dad who would be watching me from the car parked in the street. I liked ringing doorbells the best. I could fake that by just putting my finger on the edge of the doorbell ringer and not push it hard enough to engage the contacts inside. I always hope no one will come to the door. I do not want anyone to open the door and start a discussion with me. I am scared of everyone. I remember the man with a knife when I try to sell church crap. I'm scared.

November 7, 1959

I have a toothache. My gums are swollen in the back of my mouth. I told Mom and she gave me some oil of clove to rub on my gums. It took some of the pain away. I saw the school nurse today at school and she sent a note home, requesting my mom and dad take me to the dentist. Dad was very mad. He said our dental problems would be cured at Armageddon. Dad took me to the dentist anyway because he did not want problems with the school.

The dentist said I had a bad cavity and he gave me some medicine to get rid of the infection. The Dentist said he would fill my tooth next week. It is starting to feel better.

November 17, 1959

The dentist fixed my tooth today and Dad did not say much to him. It hurt when he gave me a shot. I don't like shots. Our dentist, Doctor Zuroff said I would need braces for my teeth. He also said I need to get my teeth professionally cleaned every six months. Dad said, "Okay."

After we left the dentist office, Dad said that I would not need braces because Jehovah would fix my teeth and make them all straight when Armageddon comes. He said that he would take me to the dentist if I had any more problems like the cavity, but said I will not be allowed to eat candy. Dad said it was my fault for getting a cavity. Dad was mad when he got the bill. He did not schedule me to get my teeth cleaned either. Maybe it is my fault. I sure cause my mom and dad problems. They would be better off without me. Dad and Mom go to the dentist to get their teeth cleaned. I suppose I cost them too much money. They would be better off if I was dead.

February 4, 1960

I am sixteen years old today. Brenda gave me a birthday kiss, but that is not all. After school today, we walked together in the snow towards her house. The air was cool, but the sky was clear. Everything is beautiful when I am with her. I shared my fears with Brenda. My fears of other kids, my parents and my pessimism about my future are no longer secrets from her. Brenda listened but did not question or argue with me. My parents never listen to me. I think this is what love is, and I am in love with Brenda. We stopped on the way home and walked into a wooded park where I occasionally run when the weather is good. Brenda sat beside me on the old bench behind a huge oak tree. I brushed the snow off the bench before we sat down. We were alone. People don't go to the park in the winter. Brenda leaned her head on my shoulder and put her hand under my jacket. She raised my shirt with her hand and put it on my naked back before rubbing my stomach and chest. Even though I knew what we were doing was wrong and God would punish me severely, I put my hands under her jacket and blouse. My hands cupped her breasts. She was not wearing a bra. Brenda again kissed me. It was the most sensual moment of my life. Yet, it was also the most fearful. Although I knew that I was committing a terrible sin before God, our touching continued. Our Church Elders do not allow petting, and I was not supposed to be with Brenda without a chaperone. I was committing two sins, one of which was serious and grave. I started shaking, and then told Brenda that I was not a good person, and everything in my life except her was a failure. Brenda hugged me even tighter, and told me my life will get better once I turn 18 and leave home to live on my own. I was thinking yeah, right. Then I can clean shithouses for a living, take home newspapers I find jammed behind the water closets to read and become an Elder in the church like my dad. That is if I don't get excommunicated for feeling up Brenda's breasts and sharing long kisses. I could become my dad. The thought of becoming a man like my dad scares the hell out of me. Why do I feel so bad and feel so good at the same time? I don't know. I'm tired of being so confused.

Brenda and I shared our intimacy for a short while before we got up and I walked with her almost to her home. She squeezed my hand and whispered; "I love you Nathaniel" she then let go of me, turned and walked the rest of the way home by herself. Tonight, I won't sleep well. There will be nightmares because I violated Brenda by touching her breasts, sinned against my church and God.

I feel guilty because I did not tell Mom and Dad about this incident. I should confess to the Elders, but I know I won't. I feel like shit.

I asked my parents about getting my driver's license because I am now of legal age. They said it would not be necessary, because I don't have time to go anywhere by myself. Dad said the most important goal in my life is to go from door-to-door, recruit new members for the church, and bring honor to God's glorious name. In my mind, I was saying; "Fuck God."

I cannot drive, I cannot do anything in my life I want to do. There is not much to live for and nothing to look forward to. My grades are now "C's" with an occasional "D" thrown in to boot. I never have time for homework with all the church stuff. I don't care if I learn anything. Life stinks. They say when a baby is smiling, then he or she has gas. I wish I could have gas so I could smile.

March 7, 1960

Dad said the Belcher family quit the church today because they no longer believed all the doctrines. Apparently, Fred Belchur told some people in the church he did not believe the chronology teachings by *"God's Prophets and Publishers."* He mentioned the predictions about Armageddon. Brother Belcher said the church is mistaken and Armageddon would not come in 1965. The Elders called him an "apostate" and they excommunicated him. Fred and his family said they wanted to voluntarily quit the church, but the Elders said it would not make any difference. The Presiding Elder made a public announcement at church saying Brother Belcher and the rest of the family are excommunicated from *"God's Disciples"* and must be shunned. Mom said I was never to speak to Mike and Michelle Belchur who are students in my school with me. Mom said they are now part of Satan's organization and heretics to the church and all of its members. She said they are worse sinners than a person who would take a blood transfusion. Dad described them as "dogs returning to their vomit." It will not be a problem for me to avoid Mike and Michelle at school; I never speak to anyone, except Brenda.

Dad told me I should watch my conduct or I would be excommunicated. He said if I were eighteen and excommunicated, he would kick me out of the house. He could not be an Elder in the church and have an excommunicated adult living in his household. I am scared that I may be removed from the church membership. I am scared of my parents, scared of the church, and scared of God who is an all-powerful taskmaster who requires conformity, and hates recreation and fun.

June 14, 1960

Our President of the United States is making a commitment to put a man on the moon. I still love the space program, and wish I were the one to go up there and be the first man on the moon. Once I arrived, I would disable my rocket and stay there until my oxygen ran out and I died. Just before I died, I would raise my right hand, point it toward the world headquarters of ***"God's Disciples and Publishers,"*** close my hand and extend my middle finger in a final "fuck you" directed toward them. With any luck, my hand would freeze with my finger extended forever. I don't care, my parents don't care, God doesn't care, and nobody cares. Only Brenda cares about me.

Our annual "God's Disciples and Publishers" assembly is going to be in our town. Apparently, they want smaller gatherings so it is going to be held in my high school gymnasium and cafeteria. The gymnasium can be made into an auditorium by removing a false wall separating it from the cafeteria. It is designed to allow graduation commencements. I will be going into eleventh grade next year. I talked to Dad who said I could invite Brenda to go to the assembly with us. I could not believe Dad would allow me to ask her!

I called Brenda on the telephone. I asked her to go to the church assembly with me. Brenda said she discussed it with her parents and they said it would be good for her to explore different religions and churches. That really made me excited. It is the first time I can remember being happy since my birthday party a few years ago. We will pick up Brenda and go to the assembly next Friday evening. Could it be that Brenda would become a member of our church and then I could be with her at least every Sunday? I do not wish her to be committed to our religion, but selfishly, I want to be with her whenever possible. I think I love her more every day.

June 20, 1960

I cannot believe what happened at the annual church assembly gathering. Dad and Mom picked up Brenda and she sat with me in the backseat of our four-door Chevrolet. She was wearing a light blue skirt and white blouse highlighted with a sweater and scarf. Brenda was so pretty. I carried my Bible and songbook. They open our meetings with a song and a prayer. *"God's Disciples and Publishers"* wrote their own songs because they said that all the religious music written by other people was honoring Satan. They consider the classic "Amazing Grace" to be an evil song written by a slave trader. Personally, I believe it is a beautiful song. The Elders leave out the part about how the author of "Amazing Grace" changed his life and refused to support slavery again.

For such a longtime, I had not looked straight ahead nor stood and walked tall and proud. Brenda made me feel out of the ordinary, so I was her escort and she was my angel. We entered the building and walked into the auditorium. Dozens of metal folding chairs were added to the gymnasium side of the expanded room as well as the bleachers. Dad and Mom took a seat in the third row, and I sat next to them with Brenda sitting at my right side. I could see many of the people from our church gawking at Brenda and me as we sat there.

Some in the audience were whispering. There was a crowd, perhaps as many as two thousand people. Every chair was filled.

An Elder approached the lectern and stood on the podium. He introduced the song; "We are God's Publishers" and everyone joined in the singing. After the third verse, we bowed our heads and long prayer was offered.

I sat down and looked at Brenda and she smiled at me. I felt so good and pompous with her sitting next to me. She seemed fascinated and attentive to what was happening, and did not mind being there. The speaker approached the lectern and began speaking;

"Brothers and sisters, teenage boys and girls, today we are going to spend the afternoon session talking about a subject not often discussed, but of utmost importance to your salvation. Today we will talk about sexual immorality, fornication, and masturbation. First, we shall take the next hour and discuss the sin of masturbation."

Brenda looked at me and squirmed down in her seat. She leaned over and whispered into my ear; "Is he serious? Is that what they're going to talk about? You have got to be kidding." I looked at her and could not answer. I couldn't speak. I wanted to die. This was the most embarrassing moment of my life. For the next hour, we sat listing to a detailed discussion of how God will destroy you for playing with yourself. I wanted to die right there. I felt so sorry for Brenda. I'm sure Brenda didn't want to be sitting here in the auditorium listening to this shit. Dad looked over at both of us and said; "Pay attention now, this message is important to your salvation."

I wanted to just stand up, look at the speaker and scream, "Fuck you" or better yet, "Go fuck yourself." After all, the subject was about masturbation. Following the masturbation discussion were detailed premarital sex sins, adultery, and bestiality. The last speaker talked about how some men in the first century used to sin by having sex with sheep. They finished the session with a recommendation that any person who is approaching the age of marriage should decide to remain single and go into full-time missionary work. No surprise here. Any young couple sitting in the auditorium would be too embarrassed to get married. The Elder said one should never get married unless he or she is unable to hold his or her passion. I slid down in my chair, but was unable to disappear.

We left the assembly gathering and Dad drove us home. Brenda looked at me but said nothing. I could say nothing either. I felt like a zombie. There was no thought and no contemplation of anything. I looked at the back of the driver's car seat and saw a spider crawling up the back of it. I slammed it with my Bible, and its dead body was waffled into a flat black smear. I left the spider on my Bible. I wish the spider had been me. We pulled into Brenda's driveway and I walked her to the door. She said nothing, except "Good-bye." I looked at her and said; "I'm really, really sorry. I had no idea they were going to discuss that shit." Brenda turned and opened the door and disappeared inside her home. I cannot stand this anymore. I want to die. I want to die. I want to die, I want to die. I want to die. I want to die. I want to die, I want to die. I want to die. I want to die. I want to die, I want to die. I want to die. I want to die. I want to die, I want to die. I want to die. I want to die. I want to die, I want to die. I want to die. I want to die. I want to die. I want to die, I want to die.

My Personal Notes by Doctor MG. Clinical Psychologist:

Nathaniel was admitted at my psychiatric ward at Central Receiving Hospital during the afternoon of June 30, 1960. The following analysis of Nathaniel Wilford Miller has been included as a summation of my discussions with Nathaniel and gleaned from his personal journal. Mr. and Mrs. Frank Miller gave their son's journal to me on my request for any information that might inform me about Nathaniel's personal thoughts. According to them, they are unaware of the book's contents. Nathaniel is undergoing psychological and medical treatment after attempting suicide. He swallowed several heart stimulant pills he had stolen from his Grandfather Miller's medicine cabinet. After taking the medication and running almost a mile, Nathaniel collapsed on the sidewalk near a bus stop. An unknown person saw him unconscious and called an ambulance. Fortunately, there is no permanent heart damage. This is due to his excellent cardiovascular system because he jogged almost every day. After trying and failing to make progress with Nathaniel regarding his mental health, I requested any information about his personality and daily activities from his parents and friends. This information could give me a clue about treatment for the disturbed young man.

Frank and Mary Miller requested that any psychologist who is assigned to help Nathaniel not discuss religious views contrary to their beliefs. I only examined Nathaniel's fundamentalist doctrines for my psychoanalysis of his mental breakdown and the following conclusions are made from those findings.

Nathaniel and his family are members of *"God's Disciples and Publishers"* which is a minor religion that expects the end of the world to occur sometime soon. After explaining that I'm an atheist, Mr. and Mrs. Miller were content to have me caring for their son. This discussion with the parents could indicate that religion is a reason for some of Nathaniel's psychological problems, as I shall discuss within my summary diagnosis.

Frank and Mary Miller also requested that I not use hypnosis to help Nathaniel. They claimed hypnosis opens the mind to demons and perhaps Satan himself. I explained I'm not trained in hypnosis and therefore do not use hypnosis to treat a patient.

It was not until August 2, 1960 that Nathaniel decided to start sharing and discussing his journal with me. The following summation of our conversation gives me evidence that his mental illness is a direct result of childhood fundamentalist orthodox religious legalism. Here are my conclusions, which are based on private discussions I had with Nathaniel while he was under my care and reading his journal with him.

Nathanial Wilford Miller's Diagnosis

Religion had taken years from Nathaniel's life, but he figured out a way to escape from "God's Disciples and Publishers." To Nathaniel, the only answer was suicide. He told me his childhood memories were nightmare reruns of going from house-to-house telling the "Good News" about God and his righteous plans for His earthly disciples.

I had a private discussion with Frank and Mary Miller who said Christian membership was the only way for Nathaniel. According to Frank Miller, the couple had married and later joined the "Disciples" when a member of the church had come to their door selling Bibles and religious books. Mary got captivated right away and started studying with middle-aged man and an elderly woman who seemed like a loving caregiver. The book studies continued for about a month before Frank decided to join the discussions. According to Nathaniel there was not much Bible discussion, instead they were just reading a "Disciples" published book and reciting what was found in the chapters by rote. If Frank or Mary disagreed with what was discussed, they decided it was because of their Biblical ignorance and readjusted their thinking to match those of the church. According to Mary, compromise isn't allowed. Total uniformity was required in their church doctrinarism. The integrity of the church is dependent on everyone walking the walk and talking the talk of *"God's Disciples."*

When I discussed this matter with Nathaniel, he further said the church had strict rules for family and moral conduct. His fear that God would punish him and kill him for his sins was greater than the punishment his Dad gave him with his belt. Nathaniel hung his head and spoke in a whisper when he told me about what he had done with Brenda.

Frank Miller said corporal punishment is a requirement, not a choice of their church. Nathaniel said his memories were filled with regularly getting his ass beat (his words) for making a mistake about church doctrine.

Nathaniel was forced to attend church four times a week, which did not include the time he spent preaching the "Good News" about the impending "End of the world." He was forced to go door-to-door selling the periodicals and books published by "God's Disciples." The only good recollections Nathaniel could recall about selling the books and magazines was keeping the difference between the cost of the materials and what people were willing to give him under the guise of a "contribution for covering the cost of publishing." Although it was only a few pennies, Nathaniel had something for his time spent bothering people. (His words) Nathaniel read some of the books, but found them confusing, uninteresting, and without obvious purpose and intent. From my own unbiased examination of their literature, I found the books rehashed obscure religious doctrines into something supposed to make sense for present-day humankind.

Nathaniel had a fear of Armageddon; an event that he said was going to change his future. At every church meeting he heard nothing but stories about how (quoting and using his words) "the great wonderful God of Heaven was going to bring a great horde of Angels with Jesus riding upon a white horse to mass murder everyone on the Earth except for of the members of ***"God's Disciples and Publishers."*** Nathaniel said, "God was going to spare the animals this time around and not drown, burn, or blow them away." He also told me; "Jehovah had more respect for the rats, mice, and roaches than he does for humankind." One major disturbance in Nathaniel's life was the death of his dog, Max. Mr. Miller told Nathaniel that animals would not be resurrected and forced Nathaniel to put Max in a plastic bag and leave the dead dog in the garbage can to be picked up by the trash man. Nathaniel told me he still has dreams about Max and wished he could have buried him in the backyard. He cried as he said, "Max was not a piece of garbage. I hate my Dad for what he made me do."

Nathaniel's dad told him many stories about what he referred to as the "Great Tribulation" and "Armageddon." Nathaniel told me he had nightmares about Jesus destroying 99% of humankind by hacking away with a flaming sword, with heads, arms, and legs flying everywhere. The Elders of the church told Nathaniel stories about Jesus sticking his sword into the bodies of little children and pregnant women, tearing unborn babies out or their wombs, ripping children's bodies to shreds and exposing their intestines and hearts because they were not members of ***"God's Prophets and Publishers."*** The body parts fed to birds and other animals invited to a feast of flesh prepared for them by God. The church Elders told Nathaniel if he failed to convert outsiders to the full extent of his abilities, he would be guilty of bloodguilt. God would find him guilty of second-degree murder for not bringing strangers into what they referred to as the "truth."(Church vocabulary keyword) Nathaniel told me his mind and head ached when he thought about the Armageddon crap (his words) taught at church. Nathaniel said the church taught the final battle between Satan and Jesus was prophesized to happen in 1965, and he felt unworthy to fulfill his duty of converting new members. Nathaniel said he felt responsible for the impending deaths of his schoolmates at Armageddon. He failed to tell them about ***"God's disciples and Publishers"*** warning them of the coming great Battle of Armageddon. This is an appalling mental burden to put on a young person.

Nathaniel talked to me about his dreams. At night, he would dream about a huge impetuous Jesus coming to his bedroom and giving a lecture about the sins, Nathaniel had committed. His dreams included watching his classmates killed for their sins. He dreamed Jesus murdered both sets of his grandparents including his Aunt Katie's family because they had refused to join ***"God's Disciples."*** He dreamed Brenda and her parents were hacked to death by the sword of Jesus. Nathaniel said he "tried hard to do what the church required, but sometimes he selfishly thought about his fears and fleshly desires." (His words) During his dream state, Nathaniel said he told Jesus how he was too embarrassed to explain to his classmates the world would soon end and if they did not join the church, they would die. Jesus said the blood of Nathaniel's classmates was his responsibility. Jesus would look down at him and say, "You are a member of Satan's army and don't deserve to be part of my Kingdom." Nathaniel would watch, as the flaming sword would swing at his head and his body remains briefly standing, as his head was hacked from his shoulders, falling toward the ground. He often awoke and remained awake for hours, turning on the light so he wouldn't be in darkness. Nathaniel said his dreams were frequent.

Nathaniel was taught that his only future would be with the church. He often had long discussions with the Elders of his church. He said Brother Frank J. told him he would not graduate from high school if Armageddon came earlier than 1965. The Elders told Nathaniel there was no need to plan for college or trade school, much less planning to become a profession baseball player. Nathaniel said he did concentrate on learning English in school, because a good vocabulary would help him in church. His education in mathematics was limited to the basic needs, because it took time to do the homework needed for advanced algebra and solid geometry. He needed more time for his church janitorial work. Nathaniel avoided biology classes because another Elder, Brother Owen G. explained to him how modern scientists distorted the creation teaching found in the book of Genesis. Brother Owen G. said that all biologists were evolutionists and heretics to the church. Nathaniel got headaches and was confused when he studied the evolutionary theory in school. Nathaniel told me evolution was a possibility but he never discussed the idea with his parents or church Elders. It was another dark sin he kept hidden in his mind to believe in Evolution.

Physical education was limited to what is necessary for graduation. It would be wrong to participate in sports. The ultimate vanity was to be better than someone else was, and that is the goal of competitive sports. Nathaniel discussed his desire to participate in sports as shown in his Journal. He said he loved baseball and softball. Nathaniel said he would have loved to try out for his high school team after playing softball during his early years. His church and parents did not allow it.

Nathaniel told me his physical education teacher encouraged him to become a catcher for the softball team because of his ability to throw to second base and get runners out. Nathaniel had a private conversation with one of his church Elders. The Elder told him that playing softball or baseball could never give him the knowledge he needed to help save his friends and neighbors from destruction by Jesus and God at Armageddon. The Elder reported the conversation to Nathaniel's dad who swatted him three times on his ass with a leather belt (his words) for undermining his family headship. All questions in the future were to be discussed with his dad, not the Elders.

Nathaniel told me he liked to run.(detailed in his journal presented in earlier in this manuscript) Perhaps his running kept him from attempting suicide until the incident with Brenda and the church assembly pushed him over the edge.

I diagnosed Nathaniel as a victim of severe depression. Neither his parent nor his church recognized his suicidal tendency. Although his parents did tell me the church taught that depression can be cured by being regular in the door-to-door work, attending all the church meetings, and prayer. Unless a suicide attempt is made, their church members are encouraged to avoid a professional psychologist. Even if his parents were aware of the problem, it is doubtful Nathaniel would have gotten professional help.

Nathaniel lowered his voice to a whisper and told me he didn't want to wait for Armageddon to cure him of his depression. He did not believe God would find him worthy of surviving the mass genocide of humankind. He would rather die at his own hand than be sliced to death by Jesus, he said. Nathaniel said his head hurt when he tried to ponder the meanings of life, God, and Armageddon. I diagnosed him with low self-esteem, caused by years of religious abuse. In an almost whispering voice, Nathaniel said, "I feel I'm selfish, self-centered, egotistical, and only thinking about my wants." Clearly, from my research, the church encourages members to feel unimportant and unworthy of self-betterment. A loyal member of *"God's Disciples"* would not think of oneself. If he or she did so, it is considered the ultimate in selfishness and vanity. To be egocentric, was to commit a serious sin worthy of church excommunication and shunning.

I asked Nathaniel why everyone was called "brother and sister" in his church. He told me once a person is baptized they become part of the *"God's Disciples"* family. Nathaniel told me it was a way to identify people who were not baptized. A follower would walk with pride knowing they were a "brother of sister" rather than considered spiritually immature and weak. Those who were studying are called Mister or Mrs. or Miss. Only true respect was given to baptized members. Nathaniel thought it was a way of forcing everyone to think and act alike. According to what Nathaniel told me, independent thinking and individuality within the religion is forbidden. Those human virtues are a serious sin.

Nathaniel told me his thoughts about beautiful young girls, dances, music, and dating that he began to have at age 15. Once more, he told me about his lifelong friend named Brenda. Nathaniel believed these so-called worldly thoughts were sins. He could only speak to the girls who were members of "God's Disciples and Publishers" church. The only exception was the platonic relationship he had with Brenda Fox, who attended the same school as Nathaniel. He was required and expected to attempt recruiting Brenda as a member of *"God's Prophets and Publishers."* Brother Reginald F. said there might be some young people within the church who were faithful outwardly but inwardly sinners. He told them to "beware of everyone, trust no outsiders, be watchful of current members, and only have trust in God, Jesus, and the Governing Body who established the doctrines and church legalism for *"God's Prophets and Publishers."* Nathaniel thought Brother Reginald was talking about him. How would Brother Reginald know about his sins?

Nathaniel understood the girls in his church may have evil purposes and he must be on guard to conduct himself to honor God. There were no church sponsored social gatherings. Nathaniel was lonesome for companionship. He wanted a friend, especially a girlfriend. Since Brenda was not a member of his church, she could never be his girlfriend. It would not be allowed. Brenda's parents had rejected **"God's Disciples"** as their religion and Nathaniel could only see her when his parents were not aware of it, or if she wanted to attend his church meetings. Nathaniel's secret friendship with Brenda caused further him depression and guilt feelings.

Nathaniel told me when unmarried people in the church decided to date, they must be with one of their parents. A moral code could never be broken and a mistake never made. Chaperonage rules could not be violated. Nathaniel expressed to me he was tired of being controlled and said his life was not worth living. He did not want to spend the rest of his life living without making decisions for himself.

Nathaniel said anyone in his church who was accused of breaking a sexual or moral code would be called before a Tribunal of church Elders to hold court about their sin. Every detail of the sexual event would be described and explained to these men. If the event were between a young boy and girl, each would have to explain every intimate detail of the sexual experience and be judged according to their remarks and actions. Sometimes the Elders offered forgiveness; at other times, they excommunicated the offenders. Nathaniel said a member had a better chance of forgiveness if his or her dad was an Elder. He believed the Elders did not want the publicity of excommunicating one of their sons or daughters but sometimes it happened. Nathaniel had no confidence his dad would prevent him from being excommunicated if he committed a sin, because his dad had not been an Elder except for a few short years. Nathaniel knew his dad would choose the church over his family loyalties. Nathaniel expressed his fear of excommunication for trying to commit suicide. Trying to kill yourself is a serious sin in the church.

Nathaniel gave more details than what was in his Journal about how he thought his parents would let him die rather than allow a blood transfusion to save his life. Here is a summation of what Nathaniel told me:

When he was fourteen years old, Nathaniel said he developed abdominal pain. He said his dad got angry and told him; "You are just trying to find an excuse to stay home from meeting tonight, and you know darn well I will not put up with your lying crap. You can't stay home because it's your turn to read aloud the paragraphs in study of **"Our Last Days"** book at meeting. I will not put up with your lame excuse. You're going to go to the meeting, no matter what story you come up with." Nathaniel said he remembered the conversation, because it hurt him almost as much as the pain in his abdomen.

Nathaniel said he went to meeting and read the paragraphs, while the pain in his abdomen continued to get more intense. Like most of his religious meetings, he had to pretend to smile with the pretense of being the happiest person on Earth. Nathaniel said sometimes he would go home and his face would hurt from all the fake smiling he did to please his parents, his God, and his church. It was important to leave a good impression of true happiness at the church meetings. Nathaniel left the book study with his parents, went home and took a shower. Nathaniel worked on his school homework, which was seldom completed on a meeting night. He went to bed.

Around 2:30 A.M., Nathaniel said he woke up nearly delirious with a high fever. His body was wet with perspiration. The pain was so intense he went into the kitchen to get a cold pack stored in the freezer to put on his abdomen. Nathaniel told me while he was walking back to his bedroom he collapsed in the hallway. His mother awakened by his fall, finding Nathaniel on the beige nylon carpet outside of his parents' bedroom. His dad called an ambulance and Nathaniel was taken to Mercy General Hospital. His diagnosis was appendicitis.

Nathaniel said he was conscious when he arrived at the hospital. He heard the attending doctor at Mercy General recommended an immediate appendectomy. Nathaniel told me he looked up at the lights in the ceiling of the emergency room as he lay on the stretcher. He said he tried to forget about the pain by counting the stained acoustic tiles in the ceiling. "Let's see, ten tiles back and forth and 16 up and down. That makes 160 tiles." He told me that he tried counting them individually and the answer was the same. He remembered the details about the number of ceiling tiles. Nathaniel said he listened to his dad argue with the Doctor.

"We do NOT believe in any blood products and will not allow the surgery unless you agree not to use blood during or after the procedure. It is a violation of the law of Jehovah God and if we permit it, our son's hope of everlasting life and our hope of everlasting life will be revoked by God."

"What are you talking about?" Nathaniel said he heard the doctor reply. "He probably won't need blood, but in case the appendix has ruptured and we have to spend extensive time within the abdominal cavity cleaning it out, there is a possibly, although remote, that a blood transfusion could save the boy's life. In that case, would you be willing to allow us to do all we can to promote his complete recovery?"

I listened as Nathaniel said; "My dad countered with; you can use anything or perform any procedure, except there WILL BE NO BLOOD OR BLOOD PRODUCTS. Do I make myself clear?"

Again he said the doctor countered with; "What if I just give Nathaniel blood only if extensive bleeding occurs during the surgery? Can I take the responsibility off your conscience by personally making the decision myself? You can keep your religious values by allowing me to do so. Please let me."

Nathaniel said that he watched as his dad, Frank Miller stared at the doctor. Nathaniel said, "I then looked up from my bed, first at my Mom and Dad, then towards the doctor. Dad scowled and turned toward Doctor Stein and almost shouted, "Is something wrong with your hearing? I told you NO BLOOD, and if you give him a transfusion, you will be talking to my attorney."

Again Nathaniel continued, "I saw Doctor Stein look at my parents and say; "We should not be having this discussion here in front of your son." Doctor Stein looked at me on the stretcher and continued, "Don't worry, there will be no problems and you will be feeling better tomorrow."

Nathaniel said he was on a bed that was rolled into the operating room, fearing he would die. Maybe he would need blood to live, and maybe his dad would consent if he got critical. Then again, Nathaniel knew his dad would never approve a blood transfusion for any family member. If he allowed blood, the Elders would immediately remove his Dad as an Elder and he would be excommunicated. There was no forgiveness for a blood transgression. It would be better for Nathaniel to die than break the laws of God and the church. Nathaniel said a silent prayer, and the hospital operating staff inserted the anesthetic into the I.V. tube hanging from the pole above his head. Nathaniel told me he went to sleep believing God was testing his faith. "In all honesty," he said; "I didn't care if I did die." Nathaniel slept as Doctor Stein removed the inflamed appendix and cleaned up the abdominal cavity.

Nathaniel woke up after the surgery and the abdominal pain was gone. He was going to be well. Nathanial told me as he was coming out of the anesthesia, he saw the blood committee members of his church standing beside his bed.(Detailed in Nathanial's Journal) Nathaniel said he never got over the fear that his parents and church would let him die rather than allow a pint of blood. A nurse brought Nathaniel ice chips, which she gave him to quench his terrible thirst after surgery. Nathaniel said his sleep was broken with some pain during the first night after the surgery, but he felt better the second morning.

Later, Nathaniel told me he learned Doctor Reginald Stein was a physician for many years and he many times heard this argument from **"God's Disciples"** and a few other fringe religious cults who were against blood transfusions. A few church members died, while some lived because of the skills of the hospital surgeons and staff.

The events with Brenda at the church assembly was the reason Nathaniel attempted suicide. Brenda was his link to normalcy and convincing her to attend one of his religious assemblies was the apex of his young life. Nathaniel told me the assembly gathering with Brenda would be an act of contrition for what he believed to be a serious sin of fondling her on his last birthday. My assessment is this: Nathaniel and Brenda were experiencing their peek adolescent years of budding puberty. When they were forced to sit and listen to all the evils involved in sexuality, it became embarrassing for both Nathaniel and Brenda. Especially after Nathaniel knew his relationship with Brenda had moved beyond the bounds of morality set by *"God's Disciples and Publishers."* Therefore, he attempted suicide.

Brenda visited him in our psychiatric ward, but Nathaniel turned his head and would not look or speak to her. Brenda Fox immediately left the building when his parents came to visit Nathaniel. I assume she returned home.

POSTSCRIPT:

Two weeks after being released from the psychological ward, Nathaniel was successful at committing suicide. He took one of his dad's no longer used shotguns, walked to the back of a field behind his house and shot himself in the face. I attended the funeral, but there was no sermon. According to *"God's Disciples and Publishers"*, committing suicide is a gross and terrible sin, which cannot be forgiven by God or the church. Therefore, no church Elder was allowed to give a sermon. Nathanial was in a closed casket because of the massive injuries to his face. The service consisted of nothing, not a word was said, only several minutes of silence. There were no prayers, no music, or words spoken aloud. A few flower bouquets surrounded the casket, but none sent by *"God's Prophet's and*

Publishers" church members, including Nathanial's parents. I read cards on the six bouquets of flowers surrounding the casket; one bouquet was mine, another special one from Brenda Fox. Other bouquets were from Nathanial's Aunt Katie and a couple from other relatives who are not members of *"God's Prophets"* church. At 1:05 P.M., the funeral director led us from the room. The casket of Nathaniel was carried to the waiting hearse, which took it to the Eternal Rest cemetery. Only a couple people cried, one was Nathaniel's Aunt Katie and the other was Brenda. After the burial, a meal was catered at the church. I decided to attend. The dinner resembled a party rather than an occasion to remember the life of a loved one. Nathaniel's mom and dad smiled and talked with church members, but not about their dead son. Brenda was not invited to this event, and it was best she did not attend. I stayed long enough to drink a cup of coffee and left to go home. I did not feel compelled to, nor did I wish to dine with these people.

When will humanity learn that forced religious conformity may not be in the best interest of our children? Perhaps some religions do teach love and compassion, but *"God's Disciples and Publishers"* does not fit this portrayal. As a psychiatrist, I urge parents to examine any religious group, to which you entrust your children for moral and social guidance. Children are the real victims of cults. A child of a cult member may develop anti-social behavior, become introverted, and begin to hate life. I believe this is truer of children who became members of a cult just before their teenage years. These children were free of the regimentation and religious legalism in the early formative years only to become the pawns of cult religious fanaticism.

FOR HOSPITAL RECORDS ONLY: By M.G. – Psychiatrist March 13, 1963